D1736393

PRAISE FOR
Full Moon at Noontide: A Daughter's Last Goodbye

"Old age, death, and impermanence—it seems at first glance impossible to make a reader see these timeless and universal experiences with fresh eyes, but Ann Putnam's luminous prose achieves that miracle and more, transforming pain, suffering, and loss into a literary gift of beauty and redemption."

— Charles Johnson, winner of the National Book Award

"Anyone can suffer; only an artist can turn suffering into something beautiful and universal."

— Ladette Randolph, editor of *Ploughshares*

"—this is a hard book because Ann Putnam has the courage to tell us the truth about aging and dying. But it's a gorgeous book, too, one born from the endurance of the human spirit and the capacity to love."

— Lee Martin, author of *The Bright Forever*,
Pulitzer Prize finalist (*River of Heaven*)

"Ann Putnam has given us a story of love and loss and survival that moves and instructs. . . . This is truly a work of love and devotion. A gift."

— Annick Smith
Author of *In This We are Native*
co-producer of *A River Runs Through It*

"From the beginning, *Full Moon at Noontide* seduced me. Then it sliced me open, slapped me in the face, made me cry, and enlarged my spirit. We stay with the story because it is beautifully written, because it is ultimately our story as well, and because [she] shows us that love—not—death can have the last word."

— Thomas R. Cole, PhD
Author of *The Journey of Life: A Cultural History of Aging*

"...the metaphors and rhythms of story and poetry are necessary to pull back the curtain on this numinous other world for us. *Full Moon at Noontide* is such a story."

— David Hilfiker, M.D.

"Ann Putnam's memoir, *Full Moon at Noontide: A Daughter's Last Goodbye* is poignant, thoughtful and beautifully written."

— *The Spokesman Review*

"Her tender, beautifully-written observation of old age, infirmity and death—of 'loss upon loss'—is not nearly as frightening as you might think. It is a wise and loving affirmation of life lived to the very end."

— *The Seattle Times*

"[Ann Putnam's memoir] delivers a story both profoundly painful and somehow life-affirming, lifted into literature by her sharp intelligence and luminous writing."

— Nancy Lord, *Journal of Western American Literature*

CUBAN QUARTERMOON

CUBAN QUARTERMOON

Ann Putnam

SKYLIGHT PRESS
SEATTLE, WA

Skylight Press
Seattle, WA

Trade Paperback: ISBN   979-8426476776
Also available as an eBook.

to David

CUBAN QUARTERMOON

SUNDAY, JULY 20, 1997

Cuba is Waiting For You
Havana

I step out of the plane and into a sky so radiantly blue, a sun so fierce, it takes me a moment to see the two soldiers at the bottom of the stairs, who are checking our passports as we come down, one by one. I keep my eyes lowered at the hot, oily tarmac. I don't see the dusty black boots or the black handle of the gun in the black holster, the dangerous eyes, the thick wrist, or the hand that holds my passport.

I turn back to look at the plane that had brought us here, the plane that did not, after all, crash into the sea. We'd only come from Nassau, but I'd expected disaster most of the way. Those black Russian letters across the side of the battered Aeroflot plane make me light-headed. Anybody can see this old Russian plane has tires with no tread. My stomach clenches, pushing against my ribcage.

Welcome to *José Martí Airport*. Welcome to Cuba.

I walk off the tarmac into a dark rumbling warehouse—a holding pen for luggage and tourists dazed into silence by the heat and light. I find my suitcase and roll it across the concrete floor, out toward the hot bright sunlight of Havana. And there she is, standing in the sun, holding the *Welcome to Hemingway Conference* sign—Judith herself, with her sharp eyes and strong chin, her no-nonsense clothes, and that beautiful, coppery hair, her one concession to vanity, I will learn, in an otherwise excruciatingly practical existence.

"Welcome," she says as she takes my hand. "Cuba is waiting

for you." She's smiling extravagantly. "Just like on the billboards. You'll see."

"Oh thank you," I say broadly. Everything would be all right now.

"We understand the difference between the American people and their government," she says to everyone as we gather around her with our suitcases, our trusty straw hats, and water bottles.

She had been a professor of literature once. Now she is a tour guide, since tourism has become more important than literature. I study that strong worn face, handsome in an almost masculine way, those inscrutable dark eyes, that beautiful hair.

Her English is perfect.

We've come to Havana to read the papers we've written on Ernest Hemingway to Cuban Hemingway scholars, and they to us. We're American scholars and writers, but really we're only tourists with rare permission to come to this place forbidden for so long. Most of us are excited but afraid.

I'm sorry I wrote the paper I did—what business did I have writing about Hemingway and suicide, and tangling my own mother's death into it, and hurting my father in the bargain? I'd wanted to see what one tragic life could say about the other, but I only saw my own blighted life. Of course I could have chosen any Hemingway topic. Like how his erotic life fueled his creative process or why he was so in love with death. Doesn't it always come down to either sex or death? Still, given the two, I always seem to choose the darker. Now here I am in a country with so much light I'm blinded by it.

Our bus has pulled up a short walk away. There are kids everywhere, ready for the next group of tourists hot off the plane. You got gum? Band-Aids? Soap? You have soap?

"Carry your bag, please?" the kid asks, tugging on the strap of my suitcase.

"Please don't do that."

"I will carry it, *por favor*," he says, and pulls it from me.

"*No!*" I say, and the kid sets the bag down and steps back. Just a kid with his hair in his eyes, and even I know he's way too thin for thirteen, and I see with shame he isn't stealing it, but only trying to help me lift it into the luggage compartment of the bus.

It's the only word I can think of right now, so I say *gracias* a dozen times, and pull a dollar out of my pocket. A dollar a bag was about right. What did I know about what that dollar would buy on the black market or in the dollar shops? Here's another dollar, kid, feed the family, get some shoes, go to the movies, get an ice cream.

I find a seat next to an older woman also going to this conference. She's wearing a white, pleated skirt, white heels, pantyhose. She holds a big, white purse in her lap. I feel too casual in my sundress and sandals. Something is familiar about her, but I can't place it. She smells like talcum and *Jungle Gardenia*.

"I'm Maxine Westman," she says. Her golden bracelets chime as she takes my hand. Her diamond rings flash in the light coming through the window. She has lovely golden curls and rich, brown eyes, flecked with amber.

I look at my ringless fingers, my pale skin, little freckles in an arc across the back of my hand "My real name is Annie Laurie Gallagher," I say, getting out my passport. "But people call me Laura."

There it is. *Annie Laurie Gallagher.* And there is my mother's face staring back at me. That extravagant hair, the round eyes that turn down a little at the corners in a look of melancholy and surprise. How I'd watched for signs of that despair. Around the edges of my life I'd felt it enough to imagine it. But it had always skittered off. Well, this trip would be a test.

She takes my passport and turns it to the light. "Laura's a lovely name. Elegant. Supple."

"Oh yes, and my halo of hair."

"It's beautiful. Very curly. Very *au courant.*"

"The summer I was twelve, I said from now on my name is *Laura.* I thought my mother had given me a child's name. Then she never stuck around long enough for me to outgrow it."

She looks at me with a question in her eyes she doesn't ask. Then she leans closer and confesses, "I'm really a Fitzgerald person. I think Fitzgerald people are much nicer. But here I am at the Hemingway. Secretly, I like him too."

"I heard that." A man leans over the seat in front of us and says, "I'm Bill. But people call me William." He'd been listening all along.

"You know I've never been to a country where we don't have diplomatic relations," Maxine says abruptly.

"Well you're in one now," Bill says. "Military." And there they are, guns strapped across their chests, standing side by side, in front of the terminal.

My breath catches in little snaps.

Maxine shuts her eyes and grasps her purse.

I take her hand and she pats my arm. "Might you get my raincoat?" I reach overhead and hand it to her. "I won't need this, will I?" she laughs. "It was raining so hard when I left St. Louis. I don't know why I wanted it just now."

"To feel safe. You don't have to know why."

"Are you not worried then?"

I laughed tightly. "Oh my father does that job for me." He'd called one last time to tell me how Cuba was too dangerous. No American embassy, no diplomatic relations, the caves in the mountains filled with weapons gathered up against the invasion expected now for decades. Miami terrorists blowing up hotels and planting contraband in tourists' suitcases—anything to discourage the tourist trade, stop capitalism from filtering in. Guns trained everywhere, every street a dark alley with darker doorways, the air thick with sorrow and rage. But I just looked at her and smiled.

"What did your father say?"

"Just don't go into any caves.

"Oh my no. But why?"

"Bats. Rabies, or something."

"And we must be careful what we buy. If it's anything at all, we break the no *Trading with the Enemy* law. Can you believe it? There are terrible fines for that."

"It's shocking it's an American law. It makes me want to stuff my suitcase full of cigars."

Maxine takes my hand. "You look like my daughter. Very pretty. Only taller. She has a locket like yours."

I finger the tiny golden locket I wear everywhere. "It was my mother's." Just then something brushes the side of my face. A puff of air, a whisper, a fingertip. "I grew up near St. Louis," I say faintly.

"I knew there was something familiar about you. A bit of your Midwestern accent, maybe."

I feel a little dizzy.

"You know, this is my first trip since my husband died. I am being very brave," she says with sweet irony. "But I took my little calming pills before I got on the plane."

She smooths her fingers over her purse, and whispers, "I'm carrying a suitcase full of pills. I know there is such deprivation. I went to all my doctors and they gave me samples of everything. I'm a little worried about Customs, though. I don't look like a drug smuggler, do I?" She smiles, but her eyes tighten. "I know what I look like. A little old lady who nobody notices."

Judith is working her way toward the back of the bus, counting heads. "My little chicks," she says as she walks down the aisle. "I have to see if all my chicks are here. Now," she says, taking the mic. "Your attention, please. My beautiful tourists! Your attention, please!"

The bus quiets. She narrows her eyes and fixes us with her gaze. "I will be collecting your airplane tickets. We will process them for you so your exit from Cuba will be smooth as can be. We are sparing no trouble, don't you see? Everything for you!"

So we give them over, one by one, shocked into a dazed and silent surrender. She smiles until her hands are full of tickets. Then she sweeps us over with flat, shameless eyes that belie the radiance of her smile. I swallow hard. That smile is terrifying, because now we have no plane ticket home.

Then the silence dissolves into a rising discontent that spreads from the back of the bus forward. Judith has turned around and is talking to the driver, when those mutterings strike the back of her neck. She stiffens and takes a deep breath. When she turns back around the smile is more glorious than ever.

"Ah," she says in a throaty laugh into the mic. "My little chicks." She shakes her head. "It is only for your convenience. Truly. It will make your exit out of Cuba so much easier."

"I've never *heard* of such a thing," the man behind me says in a gravelly voice that crawls over the seatback. "They can't take our tickets! This is outrageous!" He stands up, looking around wildly, hoping for some help. But the silence has returned, because there she is again, making her way back down the aisle. Her smile is fastened tight, though her eyes catch us darkly. *Don't cross me now.*

"Okay, okay," he says, hunching his shoulders and turning up his palms, then hands his ticket over too. I'd recognize that voice anywhere. I'd heard it over the phone many times these past weeks. Wallace Fiske. American Hemingway conference chair. He'd gathered up Hemingway scholars like me and persuaded us of this once-in-a-lifetime chance to see Cuba before the Canadians and Germans developed it beyond recognition. We'd meet our Cuban Hemingway colleagues, spread good will, buy cigars, *Havana Club.* But then he'd said, "Just so you're prepared. It's a virtual war zone down there."

Just before the bus begins to back out, two men hop up the stairs and slide into the two front seats across from the driver. Without missing a beat, Judith hands over our tickets, all thirty of them, to the dark muscular man with the swept-back black hair and linen jacket. He puts them into his black leather case, while the smaller man says something to the driver, who puts the bus in gear, and we make our tortuous way out of that frantic parking lot.

Bill has disappeared somewhere in the back. I'm glad for Maxine, who's wearing her large, blue-framed sunglasses that cover half her face and her frightened eyes. I want to be her daughter, the tall one, who wraps her in comfort. All these years, that sideways look toward every mother figure I ever met, but never the mother who was mine.

"We won't worry about our tickets," I tell her, but of course we do. So I shut my eyes and remember that sapphire sea from the air and Havana in its whispery blue and pink and gold in the early morning sun, a single column of black smoke carried over the water by the wind.

Then the bus pulls out onto the road, and Havana ravishes us and we can do nothing but look on without speaking. The crumbling elegance everywhere we look, clothes drying in the noonday sun stretched across tiny balconies, two men in *guayaberas* arguing under a ceiba tree, the girl in red spandex looking over her shoulder, the gold chain of her purse hot against her dark shoulder—the little girl in the faded white dress sitting on the curb, drawing something with a stick in the dirt. She looks up at me as we turn the corner and holds out her hand.

A young woman in a long white dress drifts across the street in front of us. She's wearing a white turban, her gold earrings flashing in the sun, the string of blue beads against her breasts, the matching doll in the white dress she carries before her, her dark face lit by some shining secret.

Someone from another world, slipping through that thrum of traffic without looking, as though it parts only for her.

"*Santeria*," I say. The word spins inside my head until it is everywhere. The palm trees whisper it, her lips say it, as she strokes the crucifix on Holy Days, her secret totems in her pocket, her gifts at the altar. Bride of the secret under-god—Changó or Yemayá or Babalú`. Catholic on the outside, *Santeria* on the inside. In Cuba it is everywhere.

"It's beautiful," Maxine says. The street has turned into a boulevard thick with trees and filtering sunlight.

At last we turn onto the highway leading out of the city. A billboard shouting *Patria o Muerte* broods over the nearly deserted highway that will take us to our hotel by the sea.

"*Fatherland or Death,*" Maxine translates. "Our thought for the day."

"Look at that," I say, pointing to another billboard: Lenin himself looking down this practically deserted highway. That brooding forehead and jutting chin, those piercing eyes. A little further on, Lenin and Che looking down this same road together, a future that had already become the past.

My father always said America never atoned for its sins. He never explained what he meant. He would only say, "You don't want to know, Annie Laurie, you don't want to know."

"Where's Castro?" I ask. "Why isn't he on any billboards?"

"He doesn't want that," Maxine says.

A head materializes over the backseat. "He's everywhere because he's nowhere."

"Like God," I say.

The man laughs and we shake hands over the seat. "I'm Wallace Fiske. I recognize you."

"I thought your voice sounded familiar." He's a short, bullet-shaped man, with thick wiry gray hair, close-set eyes.

Up ahead a rusty brown truck has been pushed off the road

onto the grass. The driver has disappeared under the hood; we can see only his brown back shining in the sun, an oily rag in his back pocket. No gas, no spare parts. Only baling wire and desire, and all the luck in the world. A few Japanese cars speed past a faded yellow Packard rumbling down the road ahead, and then we quickly pass it too. Five or six people cluster under the shade of the overpass. One of them holds up a string of red peppers. The rest barely look up. They know we won't stop.

We pass an abandoned Russian communications building, gray and sightless, unthinkable against this sensuous landscape. And now water-stained cinder block building after building stranded by the side of the road, set off ridiculously by a palm tree here and there.

The air conditioner spews out little puffs of cold air in between a heavy warmth full in the face. Maxine is fanning herself with a magazine. Sweat trickles down the sides of her face, her mascara dark thumbprints beneath her eyes. I've tied my hair up off my neck. My overnight bag is on the floor, too hot to hold in my lap.

Up front, the two men who'd gotten on the bus at the last minute begin to argue. The smaller man in the aisle is listening intently to the tall man with the black leather case that holds our thirty airline tickets. He's speaking in rapid authoritative Spanish none of us can follow. Now he's almost shouting at the smaller man. The man with the briefcase has turned around now too, his eyes sweeping over us so intensely it's clear we would never be his little chicks. Was he our bodyguard or something else? This man whose eyes never stop moving, whose name we never know.

Something has changed. There's a strange chemical smell just beneath the hot smell. The road is different too. I've missed something. We're headed for some dark Cuban prison, some underground cave with stockpiled weapons. I picture the headlines: *American Scholars Taken Hostage by Cuban Dissidents.* My throat tightens. I can't catch a breath in the hot air. I look at Maxine to see if she's worried too. She's fallen asleep. Bless her. I can breathe now.

Then we're heading toward a compound with an iron-gated entrance into the Hemingway Marina, just at the edge of the sea-wall. *Hotel El Vieja y el Mar. The Old Man and the Sea.* The gate swings open and we're waved in.

We pull up in front of an open air lobby next to a pond with a sculpture of a fish perpetually rising out of the water just out of reach of Santiago, the old man in a boat—variations on the theme carried out in the sculptures and mosaics and carvings on every floor. The Canadians knew what they were doing, building this hotel, working in all the Hemingway they could. It was called *Bartolomento Pier* when Hemingway met Castro that spring in 1960 before everything began to fall apart. Hemingway gave Castro the silver fishing trophy he'd won in the annual marlin tournament. Mary Hemingway always said the Gulf was strange that year. Currents of the waning moon all summer long. All the fish were drawn into Castro's net.

The wind lifts my dress and wafts up my legs as I stand there looking at that sapphire sea, glinting in the afternoon sun. I wonder if we're allowed in that water. But then I pull my suitcase inside after everyone else.

They've put me on the fifth floor. The room is freezing. There must be a thermostat somewhere but I can find none. I'm shivering by the time I've unpacked. I open the slider and step out onto the little balcony.

The aquamarine swimming pool shimmers in the sun, a blue hourglass, the shape of a woman. And beyond the pool, the ocean, the curve of the island, and then Havana in the distance. I stand in that liquid air and shut my eyes and let the fatigue and relief wash over me.

I lie down on the wide bed without the energy to pull back the covers. I settle my sweater over my shoulders and fall instantly asleep into an Arctic dream with palms trees growing out of the snow.

I wake up cross-ways on the bed, an imprint of the bedspread against my cheek.

It's almost four o'clock and I've forgotten what comes next. So I sit up and reach for the phone on the bed stand to call Maxine. "Anchors Away" plays in my ear while I wait. I laugh out loud. All these years, the weapons in the mountains, the binoculars on a hook by the door, all those years searching the sky, keeping watch over the shore. And now here we are--our own little Yankee invasion. Already I'm beginning to know the beauty and sorrow of this place. The second chorus is beginning before the switchboard answers.

I pull the bedspread up over my shoulders, tuck the phone under my chin, and try to unremember the dream.

Jazz, Baby, Jazz
Seattle 1973

I'd seen him first just standing there, running his hands through his hair before he finally sat down across from me, and propped his elbows on the table.

"I've been looking at you from over there," he said.

I didn't know what to say. I was watching the light flickering in his blue-gray eyes. "Well, I'm studying," I said with a little laugh. He pushed his blonde hair back from his eyes. I saw how they changed from blue to gray to blue again.

"You were really concentrating. Like you loved what you were doing."

I just looked at him.

"I'll bet you're a really good student. What are you a good student at?"

"Literature."

"Are you in school school? Or in grad school?"

"Grad school."

"I'm a terrible student. I'm so bad I should have graduated 5 years ago."

"What are you a terrible student in?"

"Everything except music. I eat and drink it and dream it all the time."

Don't do it, I thought, please don't do it, but I couldn't stop myself, so I said, "That's a pretty showy thing to say."

"I know. I wanted to get your attention."

"Then you're good at something besides music."

"What?"

"Getting my attention."

"I'm Brick," he said, putting out his hand. It was steady and warm and I liked his gold watch against his wrist.

I couldn't help smiling at him. "Brick from *Cat on a Hot Tin Roof*," I said, his blue eyes beckoning a confidence I didn't know I had.

"Maggie," he said softly. "Maggie the Cat."

I shook my head and smiled. "Laura," I said. "Not Maggie the Cat."

"I think you're beautiful, Lauracakes."

I could feel the heat rise and spread across my face. I brushed the hair from my face, tucked it behind my ear in that automatic way that was both seductive and self-conscious.

His sleeve touched my arm, as I reached for my coat, and I couldn't move. "Why don't you like people to say how beautiful you are?"

I just looked at him. "So what kind of music do you play?"

"Jazz, baby, jazz."

"Jazz?"

"Jazz. The blues. You want to go for a walk? I want to show you something. I was thinking about it the whole time I was watching you. You probably don't even know what's going on outside right now."

So he led me by the hand down the marble stairs of the library and outside to the courtyard. "I just wanted you to see this," he said. And there it was, a moon full and yellow and fraught with longing. We sat on the stone bench outside the library and watched it rise and lay a glistening path across the snow.

"I thought you might be concentrating so much you'd walk all the way home and not see how the moon is on everything now."

Then he walked me home in the moonlight filtering down through the bare branches and when we came to my apartment, he said, "Would you like to come hear me play sometime?" and I said yes, and he said okay then, and turned and walked away without looking back, and I knew at that moment that everything had changed.

Hemingway's Ghost
Finca Vigia

We come into San Francisco de Paula, a sleepy little village on the edge of Havana, and roll down a narrow road through an arbor of flickering sunlight and heavy green shadows, past sagging little houses on either side, then turn up the dirt road to Hemingway Museum, the *Finca Vigia*. The bus grinds into the dirt as we take the hill. Then there it is—splendid and white against the palm trees and the deep blue of the afternoon sky.

I'd been to the house in Ketchum, Idaho—that last, sad house overlooking the Big Wood River. I'd come in the back and through the little kitchen, into the living room, and walked up the stairs to the bedrooms, then back down through the living room. Jacqueline Kennedy was looking up at us from the cover of *Life* laid out on the coffee table in front of the fireplace.

Oh, go ahead, she was saying, take the picture, it won't matter now. We'd been stealing glances toward that little linoleum entryway that led to the front door ever since we came. I aimed my camera out the front door and tried not to imagine the blood fanning out across the wall, the red circle widening over the floor. And Miss Mary herself, rushing down the stairs from the bedroom in her bare feet as soon as she'd heard the blast from that 12-gauge double-barreled shotgun she'd locked up in the storage room in the basement.

Imagine finding him there, crumpled over like that, his back still warm through the blue pajamas, the red robe. What did she do before she made that first phone call? I thought of her, white-haired and tiny, leaning over.

And suddenly I think of my own tiny mother and how she must have floated across the street that day. In my dreams ever after, I'm sitting on the porch swing and my mother says, "I'm going to the neighbors. You stay here." I don't stop her even though I know what's going to happen. She's wearing her white Easter dress and her white straw hat with the pink ribbons, even though Easter is two days away. In the dream, I watch her stand on the curb and put her hand to the sky in a gesture that frightens me, as though she's either waving hello or waving good-bye. Then she turns to look at the car coming down the road and steps into the street. I look up just in time to see her pink ribbons rise up against the heartbreak of the blue, blue sky, and the sudden beauty of the shattered windshield.

That house in Ketchum was a house of the dead, all right. No spirits anywhere in sight. But the *Finca Vigia* would be full of spirits. This great white house surrounded by palm trees and bougainvillea and banyans, where the breeze floats through the unshuttered windows, and fierce animal spirits hover just out of reach of the ceiling fans turning languorously. Those sharp dark eyes full of knowing, spirits held forever on those walls—kudu, gazelle, sable, buffalo, antelope, exotic and otherworldly. And totems full of incantations and spells, magic tucked into every drawer, and everywhere a thousand curses and a thousand cures, a thousand hiding places for *orishas* and angels circling the house, heavy with desire.

We follow the walkway around the house, the late afternoon sun filtering through the canopy of green overhead. Museum proctors stand like sentries in each doorway as we peer through the windows and doors.

There is Hemingway's bathroom, books even here. And weights and dates penciled next to the scales on the far wall. He had to make *fighting weight*, he always said, yet he never did. Here before me is the story those figures tell, the ups and downs of the battle against despair and excesses too necessary to resist. Then that final winter, the spring that never came, and the last summer dry and joyless, the weight way down, no interest in keeping any records now.

And in Miss Mary's blue bedroom, somebody's portrait of her, with the nose too sharp, the eyes too narrow, a blonde-haired witch, which is what some people said she was. Oh, those wives. Wife number three, Martha Gellhorn, found the *Finca* for Ernest so she wouldn't have to stay in that tiny room at *Ambos Mundos*. Mary had warned the doctors at Mayo's not to let him go, but he'd been too cagey for all that, saying with a wink and a smile how he was all right now, he just needed to get back to Idaho and that typewriter in the bedroom, though he hadn't been able to write for way too long now, his short term memory burned away by the sizzle and pop of the currents running through his brain, then drowsy and dry-mouthed and the sense that he'd forgotten who he was.

I think of her mostly now as that tiny figure bending over in her nightgown, touching his shoulder. *Don't go, please don't go.* Jackie would know how she felt soon enough, though neither of them knew it then. That summer in 1961 when there was everything to look forward to, day after golden day, the missiles of October, the ride through Dealey Plaza in that convertible, light years away. What neighbor or friend came that morning with sponge and pail and mop while Mary lay in bed, dumb with sedatives, her face buried in the pillow?

There it is, the typewriter on the bookshelf, small and ancient-looking, on the ledge above the kudu watching over the room as he stood on the kudu skin, and typed. And on the bed, his white cap, jaunty and ready to go, as though there would be time enough for everything. And in the corner the shoe rack, and the shoes, worn down at the heel, always a size too big, the most intimate, mournful detail of all. He would have had a big fire, if he'd known he wasn't coming back, and burned those shoes.

When he left Cuba, he never knew it was for good. He didn't know it would lead to that linoleum one-way exit by the Big Wood River.

I'd get a good picture of that typewriter, though. I turn on my flash. The proctor in the doorway to the bedroom eyes me carefully.

"No flash," a stern woman in brown says to me.

"Sorry." I put my camera down. She glares at me until I move on.

"Don't worry. You'll be able to get inside." Judith is sitting in a white, wrought-iron chair next to the railing, the late afternoon sun coming through the lattice overhead on her coppery hair. She smiles up at me and holds out a mysterious green drink. "You should get one of these. I myself have already had several." She smiles again and crosses her legs. "Sit here," she says, touching my arm. "Pretty soon we will dance, eat. Are you having a wonderful time now?"

"It's lovely here," I say.

I look at the green drink, hear the chink of the ice cubes against the glass. I can't remember ever being this thirsty.

"We're coming back, you know, later in the week, when we can go inside."

"It's what I came here for."

"I have been bringing people here for ten years, and I've never been inside. Her dark eyes flash. "I love it. Showing off Cuba."

"Maybe I'll get one of those drinks," I say and get up to go. But she turns back to me and takes my hand. "That's Bernardo," she says, pointing at a dark tall man who's standing by the window to Hemingway's bedroom, explaining something to a couple of my American colleagues. "He's our best Hemingway researcher. He will translate at your conference."

He must be working very hard, because even from here, I can see the sweat trickling down his dark beautiful face. He's wearing a faded flowered shirt, no uniform. He looks like a young Sidney Poitier.

"My son," Judith says softly. "He's not really, you know. I just like to call him that since I love him like a son. I have a son already. He's very important in the government." She grows quiet, as her smile settles into a thin line. Light and shadow play across her face. She waves him over and cranes her neck for the kiss on her cheek. His smile vanishes as he bends down.

"This is Laura Gallagher," she says. "You will be translating for her."

He takes my hand and smiles. "I'm happy to meet you."

"And me also." He sits down and leans in as she takes his arm and whispers in his ear. I'm an outsider now so I move on toward the terrace.

"Look who's here," Maxine says, coming around the corner. She nods in the direction of the man who carried the mysterious leather case with our plane tickets. He's standing in the corner of the verandah with his arms crossed, as his eyes sweep over us, his black, slicked-back hair, his bronze forehead provocative and still.

"Our bodyguard," I say.

"Or internal security. We're never going to know who our friends are. Or our enemies." She leans over and whispers in my ear. "There's a gun inside his jacket. Under his arm." Then she catches herself and laughs. "Am I being melodramatic?"

"I think so," I say, as I look at him hard and he catches my gaze. I quickly look away.

A busload of our Cuban colleagues has unloaded and now the terrace is full of people we've never seen before. But the man with the cruel eyes, the swept-back hair hasn't moved. What was he looking for? And what about us, with our painful innocence and our halting Spanish? What kind of revolutionary plots did they think we were hatching right here in the open?

"Well, he frightens me," I say. We both narrow our eyes.

"'*Believe half of what you see and none of what you hear,*'" she says. "An old Cuban proverb." She's staring at him unabashedly.

I want to sit down.

Maxine touches my arm. "It's all right, Laura. Don't mind me. I'm going to check out the food," she says and wanders into the crowd.

A little band has set up against the white railing on the terrace— three men in black long-sleeved shirts and black pants, two with guitars, the singer with maracas, his watch face flashing in the late afternoon sun as they play "Guantanamera" over and over. I'm standing against the railing by the stairs leading down to the pool, watching Judith and our bodyguard, kneeling beside her. Her face is completely in shadows now, the light from her eyes eclipsed by something dark and familiar. She's talking furiously. Then I notice the music has slowed. Something has shifted.

"Hey, Laura. Hi there." Bill is weaving his way through the crowd, holding that strange green drink.

"That's looks wonderful. I'm so thirsty."

"Come on," he said, "I'll get you one."

"Do you know what it is?" I ask.

"I have no idea."

"Do you think it's all right to drink?"

"Probably not." He grins at me and takes a long swallow. Beneath all the jokes and banter, there is a longing in him that lies as cool as a sigh, and nothing to fear. I can't see Maxine anywhere. Maybe she's gone down to the swimming pool or the boat, dry-docked now where the tennis courts used to be.

"Look at that," I say, pointing to the long table being set up in the center of the terrace. "A table spread for us."

"The Last Supper."

"I know," I say. "I've heard about the food shortages. Nobody gets enough to eat. Now all this food. I don't even feel like eating."

Our group steps up to the table and piles their plates high. Only then do our Cuban colleagues approach the table and fill their plates with chicken wings, beef strips, cheese and meats, all the protein their plates can hold.

"Beige," Maxine says over my shoulder.

Bill withdraws his plate and straightens up. "What?"

"If you eat only beige food you will be perfectly safe."

According to Maxine, we must eat no beef, no eggs, chicken only if cooked off the bone, fish is questionable, and no fruits, no lettuce. Bread and rice and potatoes. Beans, maybe. It's what everybody does here anyway. One chicken a month. A country on the verge of starvation. Now all this abundance.

"And don't drink the water. Don't even brush your teeth with it," Maxine says as she moves down the line, filling her plate with bread and potatoes and pastries. "And remember the ironies. Cuba forbids homelessness and hunger."

My plate is still empty. I set it back down. All I can think about is water—cool, fresh, abundant water. It's all too much—being in this forbidden place, the spirits I know must be here. I wander away and watch from a distance. Bill is talking to a Cuban woman wearing a red sundress and espadrilles. She's laughing. He touches her wrist, now she's touching his arm, just for emphasis—she inclines her head, he touches her bare shoulder. And then that sudden spark out of nowhere. I hadn't felt that it in so long I wonder how I knew.

A little girl wanders through the crowd and stands by the woman in the red dress. "Mama?" She touches her mother's arm. Bill looks surprised and puts his hand out in introduction. The little girl is smiling. The woman's smile tightens and she laughs a false laugh.

A waiter hands me that strange green drink, the glass sweating in the heat. I lean against the railing leading down to the pool, put the glass against my forehead. I want the chink of ice cubes, the splash of water, the sweet immersion. I know what it is now. Rum, lime, mint, a spritz of seltzer and ice. *Mojito.*

I drift down the long stairway leading through the grounds to the pool. In the late afternoon sun, the ferns and palms are a golden light struck with green. In that liquid air I listen for the original stillness—the pause between inhale and exhale, the silence before the need for words.

There's the pool where Ava Gardner swam naked—as the story goes. Why would you have to wear any clothes here at all? With that innocent eroticism coming at you every minute out of this light, this heat, this sky. Of course sooner or later complications would set in. Nobody could hold onto that chastity of sight forever.

But the pool is empty. No water in the bathroom, no water here in San Francisco de Paula. You can imagine it though, that wavering blue against a whitewashed patio. I shut my eyes and listen to the whispery secret of the wind in the trees, the creaking of the bamboo, like some exotic bird shrieking annunciation or alarm. And wakened out of their cool dusky shadows for that rush into light, a red and blue and violet scattering of birds, leaving behind a strange and thrilling taste on the tongue of *mangoes* and *avocates, flamboyantes, hibiscus, frangipani, oleander.* I feel light-headed and wonder if I might sit in one of the cabana chairs under the canopy.

A bare-chested man with a white towel over his shoulder, one of the groundskeepers, maybe, poses for the picture somebody's trying to take on the other side of the pool, his arm around a little boy in brown shorts and bare feet. Then something catches my eye. A white flickering just at the edge of sight. I look over at Hemingway's boat, the *Pilar,* polished wood and brass under a sturdy wooden roof. A little girl in a white dress, peeks out from behind the guardrail around the boat, her dark hair tied back in a red ribbon. She's waving at the boy, and then ducking behind the boat, but he just stands there looking right through her. When I look back toward the boat, she's gone.

The breeze floats over the gardens with the last of the sunlight. I hear a rustling behind me and look for a white eyelet hem, a red ribbon fluttering in the wind but feel only a green, whispery silence. I shut my eyes and feel her breath warm and damp against my neck. She's hiding somewhere behind me if only I could stay still enough. The man and the boy are looking up at the house, listening to the music drifting down. My baby girl's tenth birthday would have been tomorrow.

She's shadowy now, a wraith who only spins inside my dreams, now and then, a three-day-old baby forever, a tiny hand that grasped my finger once, a wisp of dark hair, a perfectly rounded, tiny head, a hummingbird heart beating wildly against her dusky chest.

I shut my eyes and imagine the moon rising against a darkening sky. "Moonlight Serenade" is playing in my head, while "Guantanamera" skitters out over the grounds and filters down through the palms.

Then I remember my mother beside me, sitting on the porch swing, one leg tucked under the other, swinging absently in the warm night air, humming "Moonlight Serenade." I can feel her breathy and warm beside me, as I sit safely against her, sleepy in that gentle pull of her breathing or her heartbeat.

All these years, this weightless presence, this mourning not to be comforted. So little to remember—the curve of her cheek, her gossamer hair, her sigh, her lavender smell, a thousand sorrows gathered up and tucked away. I'd shut my eyes a million times, knowing she'd be there when I opened them if only I were brave enough or good enough.

I walk back from the boat across the patio by the pool, my drink in my hand, and see the stairs through the trees. I try to imagine climbing them. Maxine is coming down the walkway, waving her hands.

"No, no no," she says, taking my arm. "That drink is full of *ice*. You mustn't drink it. You must be careful of everything."

"I'm so thirsty."

"You mustn't get dehydrated," Maxine says. "There must be some water somewhere around here. Oh, look! A granddaughter cat." We'd seen it lurking around the food table on the verandah. It looks scrawny, maybe sick, and very hungry. We 're on the walkway next to the pet cemetery and the gravestones for the Hemingway dogs, *Black* and *Negrita, Linda* and *Neron,* under a low spreading tree. No graves for the cats though. Maxine reaches over to pet the cat, who is now rubbing herself against her leg.

"No, no, no!" Bill says. "*Rabies.*" Maxine jerks her hand back.

"Oh, my," she says. "I hadn't thought of that."

"Come on, Laura, you should eat something," Bill says. "Let's go back up."

It would be lovely walking that way again. A bower of green. The little band keeps on, their voices barely distinguishable now from the noise of the crowd, the sounds from the maracas and the guitars skimming over the gardens.

The heat bears down on me like a weighty hand. I can hardly climb the stairs.

"Here." Bill takes my arm.

"Thanks," I say.

"Do you want to sit down?"

"I don't know what's wrong. I feel so strange."

"Well it's been a long day," he says. "You need to eat something."

"I know. But mainly I just want water. On the other hand, ten mojitos would fix everything."

"I'll bring you something."

People are everywhere now. No place to sit but the top of the stairs. I lean over and lay my head in my arms.

Bill comes back with a plate of potatoes, pastries, plantains, and sits down. "Don't you expect to see old Hem coming around the corner anytime now? He's got a daiquiri in his hand and he's wondering who the hell we are. His birthday's tomorrow, so happy Birthday, Ernie." Bill raises his glass. "Party's on Friday, though. Hope he can wait."

And there he is, standing out of the way, in the corner of the terrace in his shorts and *guayabera,* his hands in his pockets, looking a little pissed off, and no *Papa Doble* anywhere. All those years trying to keep people like us away. Now here we are.

"He probably hates us for going through his things," I say. "He probably wishes he'd burned it all before he left."

"I'm damned glad he didn't."

"I know," I say, and think of my mother and all the things she'd burned I couldn't live without.

"But he didn't know when he left he'd never get back," Bill says.

"Maybe nobody ever does."

We sit there for a long time looking out over the gardens, the sun going down behind the palm trees beyond the stone railing, washing over the ferns and bougainvillea with a fiery, dying light.

I look at the plate of food in my lap. "I'm really not very hungry," I say. "I'm just so thirsty. I left my water bottle on the bus."

"I'll go down and get it for you."

"That's okay. I think it's locked. And we're leaving pretty soon anyway."

"You didn't try the *mojito*, did you?"

"I was worried about the ice."

Bill just looks at me. "You should. Try everything you can."

"I always wanted to be like that."

"Come with me."

"All right," I say, and we walk to the stone railing on the other side of the house to watch the sun going down. Beyond the waves of green, Havana waits.

I look up at the tower, white against that ravishing, burnished sky. Something brushes across my face—a spider web in the air. Then I glance up again and there is that familiar broad face, the barrel chest, but look at him now!—the thin, shadowy beard, the tenuous, combed down hair of that last winter when he couldn't write, the sweater against the chill, eyes full of panic and sorrow. To see him as he was at the end, fragile as tissue paper. I shut my eyes and try to resurrect him as he had been. When I look up again I see the last of the sun on the red-tiled roof, and then it's gone.

"I just saw a ghost," I say. "But not the one I wanted to see."

"Oh, well," he says. "We never see the ghost we want."

Darkness is coming quickly now. Bill takes off after the woman in the red dress, who's waved him over.

I watch him go, then walk back to the terrace, nodding and smiling my way through that crowd where no one knows my name. Those rapid Cuban syllables fall on me like rain.

MONDAY, JULY 21, 1997

Jasmine on the Wind
El Viejo y el Mar

It's after midnight. I'm standing on the balcony, looking at the sleepy arm of the island ringed with a curve of lights. Everything is so hot, so close. My pulse lags at my wrists, my heart waiting between heartbeats for what's coming next. Inside, the air conditioner is blowing hot, used up air.

I lie down, turn toward the slider, and fall fast asleep. I wake up grabbing at the dark. The room is spinning. I fumble for my flashlight and rush to the bathroom. I try the bathroom light but the power is out. The flashlight falls with a clattering, and skitters over the floor.

I can't stop. Both ends. So quick, so violent, this sudden expulsion. I can't stop shivering. I can barely get back to bed so I sit on the floor and pull the phone off the nightstand. Somehow I get the desk.

"I need a doctor," I say. "I'm really sick." I can't catch my breath in the thick dark air. My ribs ache. I crawl into bed. I'm sweating all over.

I hold onto the edge of the mattress and wait in the dark. Maybe I fall sleep, I don't know. Then I smell jasmine coming through the dark. Now something cool on my arm. Someone beside me, smelling like jasmine.

"Hello," she says, bending over. "My name is Maria. I'm going to help you."

I grab hold of her arm. "I can't stop being sick."

"Do you have pain?"

"Down here. In waves."

"Let me look just for a minute, okay? I'll be careful." She lifts my nightgown. Her hand is cool against my stomach. She presses here and there. "Does it hurt now?

"No."

"How about now?"

"No."

"It's probably not appendicitis."

She pulls my nightgown back down, strokes my arm, touches my face. "It's probably just intestinal," she says, handing me a bottle of something. "Can you take a little bit of this? It's nice and cold."

"What is it?" I say.

"Glucose and salts. You're very dehydrated. That's why you feel so bad. I can tell the way your skin feels. Like paper."

"I don't think I can swallow anything."

"You should probably be in a hospital. You need an IV to get you rehydrated."

"Okay," I say.

"Everything's a blackout so we'd have a hard time getting you there right now. Let's see what we can do right here."

I try to sit up but can't stop it from coming all over my nightgown, the bedding, the sheets.

"I'm so afraid," I say, trying not to cry. "I've made a terrible mess."

"Don't be embarrassed," she says. "It's only our humanity, you know?"

"It's awful."

"No it's not. If you can lift your hips a little I'll get this nightgown off." She draws it up over my shoulders. "Can you roll over just a little?

I turn over and hold onto the side of the mattress while she slips the soiled bedding out from under me. The room pitches and rolls. Then she gathers everything up and goes away. I lie on the bare mattress, holding onto the edge of the bed to slow down the spinning. I'm afraid to turn back over.

The air is hot and fetid. I try not to gag.

Then she's back. "We'll feel better like this," she says, opening the drapes and the sliding glass door.

"This is so awful," I say. "You don't have to stay."

"It's all right. You're very sick right now."

"I'm so ashamed," I say. "I wish you didn't have to touch me."

"Oh, I'm used to this. Did you bring medicine with you?"

"My bag on the dresser," I whisper. "My flashlight's in the bathroom. On the floor."

"No worries. I've got one." I watch the light ricochet against the mirror and shut my eyes. "You've got a lot of stuff here. That's good. We don't have much medicine in Cuba. Let's try the Cipro and some of the Compazine. That will slow things down. It's nice that you have this. You are smart to bring it."

She helps me lift my head so I get the pills down. I lie back and feel the room spin again. It's worse if I shut my eyes, but I can't keep them open.

"Oh," I hear myself saying. I lurch up. "I'm going to be sick."

She catches me and eases me back down. "Try not to be sick now if you can. Let the medicine work."

I feel like I'm dying.

"Here," she says, touching my chest. "Take a long, deep breath. Let's try to go five minutes without being sick."

"Okay."

"Breathe in five heartbeats and out ten nice, slow heartbeats. See? This way your heart slows down and your breathing too."

I can't stop the panic rising up my throat. The room won't stop spinning.

"Look at me." She touches my chest again. "Breathe with me. Keep your stomach nice and calm. Here, touch my chest too." She takes my hand and places it at the base of her throat.

So we breathe together—in for five beats, out for ten, over and over.

"Can you turn on your side now?"

I nod but I'm afraid to speak. I breathe in, then out, long and slow. The room flips upside down then rights itself. I hang on tight.

I know she's gone away because I hear water running in the sink. Then she's back. She sets a stack of towels on the bed. "I'm going to get you all cleaned up now."

She sits carefully on the side of the bed, takes a cool washcloth and washes my hips and legs.

"We better get you cleaned up down there too," she says. She hands me a soapy washcloth.

I try to clean myself and then I hand the washcloth back to her.

"Here's a nice clean towel," she says. "See? You're as good as new."

"Oh that's nice," I say. My tongue feels thick and dry. Then my stomach tightens against the pitch and roll beginning again.

"You have a lot of fever right now. We need to get it down," she says, and goes away again. Then she's by the bed with a basin and some clean, cool water and a washcloth. She slides a couple of towels under me. A sheet drifts down over me. "Just so you feel safe," she says. "I know you're hot."

Cool water washes over my face, my hair, my neck, my arms. Then I turn a little and she touches my back so softly it's like not being touched at all. The cool, wet washcloth slips down my back.

"Oh, I like that," I say.

She puts the basin at the bottom of the bed and washes my feet. "This is the farthest place from your sickness," she says. "A little acupressure and massage now."

Then she puts something cool on her hands and slides her palms down my ankles and over the tops of my feet. She takes my foot in her hands and draws her thumbs down the sole of my foot, pressing deeply and making little circles of pressure that calm the waves of fear.

I shut my eyes. The pillow floats out from under me. I can feel the fist inside my stomach begin to uncurl. The tilting room begins to right itself. I can feel my heartbeat slowing down.

"I'm going to get some candles. I'll be right back."

Don't go, I want to call after her. But then she's back, lighting candles and setting them on the dresser. "We often work by candlelight. It's how we live now."

"It's nice," I say shutting my eyes. I can see a flickering against my eyelids.

Then she's touching my forehead with hands so tender and cool they could have been my mother's hands.

"I can get a clean, dry sheet under you if you move just a little bit." Then she sidles the sheet little by little across the bed. "There. All clean now."

"I don't know how you can stay so long."

"You don't need to talk. Don't worry about talking to me. You should try to sleep."

"Will you go away?"

"I won't go away without telling you."

When I open my eyes again, I can see the outline of the chairs on the balcony, a thinning of the dark out the door, cool air blowing across the bed. The blackout is over.

She's sitting on the floor, her head against the side of the bed. I touch her short-cropped dark hair, a streak of white, like a little silver part.

She looks up and smiles. "You're better."

"I know." I'd seen her face only by candlelight. She's beautiful in the early light.

"I fell asleep too," she says, getting up slowly. "You should have some more to drink. You mustn't drink the water here," she says. "Only purified water, okay?"

"I know."

"Mix some of this powder into your water bottle, like this. Then just shake it up. It's mostly sugar and salt. It's your magic potion. It made you better."

"I know you told me, but I don't remember your name."

"We never really got around to names. There was a lot going on here last night."

She laughs a light, musical laugh. "Maria Guillot. You're Annie Laurie Gallagher. The front desk told me. You're here for the Hemingway." She holds out her hand. "I'm very happy to meet you."

I take her hand. I'm going to live.

"You should keep drinking this all day. As much as you can."

"Are you a nurse?"

"Once I was a doctor. The hotel calls me to take care of people sometimes, if nobody else can come. I live down the road so it's not hard to get here. But mostly I clean rooms."

"Oh, I'm sorry," I say, then want to take it back. I don't know what I mean. She turns away.

"Let me get you a clean nightgown. Are you unpacked?"

"It's in the drawer I think."

"Here," she says, helping me slip it over my shoulders. "Such beautiful linen. I'll bet it's from somebody who loves you."

"No," I say. "I don't know why I bought it, just to sleep. I'm glad I wasn't wearing it last night."

"You must have wonderful intuition. Or maybe you were saving it for someone special."

"I don't think so." It hurts when I laugh.

Maria looks at me hard. "Can I ask you something?"

"Anything."

"Have you been ill? I wondered about it in the night. I felt your scar."

"The new one or the old one?"

"Both."

"The new one is over a year ago. A hysterectomy."

"I thought so."

"They were going to take everything out anyway, but something went wrong, and they couldn't stop the bleeding. So. Big scar."

"That operation is so final."

"It's all right."

"Is the other scar a Caesarean then?"

"Uh huh."

"So you have children?"

"No," I say.

"I'm so sorry. I didn't mean to presume. But I did. Of course I did."

The candle has burned down to the quick. She turns on the dresser light, then sits down carefully on the side of the bed. "See? The power is back for everybody."

She holds the inside of her wrist against my forehead. "Cooler now."

"What's this?" I say, touching the shiny mark across her wrist.

"My stigmata." Then she holds out both wrists. "A matching pair."

"This is terrible," I say. It looked like she'd tried to slit her wrists.

"I was training to be a surgeon. My hands aren't so good for that now. It's all right though."

"How could it be all right?"

"Oh, well. There are many kinds of scars." She crosses her arms. "It's strange, isn't it?"

"Our history written on our bodies," I say, touching the streak of silver hair running from her forehead. "Your mark."

"It came when my daughter was born. This patch of white hair. I should have known she would be lightning."

"Your hands are wonderful," I say.

"They're good at cleaning things anyway." She's looking at me strangely. "Scars you don't see are worse." She turns toward the light breaking through the thin layer of clouds. "It's going to be a nice day."

"Thank you for my life."

She shakes her head. "You should sleep all day. Drink all you can. I should go now."

"Couldn't I do something for you? Take you to dinner or something?" I was remembering our Cuban colleagues at the *Finca* buffet.

"No Cubans allowed in the dining room."

"Why not?"

"Everything's off limits for Cubans. Beaches, big hotels, the works."

"I could buy us drinks."

"Not the bar either. I probably shouldn't be seen with you anyway. Lots of internal security in this hotel. *CDR* next door."

"What's that?"

She laughs. *"Committee for the Defense of the Revolution."*

"What's that?"

"Neighbors spying on neighbors. You know, the usual thing."

"Oh," I say, "of course." But I don't have the vaguest idea what she's talking about. Then I remember the man with sweeping eyes and the leather case with our tickets, and the gun under his linen jacket She looks at me for a long time. "Maybe you could meet my daughter. Sometimes she works here too."

I couldn't let her walk off into the new day and never see her again. "You could bring your daughter and I could order room service." I couldn't imagine eating ever again but I'd begun to get a sense of what deprivations this place held.

"Sure. We'll do that sometime."

"No. I mean really. Tomorrow? Is tomorrow Tuesday? And your daughter."

"Okay," Maria says. "We can try it. But I need to go now. You really should sleep all day."

She comes out of the bathroom with a glass of water. "I poured it from your water bottle." Then she gathers up the towels and opens the door. Air comes off the balcony, and the curtains ebb and flow.

"You smell like jasmine," I say.

"I know. It's my one extravagance. I make it myself," she says as she closes the door.

It's cool in the early morning. Everything is still quiet. No noises from the hall, no noises from the pool. The sun is on the balcony. Maybe I'd go down to the pool this afternoon, lie in the sun. I can feel sleep coming heavily, irresistibly. Then the pillow floats away again, and behind my eyes I see my little golden bird perched in the sun. She lights on the wind, a yellow flicker rushing out the window, zigzagging just above my frantic hands. Was it stunned by all that sudden space, or wild with flight, when it finally vanishes into the sky? My little girl starts to scream "Mommy!" only I don't have a little girl, so it must be me who's screaming, and there is my mother standing in the middle of the lawn in her nightgown and bare feet, clapping her hands. The bird flies right to her and she cups her hands around it. "See? I saved it for you." But then it's me with the bird in my hands, and it's the saddest thing in the world to be feeling its wings flutter against my palms.

I sleep all day. By late afternoon I manage to get up and take a shower. I stand for a long time with my head under the water, feeling it rush down my hair, my face, my neck, washing over me everywhere.

The Wizard of Oz
St. Louis 1957

The wind was turning my gold and silver pinwheel, as I waited for my father on the curb in front of the school. I'd brought it to Brownie Scouts for show and tell, the pinwheel my father bought me at the circus, because my mother had to go away again.

I looked up at the patches of sky through the leaves brushing against the clouds. My stomach clenched under my folded arms. I tried to think about the ice cream I was going to get as soon as my daddy came. My mouth felt dry. Everyone but Mrs. Blodgett and Suzanne had gone home long ago. I tucked my knees under my Brownie uniform.

Where could he be? I was too little to walk home alone.

"Annie Laurie, what are you still doing here?" Mrs. Blodgett asked. She leaned over and I could see a handkerchief tucked inside her dress between her breasts. She smelled like talcum and Elmer's paste.

"I'm waiting for my daddy."

"It's awfully late. Are you sure he's coming, dear?"

I nodded. Mrs. Blodgett sang in the choir at my father's church. Everybody knew my father. If he said he was coming, of course he was coming.

"Suzanne has an appointment at the dentist. You could come along and then I could take you home."

"But he wouldn't know where I am."

"I don't like the looks of that sky. Is your mother away again?"

"She's just visiting somebody."

"Well. If you say so."

She looked at the sky again. "But don't wait much longer, dearie, it's going to rain. Do you know the way home?" The sky looked different now. It was becoming hazy and tinged with green.

I nodded and looked down the road, at the sky and the trees beginning to sway in the wind. In the distance a dark bank of clouds was coming my way. Something was happening to the air. It smelled dusty. It was hard to take a deep breath with that tight, dry feeling in the back of my throat.

"Remember now, don't get on the bus," my mother had said, a long month ago. "I'll pick you up and we'll go get strawberry ice cream and your new red shoes. When you tap them together anything can happen." I looked down at my brown oxfords. My very own red patent leather shoes with red taffeta bows just like in *The Wizard of Oz*.

Then she'd said, "Oh, I don't want you to go to school today. Let's just stay home this morning and play hooky. Then we can get our shoes." She kissed the top of my head, my cheeks, the nape of my neck.

I loved standing there, my head in the folds of her nightgown, breathing in her lavender smell. To love her so much, to be loved so much. It left me breathless. "Let's dance," she said, and I stepped with my socks on her bare feet, one set of footprints, one heartbeat. We waltzed through the house while Ella Fitzgerald sang "Cheek to Cheek" until we finally collapsed on the living room couch.

"Oh, you'd better go to school. I don't want you to get into trouble." She laughed. "We'll have fun this afternoon though when I pick you up. We'll walk down the street in our new red shoes and swing our arms, and we'll laugh out loud if anybody looks at us at all." She laughed again. I would have done anything to hear that laugh. I sat there quiet and still, not saying anything that would break this spell. Her laugh was silvery, like water tumbling over high mountain stones.

We watched the sun flashing against the crystal chandelier and listened to the shimmer of the crystal wind chimes. Frida, my golden parakeet, sat in her cage in the middle of the dining room table scattering feathers and seed husks all over the white linen tablecloth. My mother kept her mouth shut when she looked at her. She hated things in cages. Even then I knew her silence was a profound gift to me. I knew this was the most uncomplicated pet she could think of, given her awareness of our complicated lives. My tiny mother and her moon-driven life.

We stayed quiet like that a long time. "The bus is gone, isn't it," she said at last, looking out the window. "Oh well, I'll just drive you then." I was getting that scared feeling. Something was different again.

But she couldn't find her car keys. Suddenly it seemed urgent that I get to school on time. "They aren't here," she said, rummaging in her purse, then dumping it upside down onto the dining room table. The bird flew up and smashed into the roof of the cage, then hung there on the top of the swing, panting, while my mother spun round and round in the middle of the room.

Then she grabbed all the coats from the coat stand and searched through each pocket. They lay in a heap in the hallway next to the front door. Then she began pulling out drawers, dumping silverware and kitchen utensils onto the kitchen table.

"I don't want to get you into any trouble," she said. Her cheeks were hot, her eyes filled with tears.

"It's okay, Mommy, I can walk. I know the way." I had never walked to school before, but I would have said anything to get her to sit down and take slow, deep breaths like I knew she was supposed to do.

She stood in the middle of the living room, holding the big drawer of bills in her arms and looked at me as if company had just walked into the room. "Oh. Okay," she said breathlessly. "That's a good idea." She put the bill drawer down calmly and patted it. "There. It's all right. I didn't hurt anything. I'll just walk you to school."

"Mommy, you better get dressed."

She looked down at her nightgown and ran her hands through her hair. "There isn't any time. We're all out of time."

She took my hands and pulled me to her.

"Look. Just like mine. Look at the little arcs on our hands. It's our mark. It's how we know we're the same." I looked at my pale, freckled hands and could see no arcs. "My baby, my little girl." She pulled me tighter. I held my breath. "I know," she said, letting go. "Sometimes I love you too much."

"Mommy?"

"We have to go." She took my hand and pulled me toward the door.

"Mommy, you're still wearing your nightgown."

"I'll just put on a coat. See? It's all right. Don't cry, sweetheart, I've got my coat on now."

And so she took my hand and we walked out the door, hand in hand along the sidewalk all the way to school. I watched her bare feet over the sidewalk, her thin, white legs, her coat flapping open as we walked. I was afraid to look at the houses we passed, hoping no one was looking back. Our heartbreak out here on the sidewalk for anybody to see.

So she had to go away again, and to make up for it, today my father was finally going to take me for red shoes and strawberry ice cream.

The trees brushed against the clouds that hung dark and low now, the windows of the school building behind me full of dark, angry stares. I felt a little drop of rain on my arm. Now one on my nose, my eyelid. I looked up through the trees. It was all gray. The wind was a gentle, steady purr, like a big gray cat. I tried to remember street names. I knew they were all trees. Alder, Oak, Elm, Willow. There was a mysterious weeping willow tree in our backyard that bent down and wept against my bedroom window. Willow must be the name of my street.

The sky was darker but with a green and yellow light that scared me more than the dark. The rain was coming down hard now, as the sky disappeared. I tried skipping, pretending I already had my new red shoes, on through a canopy of roaring green, past silent wooden houses and empty porch swings snapping in the wind. At the corner, Elm was going one way and Oak the other. So I turned right onto Elm and would just keep going until I came to another tree.

But where was everybody? Maybe everybody was indoors already.

A flash of lightning split the sky and I covered my ears. The boom came from nowhere and everywhere at the same time. I took off down the street.

Somebody was coming up the sidewalk a long way off. I slowed down as he came closer. There was something funny about the way he walked, like one leg was shorter than the other. I knew I'd never seen him before—his baggy brown pants hanging below his shoes, his unbuttoned plaid shirt, the hair on his chest above the dirty undershirt, the dark stubble, and his eyes! They were red where the white part should be. If I crossed the street, he'd know I was afraid. He'd grab my arm and yank me back. The clouds thundered across the sky.

"I'm in first grade, already," I said, as I forced myself to walk past him. As I did, he grabbed my arm and pulled me against him. My cheek scraped against his belt buckle as he held my face against him. I smelled his hot, yeasty, breath against my neck as he bent over me. And his cigarettes. The sky cracked open, and when he yanked his head up at the sky, I drove my fist into him. He cried out and let go of my arm. I ran and ran and didn't look back until I saw the castle mailbox my mother had made. He was standing in the middle of the sidewalk, shouting into that riven sky.

Then before I turned into our driveway, I saw the funnel drop out of the clouds, swaying over the ground like a giant elephant trunk, only to disappear into the sky. Any Midwestern child knew what that was.

I ran up onto the porch and opened the screen door. My breath was coming in hard little knots. I tried the doorknob, but it wouldn't turn. I knocked and knocked, but there was no answer. Our doorbell hadn't worked for months. What if that man was turning into the driveway right now? But I knew where the key was. "Even Daddy doesn't know," my mother had said. "The little key is for getting in, the big key for getting out. Being locked out is terrible. Being locked in is worse."

But there it was, in its little pouch snugged under the porch swing cushion. I turned the key and opened the door. I had never used it before. I rushed inside, slammed the door shut, and turned the lock. It had begun to hail. It splattered against the roof, bouncing off the porch. I crept into the living room and peeked out the curtains. A dark empty street, the castle mailbox standing guard over our lawn, the empty porch swing, twisting in the wind. No funnel anywhere in sight. The keys were magic in my hand, silver and blue, just as my mother had painted them. I put them in my pocket.

I looked at the pool of water where I'd been standing, next to the living room window. The living room was cool and dark. Nobody ever opened the curtains now. People always forgot when my mother was away.

"Daddy?" I asked the dark.

I heard something coming from my father's study. My father was talking in an angry voice. I knocked and turned the knob.

"Daddy?" I heard him saying something, but his voice was strange.

"Just a minute. Annie Laurie, please shut the door."

I inched the door shut and pressed my cheek against the cool, heavy wood. His voice was lower but I could tell he was still angry. Then I heard the phone clatter and slam. I wanted to tell him about the man and the belt buckle, that he might be trying to get in right this very minute. Then my father came out of the room and stood with his back to the light.

"You're soaked," he said. "You'd better go upstairs and get out of those wet clothes. What are you doing home so soon?"

"Daddy, it's not soon. It's late."

"Is it?" He looked at his watch, then back at me.

"Didn't anybody drive you home? Didn't you have Scouts today? Didn't Mrs. Blodgett drive you home?"

"I was waiting for you to get me for shopping."

"Oh. That's right." He looked stricken. "Annie Laurie," he said, bending down. He smoothed back my hair and hugged me to him.

"You're trembling," he said almost in a whisper. His voice was small and tight, as if he had something in his throat that couldn't be swallowed.

I couldn't stop shaking.

"How did you get home?"

"I walked all by myself," I said. "Mrs. Blodgett had to go to the dentist."

I could hear the wind against the house, a shutter banging on the far side of the house. I looked at my father. His eyes were dark, as if something had gathered up all the light. They looked like he was going to cry but they looked mad, too. There was a red spot on each cheekbone.

I couldn't stop shivering. "Where were you?" I wanted to tell him about the man outside, that I didn't care about the red shoes or the ice cream anymore.

He stood up. "You should have asked one of the mothers to take you home. It's dangerous to walk home alone. Don't ever do that again."

"Daddy, I knew the whole way home." I couldn't tell him about the man with the buckle now.

He stood up. "Well, get on upstairs now and change your clothes. You ought to take a hot bath. That will warm you up." He rubbed the top of my head. The water dripped off my hair onto my shoulders. I noticed that his shirt was wet from my clothes and wondered where his tie and jacket were.

"Is Mommy coming home now?" We were going to surprise her with my red shoes, just like hers. The question tied my mother's fate to my father's face, his voice, his dark, dark eyes, and the terrible forgetting.

"She wants to come home. She wants it so much, Annie Laurie. But she can't right now. But she'll be home soon." He couldn't hide his sorrow and fear, or turn his face.

"When?" I shouted.

"I don't know. Sometime soon." He touched my face. "You're freezing."

I knew from his voice that something terrible had happened to her.

I ran to my room. I grabbed my panda off the bed and burrowed into my closet. I huddled there, my head against my knees, and thought about the man with the belt buckle. I shut my eyes and watched a line of shiny blackbirds float across my eyelids. I leaned back against the shoes in the corner and tried to breathe through the knot in my throat. I opened my eyes and saw the man with the red eyes. I crawled out of the closet and sat on the floor against the bed, my breath scraping my throat. Not blackbirds, my mother always said. Ravens. Ravensnevermore.

That night after the bedtime story, my father sat on the side of my bed, smoothing back my hair. "I'm sorry I forgot today," he said. "We need to get you a haircut."

"I want my hair long," I said. "Like Mommy's."

"Maybe just the bangs, then. Please don't ever do that again."

"You should go get her anyway," I said. "Even if she's still sick."

"I can't do that, Annie Laurie. Her doctors wouldn't let me."

"I'd get her no matter what the doctors said."

The wind howled all night long. I listened to the unlatched shutter bang against the side of the house and the rain beat against my window. The willow tree whipped the windowpane, while I lay there, keeping watch on the shadow of the willow tree. I had lost my pinwheel somewhere along the way.

TUESDAY, JULY 22, 1997

Leaving you Softly
El Viejo y el Mar

It's the second day of the conference and already the schedule has been abandoned. I'd missed Monday altogether. Sometime this morning it's supposed to begin all over again, in the lobby this time, as it turns out there are no conference rooms. But it feels lovely to be sitting here in the cool shadows of the lounge—the dark paneling of the bar, the brass railing, that dusky purple on the carpet, the smoky glass of the coffee table, the steam coming off the cup of tea I'd brought in from breakfast. I'd had some bottled water and a pastry and was keeping as quiet as I could.

The breeze is coming off the ocean into the open-air lobby, the ceiling fans turning sleepily overhead. I shut my eyes and listen to the morning. The clicking of heels on the tile, the rush of those quick, careless syllables here and there, the faint clatter of dishes from the kitchen, and that soundless breeze, insistent, and already warm.

The sunlight off the pool lays a quicksilver pattern on the tile beyond the bar. I'm thirsty for everything—the warm steamy scent of the tea, my hands wrapped around the white porcelain cup, the shape of the morning, the edges and curves of my thoughts held easily now, the sun just outside. But I'd be blinded by that much sunlight all at once. The only light last night was the flickering light of the candle on the dresser.

I'm watching for Maria, hoping she'll come for dinner tonight. She probably spent the day cleaning rooms while I was sleeping it off. I'd know her anywhere—that short-cropped dark hair with the streak of white, those wonderfully high cheekbones, the unexpected grey eyes. Men must fall in love with her all the time. I remembered her hands even in the dark and was sure she was wearing no ring. I only know she has a daughter old enough to work here.

A woman wearing a shiny blue swimsuit, towel tied around her waist, saunters through the bar. She sits down at one of the tables by the window and lights a cigarette. She crosses her legs, a gold sandal dangling from her toes. She signals the waiter, who brings a frosty glass, slowly pours the beer and sets the bottle on the table. Foam slips down the side of the glass and he wipes it up with a napkin. He stands for a moment longer for the tip that never comes, then turns on his heel and goes back to the bar. Her long red hair shines in the sun.

Bernardo comes across the lobby and stands next to me, smiling.

"May I sit by you?" he says.

"Oh yes," I say, "I'm so glad to see you." His flowered shirt gathers the light.

He's a beautiful young man—dark shining face, intelligent eyes, his flashing smile. I'd heard about the racism in Cuba. No matter the Revolution—in Cuba, the lighter the better. Bernardo must be a spectacular exception. He speaks Japanese and German, besides English. I think of our collective Spanish. *Cerveza, por favor,* maybe *buenos días* and *buenos noches,* but *buenos tardes* is a subtlety lost to us.

Bernardo sits forward and turns to me. "I heard you were ill. Are you all right?"

"I'm going to live," I say with a smile. "How did you know I was sick?"

But he doesn't answer.

"A woman named Maria helped me. I think she saved my life. I so want to see her again. I have to thank her, or I don't know, buy her dinner. Something. Do you know her then?"

Bernardo's smile vanishes. For a moment his face closes down. His eyes shift quickly across the room. "You are lucky she came to you," he finally says. Then he lowers his voice. "Be careful, Laura."

"Careful of what?" My stomach tightens. Something turns over in me.

He waves his hand. "I meant. . . drinking the water. . .and the food. That's terrible to be sick. I am so sorry."

But he looks strangely shaken.

Then we see Maxine standing by the elevators and Wallace Fiske plunging across the lobby toward her, his shoulders hunched up around his neck. Bernardo leaps up and rushes to him. I wave Maxine over.

She sits down with a sigh. "I hate that man. It can be said."

"He was terrible on the bus," I say. "I hope he's not going to be that way all week."

"He will be." Maxine leans back in the chair, shuts her eyes and takes my arm.

We can hear the shouting from here. Wallace is waving his hands. Bernardo is standing there with his arms wrapped around himself, nodding. The elevator doors open and Wallace disappears and Bernardo heads our way.

"What a nice young man," Maxine says. "We sat together on the bus ride back from the *Finca*. He has to bike two hours every morning to work. He told me how much he misses his wife. He just got married and says he hardly ever sees her. He gets home at night only to sleep."

"That sounds newly-married, doesn't it? The missing and the sleeping part."

"Oh, it really does." She brushes the smooth arm of the chair. "This is my favorite color. This soft quiet purple."

"Amethyst."

"It's nice to think of colors." She's wearing a soft pink gauzy shift and practical walking sandals.

Then Bernardo is back, but he just stands there. His hands fly out of his pockets and will not be still. "Please sit with us. That must have been awful."

"I cannot say. I would like to, however. Maybe after I am able to quiet myself."

"We were just saying how Cuba is a good place to be in love with color."

"Yes. Let's talk about color," Maxine says, and touches my arm. "Are you all right?" Her hand is trembling.

"I have to give my paper this afternoon. I get very nervous before presentations."

"Tell me," I say as I take her hand.

She clears her throat, straightens her shoulders dramatically.

"I'm calling it 'The Great Blue River: Hemingway and the Eternal Feminine.' I'm hoping any paper with the conference title in it will do. I didn't realize that's what Hemingway called the Gulf Stream, you know, until I started writing this. It's a lovely phrase. Being a Fitzgerald person, who's only come here for Havana, my paper will seem simplistic, I fear."

"How can a true idea ever be simplistic? For Hemingway the sea was always *la mar*, not *el mar*. So of course the 'eternal feminine.' I love the Great Blue River too. I'm going to swim in it before this week is over."

"You will be wonderful, Maxine. And I will translate flawlessly," Bernardo says. He's smiling at her wonderfully.

"And then your paper will be done, and you can just have fun and see Havana."

"And tomorrow we will have a boat ride on the Great Blue River," Bernardo says.

"Tomorrow is Wednesday, then. I've lost a day somewhere. So I don't have to worry about giving my paper until Thursday. I was so sick Sunday night, I thought if I lived, I wouldn't care whether I gave it or not."

"Oh, my dear. I didn't know you were sick. We were so careful." She squeezes my hand.

"It was just too much of everything, I think." I keep hold of her hand, this casual, intimate touching so rare and fine.

She looks frightened. "But you're all right now?"

"Mostly." But as I say it I feel a familiar wave of nausea. I just need to sit here and drink this tea as slowly as I can.

"I so wish I'd known. I thought it strange not to see you yesterday, but didn't want to be a bother."

"How could you be a bother?"

"We'd just met and I didn't want to overwhelm you with my affection. But I would have taken care of you. I brought a great deal of medicine."

"I know you would have," I say, feeling the pull of tears withheld, remembering the flickering candlelight, how soft, how cool, how lovely to be cared for.

Then Bernardo leans forward, rubs the bridge of his nose. "Wallace wants me to skip the Cuban presentations if we get too much behind. But I cannot do that. My friends have worked so hard to write them. It takes four hours just to get here. And the bus only comes so far, so there is much walking to do."

"But why don't you just stay at the hotel?" Maxine says.

"Cubans aren't allowed to do that," Bernardo says without bitterness.

"But you're part of this conference." Maxine is sitting upright now. Something has clicked into place.

He goes on. He can't help himself. "We love Hemingway as you do. But we have mainly Spanish translations. In translation words can go sideways and much is lost." His eyes fill with tears. "This conference with you is very precious to us."

The three of us are quiet for the moment, gathered together in that dusky lounge.

"They told me my job is to make Wallace happy."

Maxine smooths down her skirt, then picks up her big white purse and pulls it to her chest.

"I wish he understood the importance of this conference to us."

"Maybe he does understand," Maxine says. "Maybe it isn't his understanding that's the problem."

"I would not like to think that."

"That's because you are a generous person."

"Thank you," he says formally.

"I hear you have recently married," she says. "You are very lucky. Congratulations."

"Yes, thank you. I miss her so much all the time when I'm working."

Maxine looks away. The beat of the salsa music coming from the pool drifts through the lobby. Maxine watches as the woman in the blue swimsuit and towel saunters up to the bar and orders a beer to go. The bartender watches her too, as she turns and heads toward the pool, swaying to the beat, her sunglasses in one hand, the glass in the other.

Maxine turns to Bernardo. "Do you think of me as an old woman?" she asks suddenly.

Bernardo looks at her seriously for a moment and then smiles. "You are beautiful as all women are beautiful. But you have your own beauty as well."

Maxine's eyes shimmer. "That was very kind of you. But I know what's true."

Bernardo looks to me. "Have you children?"

"No. No children. I. . . . " Maxine takes my hand, as the long cool shadows of the lounge shorten by the minute.

The sunlight is spreading over the pool and begins to spill into the hotel. Maxine softens into the cool lavender duskiness and shuts her eyes. We sit there a long time, Bernardo missing his wife, who waits every night on the porch in the shifting darkness for the sound of his bike on the gravel. She walks down the road to meet him halfway, holding their precarious lives in her outstretched hands, while Maxine waits out the night with unblinking eyes in her house weighted with grief, her husband's things just as he had left them— *why did you leave me?* she says, as she drops time after time into long soundless nights that hold no dreams.

The ceiling fan turns on and on in that warm shadowy air. I fight down a feeling of dread. I can't ever be sick like that again.

"Sometimes I didn't understand him," Maxine says.

"What do you mean?" I ask gently.

"There was so much I never knew."

"I don't think it's always possible, to understand everything," I say.

"I do," Bernardo says quietly. "It's that way with my wife." He veils his eyes against some longing he can barely contain and we grow silent around it.

"You are very lucky to have such understanding," Maxine says, touching his arm."

"She's different from me. She's always saying what she thinks. But I worry about her all the time now. In Cuba you have to be very careful of saying things. Since I married I have become much more careful."

Bernardo's words echo in my heart. Be careful, he'd said. Incautiously I ask, "Careful how?"

He laughs, a sound covering another, deeper, sound. There is a tightness around his eyes. He rubs his forehead again.

The light is spilling into the hotel from almost everywhere now. Why are we sitting in the dark with all that light so close at hand?

Maxine holds her purse to her chest. She strokes it between her fingers. "I don't know who I am," she says. "What's someone like me anyway? There isn't anyone who loves me best."

We sit there in the shadows looking out at that trembling light.

Deep Purple
Seattle 1987

"That's it," Brick had finally said. "That's the whole damned thing, Laura. You sleep like the dead even when you're awake. It's like you're not here anymore."

Brick never believed I didn't blame him. But I only blamed myself. All I could do then was turn my face to the open window and let the night air wash me over. He was right, though. I hadn't felt a thing since that night I'd gone into the bathroom and found the blood he always said was his fault.

It hailed the day he brought me home from the hospital. It was July and we were driving through a thunderstorm. I sat in the car with the seatbelt limp across my belly, remembering how a few days ago it had been taut with promise. We were waiting for the hail to stop. I couldn't go into that empty house with the yellow room and the white ducks and red tulips. Brick didn't know what to do with the baby furniture, and he'd been too anguished in the hospital to ask me what I wanted, so he just left it there. I couldn't have told him anyway. I crossed my arms over my swollen breasts. Brick dashed in for an umbrella, but he didn't come back out until the hail had stopped. I sat in the car, listening to the hail on the roof, watching it slide down the windshield like snow, the thunder cracking the sky open, then the hail turning to hard, bitter rain. I could stay here forever inside this rushing water. What would I do anyway, once I walked through that door? What would I do all night and all the next day and forever after?

"I didn't know if I should move the baby stuff or not. I can take it downstairs right now, if you want," he said.

I was sitting in the chair by the living room window, watching the water run down the driveway into the street. I didn't say anything. We were sitting across from each other in the living room. I was already wearing that impassive, empty face I would assume for years.

"Do you want to take a nap?"

I shook my head. I had been sleepless for three days now. How could I sleep? I'd have to go down the hall past that little yellow room. How could I do that and not look in or stop and sit in the rocking chair or touch the satin ribbon on the blanket in the crib?

Brick worried he would hurt the baby some way. He always leaned over me, taking all the weight with his arms. "Are you okay?" he'd ask a thousand times.

"Come here," I said. "You're way too far away." It was those first weeks after we'd known about the baby, and I wanted him, only nice and slow and easy.

"I'd better not, Lauracakes."

"Brick, the baby's just a tadpole in the middle of an ocean."

"Well, see how I'm protecting her already?"

"It's really all right."

"Okay, Lauralee." He pulled into me, whispered against my hair. "Okay okay okay."

Those months passed in a golden tenderness. He could be so intense, so present, sometimes I could hardly breathe. But those days he took everything as slow as I needed and wrapped me in the most exquisite care. Those months I was the center of the universe, not the waif, the motherless child. Everything I'd ever read said I should be missing my mother especially now, bereft of all the things she would tell me, all that womanly folklore that was my due. But I didn't. With my mother I often didn't know whether I was mother or child.

Now for the first time since my mother died, everything that hollowed out inside me all those years was filling up. I loved to touch my changing body, my breasts warm and full now, the growing little mound beneath my navel. I was hungry all the time. All I wanted was ambrosia and plums. The dusky purple skin, the sunlit flesh, the feel of the seed against my cheek, over my tongue.

She'd come as such a surprise. I'd been told by too many doctors too many times that a baby was a long shot. But this baby filled us both and made us the happiest we had ever been. Brick bought me a rocking chair, and at night I'd wait for him to come home from the jazz club, rocking in that chair and feel her move long before everybody said I could. A fluttering, a silver bubble bursting against my skin, a puff, a tiny hand.

I'd lie propped up on the bed while Brick sat by the window and played the saxophone. Long, slow, mournful blues. "Gallagher, play something happy for once."

And he'd say, "This is happy; this is the happiest sound in the world, Lauralee."

"Okay. How about this?" So he played "Saint Louis Woman," but it was gentle and soft and slow. He played it like a lullaby.

"She's a hussy already," I said.

"Okay then, how about 'Stella by Starlight'? Since that's what we're going to name her anyway."

"You know we can't really name a baby Stella by Starlight." But at that moment I would have named her anything he wanted.

"Sure we can."

"Okay, but what if she's a boy?"

"But she isn't."

Then I said, "Play 'Deep Purple,'" like I always did before we went to sleep.

"Okay, but you gotta pull down the covers and lift up your nightgown."

He wanted to watch her move against my belly, to see what she thought.

"How do you know she likes it?" I said "Maybe she's protesting."

"Nah, she likes it. You know she does."

"You want anything?" he asked, looking out the front window at the rain. I shook my head. I hardly heard him. It felt like I would never get up out of that chair.

We stayed there awhile longer listening to the silence, to the rain that would not stop, and then he said, "I just can't sit here, Lauralee. I'm goin' crazy."

"Nobody asked you to sit here."

"Christ, Laura, don't do that."

"I know you want to leave. So go ahead."

He just sat there looking straight ahead. Then he said, "I gotta go out for awhile. I'll be back." I didn't mind. It was long past dark before he came back. I pretended to be asleep when he came into the bedroom. He sat for a long time in the chair. After awhile he crawled into bed without touching me. If he had reached out to me just then I would have turned to him and buried my head in the crook of his neck and cried at last, and we would have stayed like that all night. And in the morning we would have gone into that yellow room and put away the baby things for safekeeping. But he didn't turn to me, and I couldn't reach for him. So we lay turned from each other, wakeful without words, and full of shame.

"You're pretty big now," he had said when we had just made that long, slow turn into the eighth month. "I don't want to take any chances." And so most of the time we would lie like spoons. "It's okay, it's the way I want it now," he said. "It's strange, but I like it."

But that last night he'd come in so late and slipped his hand around me, tucking it between my breasts, touching me over and down my belly. He buried his face in my neck. "Lauralee," he said, "I'm home now. "He was damp and warm from the shower, the minty smell of toothpaste against my face. He was so gentle and easy and slow I could have dreamed it.

When I got up later in the night to go to the bathroom there was blood on my nightgown, blood trickling down my legs.

"It was just a coincidence," the doctor had said so emphatically I knew it had to be true. Brick just stood by the bed absolutely anguished. "You did not start this bleeding. She has what we call placenta praevia. Premature separation of the placenta. It's not all that uncommon. It had nothing to do with you."

"What happens if the bleeding doesn't stop?" Brick looked like he wanted to take the doctor by his white coat lapels and slam him against the wall.

"We'll need to take the baby, then."

"What do you mean take the baby?" Brick was almost shouting.

The doctor stepped back into the doorway. "Do a Caesarean, that's all. It's pretty routine, Mr. Gallagher, it really is."

There were no labor pains. Just a stillness wild with fear while the blood seeped onto the pad they'd put underneath me. I wanted to put my hands between my legs and hold that pad tight. But I lay as still as I could while the blood trickled out, and she floated in that ocean of water and blood, her first and only true home. I was afraid to breathe. Then I remembered I should have lots of oxygen in my blood and breathed so fast I began to see spots before my eyes.

"My hands are tingling," I said, "They're going numb."

"You're hyperventilating, Mrs. Gallagher, just take long slow even breaths. Try to sleep. You're not bleeding very much now."

Try to sleep! My god, I couldn't even close my eyes.

Brick couldn't keep still. He paced up and down the room, circled the bed, until the nurses made him go down the hall for coffee. "It's gonna be okay, Laurie," he said out the door.

But there was no stopping it. She was born that night seven weeks too soon.

"If I hadn't touched you like that, if I'd just kissed you and turned the other way," he said, over and over. He never believed he hadn't done it. I never knew how to convince him otherwise.

Later the doctor said, "The baby's pretty small. But the heartbeat is strong. Babies a lot smaller than this can do very well. The lungs are a bit of a problem."

"What kind of problem?" Brick dropped my hand and jolted out of the chair.

They took me down to her just once. I touched her face, felt her breath against my hand, her sweet, frantic hummingbird breath. She grasped my finger and held on while her heart fluttered against her quiet dusky chest. I touched her hair. Where did she get such dark, dark hair?

Be Safe, Little Bird, Be Safe
El Viejo y el Mar

I had slept all afternoon and when I woke, all the terror of illness had gone.

"I'm so happy you came," I say way too brightly.

"Thank you," they say formally. "We are happy to be here." I would know them anywhere, this mother and daughter, their dark, dark hair, their luminous gray eyes.

But I know right away it's more complicated than I'd thought. Their eyes flick across the room, past the curtains onto the balcony, over their shoulders, before they dart in. There's a secret language between them I recognize but cannot read.

"This is my daughter, Pilar," Maria says, once the door is closed.

I take her hand. "Your mother saved my life."

Maria laughs self-consciously. "Not really."

"It felt that way to me." We smile at each other, and I feel a familiar shyness that acknowledges the strange intimacies between us.

"My mother told me about you," Pilar says.

"She told me about you, too. I'm so glad you came. I've got lots of food."

They look out at the balcony where I've set up a little table and chairs.

"It's pretty warm in here right now, but it's nice outside."

They don't say anything. They just stand there in the middle of the room. looking out.

"Maybe the balcony isn't a good idea right now," Maria says. "While it's light anyway. We aren't really supposed to be here."

"Oh, that's just fine," I say. "We can move everything inside." So we bring in the table and the chairs and the tray of food. "The air conditioning will pop back on anytime now. And this wonderful ceiling fan."

"Please don't worry. Nobody has air conditioning where we live."

"Maybe when it's dark we can sit outside." I'm trying way too hard.

"Sure," Maria says. "It would be nice to do that when it's dark." So we gather around the little table from the balcony and pull up the patio chairs. The bowls of food make steamy circles on the glass tabletop.

"Here," I say, taking a plate and filling it with slices of beef, boiled potatoes, bread, plantains. I hand the plate to Pilar. "We should eat it while it's warm." The hunger has gone so deep now my stomach aches, but I know I shouldn't eat very much, not yet. The afternoon's little set back had shaken me. Still, I love the steamy smells filling the room.

"Thank you," Pilar says courteously, laying the napkin on her lap. Her shoulder blades are like little wings at rest just above the back of her blue sundress, and below the eyelet trim beneath her collarbone, the outline of her tiny, girlish breasts. She's wearing a Mickey Mouse watch with a white band she's had to loop around twice.

I've told them at the desk I'm hosting a working dinner, and we need food brought up. And from the bar an ice bucket with cans of Coke and beer. I pick up a can of Coke and hand it to Maria. *Bottled in Madrid.*

"We're ninety miles from the States and the Coke's imported from Madrid."

"The joys of the embargo," Maria says.

"I'm learning all the time. It's very humbling to know so little."

"Could I have a beer, maybe?" Pilar asks.

"Yes, you should have beer," Maria says.

I take a can of beer from the ice bucket and pour it into two tall glasses and hand one to Maria and one to Pilar.

"This is nice," Pilar says. "I like this nice frosty glass."

"*Salud,*" we say over the clink of glasses. We sit and watch the sun slipping across the pool just before it disappears around the corner.

"Look at this," Pilar says. "Glasses *and* beer. In Cuban bars sometimes we have one, sometimes the other. Sometimes neither."

"Why no glasses?"

"No soap, no water. Who knows?" Maria laughs. "We never know. You go to the store and wait in line with your ration book and the shelves are mostly empty. Try next month. We are used to waiting in Cuba and keeping our wondering to ourselves."

I look down at the food before us, and still our plates are hardly touched. I can't imagine why they haven't finished and taken seconds. If this is a cultural reserve or politeness, it's another thing I don't know.

Pilar reaches over and touches my hair. "It's beautiful," she says.

I glance in the mirror. "This morning I wanted to cut it off."

"Your hair is very unusual," Pilar says. "You should always love that you have it."

"Your hair is like your mother's," I say. "So beautifully cut. It's like a sculpture." I want to touch her cheek, her hair, make sure she's real. "You look so much like her. You're petite, though, like my mother was. I was the tall one in my family."

"You shouldn't ever cut your hair," Pilar says. "There isn't any trouble that's too much." She runs her hand through her short dark hair, swept-back with gel. Her gray eyes are set wide and tinged with green, under whispery, dark eyebrows. With those lovely cheekbones, the tender hollow of her face, she looks like a schoolgirl, but for her eyes. In that pale blue sundress with the eyelet trim, she looks sixteen. I guess she's nineteen or twenty. How fragile she seems sitting there with that plate of food she's hardly eating, and her mother holding her close without touching.

"My mother told me you're a writer," Pilar says. "That you love Hemingway."

"Oh, I'm not really a writer. I'm a scholar."

"What is the difference?"

"I write about what other people write."

"But you write things that are published," Pilar says.

"Yes I do."

"Then you are a writer like my mother said you were."

"It's nice to think it," I say. "Once I tried to write a book about my mother's life. Or how I imagined it."

"Oh! Another way you are alike." She takes my hand. "My mother wrote a story but she won't let me see it."

Maria sits back and gives Pilar such a sharp look she's shaken into silence.

I'd pass around the food, but they'd hardly eaten anything. Finally I say, "But I couldn't do it."

"Why not?" Pilar asks.

"Oh, I think it's as hard to write about the dead as the living. Maybe harder."

"Did your mother die then?"

"A long time ago," I say.

"I'm sorry," Pilar says. "I would be inconsolable if my mother died." She sets down her fork and pushes away from the table.

Maria turns her face and looks out the sliding glass door. Her crystalline gray eyes have gone somewhere else. Pilar is watching her mother as an unexpected silence settles gravely between them.

Then Pilar turns to me and asks, "You like Hemingway very much then?"

"He's not very popular right now, but I do."

"You mean with feminism and everything?" Maria asks.

"Especially," I laugh.

"Did you see the *Finca*? My mother grew up there."

"You didn't tell me that," I say.

"You were too busy throwing up."

"I'm sorry to contradict you, but you did save my life."

Maria shakes her head. "Please don't thank me so much."

I watch them cut their food into decorous little bites they push around their plates politely, shading their embarrassment over eating so little—and wonder who this meal is really for.

I shut the slider to see if the air conditioner is working and a great puff of cold air accompanies that familiar, welcomed hum. "What was it like at the *Finca*?" I say, determined now to keep it light.

"It was only for a couple of years I lived in San Francisco de Paula," Maria says. Pilar likes to think I grew up there. She has a fascination for all things Hemingway. But Pilar isn't her real name. When she was thirteen she named herself after Hemingway's boat."

Pilar laughs. "She always says that. I didn't name myself after a *boat.* It was for Pilar the gypsy in *For Whom the Bell Tolls*, because she was so strong. Did you know Fidel read it when he was fighting in the Sierra Maestra? Hemingway is everywhere in Cuba. Like a god."

"I love seeing Hemingway without all the criticism," I say.

"In the book Maria is the daughter and *Pilar* is the mother," Pilar says. She takes her mother's hand and strokes it. "So you should listen to *me* all the time, instead of the other way around."

"When have you ever listened to me?" Maria asks. "I must have missed it." Pilar laughs again, but the laugh catches in her throat, and she begins to cough. She wipes her mouth with the napkin and quickly folds it up, but not before I see the mark of blood. She takes a sip of beer and looks at me before I have a chance to look away.

"Aren't her hands beautiful?" Pilar says, as she sets down the glass.

If Maria has seen it, her face reveals nothing.

"I know," I say, remembering how those quicksilver hands held me to earth. I look at their hands, resting now on the little glass table, tawny and smooth, without rings or bracelets, a matching pair all but in size, and the mark on the inside of Maria's wrists.

"And you both have the same beautiful eyes."

They look down and for a moment, no one says anything.

"My mother named me *Olga*," Pilar says. "Very Russian. Very ugly."

"I did not. I gave her a beautiful name. I named her *Mercedes*."

"After a *car*."

"*Mercedes* means compassion. *Santa Maria de las Mercedes*. Our Lady of Mercy. I was very Catholic back then."

"Now you're atheist," Pilar says, "and I'm Catholic."

"Half Catholic." They were talking to each other with their eyes all the while they were talking to me and I'm surprised at the longing I feel.

"She thinks I'm crazy for *Santería*," Pilar says. "Maybe I'll become a *santera*. That would be an irony."

"A virtual Mary Magdalene," Maria says darkly.

Pilar turns away.

"I changed my name too," I tell her, and she brightens.

"How did you do that?"

"Nothing dramatic, just *Annie Laurie* to *Laura*."

"Pilar is very interested in you. She wants to know all about you. I hope it's all right."

"Why did you do it?" Pilar asks "Why did you change your name?"

"I thought *Annie Laurie* didn't sound grown up enough. That's what I always tell people. But I think I was really just angry at my mother."

"Didn't she mind?"

"She never knew. I did it after she died."

"When was that?" Pilar asks.

"When I was twelve."

"Oh," she says. "Just when you were at the beginning of everything. Who was there to love you then?"

"My father. And we had a housekeeper who took care of me. A woman named Mrs. Beswick. But I was growing up by then."

"Why did she die?"

"Pilar! You shouldn't ask that."

Pilar's eyes flare. "I'm sorry. I couldn't help it."

"It's all right. It was a long time ago."

Then Pilar's eyes fill with tears. "I'm sorry you lost her."

I turn and put my arms around her and she does the same.

"It's strange to be talking like this so soon, don't you think?" Pilar says.

"I like it very much," I say. I'm watching how Maria is looking at her daughter, as if she's trying to memorize her.

The room is washed in the last brilliance of the day and soon it would be dark.

"Tell her about Hemingway and the *Finca*, Mama," Pilar says.

"Okay," Maria says, touching the inside of her arm, sliding her finger absently over the ivory scar on her wrist. "I was a little girl then," she begins. She looks at me and laughs. "We lived in Pinar del Rio, but when my parents became revolutionaries and went to the mountains, I moved to San Francisco de Paula to live with my grandparents. My grandfather was a groundskeeper at the *Finca*, and sometimes I'd come to work with him. Once I swam in the swimming pool. I didn't know how to swim and my grandfather held me on his shoulders. San Francisco de Paula is very poor, you know, just little shacks, little dusty roads. But to walk up that driveway and go through the gate and look up at that white house in all the trees. It was like being inside a dream.

"What about your mother?"

"Things happened in the mountains they never talked about. Things that separated them. So they got divorced and she went to live in Mexico. My grandfather stayed on a little while after the government took over the *Finca*. He said when Mary Hemingway came back for their possessions, she could only take a couple of paintings and some little things. She stood on the steps and cried."

The amber light is fading fast, the last of the sunset, which we have missed entirely, and suddenly it's night. "It's getting dark in here," I say, reaching over to snap on the light on the dresser behind us. Our reflections on the glass door shoot across the room. There we are, the three of us, like old friends or a little family. But I don't remember till later how they startled at the light, or the effort they made not to ask me to turn it off.

They stand up as if to leave.

"Did you ever see him?" I say. I'm weaving a net of words to keep them there.

"I was always a little afraid of him," Maria says as she sits back down. "He was so famous. But my grandfather said he treated everybody the same, don't be afraid. It didn't matter who you were." She looks to the door.

"Tell her what he said to you, Mamá," Pilar insists, taking my hand. Then she looks at her mother and takes her hand also, and now I'm inside the circle too.

"Mamá," she says, "Go on."

Maria has taken her hand back and is rubbing the scar. "I was only six or seven, you know," she begins a little reluctantly, then eases down into memory. "I watched him from the road sometimes.

"But one day he said, 'What a pretty little girl,' and he knelt down and brushed the hair out of my eyes. I'm remembering he looked sad. After we learned what happened, I thought of course he was sad. How could he not have been sad? Look what was about to happen! Nobody in Cuba wanted to believe it."

"It's terrible to be so sad," Pilar says.

I was seeing Eugenie now, how she disappeared behind her eyes when the sadness came. How I pulled her mouth into a smile, patted her cheek, stroked her hair. I turned cartwheels and fell to the ground. I pretended I was dead, and then jumped up, resurrected. I stuck my tongue out and rolled my eyes. *Where did you go?* But she had gone off somewhere too far and too dark for me to follow.

"I always thought my mother's sadness was my fault."

"Children always think they must make their parents happy," Maria says, turning to Pilar. "But when we grow up we learn it's not our job to make them happy. Only to love them."

Pilar's eyes fill with tears.

We sit there looking out at the night coming on in a rich and chastening silence.

Then Maria says, "Pilar used to ride the bus to the *Finca* to read her school books. She thought Hemingway was a ghost watching over her."

"It's true," Pilar says. "Sometimes I felt him whispering to me behind my back. Then the light changed and I saw a shadow float across my book. But I had to learn not to turn around or it went away. 'There you are,' he whispered, 'such a sweet little girl.' I didn't hear it out loud, but I felt it across my heart." She made a fist over her chest, her eyes glistening.

"Don't get her started," Maria says.

"My mother doesn't believe in anything, not even ghosts."

"And Pilar believes in everything."

"I saw ghosts out there too," I say, remembering the spider web, the shadow crossing that tender, desolate face in the window, and the wild and forsaken child edging the sunlit green, the white dress, the breathy silence on my neck, her hair against my shoulder.

"*Ghost* isn't a big enough word," Pilar says. "It sounds too made up."

"Spirit?"

"Spirit," she says, and gives me an incandescent smile. "Something that's real."

Suddenly a sound shatters the light. They push back their chairs.

"It's okay," I say. "It's just the phone."

They're standing again, moving toward the door.

"No, please stay."

"Hello," I say. "Hello, hello." A fuzzy silence and then a dial tone. "It's only a wrong number. It happens in hotels sometimes." If only I could keep talking I could hold them here. I glance at our reflection in the glass. Pilar turns toward the sliding glass door and the night spilling into the room, then quickly turns back around, her mouth tight with fear.

They exchange a look I can't read. But something has changed. Their eyes are frightened as they look to the door. Finally Maria says, "I know it's dark now, but we're used to it. May we have the dark again?"

"Of course. I like it dark too," I say, and turn out the light.

We stand there for a long moment, three shadows against the wall, attenuating the dark.

How stupid! A lighted window in the dark, just like a scene from the movies for anyone standing outside and looking up—our lives for the asking. Then I see Judith before me, her hair, her flashing eyes, her perfect English.

"Too much talking of ghosts," Maria says.

"Nobody could know we're here," Pilar says quietly. "Could they?"

"I didn't say anything to anyone."

"I don't think anybody saw us come in," Pilar says. "We were really careful."

"It's okay, Pilar, don't be so jumpy."

"Could you get fired if anyone knew you were here?"

Maria laughs out loud.

"What my mother means is losing our jobs would be the least of it."

"I don't understand," I say.

"Everybody watches everybody around here," Pilar says. "You can get turned in and go to prison for nothing."

"Pilar is being melodramatic as usual."

"I don't think that phone call means anything," I say. I have no idea what they have risked by coming here. I have no idea why they have come here at all.

"I could get that candle from before," I say. "Nobody can see us by candlelight."

Maria looks out at the night. "No candle," she whispers.

"Please stay. We could sit outside now."

Pilar taps the dial on her Mickey Mouse watch. Time glows in the dark. "I'm sorry to have to be leaving," she says softly. We've begun to whisper at the insistence of the dark, or so it seems.

"Pilar has a date. He's over at the Marina."

"Thank you for this nice dinner," Pilar says.

"I wish you didn't have to go."

"Mamá, you can stay. You never get to have fun. She's always busy busy busy. She goes to meetings and things, or she's working."

"Please stay."

"Sure, why not? For a little while. Then I can walk Pilar home."

"My friend will take me home. She has a car tonight."

"Good to go in a car," Maria says. "That road is crazy. And be sure nobody's. . . ."

"I *know*. You don't have to say it."

"I didn't say it."

"We'll be careful. You be careful too, Mamá."

They walk to the door while I just stand in the middle of the room, weighted down by that appalling light which seemed to have beckoned the phone.

"Goodbye," Pilar says over Maria's shoulder. "Thank you again very much for the dinner. I really did see his ghost."

"Me too," I say. I want to hug her goodbye but am too shy. Then she reaches out as though reading my mind and wraps her arms around me. I hold her as tightly as I dare. I touch her face.

"Thank you," I say. "I wanted this so much."

"Me also," she says, then turns to her mother.

Maria puts her hands on Pilar's shoulders and tells her something I can't hear. I'm glad we're in the dark. But I know what Maria must have said. Be safe, little bird, be safe.

Goodnight, Princess, Goodnight
St. Louis 1963

That long hot summer after my mother died, Mrs. Beswick came to live with us for good. At first she came only during the day, then she stayed through the evening. She was kind and shy, and she adored my father. I hated her because she was alive and my mother was dead. But even then, at twelve, I knew she was the perfect live-in housekeeper. Nobody at church would talk about Mrs. Beswick moving in. There had been way too much talking already. We'd had a series of day housekeepers over the years who moved in and out of my life hardly noticed, as I waited weeks or months for my mother to come home. Mrs. Beswick was tall and awkward, with large pendulous breasts, ridiculous against her otherwise gaunt, strained figure. She stood at the edges of our lives, wrapping her thin brown sweater across her chest. Her black hair was streaked with gray and pulled into a tight knot in the back. She wore rimless glasses that magnified her sad dark eyes. She wore sturdy black oxfords, thick cotton stockings and pale cotton housedresses buttoned down the front. There was no Mr. Beswick anymore and no children.

Mrs. Beswick's first order of business was to clean out what had been for the last months of her life, my mother's room and turn it back into the guest room. My father had shut the door the day my mother died. I'd stand with my head against the door and think about the smell of lavender on her bedclothes in a tangle just as she had left them, her robe on the floor, her slippers crisscrossed beside the bed, her easel in the corner by the window, her paints and palette on the chair, the sunlight filtering through the willow tree, dappling the carpet, the empty bed.

So it was up to Mrs. Beswick, because that's where she would be staying. Not a member of the family, not exactly a guest either. She said, "I'll leave you alone. You just take your time now. Your father said you can have anything you want."

I sat on the edge of my mother's bed and grabbed her pillow, and breathed in her lavender scent. I was losing her fast. My father had the kitchen repainted a bright, almost frantic yellow. But if you'd been there that last morning and seen how my mother had turned the kitchen into a sky, you'd still see the blue coming through that horrid yellow, in faint little patches here and there along the corners. I went into her closet and gathered her dresses in my arms and threw them across the bed. I lay face down and breathed her in.

For the first few weeks Mrs. Beswick stayed only through dinner. Then one morning while I slept in late, she moved into my mother's room and made it the guest room once more. The lavender was gone. Her clothes were gone. Everything was gone. All gone to the dark in the basement. The room smelled different already. Like camphor and talcum. The bedcovers were washed and starched and tucked neatly under the mattress. Mrs. Beswick's suitcase was propped in the corner, her black coat neatly folded over the chair, as though she wasn't sure she would be staying. My mother's paints and easel were gone. I had never seen this pale green chenille bedspread in place of the white satin comforter that was always slipping off my mother's bed.

She was living with us all the time now, employed as both house-keeper and babysitter, though I was way too old for that. There was no name for what she was supposed to become to me. But I hated her. I hated the way she cleared her throat in the morning, hated the sound of her heavy shoes on the kitchen linoleum, hated the way she sang church hymns in a tremulous soprano as she made breakfast.

"It is no secret what God can do, what He's done for others He'll do for you."

My family was full of secrets, but they weren't God's secrets. I had given up on God the day my mother died.

On nights my father was away, Mrs. Beswick stood in the doorway to my bedroom to remind me to say my prayers, according to my father's instructions. She was never sure how close she was allowed to come, so she just stood there, wearing such longing on her thin white face that even through my rage, I knew how much she wanted to be asked to come in and take me in her arms. But she knew how I would have wrenched myself away, so she just looked at me before she turned and shut the door.

Her longing gave me a power I did not want. I went around the house day after day, refusing to acknowledge her ungainly presence. After all, she was the excuse my father had for abandoning me too. Yet even then, I knew there was something beyond grief that hung about my father, some dark knowledge he held behind his eyes that gave him a permanent expression of remorse. Whatever it was had made him withdraw from me as surely as my mother had the day she died.

Some evenings after I'd been outside on the porch swing listening to the cicadas, I'd forget my mother was gone forever. I'd gotten so accustomed to her leave-takings, I'd come into the darkened hallway looking for her, and there in the lighted room was Mrs. Beswick in my mother's chair, and I'd stand in the hallway in the dark and feel such loneliness I thought I would die. How could my beautiful mother be gone?

The only thing Mrs. Beswick could do for us that summer was feed us. She had no words for what had happened to me. The only way she knew to fill the crater of my blackened heart was to feed me. So she baked and fried and boiled and stirred and chopped. We had never eaten better. That summer we had cinnamon rolls with white frosting, homemade white bread, pork chops with gravy over mounds of mashed potatoes, white sweet corn with a pat of butter melting on top, green beans with bacon, lime Jell-O with marshmallows, apple pie with slices of cheddar cheese, and ice cream if you wanted, or tonight for a change, coconut cake with coconut icing. For breakfast, Mrs. Beswick made pancakes and waffles and country fried potatoes, and strips of crisp bacon, and scrambled eggs whipped till they were like meringue. She fed us like our lives depended on it. And maybe they did. That summer my father and

I ate and ate and ate. The few evenings he was home, it was the only thing we did together.

"Sit down, Inez, eat with us," my father always said. "You don't need to wait on us like that."

"Well all right," she said. She always needed that invitation to join the family circle, not knowing there wasn't a circle anymore.

"How was your day, Annie Laurie?" my father asked.

I shrugged.

"What did you do?"

"Nothing."

"You couldn't have done *nothing*," he said, smiling at me in that teasing adult way that drives kids crazy. "Even nothing is something."

I glared at him until he looked away. What did *he* care? He just sat across the table from me and talked to Mrs. Beswick about the church. It was church this and church that all night long. I looked at him gesturing with his fork, never looking my way. He could hardly bear to look at me.

"Why does she have to be here?" I asked my father one night. "She's ugly. She just stands around all the time looking at me."

"Annie Laurie, I'm surprised by you. That's cruel."

"You're cruel. You did something to my mother to make her go out in front of that car."

He looked stunned. I had said the unspeakable. My heart was throbbing in my ears. I could hardly breathe. I knew I could hurt him any time I wanted now.

"I don't even know you anymore," he said, then shrugged and headed down the hall to his study. "I loved your mother very much."

"What did you ever do to love her?" I shouted after him. "You just got mad at her all the time for not taking her pills."

He stopped and looked at me. The hall light cast his shadow against the wall. He didn't answer but looked at me with such sorrow it almost broke my stony heart. I barely heard it when he said, "She loved me too."

Some nights I'd hear his car coming in the driveway around midnight and I'd hear him going up the stairs and start to go into what had been their bedroom, then he'd shut the door and go back downstairs, and then I wouldn't hear him anymore. But I never heard him cry. My father had tamped himself down so tightly he was lost to himself and to me.

But in my father's absence, Mrs. Beswick was there, her arms clasped against her trembling, expectant heart, waiting for some sign I would let her touch my hair, my face, my cheek. She stepped toward me and reached out, then tucked her hand back under her arm. "You look so like your mother," she said once, watching me staring at myself in the bathroom mirror. It was her way of letting me know it was all right to talk about her.

"No I don't," I said sharply, though I saw the resemblance more clearly every day. That's why my father ate his dinner every night looking everywhere but at me. "I'd like some *privacy*, please," I said, and shut the door against her. I could hear her on the other side of the door. *Go away, go away*, I whispered. Didn't she know that now I couldn't pretend my mother had just gone away, like she always did? Mrs. Beswick in my mother's room, my mother's bed, my mother's chair, breaking my heart every minute that long summer.

I would be thirteen next year. I stood there looking in the mirror. Any day now I would get my period. Already I needed a bra. I checked my underwear for blood every time I went to the bathroom. I knew what to expect. "There are many beautiful things to know about being a woman," my mother had said. "Pretty soon now, I'll tell you everything." I loved the way she said *everything*. Like a whispery secret unfolding before me, already full of mystery and promise.

By the end of the summer I was so desperate to be held, so hungry for any hand at my cheek, the nape of my neck, smoothing back my hair, I wanted even Mrs. Beswick to touch me.

"Good night, Princess," she said, standing in the doorway to my bedroom. "Remember to say your prayers. I hope you sleep well." It was late, well after ten. She was usually in bed by now.

Nobody but Mrs. Beswick had ever called me "Princess." Not even my mother. I had felt anything but a princess that summer. I started to tell her I never said prayers anymore and that I hated her, but something stopped me. "Okay," I said. "Sleep well too."

"Would you like a bedtime hug tonight?"

"Okay," I said, looking out the window. She moved a step closer.

It was easier in the dark. I could feel her softness and did not have to look at her. I closed my eyes and let her take me in her arms.

"There, there," she said over and over. "There, there, Princess."

I leaned into her bosomy chest, and it was like resting against two feather pillows. She sat there in the dark for a long time, rocking me back and forth as I cried and cried.

She was not my deepest heart, but every morning, every afternoon after school, every evening after dinner, she was there—a shy, awkward, finally sweet presence, who fed me and kept me warm and asked about my day, who didn't understand a thing I said, but nodded and smiled and patted my hand and said *good for you, dearie, good for you.* She fed me that first year in ways I didn't know I needed to be fed.

Jineteras
El Viejo y el Mar

"Do you want to sit outside now?"

"Sure, we can do that," Maria says, and so we bring the chairs back out onto the balcony and sit looking out at the lights of Havana.

"I'm sorry about the light. I didn't think what it would look like."

"It's nothing. Don't worry."

"The phone call couldn't be anything," I say, though I am less sure of it than ever.

The salsa beat has softened, spreading over the night. A man and woman slide into the whirlpool and she kisses his chest, swaying against him to the music. He grabs the side of the whirlpool and throws his head back.

We sit there a long time, watching the flickering blue water of the swimming pool below. Chairs are lined up around the empty pool. I've brought out another beer for each of us, still cold from the ice bucket.

"It's going straight to my head, so why not?" Maria says.

We both snap open another can. Maria makes the sign of the cross.

"Oh, so you're religions then."

She laughs out load. "My religion is this great beer. Communism forbids religion, you know. Catholicism is mostly a disguise for *Santería* anyway. Even Fidel believes in it. Pilar, though, she believes in it so much it scares me."

"All my life I've tried to believe in things. Too much sorrow. Too much everything."

"Isn't it funny how you drink enough of this beer and you can say anything?"

"I like how we're talking just like old friends."

"That's what Pilar would say. In some other life, we would have been."

We've settled into the soft dark air and a sweet familiarity so strange and new.

"My father was a minister," I say. "You know, like a priest. So it was church morning and night when I was growing up."

"Do you believe in it then?"

I could feel my head getting heavy. "No. I never did."

"Do you resemble your father?"

I take the last sip of the beer and it slides down my tongue, tasteless and warm.

"No, only the color of my hair. He had beautiful, silky blonde hair. Not curly blonde like mine or my mother's." My sudden adolescent height made me ache with self-consciousness, as I inched toward the modest height of my father and past my tiny mother. Where did this tallness come from? No ordinary child would think about it. Even so, I had always been thankful that people could point to my blonde hair.

That whole summer after my mother died, he couldn't even look at me. But the smell of lavender, the sound of wind chimes, a whisper in my ear. Or the worn imprint of her ring inside my father's wallet. She haunted us both no matter what we couldn't say.

I think of him now, permanently retired to his study, that dark, oak room, with his Mozart and Bach and Saint John of the Cross. And Gerard Manley Hopkins, that day brightener. All that dappled Hopkins light filtering through the willow tree into every room but his. He knew the dark night of the soul, the hour of the wolf, and still couldn't come into the light.

"I like how soft everything is, you know?" Maria says. "Like in a dream." She's watching the sea swallowed up by the night.

I don't know if I'll ever see her again and want to remember her exactly—her strong, smooth hands, her cool voice in the dark, the scent of jasmine. She's so beautiful, sitting back in her jeans and lavender tank, the sandals she'd kicked off long ago.

"There isn't any more beer," I say. "But I could call down for some."

"Oh, no thanks," she says.

Then I realize it would mean someone coming to the door. "Or I could go down myself."

"I think it's been enough beer. But you are very kind." She swishes the last of the beer around in the can. "What about your father?" I ask.

"We are from Pinar del Rio. But my father moved to Havana, then the Sierra Maestre. He was a revolutionist. He wanted so much for things to be changed. But he liked thinking better than fighting. So after the Revolution he studied economics at the University. He was always a dreamer, you know? Also very funny. In his heart he wanted to be an actor or a poet. But he became an economist instead. Now he's in tourism like everybody else."

"My father liked to think about things too. He was nothing like my mother. He was always so theoretical and practical. I mean he still is."

"My mother wasn't like my father either. She was in the National Ballet before my father. When I was little I used to tell people, I was so proud of it. But she gave it up to go to the Sierra Maestra with him."

"Is that when you stayed with your grandfather?"

"They tried to explain why they were leaving me, but I couldn't understand it. Anyway, when they came back my mother was different. She tried to love us after that, but she couldn't. She said she dreamed she was still tangled up in the mangroves. She said that's how my father made her feel."

"We're going to Pinar del Rio on Sunday," I tell her.

"You can't believe how beautiful it is. It's like another world. But getting there is very difficult. I could ride the camel bus part of the way or hitch a ride on the handlebars of somebody's bike."

"We're going in our air-conditioned bus," I say cheerlessly.

"Don't feel guilty for nice things. Enjoy yourself. In Cuba it's all beautiful."

"American guilt is so easy."

"I think you are a very nice American. I could take your hand that night but not now, because we are in ordinary light. You would misinterpret. So I will tell you that my mother died also. My mother Allegra. You can picture her. Beautiful long black hair, tiny like Pilar, but strong. It hurt when she hugged you she was so strong. She had wonderful hands."

"Your hands are from her." A rush of warmth has settled in my throat and I can hardly swallow.

"Yes, I know. I used to love her hands when she talked. She died in Mexico." Maria spreads her hands in front of her, turns her palms up. In the dark there are no pearly scars edging across her wrists. "When she left I missed her so much I thought I would die. But you know all about it."

"Isn't it strange to be the same?"

"It's why I told you."

"My mother's name was Eugenie. I always loved how you say the *g* softly against the roof of your mouth."

"It's beautiful," she says. "I always thought my mother's name sounded like an alarm. *Allegra! Allegra!* Here is *Allegra!*"

"I'm sorry there's no more beer, but we're doing very well without it."

"Yes, we are."

The railing is cool against my bare feet, my arm on the glass table-top. I breathe in deeply and smell the sea. "My mother smelled like lavender."

How did she sit all those years, so quiet like that in the front row pew every Sunday? Then she'd follow him out of the church afterwards, in those black patent leather high heels skimming over the carpet, those tiny white legs. At that moment he always seemed to forget she was there.

"Maybe my father felt like mangroves too," I say.

Maria nodded to me. "Our mothers. My mother smelled different when she came back from the Sierra Maestra. Like coffee and cigarettes, and something else I'd never smelled before. I remember it scared me that she smelled different."

We are weaving in and out of remembrance, creating a fugue of memory without segue.

"My father tried to save her. But not hard enough."

"How do you know? Maybe he tried as hard as he could."

"I think it was me who didn't try hard enough."

Maria shook her head. "No," she says. "No."

We sit there for a long time without saying anything. It's quiet and a little cooler now in the dark. "Pilar put on that blue dress for you," Maria tells me at last. "She wanted to meet the American Hemingway writer. She didn't want you to get the wrong idea."

"What idea?"

"The idea you'd get if you saw the red spandex and her black skirt."

"What do you mean?"

"She doesn't have a date. She's going to work."

"Oh," I say. My breath spins furiously on itself. All I can see is that beautiful child in the pale blue sundress, the Mickey Mouse watch.

"Please don't be shocked or think of her badly. It's very different here. We're all doing the only things we can."

"But don't you worry if she's safe?"

"Here in Cuba, everything is to worry about."

"Is she ill some way? When I touched her face she felt so hot."

Maria waves me off. "Tonight all she has to do is collect her money. She's determined to do that." Maria's voice is sharp, and I can feel my face redden, my eyes sting with tears. I have spoken the unspeakable.

"I'm sorry. I didn't mean it harshly," she says after we have grown silent for too long.

"I love watching how you are together," I say, and try to smile. I couldn't bear to lose them and am afraid in my ignorance I have.

"You want to ask me how I can let her do this."

"Okay."

"For a long time I tried everything. Then I finally had to let her go. Children won't have it any other way. So I just love her. The worst has already happened anyway. But her dates give her things."

"It must help to get things," I say, trying to keep my voice steady.

"She thinks black market dollars all the time now. She's saving everything she can. They all fall in love with her. She doesn't sleep with them anymore though. She tells them right away so there won't be any trouble. She laughs, tells jokes, dances a little bit when she feels all right. She can do other things. She knows it comforts me to hear all this. But I only half believe it."

"But is she safe enough?" I realize as soon as I've said it what a stupid question it is.

"She never tells me. I worry all the time what will happen when they find out she won't really sleep with them. That they'll think it's part of the tease."

"She looks so fragile to be living so dangerously." I feel a tightening in my chest.

"I know. We all are."

"She hardly ate anything. You didn't either."

"The stomach is very good at adjusting to the supplies at hand."

"Please take everything. Please take it back with you."

Maria smiles at me with sweet tolerance. Whose emptiness was I filling anyway?

"You know why she cut her hair? You can see that mostly we wear short hair down here. It takes less shampoo to keep it clean. In Cuba our hair is part of our sensuality, so short hair is a great sacrifice for somebody so young."

I feel my hair soft against my neck and can't remember when I last cut it.

"She didn't want anybody to be jealous of her shampoo dollars. I think she cut it also for absolution."

I think of her in that blue sundress, the watchband doubled around her wrist, what her eyes have seen, what language of the body she knows.

Maria turns to me bitterly. "Let me tell you something. What you said about not saving your mother? When I heard people whisper *jinetera* behind Pilar's back—you know that word by now? Cuban for jockey, hustler, people trying to get ahead. Not just prostitute. I tried so hard to save her. But mothers can't always save their daughters. And daughters can't always save their mothers no matter how much they love them."

The stars have spread out in lacy, untroubled patterns. In this dark secret place I tell her how in my dreams, I watched my mother step out into the street, knowing all the time what's going to happen. How I'm sitting on the porch swing watching the car come down the road, then the ribbons from her hat float up over the top of the car. Then the only thing I see is the windshield, and the sun gathering up the splintered glass.

"I used to think I could bring my mother back if I ran around the *ceiba* tree one hundred times. Your mother died before you could know you couldn't save her. So you are always reaching out to catch her and she's always just out of reach."

"I still feel like there's something I should have known."

"So you think if you knew this you can go back and change the way things turned out?"

"Maybe I'd find absolution."

"Maybe you already have it."

I feel an ache gathering behind my eyes but will not cry.

"I'm thinking about Pilar all the time. That if I could wrap her in enough magic, I can keep her safe. I know all the tricks. Cowrie shells, coconuts, beads, crosses, the works. But I have no belief. It's a great failing."

Maria holds the sweating can against her face and leans back. "When Pilar was fifteen, she was still a child, you know? Impatient, restless, but also beautiful like a woman, and so one day she couldn't find soap to wash her hair. She was invited to a dance and couldn't stand a second more of doing without, so she pulled her hair up and tied it in a knot and learned how to get more money in one night than in half a year of scrubbing all those floors.

"And the second month of slipping out of the house, a German businessman beats her up. 'I won't do that no matter what you pay me,' she says to him, and he says, 'Oh yes you will,' and so she comes in the window early in the morning and falls asleep on the bed outside the sheets. She's curled up like a baby, her hand under her chin, so I come into her room and the sun's streaming in the open window, and I see this purple blooming all over her throat and her chest and the side of her face and I know everything. All those months and years of doing without, piling up and weighing her down. She was so beautiful, so hurried she couldn't wait for it to be morning, or night, or sunset, or her birthday, or the next breath.

"'Things will get better,' I told her."

"And she says, 'When? When will they get better?'

"I was crying and she says, 'Please don't cry, Mama, that hurts worse than these bruises. I know how to do it. I just close my eyes and go someplace else.'

"You'll get more than a slap or a few bruises. You'll get yourself arrested or killed. You'll get pregnant or get some terrible disease. Then what will you do? Go to Helena's dirty back room and lie on her kitchen table and just close your eyes? Where will you go while she does her chicken blood magic on you?"

Maria leans forward and puts her arms on the railing, and looks out. "She's always careful. She takes all the precautions." Then she speaks so quietly I can hardly hear her. "But now. . . ."

My heart clamps into a fist. I try to catch my breath.

"I know you can see she isn't well. She's so beautiful, even now. She's very brave. She jokes all the time. She's preparing me, you know? It ought to be the other way around."

"I think she's very strong."

"She is. Even with her illness."

"Can you tell me what. . . .?"

Maria waves her hand, shakes her head. "I'm sorry to mention it. Not so good to talk about it right now, okay?"

I want to put my arms around her or take her hand, but I just sit there blinking back the tears. We're there for a long time looking out over the water.

"I'm watching her all the time now," Maria says. "She's being burned down to the quick right in front of my eyes."

"There's a kind of splendor about her," I say. She's so achingly beautiful you can't take your eyes off her. But it's more than that. There's a fierceness about her, too."

"She's a chrysalis becoming a butterfly," Maria says. "She's becoming who she'd be if she had all the time in the world."

Then I know what it is. It's the radiance of death. She's living in a circle of light, a deep and splendid sorrow that is transcending her girlishness yet doesn't seem to touch her strange and haunting innocence.

"You should see how men look at her. At first they're afraid to approach her, but they can't stop themselves. They just want to touch her and they don't know why. They don't know what it is, only how much they want it. Then they will do anything for her."

The night has settled finally upon us. The lights off in the distance tremble.

"Look at the blackout. On and off. Just like our lives. Look. Way out there to the right. The flashing across the water. Can you see it? Or imagine it?"

"What is it?"

"That's *Castillo del Morro*, the lighthouse that guards the harbor. The waves crashing on the rocks under *El Morro* are very dangerous. You would never want to be in that water." Maria sets the empty beer can on the table and wipes the table with the palm of her hand. "Once I dreamed I died in it."

I look at her, then back out at that water. "That's terrible." I wrap my arms around my waist.

She shakes her head and smiles at me. "Too much beer already. Too much melodrama."

I want to smile back but can't stop the terror building inside. I squeeze her hand, which she returns. "What does she need?" I ask. "I have lots of things."

"People are generous, you know? Now I can bring her all the soap and shampoo she needs. When they know how our lives are here they leave us lots of stuff, even medicine sometimes."

We go back into the room and I close the drapes behind us and turn on the light. Then I bring my overnight bag out of the bathroom and dump everything on the bed. I scoop up bottles of pills and hand them to Maria. "Please give her everything. The antibiotics, the vitamins, the aspirin and Tylenol."

She reads the labels of the bottles in her lap. "You don't know what these are to us."

"I know I don't."

I take the leftover slices of beef from the little hotel refrigerator and put them between slices of bread and wrap them in a napkin. "Make her a big thick sandwich or some broth out of this beef."

"I do this from the hotel every time I can." Maria is smiling at me. "I know you're a little in love with her. She's that way with you too."

Just then I want to be smoothing back Pilar's hair, letting lush smells from the kitchen wake her up with an appetite for all the food in the world.

"Please take everything there is."

"Thank you. I don't know what else to say."

"Do you have far to go to get home?"

"No, we live up the road from the Marina. That's why we moved here. Otherwise it's bicycles in the dark and potholes all over. It's dangerous to be riding on these roads at night."

"Will you have trouble getting out of the hotel?"

"I'll just say I'm working the late shift. It's nothing to worry about."

It doesn't occur to me until much later that maybe she really is. That the late shift she's working is right here in this room. Maxine had said, "Believe only half of what you see and none of what you hear." But right then I'm in love with both mother and daughter. Right now I believe in everything before me.

"Please come back," I say.

She's looking at me in a way I haven't seen before. Her eyes have cooled. The light has gone out of them. "Maybe it's a little tricky. I don't know yet. I want to, though."

"Tomorrow we're going to Cojimar, but maybe you could come back Thursday night? I don't think that phone call meant anything."

She just looks at me. "No. Of course not. Anyway, please just be careful."

"What do you mean?"

"I mean generally, you know? Like looking both ways before you cross the street, saying your prayers, not drinking the water."

"I'm always careful. That's my problem." We're standing by the door in the dark. I've turned out the light just to be safe. "How tricky is it for you to come here?"

"It's not so hard," she says. "Thursday night I will try. But if you see me around, you don't know me, okay?"

"All right," I say, and feel a shiver down my neck.

"If someone saw us together. . . they might think things that aren't really true."

I look at her hard and slip a twenty dollar bill into her hand.

"You shouldn't do that. Do you know what this is? A doctor's salary for a month." She puts her arms around me. I can smell her jasmine perfume. Outside the night rushes on.

I don't know if I'll ever see her again. I stand with my head against the door, the air conditioning pouring out of the vent. Then I notice the twenty dollar bill tucked safely back inside my hand.

It's near midnight now, and I'm still sitting on the balcony in my nightgown. I'm getting to know that sensuous curve of the island, where the shortest distance between two points is never a straight line. I'm getting sleepy, listening to the night, watching the lights of Havana in the distance.

Then smoke is pouring through the crack under the door, curling up over the wet bedding I've stuffed around the corners. I'm on the balcony waving my arms and shouting *help me help me!* but my throat is full of smoke, and I can't make a sound. Then I'm outside the hotel looking up at myself from below, surrounded by a hundred windowpanes flickering with fire, my white nightgown caught up in a hot wind. I wake up with my face in the pillow. The air conditioning has gone off again. I stumble across the room and open the glass door to the balcony and take in big gulps of warm dark air. I touch the railing. It's cool under my hand. No fire anywhere, only dark and quiet and now a little breath of air from the sea.

The Fire-Eating Dragon
St. Louis 1963

The moon is filtering through the leaves in the wind across her bare white legs. She's sitting cross-legged in the backyard under the willow tree. My mother's in her nightgown and red coat, holding a black chest with a fire-eating dragon in her lap. "Beware the dragon, lest he devour you," she's remembering from long ago. "We go to the Father of Souls, but it is necessary to pass by the dragon." That's St. Cyril of Jerusalem, she remembers from Catholic school. She knows she's all right if she can remember that. Dragons have such power, she's thinking. She'll need all of it for what she's about to do.

First she opens the black chest and stares at the letters inside for a long time before she drops in the lighted match. It flames up for a second then extinguishes itself, and a little puff of smoke floats up into the night. She tries to light it half a dozen times, finally holding the match against a corner of the stack of letters, white in the glow of the flame that creeps along the paper, curling the edges. She doesn't notice she's burned the tip of her thumb. She holds her hands over the flame, feels the heat pulse against her palms, feels it bite into her fingertips, then she leans over close to the flame and closes her eyes, feels the heat against her forehead, presses her fingers against her temple.

She seeks the blue light in the center of the flame and doesn't find it. She runs her hands through her short-cropped hair, feels the night air across her shoulders. She isn't even cold. She feels calm and peaceful now. She sits for a long time, watching the flames edge around the letters, slowly, exquisitely, like an orange scarf in the wind. Then she says, "That's enough," and closes the lid. The flames extinguish themselves against the lid with the orange dragon on the front, making smudges like long fingerprints against the metal. The moon has gone behind the clouds, but it's still there, she thinks, like the beloved dead. She can hardly see to find her way back to the house. She goes downstairs and hides the box where it stays until I find it. Next she goes into the garage and gathers up the sky-blue paint and makes her way to the kitchen.

WEDNESDAY, JULY 23, 1997

The Big Blue River
Cojimar

We step off the bus into sun so hot it makes your skin hurt. So this is Cojimar—a sleepy old town, tucked away at the edge of the sea, dust settling over everything in the white-hot noonday sun. Just a few dozen houses overlooking the harbor and the fortress down the promenade. No wrought iron balconies or indigo shutters on lavender or coral-colored houses. It's a fishing village, inclined neither to poetry nor color. But all you have to do is look out to sea, where the sun glitters over the water. A few boats in the harbor tilt in the little swells from the tide, their masts making a weary arc against the sky.

I walk down the promenade past bleached out water-stained little houses baked into submission by the sun and salt air, their sagging tiled roofs over sagging porches. A blue flickering light from deep inside a darkened room in a shack here and there, the only sign of habitation. A surprising number of dogs of indeterminate breed sit in doorways or on porches or stand in the road, looking on.

Then on the boardwalk toward the Hemingway monument, Hemingway's old friend, Gregorio Fuentes, the skipper of the *Pilar*, is sitting in the shade in a white plastic deck chair, waiting for his cue. He'll place a wreath at the monument. For now though, he's sitting with his hands resting on his cane, watching us with a drowsy, amused expression through the smoke from his cigar. He's wearing his Sloppy Joe's blue baseball cap and, improbably, a white dress shirt. He's ninety-three now, the same age Hemingway would have been if he hadn't found the gun that early July morning while Mary slept.

We pay our respects and cross the little road to the boardwalk next to the old Spanish fortress at the end of the promenade to watch the Cuban military patrolling the rooftop. The Cuban flag and the requisite satellite antenna wrench the fortress out of the past.

I aim my camera at the rooftop of the fortress that guards this little harbor.

Someone touches me on the shoulder. "My dear," she says. "You really shouldn't do that." It's Maxine.

"Oh," I say. "You're right," and put my camera down.

"Hand it to me," she says as cool as you please. "Now you stand here, and I'll pretend I'm taking your picture." She kneels down a little and aims the camera just over my head. She aims it right at that those soldiers on the rooftop.

"How did you know to do that?"

She's smiling conspiratorially. "I know a lot more than people give me credit for."

We walk back down the boardwalk toward the tour boats rocking in the little wind off the water. There are people everywhere.

"I just look like a little old lady. I'm really quite rebellious at heart. I never got to show it before." Everything about her has begun to soften, her white dress, her white sun hat against the backdrop of the sapphire sea. She is seeing herself as she was to him who loved her best, the days spreading out before them, sunlit and full of grace.

"You look so happy," I say.

"I am. But it surprised me. I feel a little guilty."

"Guilty for being happy?"

"For not feeling sad."

"After my mother died, grief was the only friend I had."

Maxine touches my cheek. "I like you very much." She looks up at those soldiers on the rooftop then back at me. "You should be careful."

"People keep telling me that. But I don't know what any of it means."

"You look wonderful," Maxine says. "But I got your message. I'm sorry you had to go through that again."

"I started to feel sick after the lobby yesterday and it kind of frightened me. But I slept all afternoon and I'm fine now. I was sorry to miss your paper, though. I know it was wonderful." I didn't tell her about Pilar and Maria coming to my room and didn't know why.

"Oh, yes it was completely wonderful," she says with a smile. "But I'm only happy that it's over. Bernardo was marvelous. I wasn't even nervous."

Less than half of us have signed on for the Big Blue River boat adventure, so the other boat lies empty, tied to the dock. We want to see where Santiago caught the great marlin. The others are either having drinks at *la Terreza,* seeing where the remains of Santiago's marlin washed ashore—or lining up for Gregorio Fuentes's autograph and kiss for the ladies.

"Obviously we are the more adventuresome of the group," Maxine says. "But why aren't we taking the other boat? It looks much sturdier. I suppose the smaller one takes less gas."

Maxine gives me a hug, boards the boat and heads for the shade in the cabin. I climb in after her and take a bottle of water from the cooler. Judith climbs in and ducks under the canopy and into the cabin. I move to the back of the boat and sit on a little bench by myself. I don't see Bernardo anywhere. But standing on the dock is our bodyguard, with his dark eyes, thick, swept-back hair, the bronze face. He climbs in last and disappears into the cabin.

The wake of the boat spreads out behind us and that sad little town dissolves into the distance, as we slowly gather speed, the faded Cuban flag at the stern of the boat snapping in the wind. Hemingway said the waters of the Gulf held strange, healing powers. I lean over but can't quite reach it as we chug our way to the center of the harbor. I shut my eyes and turn my face to the sun. We're drifting now in a wide gentle circle, a tender roll and sway, sensuous as an embrace.

"What are you dreaming?" Bill asks, as he sits down beside me.

"I'd rather be in the sun than under there in the dark."

He takes another sip of beer. "It doesn't stay cool very long," he says. "That's why I have to keep starting over." I can hear it in his voice.

"It's been a strange couple of days," I say.

"You think things are going pretty slow because of all this heat. They feel slow. They *are* slow, then the next thing you know you've gone someplace you never wanted to go and you don't know how you got there." Bill runs his hands through his hair.

"Isn't the light incredible?" I say. "It does something to you." My hand goes to my locket. I flip it open, then snap it shut. I hold it between my fingers against my throat. Bill is watching me.

"You were wearing that on the bus."

"It's from my mother. It was my French grandmother's."

After a long time, Bill looks at me and says, "You just stay quiet and watch everything. I'll bet a lot's going on with you down deep."

"Too much beauty and too much sorrow around here."

"Too much of everything," he says. "And too little."

"Don't you get sent to prison if they catch you trying to escape?"

"They used to. But of course you could always drown. Or be eaten by sharks."

Then Pilar's face rises up, the haunted eyes, the imperious cheekbones, the tender hollow of her throat. A hundred such faces rise up.

"Cuba's a strange place, isn't it?" I say.

"That sun. It's got everything all washed out."

The water goes on and on. It seems like we've been out here forever.

Then Bill says, "I got kind of tangled up in something."

"Do I want to hear this?" I ask, smiling against the turn he wants to take.

"No, you really don't. I shouldn't have said anything."

But he looks so despairing there's nothing to do but tell him to go ahead.

"It's okay. I don't need to talk about it."

"You can if you want though."

Bill takes off his sunglasses and rubs his eyes. "It's just that one of those Cuban women, she teaches English to doctors out in Camagüey. She's just here for the conference, see? I met her at the *Finca*, then last night down by the bar. God. She has this beautiful little girl, about five or six, and she's got nothing for her. This woman has this beautiful reddish-blonde hair and these amazing eyes.

"It was like she was waiting for me. I didn't even see her little girl. And then after a while, and too many drinks, she said, 'I would like to be with you. I've been watching you since the night at the *Finca*.'

So I thought what is this? I wasn't thinking too straight anyway, so we went up to my room and she said, 'I'm very sorry, I'm so very sorry, I would like to make love to you all night, but my little girl is downstairs in the lobby,' and I said, 'Where in the lobby?' and she said, 'Oh, she's asleep in one of the chairs, it's all right.' 'Are you sure it's all right?' I kept saying, but I knew she was really worried about her the whole time. She wasn't even supposed to be here, you know, being Cuban and everybody watching everything. It didn't even matter that she was there for the conference. But I just went ahead just like she asked me to.

"I couldn't stop thinking about that little kid asleep waiting for her mom or waking up and not knowing where her mother was, and maybe both of them getting kicked out of the hotel, and so I gave her this money when she left. I knew how much she didn't want to leave her down there. After she left I lay there for about a second and thought you *prick*, and I pulled on my pants and shirt and went after her. I had to see if that little girl was okay. But the kid was gone. Everybody was gone. Then I thought, yeah, right. There wasn't any kid. It was all part of the trick. So I just sat down at the bar and had another beer."

All the light has drained from his face. His shirt is clinging to his chest. "But there really was a kid," he says. "This beautiful little kid. I saw her this morning. I saw them across the lobby with the translators just before we got on the bus."

The sun seizes its hold on the sky while the waters shift and dissolve beneath us.

"What can I do? Give her more money? I can't *marry* her. I don't even know her. But it's the only way she can get out of here. God, I hate this government. I didn't realize how much till now."

"Here," I say, reaching my hand over the railing. "Put your hands in this water. You can reach it."

"Anything for redemption." He wants to turn the phrase into a punch line, but it falters on the half-smile he's trying to hold.

Poor Bill. Now he was responsible for her, one way or the other. We're drifting on and on, in more ways than one, and no land in sight.

I look at that flat indifferent sky. We could drift out here forever.

Now we're moving again. Bill has turned around and is watching the treacherous wake. I hold onto my hat. I can't believe how fast we're going. Then the boat cuts an arc in the water as we make a sharp turn. Everybody shifts to the left. I grab the railing and hold on.

"Geez," Bill says.

A spray of water shoots over the side. The back end of the boat sinks low in the water as the engines dig in. Gregorio and Ernest in the *Pilar*, chasing German submarines off the coast. Now here we are, making a run for it, giving those soldiers on the fortress something to do. They're scanning the Gulf for that roiling arc of water before they call the patrol boats with the machine guns. But the boat straightens out and begins to slow down.

I've finally let go of the railing, and flex my fingers. The boat is drifting smoothly over the Gulf now. My heart is beating frantically, even so. I look at this smooth, blue water and will my heart to ease.

Nothing now but sky and endless water. The sun is on everything—my arms, my neck, my back through my sundress, the tops of my sandals. We'd be turning for Cojimar soon. I move into the shade of the canopy and think of that nameless Cuban woman with the little girl. And Maria and Pilar—the smell of jasmine, those beautiful hands with the pearly scars, the Mickey Mouse watch on that slender wrist, the quiet of the evening shattered by the splintering ring of the phone.

I think of the way we seem to be tangled together under this heartbreak of a sky, this extravagant, treacherous sun, our brief, fragile lives.

Fast as I Can
Seattle 1975

The wind was blowing so hard the waves kept crashing over the side of the bridge and spouting into the air. We were racing through the storm to the Space Needle, to see what it was like six hundred feet high in a wind like this. We'd been studying by candlelight in Brick's apartment, listening to jazz on the radio. The power had long since gone out. The DJ was reporting live from the top of the Space Needle. "Come on up," he was saying. "You can still get out onto the deck." We were racing to get there before they made everybody go down below. Falling trees had downed power lines all over the city. Most traffic lights were out. But we inched our way along while I huddled into the seat. I swallowed my terror and looked over at Brick. "God, this is great," he kept saying. I thought I might be sick. He pulled me into a hug and laughed. "Annie Laurie, you scaredy cat. I'm gonna show you how not to be afraid."

They were still letting people go up in the elevator by the time we got there. I could feel the pressure inside my head as we floated to the top and stepped out into the lobby. Incredibly, people could still go out onto the observation deck.

"It's all right," Brick was saying as we stepped out into the wind. "This was built to survive hurricanes."

The Needle was swaying in the wind, blowing my parka hood off my head, my hair against my face. I shut my eyes against the wind and leaned into him as we worked our way to the edge.

"You gotta look," he said, and I opened my eyes at last. Lights blinking all over the city like stars. It was like looking down at the sky. You could see them flicker and go out. Then blue explosions of light, like puffs of blue smoke.

"What are those blue flashes?" I shouted.

"Transformers blowing," he said, above the howl of the wind. "Don't think about that. It takes the magic away."

"It's beautiful," I said. Those blue explosions of light against the night sky, those few trembling stars breaking through the clouds. I wrapped my arms around him and held on tight. I knew nothing in my life would ever be like this again.

Finally they pulled us back in and we went to the bar and sat drinking hot buttered rum until the restaurant closed down. We rode down the elevator holding hands, and I thought I would never be afraid of anything again. Then we drove back through streets criss-crossed with downed power lines and branches and road signs. I fell asleep and let him guide us home. We were safe and warm inside the eye of the hurricane. He was magic like that. Later, though, when he said, "You're always afraid of everything," it was already true.

Dangerous Liaisons
Havana

"Welcome! Welcome! Everybody, come!" Judith is standing on the veranda, her arms outstretched, as we make our way up the stairs. Bernardo stands beside her looking grave. She motions for us to gather in a circle. White wicker chairs line the veranda, but Judith motions for us to remain standing. Music from a far-off room floats out the doorway and is caught up in the sunslept air. We're weary from the long day in the sun, and a stop at the *Floridita* for drinks, and so we stand there shy and expectant, watching the open doorway.

It's a beautiful old mansion, set back from a residential street lined with palm trees. I'm standing near one of the white columned archways on the marble floor, watching the water spill out of the fountain on the front lawn into a marble pool. The sun washes the white archways in a pink glow, the palm trees filtering the last of the sun going down.

Then there he is, the mayor of Havana, grinning boyishly, with his hands in his pants pockets, looking us over. His dark hair is combed to the side with a matinee idol curl, the white *guayabera*, one pocket full of pens, the other with a pack of cigarettes. He looks like a larger Ricky Ricardo. We're here to receive the keys to the city. Bernardo's doing the translating. He's wearing that blue tropical print shirt, his face luminous in the falling sun.

The mayor is saying something too fast for Bernardo to keep up. What a momentous occasion to have such esteemed Hemingway scholars as his honored guests, and so he would like to present us with keys to the city. On cue, two women appear, carrying trays of cellophane-wrapped metal figures. The speech goes on and on while the sun drops behind the palm trees. It's the usual—new streetlights, repaired post offices and warehouses. But it doesn't take us long to remember the ironies. New streetlights but no electricity, new warehouses but no goods to store in them.

As he steps inside, the mayor turns back, as if he's just thought of something. His voice is quieter now. Bernardo leans close to him.

"Hemingway is the only bridge between our two countries now," Bernardo translates. "When our governments begin new relations, we want the signing to be at *Finca Vigía*."

Bernardo's eyes glisten with tears. The mayor places his hand over his heart in such a completely ingenuous way, a strange wistfulness replaces our skepticism.

"Please sit down while preparations for you are completed," Bernardo says. Sweat runs down his face. Judith has disappeared. So we sit in the wicker chairs at last and watch the twilight grow soft, while beyond the lights of Havana, night is coming fast.

Finally Judith motions us to follow her into a reception room. Silver tiers of pastries, silver plates of all kinds of food spread over a long table. The little band strikes up a song as we go inside. Our bodyguard is standing just inside the doorway, with his arms crossed, his feet apart, that little leather case tucked under his arm. The female singer in a blue taffeta dress begins a wistful song, while two men in white *guayaberas* and black pants accompany her on guitar and softly held maracas, their white shoes tapping out a slow, insistent rhythm.

My illness has faded into a barely remembered dream. Only beige food was safe, Maxine had said. But there she is, holding a plate full of meatballs on little cellophaned toothpicks, steaming brown rice and black beans, chicken wings, pineapples, and mangos and plantains, and little pastries with strange sweet centers. The band plays on.

There are twenty Americans here and I only know a few of them. "Who's that?" I ask Maxine. "The tall man in the corner by the musicians? His eyes are beautiful. Blue or green? Maybe both?"

"His name is Michael something. He's lovely though, isn't he.

He's a psychiatrist. He gave a talk right after mine, on Hemingway's mental illness. He was pretty sure it was manic depression. He wondered what it did to Hemingway to have to leave Cuba. It was very sad. I couldn't stop looking at him."

"I wish I'd heard it." Then I remember what I'm going to say tomorrow in my paper about my mother, and am glad I didn't.

Then right out of a Hitchcock movie, the butler floats through the crowd. He's all seriousness in his black shoes and tuxedo, his jacket a size too small, and eyes that saw you without looking. He's carrying drinks on a silver tray—that liquid sunset made of earth and sky—*Havana Club*. We say *yes oh yes* to that cool bronze taste on the tongue that turns hot going down.

A short Cuban man with a horseshoe of dark hair appears next to me, rocking back on his heels and smiling at me until I acknowledge him. I've never seen him before. "Hemingway," he says, tapping his conference badge. His smile is strange and tight. His eyes keep darting around the room. He seems to be having trouble keeping his balance.

"Would you like a little more?" he asks, pointing to my plate. "I would like a little more also." But he has no plate. His eyes are wide and glassy.

"Would you like me to get you some food?" I ask, ashamed I haven't thought of it right away.

"A plate of food would be most grateful. You are very beautiful. Thank you most wonderfully. And a drink, *por favor?*"

I fill his plate as high as I can and walk back. He's holding an empty glass and staring at his shoes. "I thank you most sincerely," he says without looking up. My American guilt, as Maria said, is so easily absolved. And then I remember what she had said about how hunger works. He might be able to eat only a little. Then I notice the name on his Hemingway badge: *Bill Tucker.*

Bill Tucker? "Bill Tucker" puts down his glass and takes hold of the fork.

I shoot a look across the room. Bill is staring back from the other side of the table. My eyes shift over to the Cuban and back to Bill. What's going on? Come here, he says with a tilt of his head. The Cuban has not looked up. His hand holding the fork is trembling.

He's eaten very little. Finally I maneuver my way to the other side of the room. None of our Cuban colleagues are here. Only the interpreters and other Cubans of indeterminate status. *Bill Tucker* sticks out like the proverbial sore thumb.

"That was nice of you," Bill says, pulling me over. "Anybody see you?"

"I don't know. Who is he?"

"Stay here, okay? Stay on the other side of the room from him. You don't want to know who he is." Then Bill works his way back through the crowd. Bernardo shifts over to the Cuban and leans over, whispering furiously. The bodyguard's head jerks up and looks from the Cuban to Bernardo. Bill has eased back out of sight.

"What's going on?" Maxine whispers over the beat of the Cuban trio's "Guantanamera."

"Something strange is happening," I say, and narrow my eyes.

Bernardo is swinging his gaze back and forth from the Cuban to the mayor. Our bodyguard has disappeared.

"Who is he?" Maxine says. "Isn't he wearing a Hemingway badge?"

"He's Cuban."

"I didn't think they could invite the Cubans," she says, setting her plate down. "I'm going over there."

A thin murmur unsettles the air.

"Maybe you better not," I say, but she's gone.

Maxine drifts through the crowd as free as you please. She picks up another Havana Club on the way.

I look over at the three of them. She's talking to Bernardo while the Cuban makes another attempt at his plate. Two men in dark jackets are standing on either side of the doorway. Our bodyguard is back, leaning against the wall, his legs crossed, looking right at Bernardo and the Cuban. Bernardo says something to Maxine and she shuts her eyes. Then she quickly puts down her drink and heads toward Bill at the back of the room, shaking her head.

"Who is he?" I say as she finally comes back.

"A Cuban dissident," Maxine says tightly. "He was in prison for four years for protesting the mayor. He wasn't the mayor then, however. He's had far too much to drink."

"What's he doing *here*?"

"It was Bill's idea," Maxine says. She looks a little shaken. "He met him on the street outside the *Floridita*. This is very foolish. He claims he looks different now, so nobody will recognize him from before."

I could see Bill doing it. He's at a bar and says, *¿Habla usted inglés?* to the guy next to him, and the guy says sure, okay, I speak English good, and Bill says, you hate the government? You hate Castro? Come on with us. Free food. Cheese. *Meat*. All the drinks you want. Fuck the government. And Bill slaps his conference badge on the guy's shirt and *Bill Tucker* and his new buddy walk into the house of the mayor of Havana, a smile breaking out on his face.

The singer in the blue taffeta keeps throwing looks at the dissident. She can't stop looking at him. All through the song, she wears a frightened look.

"What if he gets caught?" Maxine says. "What if they blame us?" She looks toward the doorway where the two men in black linen jackets are blocking the way.

Somebody has grabbed my arm.

"Laura. Dear Laura," Judith says. "General Cabrera wishes you to know how beautiful you are, and also that Cuban men are very particular about women. So it is the highest of compliments. He is a hero of the Revolution, you know."

Then Judith nods at a lean, gray-haired man in a tan wrinkled jacket and baggy black pants. Even heroes of the Revolution have seen better days. I can feel that look before I see it. Those dark eyes burning into me while I try to look away. He nods and raises his glass. I swallow and feel my face pulse with heat, though I smile courteously. He nods again, gravely this time, then comes across the room.

He smiles and hands me a drink. Judith makes introductions, and he takes my hand. "You are so beautiful I cannot keep my eyes from you. Your hotel room number please. I will call later tonight if possible, tomorrow for sure. It is true," he says. "I am going to see you again."

He brushes his hand across my bare shoulders as he turns to leave. I don't have to try to forget my room number. I can't remember the name of my hotel. And later I can't remember what I said. Judith's eyes snap. She knows how I've lied. *Please*, I say. My eyes ache.

But Judith's face is a mask behind her brilliant smile. She says something in Spanish she doesn't bother to translate and he laughs, a gold-capped tooth glinting absurdly under the light from the chandelier. And then he's gone.

"Thank you for making him go away," I whisper to Judith.

She looks at me with the coldest eyes I have ever seen.

"You *should* have received him," she says and turns away.

I sit down in a corner chair with the Generalissimo's untouched drink in my hand. He's watching me from across the room.

American men look at you with a flicker that slides up and down then quickly looks away. But this look doesn't skim over your body in a furtive, self-conscious way. It apologizes for nothing. It locks you in and your eyes can't do anything but look back. The only one who ever looked at me without turning away like that was Brick. I had looked up from the book I'd been reading that night in the library because I'd felt his gaze long before I saw it. And half a dozen tables across the room, there he was. *I've been waiting for you. Where have you been?*

The interminable verses of "Guantanamera" go on, as Judith begins pulling people against their American reluctance into the dance. Then somebody signals for the music to pick up after those slow, friendly choruses. There is a fierceness to her now, as she begins clapping her hands above her head, dancing in a little circle by herself, her head thrown back, her hair bouncing under the light. Then she hikes up her skirts and moves to the center of the room. She's moving her hips in that sensuous figure eight, until the music plays itself to the end, and she collapses against the wall. Everybody applauds. She covers her face with her hands and shakes her head. "I'd better sit down," she says, sinking into the chair beside me. "I don't dance so much like that anymore." She stretches out her legs and crosses her ankles. She looks over at me and smiles.

"Now can you see what it is? This music? What it means to us? We drink, we dance, we make love. Nobody can stop us."

"It's beautiful," I say.

"Come," she says, taking my hand. "Time for you to dance. No staying in corners tonight!" She pulls me into the center of the room, lifts my arm and turns me round and round as the room whirls by. My dress fans out around me. "Bravo! Bravo!" she shouts. She can't stop laughing. "Like this!" she cries over the music, and claps her hands above her head, swaying her hips. The circle widens for us, and we're in the center dancing together, my hands above my head, my body swaying too, my breathing caught up in the beat, going fast then faster until I'm inside the music, there is no stopping it, and now I know exactly what Judith meant.

Judith gathers me in an embrace. There is a transcendence to her now, an otherworldliness in her eyes on fire with that music—how purely a matter of sex and death. And then I know why it's the music of revolution. Or any orgiastic destiny.

"We do not want to kill," she breathes in my ear. "We do not want to be killed."

"What?" I say. "What?" The sun has dropped from the sky.

I look around. Generalissimo is gone, the dissident is gone, the men by the door are gone. Michael with the beautiful eyes has gone.

Bill is standing where the dissident had been, an untouched Havana Club in his hand. His shirt is soaked through. There is such a look of sorrow on his face, he would have to live with this, too.

The light is gone now. We will be going soon. We're standing out on the porch, waiting for the bus which, after one more stop, will take us home. Someone inside has turned out the lights, and we stand in the dark.

Soon Bernardo comes outside. He looks exhausted. It's almost eleven, but he's going to stop with us at the *Bodeguita* in Old Havana, then ride back to the hotel, and then bike all the way home.

"How long before you're home then?"

He just shakes his head. "Always too long." He lets out an unguarded sigh. I put my hand on his arm.

"My wife," he says. "I have been going without her all day now and half the night. I don't want it to be any longer." Maria had warned of those dark, treacherous roads. So he will make his perilous way home to her on his bicycle, no headlight or streetlamps to light his way.

"I'm really sorry about what happened tonight."

"It wasn't you," Bernardo says.

"What will happen to the dissident?"

Bernardo rubs the bridge of his nose. "Don't worry. Probably it will be nothing." But he looks so despairing even I know it isn't true.

"What about Bill? He was wearing Bill's name tag." Bill has disappeared into the night.

"I am *responsible* for you. My job is to make you safe. I should have been able to stop it. I tried to edge him out the door when I saw him." Bernardo leans back against the wall. "They saw me with him too."

What about Judith? Was her job to make us safe? Her revolutionary idealism read like a proclamation. The secret pragmatist who would do anything she had to was invisible behind that dazzling smile. Beware those eyes, though, and that coppery hair shining under every light.

I want to ask Bernardo about Judith. But he's so anguished standing there waiting in the dark, so troubled for our well being, and for his own, I cannot. I like him very much, and now Bill's joke would probably bring him a kind of trouble we would never understand.

"Is Bill safe, though?" I ask.

"Bill should be very careful. What happened was very bad."

"Oh," I say. Suddenly I feel hollow inside.

Bernardo takes my hand. "You need to be very careful too."

"Okay," I say, but have no idea what he means.

He squares his shoulders and gives a shy smile. "Not to worry, please. Tomorrow I will translate perfectly for you."

We stand there on that porch holding hands, moonlight falling all around.

Finally we're safely on the bus, winding our way toward *La Habana Vieja*. Maxine and I are sitting in silence. Before he'd buried himself in the back of the bus, Bill had said, "I just wanted to say, *fuck the government*, you know? I guess I did." We have all been chastened. Even our jokes about pooling resources to get the dissident a lawyer fall flat. Bill is sitting by himself in back.

It all happened so quickly, once the dancing began. Hardly anybody noticed when the two men in the doorway eased their way toward the dissident, who was already heading toward the exit. Hardly anybody noticed the way they put an arm on either elbow. He didn't say a thing.

"That poor guy. It wasn't any joke."

"He'll probably get sent back to prison," Maxine says.

I'm remembering the way he stared at my plate, the extravagant way he asked for my help, how he looked down at his shoes.

"Do you feel we're being watched all the time now?" she says.

Our bodyguard is leaning into the aisle, saying something to the driver nobody would ever be able to translate.

"Don't you think there's a terrible innocence in what we do?"

"Sometimes I'm afraid," I say.

"Of what?"

"All of it." I look out the window. "Everything."

"It's like a dream," she says.

"Or a nightmare."

"No, not a nightmare."

"You're right," I say. "It's too beautiful for that."

"Please don't be frightened," Maxine says.

I feel the sudden urge to put my arms around her.

I look out the window at Havana going by. Soon we will turn off the Malecón and start down those narrow streets toward Cathedral Square. There's no stopping it.

Havana Bay is to the left, and beyond, the dark seductive mirror of the sea. Across the bay, *El Morro* Castle stretches out over the water, the lighthouse a candle flame against the night, and those guns, trained at the Straits of Florida all these years, waiting for the American invasion that never comes. In a storm the sea would crash against those rocks. The lighthouse would lay a violent path of light across that dark water. We drive on and on.

The air conditioning is blowing fiercely now, when I'd be glad for that tender night air coming through an open window. We look so clearly what we really are—ghost figures, holding every promise, every fear, floating down those dark, edgy streets—as we wind our way down the Malecón toward Old Havana.

Then we round the corner and everything changes. Heads turns in slow motion, a shadow darkens an entryway, the flickering arc of a cigarette, whispers in lost languages spread out over the cobblestones, and a feeling of coming dread. I put my hand against the window and shut my eyes. The glass feels cold under my hand.

Bodeguita man
Old Havana

It's slow going down Empedrado Street packed with people waiting out the hot Cuban night. Judith said there was a carnival going on all over Old Havana, so please stay together. In the crowd we get separated, so Maxine and I head for *La Bodeguita* on our own, holding our purses tight, as Maxine leads the way. Bill has gone right into the *Floridita* and headed for the bar.

The Cuban flag hangs listlessly in the night air from one of the balconies across from the *Bodeguita*. We work our way inside through the group of people crowding the doorway. No place to sit, so we stand next to the singer entertaining the people at the bar. We'd sign our names on one of those walls covered with signatures. Why not? Everything about this week is a hot, trembling dream.

"Okay, Laura, big smile," Maxine says. I hold my pen up and turn to sign my name. The flash illuminates a wall of names, and the insistent *I was here!* The lights flicker once and suddenly I don't know where I am. My name has disappeared in the curves and loops of all the other names.

The lights flicker again and go out. A communal sigh ripples through the air. The music keeps on. All the electricity gets funneled into the tourist hotels by the sea.

The dark is a thick, hot buzzing in my ears, making it hard to breathe, so I feel my way toward the doorway and flee into that narrow, crowded street. The night is full of shadows, breathless and still. The crowd from the *Bodeguita* is spilling out into the street now. Even the little band has moved outside. Maxine has disappeared.

I'd just stepped across the street when I feel it. Only a little tug at first across my neck. Then somebody yanks my purse hard across my chest, spins me around, and jams me tight against the wall. It burns where the bricks scrape my back. The red tip of a cigarette flicks through the air.

"I'll break your neck getting this purse off," he says, in a dark voice against my throat. Then he lifts the strap gently over my head. He fingers through it for a moment then throws it on the ground. His hard, quick hands reach under my skirt, darting up and down between my legs, then around my waist, and up between my breasts, quick and purposeful and light. I can't breathe. I keep my back tight against the wall.

He's looking for the money belt against the small of my back I keep pressed into the wall. He's sure he hasn't missed anything now. So he just holds me there against that wall, one hand around my neck. I can feel my knees give way. He grabs my elbow and yanks me back up.

"Don't do that," he says slow and cool like a love song against my ear. I smell aftershave. Something like Old Spice, sweet and familiar as grandfathers.

His strange, hot breath smells of cigarettes and something else. He steps back and strokes the side of my face with the back of his hand, his ring smooth as gunmetal against my cheek. I try to scream but it's so noisy nobody would hear me anyway. We'd look like lovers. We'd be just another couple despairing of hope, passing the night against that wall, while the music plays on.

The narrow stretch of sky above the rooftops holds no stars. Then everything starts to spin and I press my hands against the wall. This man with the dark eyes, the hard, coiled body, thrusts against me. Then just as it was when I was six years old—the smell of cigarettes and beer, and the belt buckle hard against me, as the sky disappeared.

"You mind your own business," he says.

"What?"

"You know what I mean. You stay away." Then he snakes his

hand down my neck and between my breasts. He picks up the locket and puts it in his mouth. Then he lets it go. It's hot and wet against the hollow of my neck. I'm going to be sick and swallow hard.

"I could do anything I want to you."

Then he slips away into the crowd. The back of his head, his ponytail against the white shirt, vanishes into the night. The moon rises quickly and slides over the white bricks. The pulse of the music is at my temples, my throat, my chest. Nobody has missed a beat. I touch the locket with my hand.

My purse is on the ground, the contents spilled over the cobblestones—a lipstick, some small change, a few bills, the figurine. But he didn't find my money belt with my passport and room key. Then I know. He hadn't meant to rob me. *Mind your own business,* he'd said. *What* business?

On the bus ride back to the hotel, I don't say anything. I'm afraid to speak. How long did it last anyway? In the quiet of the ride home, I'm inside the nightmare inside the dream.

We start up the long road before we turn into *The Compound,* as we've come to call it. The road is empty of everything but a solitary biker. A girl is sitting on the handlebars holding a paper sack. The bus turns the corner toward the Marina and the headlights shine on the Hemingway daughters of the night, in their spandex tops and biking shorts, and red high-heeled shoes, the fearless, veiled eyes looking into the lights of the bus. *Hey you, you wanna good time? Sure you do, you know you do.* I don't see Pilar because my heart would break if I did. Up ahead is our hotel, lighted outrageously against the night.

My room is hot and stuffy so I open the sliding glass door onto the balcony. Lights are going out all over the island. Everywhere but here. I get ready for bed and listen for a tap at my door, hoping it might be Maria, but it never comes. The guy was probably drunk or on drugs or crazy in the dark, thinking the whole time I was somebody else. I slip off my dress and untie the money belt. I empty my purse and money belt onto the bedspread—my room key, my passport, three ten dollar bills damp with sweat, all safe. The mayor's figurine has lost her hand. So now I've lost the key to the city she was holding.

I touch my mother's locket. Nothing missing. I unclasp the locket and put it in the safe on top of my passport and click the lock.

The light in the bathroom startles me. A scrape on my shoulder I don't remember, and my frightened eyes. I touch the hollow place on my neck where the locket was and the red welt across my collarbone. I sit on the edge of the bathtub and think about all the things gone missing.

In the shower I feel the burn of the scrape on my shoulder. I put on my nightgown carefully and sit on the balcony. I'm trembling in the warm, humid night. A couple in the whirlpool is having a go at it. She's dark and exotic with long black hair and a red thong bikini. She wraps around him as he holds her. Then her hands slide down and disappear in the water, and he loses his balance and they both go under. They don't care what anybody sees in that blue spotlight under the water.

A Turtle Without Its Shell
Seattle 1972

One time we made love for a whole weekend. I was standing in the doorway of the bathroom in my parka, my ankles pressed together. I looked down at my boots and wished for my mother's red shoes. Brick turned on the light by the bed. He looked at the bedspread in the musty light.

"I'm sorry," he said. "I should have gotten someplace nicer. It's too dark in here." The heavy curtains were pulled against the late afternoon sun, but I was glad of the dark. To do this I needed the dark. I took off my coat and laid it over the chair next to the desk and sat down.

"We're gonna take our time, Lauracakes, we've got all the time in the world. So come here. It's all you have to do." It was like coaxing a puppy out from under the house. Then he turned out the light. The day vanished and I had no idea where I was.

After it was over I remember thinking it wasn't so bad after all; I was still safe and no harm had come. We could go on with the business of loving each other and seeing where our lives would take us.

But he said, "No, we're not done." Then he touched the hollow place where my locket was and let his fingers flicker across my breasts, down and down, and I sat there on the edge of the bed ready to grab my clothes and bolt for the door while he sat beside me and touched me all over again. "From now on everything is for you," he said. "Just for you."

"Me?" I said.

"I want to love you till you can't stand it anymore. I want to touch you everywhere." Then he got up and opened the blinds, while my heart was gathering itself against him. My breath was coming in quick little bursts that caught in my throat. I tried to look away but couldn't take my eyes from his face.

He was touching me again in the same way as before, but differently. Something strange and warm washed over my chest, my neck, my face.

He was looking at me smiling.

"What?" I asked.

"Laurie, you've still got your socks on."

"Okay," I said.

He slid them off, first one then the other.

"I want to see everything," he said.

I wanted to put my feet under the covers and pull the sheet up tight, but he'd taken all the covers off. I wanted to shut my eyes against him but I couldn't. So I held to the look on his face that said *trust me*. Everything was sliding and turning and I shut my eyes and held on tight. Then I was hopelessly, achingly, inside whatever was spinning me toward a light so warm, then so hot and bright, it broke into a thousand fragments, and I was inside a terrible and beautiful shattering light.

I came every time. I couldn't stop myself. "Here, I can do it again for you," he said. I was like a child being tickled to death. What if I couldn't stop? When I finally got up and went into the bathroom I knew what it was. I sat down on the edge of the bathtub and knew where I'd seen it before. That light. It was the light of the sun on that shattered windshield.

I sat there a long time trying not to cry. There was no end to it. I flushed the toilet and washed my face and stood there holding my wrists under the water to cool down. "You're always going to the bathroom," he said, and laughed, so I had to shut the door. Then I came out again and got into bed. This is how it would be with him from now on. I would just have to hang on for as long as I could. How many times could I break open like that—a turtle without its shell beneath a longed for sun?

Finally I couldn't feel anything anywhere, but by then I knew all the moves, and I was very good, and for a long time he didn't know I wasn't good for anything anymore. "Remember that winter we made love all weekend?" he'd say over and over. "That weekend started our life." He smiled and I gave him that secret smile that said I remember it too. But I always felt a little sick because I knew I wasn't who he thought I was. He was right. That weekend started our life together.

THURSDAY, JULY 24, 1997

The Need in This Place
El Viejo y el Mar

The lobby is heating up with people delivered from the night into the safe passage of the day. The fan overhead turns languidly in the sunlight, spilling shadowy light. My stomach tightens. A whiff of jasmine comes in on the ocean air and I look up. But she's not there.

The salsa music from the patio is competing with the TV in the bar. It's Che all over again. A wave of upturned Cuban faces, commentary in rapid-fire Spanish, news clips, photographs, some kind of funereal music.

I'm sitting at the head table, waiting for the conference to begin. Or not. Everything in Cuba is something slow trying to go fast. I'm imagining the four of us at the head table, looking out over a packed audience—the student scholar from Camagüey, the professor from the University of Havana, Bernardo, and me.

People are beginning to filter in and take their seats. Mostly Cubans, few Americans so far. We're already half an hour late. The other translator is sitting in the audience in the front row next to her little girl. But no Bernardo. A tall, young man of nineteen or twenty comes up to the head table and extends his hand.

"Professor Gallagher, I am Antonio Ferraro from the Hemingway Pedagogical School in Camagüey," he says. He takes a deep breath and lets it out slowly. "It is very long from here."

"I'm happy to meet you," I say seriously. "I've been waiting for you."

"You are the chair of our presentation. I am very interested in what you will be saying."

"Please," I say. "It's Laura."

"You are giving a paper on *The Old Man and the Sea.*"

"Well, sort of," I say. "I'm afraid the connection is pretty loose." I'd written it in fear and trembling weeks before. I had wanted to show that what Hemingway was saying in *The Old Man and the Sea,* he was also saying to me.

I remembered the long pause while the phone line trembled, then my father's intake of breath, the sigh he didn't hide. "Can't you just talk about Hemingway and leave your mother out of it? You can't unbury the dead." My stomach clenches into a fist with remembering. I'd wanted to lay her to rest, not unbury her. But maybe I've unburied her after all.

Antonio sits down beside me and smiles shyly. "It's good to connect things not easily connected."

"Thanks for saying that. I see you're going to give your paper in English. I couldn't give my paper in Spanish if my life depended on it."

"I worked very hard to say everything correctly. It is difficult to say things truly in another language. Sometimes there are no words for what must be said."

"Sometimes there are no words even in your own language." I had tried and failed to do just that in these imperfect pages I would soon be reading.

Antonio starts to say something, then slumps forward, but catches himself at the last moment. He puts his head between his knees, and gives a whisper of a moan, a sound held back as much as a sound like that can be. Then he vomits onto the floor.

I touch the back of his neck. "It's all right, Antonio, it's all right."

He can only nod. He's holding his head in his hands. I rub his back and whisper, "It's okay. No one can see you."

A man rushes onto the stage and leans over him. "Here, son," he says, helping Antonio back up. "Take some slow, deep breaths." The man kneels down beside him and holds his wrist, counting his pulse. He touches his forehead quickly. "Can someone bring some water? And some towels?"

"I'm sorry," Antonio says. "I am most ashamed."

A waiter hands the man a glass of water. "Drink this," he says quietly. "You'll be all right in a minute. But you have a lot of fever."

Antonio shuts his eyes and takes a sip of water. The man sits down beside him and puts his hand on Antonio's back. Then he rubs his hand over his arm and pinches the skin lightly. "You're pretty dehydrated," he says.

Antonio's eyes slide over the room, hoping no one has seen. "Yesterday I was very sick."

The waiter returns with towels and the man leans over and wipes Antonio's pants and shoes. The waiter takes the soiled towels and puts them in a bag and leaves.

"I'm so embarrassed for you to do that," he says.

"It's nothing," the man says, rubbing his back. "I'm used to it." It's the tall man with the beautiful eyes from the mayor's party.

"I give you a thousand thanks," he says. He's ashen even through his Cuban skin.

We sit for a few minutes without speaking, one of us on either side of him. My hand is on Antonio's back too.

"I'm getting much better now. My fever has been very great. Also I am exceedingly nervous."

Antonio's crew cut makes him look even thinner than he is. There are dark circles under his eyes. "Try some more water, if you can," the man says.

I hand Antonio the glass of water.

"I saw you at the mayor's house yesterday," I say to him, as he stands up.

"I saw you too," he says. "Michael Ryan."

"Doctor Ryan?"

He nods.

"Laura Gallagher," I say. "It's good you're here."

"I'm glad I'm here, too."

"I'm going up to my room and wash my hands and get some things," he says. "We need to get that fever down and something for dehydration." He touches the side of Antonio's face. "It would be good if you could lie down."

Antonio looks shaken. "I could not do that," he says. "This is my presentation. I have worked so hard." His lip with the fledgling moustache quivers.

"I'll be right back," Michael says. He steps off the platform and heads for the elevators.

Antonio looks out at the audience, still just a scattering of people. No one's paying any attention to the drama at the head table. He takes a long, deep breath. Bernardo isn't anywhere.

"This book gives me courage," he says, touching the worn, hardbound book in front of him. *The Short Stories of Ernest Hemingway.* "It's the only one in Camagüey. I have received special permission to bring it."

He picks up the paper he's going to present and takes a deep breath. I look away so he won't know I see his trembling hands.

"I am speaking on Hemingway's compassion. I want so much for my words to be worthy."

"Your topic is a fine one," I say.

"Yes," he says quietly. "I am most passionate about it."

He smiles unabashedly and lets out a sigh. Something is settled now. His shoulders ease and he leans back in his chair. His hands have stopped trembling.

Then Michael is back with a bottle of water. He shakes it up and it turns cloudy. "Now just sip on this as you can until it's gone." He hands him two white pills. "These will take your fever down. And these for later, if the fever comes back." Antonio tucks the little bottle of pills in his jeans pocket. His eyes fill with tears.

"I shouldn't have come with this sickness to be so much trouble. But we have no medicine for fever."

Michael looks at him with a kind of tenderness. "I'm going back to the audience now," he says. "But I'll be right here in front. And please. Know you're fine now. Enjoy this moment."

Then Antonio reaches to shake Michael's hand. "I most heartfully thank you for saving me."

"I did nothing. You're the one who wrote your Hemingway paper."

Antonio takes a long sip of the cloudy liquid and shuts his eyes.

A woman in a green dress has come in while we're talking and takes her place next to me. The busload of Cubans has arrived.

"I am hoping I'm not very late," she says breathlessly. "Our bus." She rolls her eyes. "I had to wait so long. It's too hot." She takes a handkerchief out of her straw bag and wipes her forehead and neck. "I am happy to meet you," she says, extending her hand. "I'm Teresa Diego from the University of Havana."

I remembered her from that first night at the *Finca*. That green dress with the wide gold belt she's worn every day of the conference, her dark hair brushed into a curve at her cheek, the other side tucked behind her ear. And her shoes—espadrilles that crisscross her ankles. Imagine walking for miles to wait at a bus stop in shoes like that. It's what all of them wear—shoes that make no compromises. Elegant, high-heeled shoes designed to set off the curve of the ankle, the shape of the calf.

Teresa picks up Antonio's book of Hemingway short stories. "Your own copy?" she asks.

"Oh no," he says. "It belongs to all of us. In Camagüey it is the only one."

Teresa nods. "He means it is the only copy in English," she says to me. "We have Spanish translations, but they are of limited value."

"I've heard translations are a great handicap," I say. Yet how rich and fine to have words to catch the things that slip around the corners of one's own tongue. How awful not to be understood.

"You know *Winner Take Nothing*, no? I will be speaking of it today. In Spanish, *Winner Take Nothing* is translated as *Earnings of Nothing*. The poetry is gone, you see. Also the meaning." There's a sudden fierceness in what she's saying, as if she finds herself responsible for bearing witness to this work with Hemingway.

Now the seats are filling up. Maybe a hundred people, mostly Cubans. A scattering of Americans, most of whom have ditched the conference in favor of more exotic pleasures. But Bernardo is not among them. Neither is Bill. He's probably up in his room sleeping off yesterday.

Maxine is in the front row, sitting next to the translator's little girl. She reaches in her big white purse for a box of Mickey Mouse Band-Aids. That beautiful little girl had sat in that front row seat every day of the conference while her mother translated. Every day that white dress with the green polka dots, the black patent leather shoes, the white anklets. Every day that dress looking as clean and crisp as the day before. She opens the box of Band-Aids and dumps them into a pile on her lap. For some things there is no need of translation. A doll with no clothes and enormous blue eyes lies on the floor in front of her chair, abandoned for the moment for the Mickey Mouse Band-Aids. The translator gives her daughter a behave-yourself look and steps up to the platform. She's worn the same white sleeveless blouse and white culottes all week. Nobody it seems has a change of clothes. Yet they're always beautiful. No cosmetics or deodorant or shampoo, hardly any soap. Are there potions and spells for lipstick and rouge and creams that grandmothers hand down to their daughters and daughters to their own daughters? It's so clear how deeply held this female beauty, how cruel the deprivations. *Soap? Do you have soap?* I think of what Pilar had done for it. All morning I see her everywhere—her blue sundress, her watch, her short-cropped hair.

"I can translate for you if Bernardo doesn't come," she finally says. Her name is Tani. "I don't know why he's not here."

"Last night he said he was going to bike home from the hotel."

"He lives far from here," she says. "But he's always on time. We make jokes about how he always has to be on time."

"We can sit side by side and I can translate as we go. You read a paragraph and I'll say it in Spanish."

"Will your daughter be okay?"

"She knows how to be patient." Tani looks down at her daughter, the Band-Aids in her lap, and Maxine with her arm around her.

I wonder if she'd heard about what had happened at the mayor's. "Do you think Bernardo's all right?" I ask.

She looks at me sharply. "In what way all right?" she asks, then draws back and crosses her arms.

What do I know about the perils of the day or night? But I can't help it. "It's late now, isn't it, for him not to be here."

Her eyes sweep over the audience and to the front desk and the entryway beyond.

"Yes," she says softly. "It's very late."

Something drops in me. I imagine him on that bike riding home to his new wife, then catching a slow bus back to the hotel in the early morning. How anguished he was, standing on the mayor's porch in the moonlight. What have they blamed him for?

I look over the audience and feel unexpectedly ashamed. All those empty chairs, the audience down by a third. "Have you seen much of Havana?" Tani asks. "If there is some place you'd like to go I could be your guide. Did you see Old Havana?" There it is, the old hustle, I'm thinking, then catch myself.

"We were there last night but only for a little while. There was a blackout."

"Maybe you'd like to try again."

"Oh, I don't know. I thought it was kind of scary."

Tani looks at me oddly. "How was it scary?"

"I couldn't see where I was." That hot cigarette breath against my face, the Old Spice, the hard, thick hand, all of it coming in a rush.

"Night things lose their power by day," Tani says.

"We could go tomorrow," she says. I know what she's doing. God knows she wasn't getting paid much for translating. Fifty cents a day.

"I don't know about tomorrow," I say, touching my locket. "Maybe some other day. I don't know if I could go back there. It's hard to explain."

"Aren't you all going to the Finca on Saturday? And Pinar del Rio on Sunday. So maybe tomorrow?"

"Let me think about it, then."

"Okay," she says. But her face has clouded over.

By now the lobby is full of the morning bustle. I'm looking for Maria everywhere. It's so late now Wallace is standing in the back, waving his arms and pointing to his watch. It's clear we can't wait any longer.

Finally I stand up and walk to the podium. "Welcome to the Hemingway Colloquium," I say over the beat of the salsa music coming in from the pool.

I hand the microphone to Tani for translation as Teresa walks to the podium. She takes a deep breath, and looks out unblinkingly. She lifts her chin, takes another deep breath. No matter what, she would be proud to present her paper to the Americans. I wonder if she realizes most of us aren't even here. I resent Bill sleeping it off.

"In Hemingway's story 'After the Storm,'" Teresa begins, "there is the image of the floating body of a woman. You can see her through the window of a sunken boat. I want to ask: why always a woman? Why are the women in Hemingway objects of desire only? Why do they only smile at death and never speak?"

And then she bravely takes her audience through the stories of the 20's and 30's. I look out at this audience, mostly male, and am sorry for the faint, polite applause. I tell her I was very moved by her work and she puts her arms around me. "Thank you," she says.

Tani's little girl has taken off her shoes and socks and has wrapped a Mickey Mouse Band-Aid around both big toes. She sits there with her heels tucked under her skirt, looking at her feet. You can see the tug between childhood and what would come all too soon. She smiles puckishly at her mother and puts her feet down.

Then Antonio turns to me. "I'm ready now. I am most ready." He has drained the bottle. His eyes are bright now with something more than fever.

"Okay," I say, and touch his arm. He smiles at me gravely, gives Teresa a respectful acknowledgment, and makes his way to the podium.

He's all authority and presence now. He clears his throat and looks out. He is a Hemingway scholar. He's almost twenty. He has important things to say. He will say them in English. He pulls his shoulders back and begins what I'd expected to be a vigorous defense of Hemingway's bravery and manhood.

But there is no machismo in his first line. "Hemingway makes me weep," he begins. "He makes me weep for those caught in war, for fathers who do not understand their sons, for those pushed aside through homosexualism and other races, for those who are poorly treated, for those going without understanding, for all those who are on the outside of life. He makes me weep for the sea and the sky. Hemingway was compassionate for all of these."

His eyes blaze with passion and the fever that has no doubt returned, his voice only gaining strength as he touches the deep center he's drawing from. When it's over, he sits down and doesn't raise his eyes as the applause goes on and on.

Michael Ryan is applauding too. He looks at me and nods. I can't help but smile.

Wallace is standing up, clapping wildly, and for the first time I'm glad for him.

Then Antonio turns to Teresa. "What is your opinion?" It's her approval he wants most of all.

"He was not compassionate of women," Teresa says, "neither in his life or his works."

Antonio looks shaken. I can see he really is quite ill—the tightness around his eyes, the dark where all the light had been.

"Then I am very sorry to have disagreed with you."

Teresa puts her hand on his arm. "Oh, no," she says. "I meant to offer congratulations. You did very well. It's all right to disagree. And your English was beautifully rendered."

He pauses for a moment. "Thank you for the compliment," he says. He's still trying to phrase a way to disagree with her respectfully.

"It's good to have heroes when you are young."

"I know I have neglected to think about the women," Antonio says at last. "I would like to show how Hemingway was compassionate of women also."

Teresa looks at him and smiles wearily. "I hope for it too."

Now people are coming up to congratulate Antonio and he's smiling and shaking hands.

Then the long table with the pastries and coffee appears and everyone weaves their way to the back, all but Wallace, who is pushing his way against them to the front, shaking his head and pointing to his watch. "For *godsake*, Laura. Don't let them take a coffee break *now*. We're way behind as it *is*." But it's too late. They can't be called back. "That *goddamn* Bernardo. He held the whole thing *up*. I do not *understand* these people." His head jerks with every accented syllable. Then he catches himself and turns to Antonio.

"That was a *fine* paper you gave, son," he says, reaching across the table to shake his hand. But he can't quite make the shift in tone and it comes out in little bursts of dissipating anger. Finally he shrugs and throws up his hands.

"Well *hell*. I might as well get some coffee." So he turns and wanders off, his shoulders bunched around his neck.

We watch him disappear into the crowd. Antonio stands up shakily and a friend on either side helps him down the platform and toward the long table. Maybe pastries and coffee are what he needs.

"Wallace is not a very agreeable person," Tani says.

I laugh, but her candor startles me. "No, he's not." I feel I should apologize. "His nerves are shot. He's brilliant, though. He's something fast that cannot go slow."

"It was nice what he said to Antonio," she says. "Show me your paper while there is this little break."

"I'm worried about saying it," I tell her, because she's so earnest, so careful.

"Why did you do it then to worry like that?"

"To bring a dark place into the light."

"We will be side by side and you will say your paper nice and slow and everything will be fine."

"Okay," I say, though I know these words might ravage my heart. Yet how can they matter to anyone more than to me?

"Your friend is taking good care of my daughter," Tani says. She's gone off with Maxine for pastries and juice. I don't ask about the father, or grandmother or aunt or friend to watch over her. It's clear Tani is on her own.

"She's beautiful," I say. "What's her name?"

"Paloma. After my mother." That little girl is gathered up in her mother's smile and settles into it. She will keep her daughter safe in that smile for as long as she can. Then one day this child will get tired of so much doing without, and she'll wrench away from that look—angry, impatient, a little afraid, and take her own path into harm's way.

"She's beautiful, so she needs a beautiful name," I say.

"She is beautiful, isn't she? She's only dark from going to the beach." There it is again. The crucible of race Cuba has forbidden, now that the Revolution has made everybody equal. But it's the hierarchy of color anyway, light to dark, top to bottom—Bernardo a shining exception. That radiant smile, those compassionate eyes, but no young Sidney Poitier in sight.

"That's all she wants now. Every day, go to the beach. All the time she's more and more restless."

Maxine and Paloma are coming back. She's holding a pastry in either hand. Maxine holds her pastries while Paloma spreads a napkin over her polka dot dress. She's already discovered the comfort of that soft, yielding body. Maxine has stilled her restlessness. Paloma looks up at her mother and waves a shy hand. *Look at me. Look at my new friend.*

"I'd like to go to Old Havana with you," I say. "I didn't really get to see it before."

"You can do it then?"

"Sure," I say.

Tani looks at me, then breaks out in a smile. "You won't be afraid in Old Havana. You will have all the light you need."

Then we can wait no longer, and I begin. I think of Teresa and Antonio and know I can do no less.

"By trick and by treachery, Santiago, the old fisherman, calls the great fish up from the sea. Now having seen him, and loving him all the more, he gathers all his strength and drives the harpoon down and down until heart touches heart. It is the parable of the artist, and the great sin of art—to call up from the deep what must be kept hidden, yet bring it to light."

Then I take a deep breath, as Teresa had done, as Antonio had done, and turn the page. I take another breath, shut my eyes, and open the black metal chest with the fire-breathing dragon.

"Hemingway knew great despair. My mother knew this also. On Good Friday, when I was twelve, she stepped off the curb into a fast-moving car. Have I come this far to say what I have never been able to say to anyone, this thing that lies like a shadow on my heart?

"Then I wonder: what truth might my mother's story tell I could not bear to hear? Must I tuck it deep inside a bottom drawer? Yet some day couldn't a tale be made even of failure, with a completion and beauty of its own? So I stand here in the open with tears streaming down my face, looking toward the vanishing sun."

I sit down and listen to Tani settle that final paragraph into elegant Spanish rhythms. Was the truth I couldn't find elsewhere, in the rise and fall of these strange syllables? But I'm an outsider to my own story. I'm still the little girl with the unopened chest buried under her bed.

What are bones anyway? Precious bones. No wonder everyone believes Che is finally coming home.

Then I come back to myself, and blink back my tears. Maxine is at the center of my vision, blowing me a kiss. I whisper thank you and touch my heart. Michael catches my gaze and turns it back to me. People are standing and he's standing too, and then he's walking toward me as I'm walking toward him.

"Your paper. . . ." He swallows hard, reaches to take my hand then stops himself. "Your paper was wonderful. I'm so glad I got back in time. I'd been out in Havana with my friends. I came with them on their sailboat from the Keys. We've been going back and forth from the Marina to the hotel all week." He takes a step back to stop this rush of words.

There are bright spots of color on his cheekbones. His eyes have gathered up the light. "What you said about your mother…."

"I don't know about that," I say. I'm trembling and wrap my arms around myself.

"Maybe we could talk sometime. I'm a psychiatrist." He's turning a wedding ring round and round.

It feels like I've swallowed a stone. "Are you interested in Hemingway then?" I manage to say.

"Since college. I was asked to give a little talk on Hemingway's mental illness. It was nothing much. I gave it on Tuesday. Mainly I wanted to see Cuba. I'd like it if we talked sometime."

"Okay," I say. "Sure."

"I'd like that," he says. "But I need to go right now."

He turns to leave and I say, "I'm worried about Antonio. I brought antibiotics but I've already given them away."

"I've got some in my room. I forgot them in all that rush." He looks at his watch. "I'm so sorry. I've really got somewhere to be right now. I'll dash up and get them. Could I give them to you for Antonio?"

"Of course."

He turns to look back at me as the elevator opens, then steps inside. He holds the door open for a moment, before he lets it shut. Such beautiful eyes. Sea green, or maybe blue.

Then I see her. Judith is making her inexorable way through the crowd toward the platform, her face impenetrable and grim.

Tani has turned around to get her purse and doesn't see her coming. She flinches when Judith touches her arm. "*Tani,*" Judith says.

Tani's face grows pale. "You can't leave now. You're going to have to do all the afternoon translating. Bernardo isn't coming," she says in a voice, low and heavy with emotion. Her face comes and goes in the shadow of the ceiling fan. Maxine looks up.

Tani swallows the solitary question rising in her throat, fear gathering behind her eyes. Then a veil comes down and her face goes completely blank.

"We have tried to get another translator," Judith is saying, "but we don't have permission yet."

I can see the weariness wash over Tani as she calls upon the long practice of patience. Resignation has already set in. "Okay," she says. "I'll need to tell my daughter. She's getting restless."

I start to speak but Tani touches my arm. *Please don't ask her. You'll only make whatever it is even worse.* Tani and Teresa are looking everywhere but at Judith. So I pull back and look away too. They have moved over to let me in. I am one of them against her too.

"What's going on?" Maxine says. I can see the panic in her eyes. She's come up to the platform right away. I try to signal her with my eyes. But there is no stopping her.

"Judith!" Maxine has taken her arm. "Where is Bernardo? I want to know why Bernardo isn't here."

Judith's eyes burn cold. "You don't have the right to know anything you want. You are a *guest* here." She shakes off Maxine's hand and turns to walk away, then whirls back around. "You Americans are *careless.* You don't know what you've done." Her eyes have turned black. Maxine stands there, clutching her purse to her chest. She can't think of a single thing to say.

The salsa music has stopped. The television with Che's funeral has stopped. The noise from the pool has stopped and I can't hear anything but the thrum of my heart.

Maxine touches my arm and I realize she's shaking. "I've really done it now."

"No," I say. "No you haven't." She sits down and closes her eyes.

I look everywhere for Michael. Then there he is, coming with a bottle of pills he puts in my hand. He covers it with his own and holds it there. "I wish I'd brought more," he says. "I really had no idea."

"Nobody did."

"But I'll see you," he says, squeezing my hand. Then he's gone. I want to think he gave them to me to touch my hand.

I'm afraid I'll never see him again, then remember the gold ring turning round and round.

The morning is over and I walk back to my room. All those words gone slantwise into Spanish, or face forward into English, are swept up by the ceiling fans and cast into air. A rush of blackbirds whir across my face and something burns in my throat.

I shut my door and lie down. I say prayers for Bernardo, and for Antonio, who will go back to Camagüey and give up that book. And Teresa? Would she finally commit the *crime of dangerousness?* Saying the wrong thing, or buying the wrong thing, or talking to strangers, or having the wrong kind of money, or your eyes showing what you're really thinking. And for Tani also, who'll stay in the growing heat of the lobby all day for fifty lousy cents, and for that beautiful little girl and her doll with no clothes, and her Mickey Mouse Band-Aids.

Leon the Owl
St. Louis 1963

I knew my mother wrote my father letters I wasn't supposed to read. But her letters to me during those times she went away weren't letters so much as a scattering of notes scribbled on lined tablet paper my father brought back from his visits, or tucked in letters she sent him. "Dear Annie Laurie, my dearest heart, I miss you more than any number. I'll be home soon. I love you, Mommy." It was all right. How could you get tired of hearing how much you were loved?

But what did my mother write to my father that she didn't write to me? What were they to each other and why had I suddenly lost them both? She had put the letters in that black metal chest with the red-orange dragon breathing fire. "My secrets," she had said, smiling mysteriously, as she snapped the lid and clicked shut the tiny gold padlock.

My mother was always magic, and maybe she was only pretending to be dead. Her scarves and nightgowns, her lipsticks, her brush, her comb, her red shoes—they were tucked away in my room for safekeeping. I hadn't actually seen her walk into the street, though I had rushed after her a thousand times in my dreams.

That summer I was a spirit floating through the house, looking for what I feared I would never find. Then one night late in August, I grabbed my flashlight and went as quietly as I could down the dark narrow stairs to the basement. This journey into the netherworld had to be taken in the dark. A light might frighten her away.

I snapped on the flashlight, but soon could see by the moonlight coming through the basement window above the little cot on the far side of the room. There was her big box of paints and her easel propped up in the corner next to the furnace, her canvases stacked along the far wall, and boxes of paint brushes, thick with red and blue and violet paint, now flaky and stiff, and the paintings themselves. I turned them over one by one.

"Do you like this one, Mommy?" I would ask.

She'd usually shake her head. "Not very much."

"I like it."

"Okay then, we'll keep it."

But mostly she took them to the trash to be burned. We would make a fire in the fire pit in the alley behind the garage. My mother liked to burn things. "I feel so nice now. Burning things is a good way to change things without waiting." So we would watch the sparks float up over the roof of the garage. "See? We're making our own sky. These are our stars."

My mother didn't paint bowls of fruit or sunsets. Her paintings were mostly swirls of color and movement.

"But I can't tell what it is," I sometimes said.

"They're meant to make you see something but not just with your eyes. Like you don't know what it is, but it changes you anyway. Like this blue. It's a cool, high sound." She laughed and turned around on her painting stool and looked at me. "You don't think I'm crazy, do you?"

"No, Mommy," I said, but I was beginning to feel scared, so I picked up another painting and sat down on the cot. "What about this one?"

A shadow came over her face, and her eyes darkened. She ran her hand through her hair. I could see her chest rising and falling. She went on in her usual way of talking without really remembering I was there. "Sometimes our eyes are the enemy. Do you know what I mean?"

Of course I didn't, but I nodded like always. Most of the time I didn't understand her, but once in a while for some brief moment, things made the most astonishing sense, and I knew we were together in some magical place she had made. And then it would pass, and

I would only feel the weight of trying to understand her and the emptiness of not being where she was.

She handed me another painting. I propped it against the wall, and stood back to look. I wanted to feel calm again but I felt something grave about my mother then, and something strange and frightening about myself.

"It's okay, Sweetie, I don't want anything down here to scare you. I don't have very many quiet paintings." Sometimes my painting mother knew how I felt. But mainly she didn't.

"It's pretty," I said, my heart a wild thing in my throat. It was a woman I didn't recognize. Is it you? I wanted to ask.

She smiled mysteriously. She didn't snatch the painting away or say anything. A woman with her eyes closed, rising over a black narrow bed, her arms outstretched, a halo of golden hair fanning out around her head, a ruby in each open hand, or maybe teardrops of blood. A gauzy white nightgown had slipped off her shoulder and was threatening to fall to her toes, pointed in perfect grace. Flames licked the corners of the dark narrow bed where a white owl kept watch, the light flickering in its amber unblinking eyes. The painting was so terrible and beautiful I both desired and feared it was my mother who floated above the flaming bed.

Most of her paintings frightened me like that. I saw only wild, bruised, and luminous eyes, and mouths painted over into silence. I kept waiting for the secret that would let me understand them, but for the most part they remained frightening and closed.

I always knew what would come soon after those days of painting and then burning the paintings into the night. She would gradually spin down like an overwound top, or she would plunge and crash. So one morning soon after, it would be my father who got me up for school and set out my breakfast.

And when I came home from school she would still be sleeping. I would creep into the bedroom and sit on the edge of the bed and touch her shoulder.

"Mommy? Can you get up now?"

"Hi, Sweetie," she'd say, her voice slow and far away.

"Did you get up today?" I asked, devoutly hoping this was only a little nap, but knew it wasn't.

"I'm getting up pretty soon now. I just have to sleep a little bit more. Give me a kiss."

So I'd burrow into the covers like a little forest animal and put my arm around her. She'd feel hot and damp and strange now, and I was afraid because I knew something terrible was going to happen.

"Daddy, please make her get up," I said. Sometimes he could, but mostly he couldn't. And then I would hear the doorbell ring, and there was Mrs. Bell or Mrs. Perkins, or Mrs. Beswick standing on the porch with her handbag and her apron over her arm, and I knew we were in it for the long haul.

I sat on the cot and breathed in the cool, damp basement smell and looked at everything. The basement was a museum to my mother's illness. Twelve hummingbird feeders. Half a dozen sacks of ribbons of all colors lying in snaky tangles. A big wooden crate full of dolls' heads and legs and arms. Paper mâché masks of doll faces propped on the drying rack in the corner. Bags of soft, gray dog fur. Where did she get dog fur? We never had a dog. A hundred pairs of shoes, or so it seemed, stuffed into bags and cardboard boxes. Shoes of all colors purchased from flea markets and thrift stores and church bazaars and department stores and shoe stores. Eventually my father worked out an agreement that authorized purchases only from him. It made my mother furious. She found ways, even so.

And watching over everything was the stuffed owl my mother called Leon. She said it had fallen straight out of the tree, struck dead by lightning. "It's dead," my mother said one morning, coming into the kitchen. She was wearing her red coat over her nightgown. Her feet were bare.

"What's dead?" my father asked. The alarm on his face was so clear and automatic I knew more deeply than ever what he lived with too. We followed every siren we ever heard home to our front door.

"My owl," she said.

"What owl? Eugenie, what owl?"

"My owl in the tree out back."

"You had an owl?"

"Look for yourself," she said. And there it was, lying on its back under the tree in the backyard, its eyes two amber beads, its talons splayed in death. She wasn't sad or surprised to find it dead on the ground. But now that her spirit animal was dead, she had decided it wasn't her owl after all. This owl was gray with dark brown stripes. "This isn't really my owl. My owl is white. It's a Snowy Owl."

"We should bury it," my father said.

"No. Don't put it in the ground."

So one day a few weeks later, a box arrived from *Leon's Taxidermy* addressed to *Mrs. Peter Lindstrom* in thick black pen. But she couldn't stand having the owl in that box. To her, it was caught somewhere between the living and the dead. So she brought it down here and propped it on the ledge in the corner across from the furnace, where it stood watching over the fire and the nocturnal life in the basement that went on while we slept. After she died, my father took it away.

My eyes kept going back to the furnace and remembering how my mother loved fire and moonlight. If she could only touch me or say something in my ear. I listened to the stillness inside the basement sounds, and heard the tiniest exhalation against my face, and the scent of lavender rising in air. I whispered, *Eugenie?* And went straight to the dark space between the furnace and the wall, right to the little black metal chest with the red dragon, waiting in its secret hiding place.

I pulled it out from the wall, dusted it off with the sleeve of my pajamas, and carried it upstairs to my room, where I slid it under my bed.

My mother had come back.

I kept it under the bed until the end of August, hidden by the bed skirt and the *Do Not Enter* sign on my door and upon my heart. Unopened, it told me everything I needed to know. And neatly tucked in a corner at the bottom of that chest, the thing dark and bright that would explain our tangled lives.

What Comes After
El Viejo y el Mar

I watch the ceiling fan over my bed turning in the warm breeze from the sea. I'm trembling and can't quiet my heart. My father is standing before me. His slender hands are folded against themselves, his wedding ring catching the light. There is an aching loneliness behind his shy blue eyes. *Why did you have to unbury the dead?* he asks. *Why did you do that?*

So I think about shoes, and the red shoes I never had. That errand was forgotten in the swirl of the new developments in my mother's illness and the drama of her coming home. But when my mother died, I grabbed her red shoes and kept them hidden under my bed all those years while I finished growing up.

I'd put them on every week and click their heels, like Dorothy, and walk around my room, waving my arms like a ballerina. I could imagine anything. Mrs. Beswick dead and gone. My father loving me again. My mother come back for good. I was glad they were too big because there was still room for me, but then when they fit just right, I knew soon they wouldn't fit at all, and the magic would be gone. I gauged my shoe size with my growing height, and was always afraid when my head reached higher than the latest mark on my closet door. I didn't ever want to outgrow my mother. I always wanted to fit tucked in her arms. When I grew up and moved West, I packed those size five, red patent leather shoes in a cardboard box, and buried them in the back of my closet.

Then I think of the shoe rack in Hemingway's bedroom and

feel the threat of tears. Imagine if he knew we'd be standing in his bedroom looking at his shoes, taking pictures like that. It would be like stealing nail clippings or locks of hair. Sandals and loafers and white bucks and wingtips, worn down at the heel, all but the wingtips, which I imagine he hardly ever wore. I thought again that if he knew he wasn't coming back, he would have had a big bonfire before he left, and chucked in the shoes.

Couldn't I see that face one more time, no matter how frail he looked? Just for a moment, his face in the window of the tower where he was supposed to write? Some days he must have climbed those wrought iron circular stairs to the roof to see the sun setting over Havana and maybe, once or twice, to look down, and think of the whispery rush of green rising to meet him. Or rocking back and forth on the balls of his feet, wondering if there was still too much bulk of him to die in such a fall.

I turn over and bury my face in the pillow. What had I done? I feel empty, cored-out. Like I'd just given away the most precious thing in the world.

Letters from the Looney Bin
St. Louis 1963

I locked the door to my bedroom, wedged a chair under the door-knob, and listened for the still, cool silence of that late summer morning to be sure no one was home. Then I slid the little chest from under the bed and set it on my lap. I jammed the point of my knife into the tiny gold padlock until the tip of the knife broke off. Then I ran to the garage for a pair of pliers, twisted the lock back and forth, then finally gave up and jammed the knife under the lid and pushed down as hard as I could. By then I didn't care what I broke. Finally the tiny padlock split open and fell to the floor.

I sat there for a long time, smoothing my hands over the cool black tin, the rivulets of fire rushing out of the dragon's mouth across the black metal. I shut my eyes and opened the lid.

It couldn't be! Who would save ashes? Bits and pieces of paper with words and lines here and there, lying in a bed of black and silver feathers. One puff and this record of our lives would disappear. If she had wanted to save them, why would she burn them? If she had wanted to burn them, why would she save them? It was as contradictory as everything else in her life.

And where was the snip of baby hair, the peach beaded baby bracelet, the baby tooth? They must be someplace else, because all this time only these pieces of letters and a snippet of a picture of a man with dark hair I had never seen before.

I carefully lifted each letter. Some crumbled in my hand, others were just fragments, and several miraculously whole. I brought them out of the ashes and laid them carefully on a white towel over the rug.

All the letters were from my father and mother except for one I couldn't place. I wondered how my mother had gotten hold of her letters to my father. I tried putting the letters together chronologically, hoping I could see what had passed between them. But the letters would not speak to each other. Their parallel but separate lives were etched in these half-burned letters snatched from the fire. And where were the letters that would tell me how to live without her? And where were my letters to her? She wouldn't have tried to burn these! They were tucked away, along with my baby things, in a place too safe to ever find.

And who was G? He had printed his letter in bold blue pen, unlike my father's careful, crisp handwriting and my mother's broken script. I had brought artifacts out of the dark and into the light. But they only showed the thing that had broken in my mother and could not be fixed. Even I could see my mother and father falling out of love, worn down to the nub by my mother's illness.

What are letters anyway, but fingerprints or palm prints, or bones? I thought of our small collection of family photographs in a jumble at the bottom of a small cardboard box under the stairs. Would we have rushed to save them in a fire?

> **DECEMBER 25, 1949**
> CHRISTMAS DAY AND I AM WITHOUT
>   MY ONLY WISH NOW   AND TO BE
> WITH YOU. I AM RIVEN. ALL MY LOVE AND
>   HOPE   LIKE THE EARRINGS. I WANT
> TO THINK   WEARING THEM ALWAYS.
> G.

So somebody named G had loved my mother before my father did, and all this time she had saved his letter. My mother was beautiful. Why wouldn't lots of people fall in love with her?

May 25th, 1950

Dearest Eugenie,

I think about how you came to me in the moonlight.
    no good for anything else now. Two weeks ago I
didn't even know   Now I can't imagine how
    without you.   truest thing I know.

Peter.

So this was how my father sounded falling in love with my mother. But this letter told me what I wanted to know. That he had loved my beautiful mother. That I had come into the world because of it. And what of my own, unremarkable life? Turned this way, my life was a star exploding into being. But what was the key to the mystery of their lives? Their terrors of the night, the long, strange absences, all the things that led finally to that shattering in the sun?

January 2, 1951:

The New Year!

   Dearest Eugenie,

You were so brave so beautiful.   so proud   She
    looks just like you. I have two girls
      am happier than ever.
  I love and   for both   forever.

All my love, Peter

There it was. My mother saving it all these years, the card saying my father loved us both. I read it over and over. But something dark kept flickering past my eyes. I looked at the first letter, then back and forth between the two. How could that be? I looked at the dates again. My father had made a mistake. Maybe it was March not May when he knew he couldn't live without her.

August 8, 1952

   Eugenie, I want you to know how much I want to
be home with   church session will only be a week
    longer. Please be my good girl   try not to   too

much. leave paints alone. I think   makes the   worse.
Please   call Mrs. Schulz for help in the   if she's
Love

Who was Mrs. Schultz? I did not remember any Mrs. Schultz.

June 10, 1957
Dearest Eugenie,
Truly you suffer, I know   and missed the signs
     sometimes and   have to you in ways not good
     for you   or   For   truly sorry. such cour-
age to stay in spite of   fears. pray for   daily and
to know you are my   and my heart always.
All love,

I always knew the signs. I had watched him miss them over and over. I would never ever have sent her away.

June 5, 1958
Dearest
The carpets cleaned   will love   I   don't
     be disappointed about the blue one. We can find
another and everything will be as   I returned
     the shoes   a strange day, as I'm sure you
   Till next week   Annie Laurie is
       Such a big girl to be finishing first grade.
Love Peter

A log must have rolled out of the fireplace after my mother had lit the fire, after my mother had gone to bed. How dark and still our house must have been, so quiet the crackle and snap of the fire, and only the smoke to wake us up. Now it was the first day of summer vacation and my mother had gone away again.

September 14, 1961
   Dear Eugenie
I've been busy   church as I'm glad   better and

> will be glad for   home. Just a few   Annie Laurie
> misses you always. Mrs. Beswick   everything   such
> a help, as you can   Till next week, then. Peter

This time he had forgotten to sign love. What had happened to love? I thought of all the letters burned to ashes.

Then the last letter, rolled up tight in the center of the little stack of letters—the one that should have burned all the way through but was perfectly, horribly intact.

> March 27, 1963
> Dear Eugenie,
> How could I send you back there when you told me
> how it was? You told me and I didn't believe you. I
> have betrayed you a thousand times. I have heard the
> cock crow and I have been true to my name.
>
> I will be home before this letter arrives. But Mrs.
> Beswick will take care of everything. I'm glad you are
> safe now and that all is well. You should remember
> it's over now.
> All my love, Peter

What terrible thing had my father done? Here was the secret that would unlock everything if only I could find it. My father, who in the end knew exactly where Eugenie had gone, and what had happened to her, and his pure and ravaged part in it.

Then the letters from my mother to my father, tied with white ribbon and only singed about the edges, as though they had been placed on top, after the fire had gone out. There she was, breathless and out of time, her frantic script across a gilt-edged page, her voice moonthrown even now. Why did she want to save these above all others?

> *May 29, 1950*
> *Dear Peter,*
> *You have saved my life. I will always love how you found me*

in the moonlight. How could you know I would be there? My broken shoe and everything.

My mother had said May too. They couldn't both be wrong. If they had met in May how could I be born the first of January? My star rushing into being too soon! I couldn't think what that meant.

August ? 1952
Peter how can I get well if I can't even breathe? They won't let me write anything down without watching, I know I have to be here but the sky is gone every day, it is so sad I can't stop crying. Terrible things happen all the time now, they would never let me write it down though. When I come home I won't even remember it.
Eugenie

*

September Dear Peter,
I'm coming home in two weeks but you know that already. They've burned it all out of me and now I'm fire-scarred everywhere. You should see the holes in my hands and my side, my crown of thorns. Ha ha. It's gone this time, and I'm glad, I know I couldn't come home till then. I don't know who is this dead person looking back at me in the mirror but they said the spinning one wasn't me either. Did you get her shoes, the red ones like mine? I don't know what year it is. You'll tell me when I come home.

*

February, is it ?
Peter—But all this time away from her, all the things I missed, where did they go? I can't bear it, this grief. It's February I think, I can't remember what day. They make you feel stupid if you can't. I know it's February though.

*

Peter Peter Peter—

I wrote you a thousand letters but I couldn't really. They were all in my head. For a long time I couldn't hold the pen still enough. Now everything is so still I can hardly write. The pen can't even move across the page. They're always telling me to take deep breaths and I do I put my hand over my heart to check but my chest doesn't even move, all the air is already dead, I know you don't believe me but the moon doesn't move across the sky or anything. Why be alive if you can't feel anything at all? When I was spinning yesterday I think it was yesterday, I could feel everything. I stood out in the rain today and shut my eyes so I could feel something that was alive.

*

Dear Peter,

Montréal. I wouldn't know if it was beautiful or not, how could I? You said these are the only letters I ever wrote you. The ones from this place with that unspeakable name. That's not true. But my owl saved me all the time. It sat on the bed even when that man was there. It kept the ravens away every time. My hair's gone now, or did they tell you? It's coming back a little. I don't know my face in the mirror, they only let me look once. They make you sleep all the time. That man watches me when I'm sleeping I can tell even when my eyes are closed, his horrible breath. That Frankenstein. I know what this place is.

*

March 15, 1963

They fixed it now so I won't ever have to come back here. I never could take the shoes back, you know I couldn't. I would be so ashamed. But you did it again, didn't you. I was wondering if maybe I could keep the red ones. You know how I am about always having those shoes. I know what day it is. Today is the ides of March. What is that? I used to know. But I forgot. Next week it will be all finished.
Lunatic from the Looney Bin

*

I read them through start to finish. I couldn't stop. Because that was it. Fourteen letters and one fragment. Why did she have to burn them? If she'd known how much I was going to need them, she would never have done it. She changed her mind at the last minute though, and put out the fire. I had to believe it wasn't the other way around—that the last minute she changed her mind and lit the fire.

FRIDAY, JULY 25, 1997

Love in the afternoon
El Viejo y el Mar

Friday is slow to come, and sullen when it does. But finally the day is born, and we are in it. You can hear people counting the days more in anxious relief than regret. Tonight is Ernest's birthday party by the pool. And tomorrow one more visit to the *Finca*. Then on Sunday the trip into the mountains to see the caves. We fly home Monday.

I'm in the dining room, looking onto the patio and the seawall and the water beyond, remembering the sapphire sea of Cojimar, two long days ago. My buttery scrambled eggs and plantains and fried potatoes are half-gone, but the scent of my *Cubito* coffee is rising in a steamy cloud.

I'd waited for Maria all evening but she never came. So many people to wish safekeeping for. Such unexpected sorrow as they urge their lives upon us, and ask us not to forget them. Nothing like the ordinary way people slip in and out of your life with no wake to mark their passing.

Maxine waves at me as she's going through the buffet line. She's glowing. Today she's wearing a fuchsia dress that drapes in little pleats, brushing her pale white legs flirtatiously as she walks. Her golden blonde hair has lost its curl and lies softened now, against her face.

She puts her plate down next to me and pulls up a chair. She props her purse in the empty seat at our little round table. "There. Now nobody can bother us."

There it is—the sweet smell of her, like talcum and sugar cookies and *Jungle Gardenia*. The rings of alabaster bracelets clink as they slide up and down her arm.

"Oh I must have coffee this *instant*. Do you suppose one of those nice waiters would bring me some right now?" She turns to wave one of the waiters over, then leans toward me and whispers, "He's my favorite. His name is Winston. I've not learned his last name."

She's already caught his eye. It's clear he's been watching out for her. She's probably tipping him grandly.

He ceremoniously pours her coffee from the silver coffee urn, then looks at me. "Another?"

"*Nada*," I say. "*No más, gracias.*" He gives her a quick little bow and pauses just for a moment to look at her, a shadow of a smile, as he turns on his heel and strides back to his place against the far wall. A white towel hangs perfectly creased across his starched, white-coated arm. "Isn't he adorable?" Maxine says. "I like to think he's watching out for me. I know he isn't really."

"Oh, I don't know, Maxine. I think he's looking right at you."

He's short and muscular, broad-faced with wonderful cheekbones, and dark eyes. "He really does have a very sweet face."

She smiles and pats my hand. "I love you for not laughing at me."

She picks up her fork. "I'm throwing caution to the wind." Her white china plate is a splendid mosaic of colors. Mangoes, oranges, papaya, pineapple, banana slices covered in grated coconut, limes, a croissant filled with guava paste and chocolate, a mound of scrambled eggs, a little scoop of black beans, a thin slice of bacon, little triangles of cheese. My plate is ascetic by comparison.

Of course none of our Cuban colleagues are permitted in the dining room, with this wall of windows facing the sea, the marble buffet table, the white linens, the silver, the china, the armada of white-coated waiters.

"I missed you yesterday after the conference," Maxine says, putting down her fork. "You were going to go with us to the Marina."

"Did you have a good time?" I say.

Maxine smiles at me and touches my hand again. "It was wonderful sitting in the sun. The Hemingway Marina girls. They are quite irresistible."

I haven't told her about Pilar or any of it. But in a flash, I imagine her leaning against that Marina bar, the music so loud she can hardly think. She isn't wearing her blue eyelet sundress, but there it is anyway—the Mickey Mouse watch, the white band double-looped around her wrist. And there, the tender cut of her shoulder blades above the red spandex, her dark, close-cropped hair. Pilar was only sixteen when all this began—in school by day, her life barely beginning, yet all the while coming to a close, as she waits impatiently for a future that has already passed.

"So many men," Maxine is saying. "There were so many men. Canadians and Germans, a few Americans, I imagine. They were looking things over, all right. It's strange to think, though. Beauty as a natural resource. A national export also."

"So much for Castro's ban on prostitution."

"The Cuban government just looks the other way," she says. "They love the dollars. The problem is always us. We're the enemy."

I love her sweet authority, the way she's becoming beautiful before me. I can see she's beautiful still, yet invisible now to the world. All those years of telling it slant. Now she can say anything she wants. Still. The waiter has seen it. It's more than flattery for a tip. And Bernardo saw it. But what do they see that her American colleagues do not? Her liquid brown eyes flashing with gold and green, her knowing smile, her imperious nose. Or is it a secret beauty, now a thing apart, emerging like frost out of the ground under a new sun? Her body is softening into a lush and tender fearlessness. What joy to be rid of leanness and angularity, the cinched waist and taut thighs, the high, firm breasts. This never was the landscape of desire, as we have always been taught. Instead it's this: an ivory softness yielding to this air, this light, to life itself.

The dining room is full now, and we can say anything we want. We're safe inside the rising and falling syllables of a thousand languages, the clatter of knives and forks, and the disco music coming now over the loudspeakers.

"This is my first trip without him. But I already told you that, didn't I?"

"Yes," I say. "I thought you were very brave."

"After he died, I lived in a desert. I cried all the time but there were no tears. It made such a terrible, ragged sound. It felt like I couldn't swallow. I could, of course, but it frightened me all the same." She touches her throat, and her bracelets slide down her arm.

"It's good you can talk about it," I say. I've put my fingertips on my wrist and am counting my heartbeats. Too fast.

"I thought I would stop breathing in my sleep. I could feel my throat closing up. How could I go on living if I couldn't breathe?" She brushes her wedding ring with her finger and takes a deep breath.

It's all familiar, this losing someone so suddenly your breath rushes out of you, as you run out of your sixth grade classroom and down the hallway, but there is no air until you run into the rain and stand against the wall, banging your head against the bricks, until you gasp in pain, and take in air at last.

"You know all about it, don't you," she says, her eyes filling with tears. She wipes them away with her napkin. "Oh my. It's only still breakfast," she says through a light and silvery laugh. "I've only recently been able to cry. It's a great accomplishment. Now it comes all the time."

"I like it when you laugh," I say. My mother's laugh was always a stream tumbling over pebbles. My heartbeat has slowed to it, that soft ripple of water over stones.

"My dear," she says, folding the napkin back across her lap. "I must ask you because I love you. You were married once, I think."

"It wasn't anybody's fault," I say against my trembling heart.

"Someday you'll tell me about it." She strokes my arm. "It's all right. Everything is all right."

I hadn't known how much I'd missed it. These little pats and caresses, the way she says *my dear*—all this could not end with Cuba. But I didn't want to frighten her away with my too apparent longing.

Her wedding rings flash under the light. "I miss it so," she says. "The rollercoaster ride of it. Did you think an old lady could wish for such things?"

She looks off toward the ocean. "I hadn't expected it. I hadn't expected to love him. Well, he was difficult to live with. He took up so much room, you know. I had worked so hard to change him. Then one day years after we married, it came, like a thief in the night. All my resistance to him was taken away. And in its place a ravishing life. You would never know it to look at me. If a Jewish woman can be born again then that's what I was.

"I don't think he ever really knew me. I had acted my part so well. Then one day I let him love me in the way he had always wanted. You know, with nothing held back. He was. . . I cannot tell you. Until the year before he died."

She closes her eyes with remembering. "Love in the afternoon. That slant of the sun across the bed." Her bracelets have gone silent.

"In my marriage I always held something back," I tell her. "I knew so little, and he always went so fast I could never keep up. I just pretended I did."

"Maybe he didn't know how to be careful so you could go as fast or slow as you wanted." She's whispering now, speaking to the memory rising inside her. "You know. In that way. Slow and fast at the same time."

Saxophone music and I was a goner. Even now, after all this time, I can't hear it without my voice betraying itself with a thick, smoky sound, my heart a hollow place inside my chest. *Lauracakes*. I was still *Lauracakes* whenever I heard that bluesy sound—all the sad young horn blowers filling the night with that burnished, mournful sound. "One time I didn't though, hold something back."

Maxine smiles then looks out to the water. "I didn't think I would ever be able to live in the world without him. But I'm not afraid of grief anymore. It's teaching me who I am." She touches the table with her palms. "I'm here, you see. I'm here."

Then she takes my hand between her hands. It's what I've missed more than any other thing. This language of mother-love. "I like how you take my hand."

"My child," she says. She's studying my hand, tracing the heart line on my palm, then turns it over. "These little freckles make an arc. Right there. You have a little sign."

"That's what my mother always said."

"You have never healed from it, have you? How could you?"

I rub the locket between my fingers. It's smooth and cool in my hand.

"Now I've made you sad, haven't I? I didn't mean to go on like that. We should walk to the Marina. See? The clouds have almost disappeared."

La Petite Mort
Seattle 1976

Sundays were for sleeping in, with all the time in the world for coffee and the chocolate croissants he'd bring home before I woke up. That morning he'd tried to make the eggs but he'd forgotten to turn down the heat so they'd burned and the smoke set off the alarm and when I came rushing into the kitchen, I saw him dashing outside with the smoking pan. I opened a window, and a little wind came up and whisked the curtains and took all the smoke away.

He came back in with the dishtowel over his shoulder, holding the blackened pan, the eggshells scattered on the counter and my croissants in the little deli bag by the sink next to the brewing coffee. He set the pan down and reached for the croissants.

"I was going to warm them up but thought I'd better stay away from heating things. Coffee's ready though." He looked at me and tears came to his eyes. "My own true love," he said, and then I knew it had really happened.

"Laurie," he had said. "Could you be awake for me right now?"

He'd asked me for this once before, and I'd turned away playfully with a joke on my tongue and he never asked me again. I was deep into sleep but roused to him anyway, and reached for him to say yes because my mouth wouldn't work, nor my eyes open and because what happened then came from a place so free from mind or thought it was the deepest, purest thing I'd ever known.

My unguarded heart tumbled so fast out of time I slipped down and down and gathered him up the way he'd always wanted me to, for how could I touch him unless it was everywhere? How smooth and strong he was, and I wanted it to go on and on, until finally the strange, salty taste of him, like tears.

We sat down at our little kitchen table without touching, the sun coming through the gauzy white curtains. We knew even then that words might break it apart because we had made love in a silent dream lit by day blind stars.

"*La petit mort*," I said, and then felt the fear of it.

"The little death," he said, reaching for my hand.

"Let's not talk about it."

"We're talking about it now."

"What if we forget?" I said. "Maybe we should have a secret word for it."

"Paris," he said.

"I've never been to Paris."

"Me either."

"I've always wanted to go."

"Now we have."

"Un Bel Di"
El Viejo y el Mar

Finally I tell her how Maria came to my room when I was ill, then later, how Maria had brought Pilar to my room, and how I'd stupidly turned on the light so anybody outside could see. And then the phone call that shattered the air, and the *Bodeguita* man who'd shoved me against the wall and said, *mind your own business.* "Maria is caught up in all of it, I think. I haven't seen her for three days now."

"Like Bernardo," Maxine says. Then she touches my face and whispers, "Don't you know who I am?"

I can't stop looking at her eyes. My knuckles ache from gripping the table. I tuck my hands in my lap. Who was she, sitting there with the sun filtering over her golden hair, her tiny white hands and then, a flicker of blue behind her amber eyes? I touch her arm. It's soft and velvety and cool. I breathe her in and wait for the smell of lavender. But I smell only talcum powder and *Jungle Gardenia*. Maxine is Maxine after all. No tight, nerve-drawn muscle and bone, no current humming over her skin, no breathless air buzzing overhead. Still, I'd seen something behind the eyes—a little pulse of blue. Just for a second her eyes had changed. Possession. They believe in it down here.

"That terrible man," Maxine says. "We should have reported it right away."

"But how? Who would we tell?"

Maxine's hand reaches for her throat. There is a new level of awareness now. "I'm afraid for Bernardo. Why is he gone when his job is this conference? That mayor's party. If anything happens to him, you know we're also to blame."

"Maybe we've put everybody in harm's way."

Then the lights flicker and go out. No clatter of forks and knives, no ripple of syllables floating on air, no salsa bump and grind, or whisper of the ceiling fans.

"Do not be alarmed by the absence of light," our waiter says, rushing over. "You are always safe here. We have the greatest of generators. At any moment the lights will return. And the coolness of air. The sun is already almost completely here. I am curious, however. What do you say in America when the lights go out?" Maxine and I just look at each other.

"Oh, shit," I say.

"Ah! *Shit*! Yes I know that word! Thank you!" he says and returns to his post.

"He's studying to be an opera singer. He's going to make his way up in the world."

She smiles a new, secret smile. "He said he would like to sing for me someday. What would I wish?"

"What did you wish?"

" 'Un bel di.' Do you know it?"

"*Madame Butterfly*," I say. "Not exactly a tenor's song."

"How did you know he was a tenor?"

"Doesn't he look like one?" She searches the room for him but can't find him anywhere. "Even so. I would love it more than anything. He said he knows it well."

She sings in a sweet, timid voice,

> "*Un bel di, vedremo*
> *levarsi un fil di fumo*
> *sull'estremo confin del mare.*"

"You know Italian," I say, and sing back in English,

> "*One fine, clear day,*
> *we shall see a thin wisp of smoke arising,*
> *on the distant horizon, far out to sea.*"

"You know it too," she says through tears in her voice. "The despair of love. The transcendence.

> *'n po'per celia,*
> *e un po'per non morire'"*

Then I say softly, because I can no longer hold the note,

> *"'I shall stay on the hillside and wait. . .*
> *A little to tease him*
> *And a little so as not to die. . . .'*

I only know the despair part. I'm still waiting for the transcendence."

She's looking out at the water glinting in the sun. "The ship on the edge of the sea just appearing." Her face has softened into a pure, radiant sorrow. "My husband," she says. "Maybe he knew me after all."

Nothing to Fear
El Viejo y el Mar

When I step out of the elevator, I see the housekeeping cart outside my room. *Please*, I say and slide in the key. Maria is inside changing the sheets.

"I was afraid when you didn't come," I say, without thinking. Dark things rush at me from every corner. Bernardo in the moonlight, the dissident at the mayor's, the man in the alley whispering, *mind your own business.* The room tips over and then rights itself.

I sit down on the half-made bed and cover my face.

"I'm sorry," she says, dropping the sheet back on the bed.

"I was so worried when I didn't see you." Tears fill my eyes. I'm remembering the three of us in that tender, lighted circle as night came on behind us, and the phone call that shattered the air.

She sits down on the bed and puts her arm around me. "I wanted to come last night but I couldn't."

"I never cry," I say, wiping my face with the back of my hand. "Too many people just gone and nobody knows where they are."

She should have said, *what do you mean?* but she doesn't. She just sits there strangely silent, looking out at the ocean through the open sliding glass door.

"Is Pilar all right?"

"Pilar is okay," Maria says without smiling.

We sit there on the bed in the cool air.

The sun is dissolving now, after its brief appearance at breakfast.

"These clouds are a great relief from sun all the time. But it will be back by noon."

I stand up and smile. "At least I can help you make up the bed."

"That's my job."

"No it isn't. Let me help," I say again.

"I'm almost done now. I've been hurrying in the other rooms so I could stick around a little bit, you know? In case you came back in time."

She gathers up the old sheets and puts them in the corner.

"I don't want you cleaning my room," I say, feeling my face turn hot. Those beautiful hands cleaning my bathroom, picking up my things.

"I already did. Besides, somebody has been doing it all week."

I had no idea who'd done my housekeeping. I'd left my dollar on the dresser each day for whoever she was.

Then we gather up the fresh top sheet between us and let it float onto the bed. We lay the bedspread out and tuck in the pillows.

"There. Now it's nice for you tonight." Maria looks over the room and smiles. "Making things clean again is something you can do for people. It heals them and they don't even know it."

Maria looks back toward the bathroom and starts to speak, then turns to gather up the bed linens. But she stops. Something is being decided, and now she's rushing toward it. "I have to be going pretty soon," she says. "Nobody should see me on this hall for too long."

"Can you stay a minute?"

"I've been in your room too long already."

Maria looks at the door then motions to the bathroom. "Could we go in there, please? I'm going to move my cart down the hall, then nobody thinks I'm in here too much."

"Are you all right?" She looks weary in the shadow of the doorway, but there's something else.

"There is a little trouble now, that's all. But not much."

"Is it the phone call? Are you in trouble because of me?"

"Just politics like always. Too boring to talk about."

But she looks at me strangely. "I'll be just a minute," she says, and goes out the door. Something cold and hollow is gathering in my stomach. Then she's back and we move into the bathroom and shut the door.

"The bathroom isn't bugged, is it?" It's a funny and terrible thing to say.

"Cops and robbers," she laughs. "I'm a little crazy today, don't you think?"

"Why are we in the bathroom, then?"

She smiles and shakes her head. "This way nobody from housekeeping can walk in and see us. Lots of people have keys to your room." Just then I have the sense that Maria's housekeeping assignment has never included my room.

"Have a seat," I say, and point to the toilet. She laughs again and sits down. I sit down on the bathtub next to her.

"In this hotel there is soap everywhere. It's what women in Cuba are always wanting. To have things nice and clean. A bath every day. Wash your hair also. I wish I'd had this job a few years ago. I could have brought home all the soap in the world."

Maria is sitting with her elbows on her knees. She's rubbing the scar on her wrist with her thumb. "You're leaving soon now, aren't you?"

"Not till Monday."

Then she takes my hand and says, "I have liked knowing you."

"Please don't say it in the past tense."

"I'm sorry I missed last night. We could have had beer and some laughs. So I came by to see you this morning, but also to ask you something." She turns from me, then stands up.

"No. Please don't go. You can ask me anything."

She sits back down and looks into my eyes. "I wrote a story about my life and I was wondering if you would have it."

"That's wonderful," I say.

She looks at me bitterly and shakes her head. There are tears in her eyes. " No. It's not wonderful." Then she holds out her wrists. "My writing is about these scars. Others also. I'm sorry to be so dramatic. But it's my power now. Is that too self-important?"

Her suffering, her passion blaze in her eyes. I take her wrist and run my finger along the pearly smooth scar. "What happened to you?" I ask as softly as I can.

She tucks her hand under her arm. "I was stupid. And there was too much despair."

I want to touch her but stand up to look in the mirror.

She dampens a washcloth and lifts my hair and puts it cool against my neck. Then she splashes water on her face and buries it in the towel.

"It smells so nice. I love things when they're fresh and clean."

"Who did this?" I ask. I can't help myself. "Why would anybody do this?"

"Me. I did it."

"But who made you do it?"

"I couldn't keep quiet. I was just out of medical school, and I thought I knew everything. But look at me now. Prison made me very rehabilitated. Now this great job. All the perks. All the soap I want."

She's standing with her back against the bathroom door. "I think the hotel is watched all the time now."

"Who is being watched?" I sit down on the bathtub and lean over.

"Just in general. Lots of Americans. But Hemingway people especially."

"Why Hemingway people?"

"I think maybe when you were at the mayor's something bad happened, even if it wasn't truly bad. Maybe it was the beginning, you know? Also maybe people saw me, maybe coming here with Pilar? Probably not though. We know how to be careful."

"How can you tell about the watching?"

"By who's hanging out in the lobby. Lots of internal security."

"Like who?"

"Everybody watches everybody in Cuba."

"There's this man who comes with us everywhere. Nobody's ever said who he is. He carries this leather case, but mostly he just watches."

She sits back down on the toilet seat and takes my hand. "You probably shouldn't see me, even now you shouldn't."

"But here you are anyway, right on my very own toilet seat." I can't stop smiling at her.

"I would like to read your story sometime."

She just looks at me. *Don't you see? There is no sometime, there is only now.*

"You don't know what I'm asking," she says. "I want you to *take* my story."

"What do you mean?"

"Cuban women are strong. But our daughters are becoming *jineteras*. We're dying, you know? From the outside in. My story is what's left of me."

"Please don't say that."

She manages a laugh and stands up.

"I'm just being melodramatic." She turns me to the mirror. "Look at us. Aren't we a pair?"

"One light, one dark."

"But see? We're exactly the same height."

"We don't need a picture. This is all we need." Still, I would have liked a picture.

"I copied it over very carefully," she says, "so it wouldn't take up much room. And there is an address of where it should go if you can do it. People carry things out of the country all the time."

A shudder passes through me. "Something happened," I say, and see alarm flicker in her eyes.

"What? What happened?"

My heart is thundering. Bernardo holding my hand, *be careful, be careful!* The man in the alley, *I'll break your neck getting this purse off.* Our three faces in that circle of light as night pooled at our feet and the phone rang on and on.

Shadowy figures move through the dream with darkening breath. A heavy ache of a dream that will not incline itself to words.

Maria just sits there, holding her face in her hands. I swallow hard and tell her everything.

"Oh, that's terrible," she says. "That's terrible."

I'm breathing so fast my hands are tingling. "I'm going back to that alley today. One of the translators is taking me to *La Bodeguita*."

"It's not really an alley, you know. It's Empedrado Street. Very respectable. Alley sounds too dangerous."

Then the ghost man walks out of the shadows of the ghost dream and whispers in my ear, *mind your own business.* "Did that man in the alley mean you?"

She turns sharply toward me. "Oh, no. I don't know anybody like that."

Then I remember. "He wore Old Spice." I watch her gray eyes turn dark with recognition.

"He was just having too much to drink and thought you were somebody else. Or just a crazy person. You know. Somebody like that."

I want to touch her wrist and say, I will do anything for you. But I can't say a thing.

"You should think about it then. You should really do that." I can see her edging between hope and despair. Still, she rushes ahead and tells me the thing that would discourage me for good.

"That man in the alley? Maybe it was a warning for you, even if he didn't know it."

"Like a warning from the universe?"

"It's what Pilar would say. She believes the universe talks to us always."

"Empedrado Street," I said. "You called it an alley too."

Then she says, "Maybe it was an alley. Maybe it was a dangerous place. Maybe I'm afraid for you."

"Bringing that Cuban to the party? I know it was stupid. It was meant to be a joke."

She shrugs. "No jokes like that in Cuba. No joke for him. No joke for Bernardo."

"Do you know Bernardo?"

She nods but says nothing. Then she says, "I think everybody ought to be very careful."

"What do you mean?"

"Like nobody seeing me here." She turns her hands over. "These wrists," she says. "I just wanted you to see how they are my story. I didn't mean to manipulate."

"Oh, no. I never thought you did."

"All right. Maybe a little."

Things are moving fast now and I'm holding on tight.

"I'm really not very brave. Please let me talk to somebody first." I can see Maxine figuring out how to carry the manuscript in her big white purse perched like a manifesto on her lap. *Don't you dare touch it.*

"Please don't do that. Don't talk to anybody. Even you shouldn't know what you are doing." Maria puts her hand on my arm. "One thing more I must tell you. Pilar has nothing to do with it. She doesn't know a thing. There are others, but not her. She's safe in her innocence. I have to believe it."

"I wouldn't ever say her name."

"That's good. I'm glad you understand. I'm worrying about her too much. Since before she was born."

"But is she all right?" I ask again.

"Ever since our dinner not so good. All week a fever that won't go away. It's pretty high right now. She has no immunity anymore."

I know why she's sick, I want to say. Bring it out of the dark.

"I know what you're thinking about Pilar, but it's not that," she says, rubbing the back of her neck. "Such a beautiful name, *Annie Laurie*. Pilar thought it was the most beautiful name she'd ever heard. I know how you fell in love with her." Tears are gathering in the corners of her eyes. "She has leukemia."

Something hits me hard in the stomach.

"Isn't it strange? I worried so much about the other. But instead now it's this."

"Are there things that can be done for her?"

"We've already tried everything there is. She's got the fast kind. One day it will go very quickly. Soon, I think. She's in the hospital now."

"Oh," I say from such a deep place it comes as a great pain against my heart. I put my arms around my waist and lean over. Black spots swim before my eyes. I can barely whisper. "I'm so sorry."

Then there she is. Her dusky breath, her hummingbird heart. "I had a baby girl once. I had her for three days before she died. I wasn't allowed to hold her until after. But once she held onto my finger. She had a tiny fairy hand and the strangest dark hair. Monday was her birthday. She'd be ten now."

Maria doesn't say anything for a long time. She's running her thumb over the quarter turn of freckles on the back of my hand. "You'd know how to love her and then when you had to, let her go."

A familiar terror rushes through me. Something most loved on the edge of being lost. I rub my locket between my fingers, like a rosary, as I feel the sting of tears.

She's watching me, and says, "Monday was Hemingway's birthday too. Can you be all right now?"

"It's only once in a while I feel like that."

"I knew you would understand how we are here. How many secrets there have to be. I knew you would understand about Pilar. Don't you know what is happening? She is breaking your heart. She is healing you also."

If I were her mother I would lay down my life for her. I would put my arms around those shoulders, so urgent and frail. Where could she fly to, with wings like that?

Then she says, "There is maybe some danger here. A little. Not much. It's all right if you can't." We sit there a little while longer as the fatigue washes over her again, her dark eyelashes shading her eyes. Then she gathers herself and tells me the last thing. "There are names in my story."

"What do you mean *names*?" I feel myself drawing away from her.

"Names of people who did bad things. Government names. People who are powerful, cruel."

It's too much effort to stand up. Then I think of how we were the other night, leaning back in our chairs, our feet propped up on the railing, and now here we are, sitting on this bathtub.

"I liked lounging in chairs a lot better," I say, as something tight in me begins to ease.

"Me too. My legs are numb."

"We're really something."

"So what happens now?" she asks, getting up at last.

"Tonight's Papa's birthday celebration, and some kind of water ballet in the swimming pool. Can this be true?"

"You won't believe what they can do. Like defying gravity."

"I didn't know there were such things at hotels."

"The arts are very important in Cuba. But it's difficult for artists."

It's everywhere. In the music, the air, in the way the light makes love to the sea. I think of Teresa and Antonio All that hope urged upon all that despair.

"Will I see you again?" I ask.

"I would like that. But I really have to go now."

"Are you working tonight?"

"I don't know yet. I go back to the hospital now. But I will see you, maybe." She reaches into the pocket of her uniform and pulls out a little copper vial and puts it in my hand. "Jasmine," she says. "Now you will remember me."

She opens the bathroom door and we stand by the balcony. I look out at the ocean stretching before us, flat and noncommittal.

"I'll figure out how to do it. Just bring it to me."

She points to the bathroom. "I already did. The stack of towels on the counter? It's in there."

A Blue Stone
Old Havana

Tani is waiting for me outside the hotel entrance. Her daughter is peeking out from behind her, one thin brown leg flashing in the sun as she scuffs her shoe in the gravel. "This is Paloma, my daughter."

She almost comes up to her mother's shoulder. "She's shy," Tani says. "She's tall for people in my family. She's almost eight."

"I like your socks," I say. She looks at her anklets trimmed in lace and leans into her mother. "Your long hair is really pretty."

Tani gives her a nudge. "Thank you," Paloma mutters, looking at her feet.

"Paloma is mad at me because she wants to go to the beach. I told her Old Havana is a cultural experience. She thinks she's seen it too much already." She's looking up at me with cautious eyes.

"Maybe we could get some pizza for lunch," I say.

"I don't know," Tani says.

Why had I phrased it that way? "My treat," I add too emphatically.

"It's her favorite thing. Next to the beach." She gives her daughter an ironic look and pulls her into a hug. "There are lots of places we can go for pizza."

Paloma is trying to stop the smile by looking at the ground again, but she can't.

What's pizza anyway, to bring such joy? Tomato sauce and cheese on a circle of dough.

How easy it is to feel important.

I point to Paloma's wrist. They're wearing identical red and white beaded bracelets.

"Your bracelets match."

Paloma slides her arm behind her back and gives her mother a look that says there's a secret here not meant for me. I look away.

Then Tani asks, "You want to take a cab or the camel bus? No more tourist vans for you. You want the authentic Cuban experience."

"Sure," I say. "Why not?"

She laughs. "I was kidding. You don't want to take the camel bus. I can tell you what it's like though. Three hundred people packed like sardines."

We move out of the sun while Tani finds a cab. She points to a dark, muscular man in a black tank top and faded Levis, leaning against the hood of his cab. "He's our ride, but don't let him know it yet." She waves to him and he sends a radiant smile our way.

"She is Marguerite," he says, patting the hood of his pale green 1957 Chevy. "I love her so much. See this? Like Fidel." He's pointing to his car ornament, a white porcelain dove perched with outstretched wings on the front of the hood.

"Fidel's victory speech," Tani says "when they let those white doves loose and one landed on his shoulder? You know. The great omen. It was a trick though. They tied weights onto its leg, so it would drop out of the sky." She narrows her eyes and shakes her head at the cab driver. "Not necessary."

Then she turns to me and whispers, "He thinks you'll be impressed if he's *Fidelista*, and so you'll take his cab. He's not *Fidelista*, though. Nobody is."

Now he's smiling his way around to the other side of the car to open the back door. "Yes?" There is no denying him. "I am Gabriel."

Tani hesitates and then nods. I have no idea what she's done, but things are settled now, so we slide into a backseat so plush I wonder if Gabriel sleeps here.

He punches the horn. "La Cucaracha" plays slowly in the hot Cuban air.

"*Hola*," he says and punches the horn again, hanging his head out the window and giving the thumbs up to every cab driver we pass.

Ancient Buicks and Chevies floating past boys on bicycles pulling carts, the rush of Russian Ladas and Toyota *turista* vans, then the slow-motion mirage of a camel bus caterpillaring its way around an impossible corner, as people queue up for blocks. We drive on, past Russian obelisks, outrageous and eerie against this extravagant sky, the heartbreak of that crumbling skyline, the sapphire sea nudging lazily against the Malecón.

We step out of the cab into the heat, the sun uncompromising and granting no favors. Old Havana by night was cobblestones, alley-ways and shadows, and music urging itself onto the night. Old Havana by day is sunlight and heat, no shade except in a doorway or the filtering shade of the ceiba tree.

Then we turn down a nameless street, and a woman appears out of the shadows, wearing a white ankle-length dress and white turban. Her eyes widen as she passes me. Paloma tugs at her mother's arm and stares.

"Who was that?" I ask.

"She's becoming a *santera*. She has to walk through the streets like that for a whole year. Change her clothes all the time. Keep very, very clean. Shave her head. It costs a lot of money. But then after the year she is a *santera*. A priestess."

I wonder how she manages all this without soap, without money. "What else must she do?"

Tani laughs. "Oh, the usual stuff, like not look into mirrors, wear only white. Sacrifices. Purifications. Offerings. No sex."

"Is this the chicken blood part?" I ask. Then I see how Tani's face changes, and know I've been irreverent.

"All this sounds crazy, doesn't it?" She smiles at me like I'm a small child needing translation. "Animals take on the sins of the *santera*," she says. "They're passed over her body, and then sacrificed by the *babalawo*. The high priest. That's why they are never eaten afterwards."

"I'm sorry," I say. "I didn't mean to make a joke."

"It only feels strange. She is learning to die and be born again."

Tani takes hold of Paloma's arm now. "Be careful here. Traffic is crazy on this corner. Fidel is the worst. You see his black Mercedes coming and you better get out of the way fast. He won't slow down for anybody." So we stand on the corner, waiting for a break in the traffic.

I turn around to watch the woman in white disappear into the crowd, her white turban floating down the street. When I turn back around, everybody else has already dashed across the street. I stand on the corner, waiting for another lull in the traffic. The sun is in my eyes and I need my sun hat, which I probably left in Marguerite's back seat.

Everything is in slow-motion. A woman laughs into the sun as her yellow Buick convertible slides into the turn. Her golden earrings flash as she turns her face. A motorbike roars, thrumming the air. An old man in a sidecar holds onto his straw hat, his eyes blinking behind thick glasses. A boy in a Mickey Mouse T-shirt turns his head and bikes into the curb, his wooden cart bouncing over the pavement. A blue Pontiac rumbles past, sticks of sugarcane tied to the roof.

Then someone touches my arm. I turn around and there she is—the woman becoming a *santera*. She looks at me with shining eyes. She's saying something in musical, liquid Spanish, as her smile grows wide and soft. She has freckles over the bridge of her nose.

"*No comprende,*" I say turning over my hands. But her eyes hold me. She takes my hand and strokes my palm while she says something incantatory. Her hand is cool and light against mine. Then she places something smooth and hard in my hand and tucks my fingers around it. I drop it into the pocket of my skirt and fish in my bag for something to give her.

Tani is staring at us from across the street.

"*Gracias,*" I say and hand her a wilted dollar bill. She looks at it for a moment as if she doesn't know what it is. "*Buenos días,*" I say.

She makes a gesture over me, like a benediction. She says something else and turns to go. Then she stops to look at the dollar bill again. There is something I need to say, but I can't think what it is. If I open my mouth I'd speak in tongues.

Then everything becomes as unreal as an overexposed photograph. The white-hot sky, the breathless air, my heartbeat pulsing in my ears. I can see only the sharp edges of things. Sounds are breaking up like a bad phone connection—the honk of a horn scraping the air, the *thump thump thump* of a bicycle over the cobblestones, a hot murmuring at my ear, a whispery breath on my neck, a solitary bird splitting the sky with a sound singular and strange.

I bring up the stone she had tucked in my hand. Just a smooth, blue-gray stone, ordinary after all. *Gracias*, I say again, and turn to rush across the street. When I'm safely across I turn back to look. She's standing on the corner staring after me, as though she's trying to remember something she's just forgotten. Then she darts out across the street, calling after me. *Laura, Laura, Laura.* But how can she be calling my name?

Tani puts her hand to her mouth as everything shifts into slow motion, and sailing down the street, is that big black car that would not stop for anybody, the sun flashing across the windshield. Now it's rushing into the turn.

"No!" Tani shouts. "Go back!" she motions with her hands. But the woman in white keeps on. Tani grabs hold of Paloma and pulls her tight.

The woman is in the middle of the street now. She's looking straight ahead at me, carrying something in her outstretched hand.

I could not stop it. The sun flashing on the splintering windshield, her white Easter hat floating up into the sky.

That black car sails right on by. It passes so close the wind gathers her white skirt and it flutters in front of her. She hasn't noticed a thing.

Then she's made it safely across, and she's standing in front of me, wearing a strange little smile. She pats my chest and hands me what she has so perilously carried. It's a postcard of Che Guevara. He looks like a young Errol Flynn smoking a cigar.

"Gracias," I say. I begin to search my bag for another dollar.

She touches my wrist and shakes her head. Then she smiles again and turns to go back across the street.

I put my hand out to stop her. "It's all right," Tani says. "Nothing can touch her." And it's true. We watch her weave her imperious way between the cars, and then disappear into the crowd. Tani turns her face away and wipes her tears. "I wish everybody could be like that," she says. "In a state of grace."

"What is it?" I ask. "What's wrong?" She's still holding onto Paloma, who's wriggling her way out of Tani's arms.

She looks at me with such recognition and sorrow I don't know what to say. "I have to tell you something that's terrible," she says. "Not now though."

"Okay," I say. But of course it isn't.

I feel in my pocket and bring out that blue-gray stone.

"What is it? Why did she do this?"

"It's a sacred stone to her. She has blessed you. Now you will see what you couldn't see before." I have Che in one hand and a blue stone in the other. So who am I now?

Altar of Lost Children
Old Havana

"We should go to the plaza," Tani says. "No more walking on the streets." So we set off for the *Plaza de la Catedral*. The craft sellers setting up their tables are already baking in a sun so high it's snatched up all the shadows.

We wind our way between the red and yellow umbrellas standing guard over the tables, and across that sunlit square toward the great cathedral, ancient and white against the cloudless blue sky.

"*Catedral San Cristobal de la Habana*," Tani says. "It's the cathedral on all the postcards." Up close its grandeur is only slightly dimmed by the dirty limestone façade.

We're standing on the stone steps leading up to its massive wooden doors. On either side of the cathedral proper is a bell tower with a cross at the peak.

"Cuban Baroque," Tani says. "Somebody said the architecture is like music turned to stone. They meant curves going all over the place."

Under a gray sky it would look haunted.

"It's beautiful at night here," she says. "Or we could go in now if you want to."

"Oh, I don't know," I say. There is something dreamlike here that frightens me. Something my mother told me I'm trying to remember.

The white hot of noontide is softening now into a strange light, and a metallic, echoing silence. I'm listening for the music turned to stone.

"Truly. You should see it at night. The soft lights coming through the stained glass everywhere. The moon on the cobblestones, on the cathedral. The sound it makes at night isn't like stone. It's like water. You can shut your eyes and hear it."

"Okay. Let's go inside."

So we climb the steps and slip through the heavy mahogany doors into the dimly lit cathedral.

"Altar of Lost Children," Tani says as we stop in front of the statue of the Madonna and Child. "See?" she says, pointing to the white notes tucked into her arms, laid in her lap. The white candles circling the offerings tremble against the purple flowers languishing in the cool dank air.

We take the steps quickly back out into the sun. Was she there when we went in, sitting under the red and yellow umbrella, puffing away on that cigar? Her dark face against the white turban with the red flower, her white dress spread out around her, beads of all colors around her neck, her wrists. She's all set up for business in front of a little card table covered with a red tablecloth, Tarot cards fanning out in front of a tall glass of water. She looks up at me and draws a long breath. One of her eyes has come unmoored. I shiver in the sun. Voodoo, curses and hexes, dolls pricked to the heart with knitting needles. It's only local color. A teller of fortunes for those holding unanswered prayers in their damp, cold hands.

"A *santera?*" I ask Tani.

Tani shakes her head. "Don't bother with her. She just wants your money. If you want the real thing, I can take you."

Now we follow smells so strange and familiar you begin remembering things you never knew—jasmine, cinnamon, pastries filled with guava and vanilla and almond, plantains, *guarapo, café cubano,* Coppelia ice cream. Then I remember cherry pies. When were there cherry pies?

Tani touches my arm. "What do you want to buy?" she asks, but I sense we need to move on.

"Now you can buy whatever you want." Beaded gourds, maracas, dolls with dark faces and yellow turbans, feathered masks, shawls, rugs, beads, all color and sparkle catching the sun. Buy my wares, feed my family.

So I buy a peasant blouse, a scarf, a pair of earrings, a little doll— tourist exotica, and nothing that calls my name.

I give the doll to Paloma, the blouse to Tani.

Tani just stands there with her arms crossed. She's smiling mysteriously. I can't interpret the way she seems to be guiding me toward something.

"I don't know," I say. "I think I want to go back and buy those beads."

"The blue ones with the crystal? They're her colors."

"Whose colors?"

"That blue stone the *santera* gave you? I think she was bringing it for her *orisha*. Her personal saint. See how it's really blue not gray? That's her color. Her stone. That's *Yemayá*. Goddess of the sea."

All right, I think, I could use a patron saint. So for two dollars I buy the necklace with the repeating pattern of seven blue beads, seven crystal ones. The cathedral shimmers in the background.

A boy about twelve or thirteen has run up alongside as we walk through the square. Now he's jogging beside us, sketching on a large paper pad. His shirt is clean and white, neatly pressed, and so are his khaki shorts. His eyes widen behind his wire-rimmed glasses.

He sketches me first. Then he flips the page of his sketchbook and dashes around to the other side and begins sketching Paloma. I watch her face come to life on the page—her round dark eyes, her pleased, shy smile, her perfect oval face, her ponytail.

He tears off the page and hands it to Paloma and then one to me. Sale or no sale, they are ours. He begins on Tani. She shoos him away and he darts off a few feet, sketching her the whole time.

"*Por favor?*" Paloma says.

"My treat," I say. "They're wonderful sketches."

"All right," Tani says, but I can tell she's not pleased.

She stands there looking at hers critically.

I hand him three dollar bills. He pockets the money, flips to a new page in the sketch book, and takes off.

The drawings are remarkable. Imagine an artist sketching in the shade at some festival. This kid did it in a couple of minutes on the run.

There is my crazy hair, my melancholy eyes, my half smile. And Paloma, her nascent beauty captured in outline. She points to her mother's picture. "Just like you, Mama." Her hair pulled back from her unsmiling face, her serious eyes.

Tani doesn't say anything. She just folds up the picture and puts it in her pocket. Paloma wanders off toward the craft tables, studying her picture as she goes. Tani watches her with a strange reluctance.

"Did it bother you that I paid for these?"

"Oh, well. It was very nice, but I don't want her to get the wrong idea about work. Do you know how much I am paid for a day of translating?"

"Fifty cents a day is an outrage."

"It is very hard work, but Paloma, she doesn't see it. She just sees her mother sitting around talking into a microphone. My days are long, but hers are longer. It's all right though, to pay that boy. He's probably feeding his whole family."

I don't know what to say.

"I know I'm a hypocrite," she says. "We're all hustling. I wanted you to ask me to take you out today so you would pay me."

"But I wanted to. I wanted to be friends the way women are sometimes," I say gently. "I wasn't trying to buy anything. Not even your time."

Tani takes my hand. "It's way too hot to be standing here anyway," she says, and leads me across the plaza.

"Paloma!" she calls. Conjured by a single word, her face pops up out of the sea of umbrellas blinking in the sun. This child would never be lost. Her mother would always call her back no matter how she strayed. Now she's smiling beside us.

"Let's walk down to Obispo Street," Tani says. "We can see *Hotel Ambos Mundos* and the *Floridita* on our way. Then after lunch we can take Empedrado Street to the *Bodeguita* and see where you got lost. It helps to name the places where you are.

"Be careful crossing," Tani says. "It's that pink building up ahead. *Hotel Ambos Mundos*. Room 511 where he wrote *For Whom the Bell Tolls*. I'm in love with Hemingway too."

We're on the *Hemingway Trail*—light years away from the *Catedral de la Habana* and the Altar of Lost Children, the fearless *santera*, the ghosts and sunstruck light of *Finca Vigía*.

We step inside *Ambos Mundos* as the strains of "New York, New York" glide on a slow, melancholy beat across the lobby. A woman sits at the piano by the open shuttered windows, a violinist on a barstool next to the piano, a crystal bowl on top of the piano stuffed with dollar bills. The lobby is cool and elegant, all brass and dark polished wood, tile floors.

"I'll wait for you here," Tani says. I treat her to a beer and Paloma a soda. They sit down at one of the tables near the window. Tani looks exhausted.

The elevator isn't working, so I take the marble stairs up to the fifth floor, room 511. It's stifling and I have to catch my breath at the top.

Room 511 is a monk's room, with its snug-sheeted, narrow bed in the corner, trim white walls. No wonder 3rd wife, Martha, bought the *Finca*. No room for a woman here.

But what you climbed those five flights of stairs for is in a glass case sitting on a little mahogany table in the center of the room. I want to stand before that typewriter forever. But it's so hot, I go to the window to breathe that air and see what Hemingway saw—those pink and white stucco rooftops glinting in the sun, the Cuban flag on top of the fortress waving in the breeze, *El Morro* across Havana Bay, *El Cristo* on the far right. I look down the five floors to the street below. "The world is a fine place and I hate very much to leave it," he wrote in this very room. When did he stop believing that?

But it's too hot to breathe now, so I get back down those five flights of stairs into the cool lobby, then out into the hurly burly of Old Havana. Then we're walking down Obispo Street to *El Floridita*, home of Hemingway's famous daiquiri. "The drinking woman's tour of Havana," Tani says, as we walk on by.

We're standing on that frightening corner in front of *El Floridita*, traffic going every which way, while Tani is deciding something. Paloma tugs at her arm, and Tani leans over and whispers in her ear. Then Tani takes my hand and says, "I want to show you something not on the Hemingway tour. But it's just a few blocks. I want you to see the *Prado*. We can still have time for lunch."

Then we're walking down the *Prado, Paseo de Martí*. Paloma smiles up at me shyly and takes my hand.

"Our favorite place in Havana," Tani says.

"The Prado, like Madrid?"

"Like Madrid."

We walk under that leafy bower with the sun filtering through the laurel trees casting gauzy patterns of light and shadow on the walkway. Building facades slip in and out through the trees—turquoise, green, orange, pink—and the green gas lamps along the promenade, the bronze lions looking out from their pedestals, the marble benches, and then the wrought iron benches in red, yellow, blue. It's a country in love with color, with everything to comfort and astonish the eye. Tani opens her arms. "This place restores my soul. These are still waters to me. I'm such a good Communist to be quoting the Bible."

I smile at her, knowing we have moved to a deeper place.

"It's our syncretism, the way we gather up everything we can. You can never unravel it. You can be both Communist and Christian. You can believe in *Santeria* also."

"I'd like to be something," I say.

"Someday you will."

"Sometimes I can hardly breathe. Everything in Cuba is too beautiful and too sad."

"I wanted you to see it, though, before more Old Havana. The poverty you can't see so well here."

Tani looks away, but I can see the tears in her eyes. We walk on through that wavering green in a strange and beckoning silence. "I told you I need to tell you something," she whispers. Paloma has not let go of my hand.

"I know," I say. But I don't.

Then we walk back near the *Ambos Mundos*, down those narrow streets in the shadow of all that elegant, crumbling desire. The sun has taken the sky but casts no light.

On the way to lunch, we duck inside a Cuban shop with the sun coming dustily through the windows. "See?" she says. It's a sort of

Woolworth, five and dime. On the middle shelf behind the counter a solitary goldfish swims listlessly in a cloudy fishbowl. "No toilet paper, no toothpaste, no cosmetics for so long now."

We smell the pizza long before we come into the little courtyard restaurant. I ask Paloma what kind? Anything you want. "Cheese and pepperoni," she whispers "Extra pepperoni, please." Her eyes wait for a silent rebuke but it doesn't come. Paloma looks at our three little aluminum plates and the empty center of the table, and back at her mother. She slides down in her chair and puts her head back. Her mother narrows her eyes, and she sits back up.

I'm fingering my crystal and blue necklace. "Tell me about *Yemayá*, if she's going to be my patron saint."

Paloma leans her head against Tani's arm and looks off. She knows we're in for it now. "She's goddess of the sea. In love with the moon. Very beautiful. Very sensual. She's mother to many children not her own. Her sister, *Oshun*? She was too busy with all her love affairs to take care of her children so she gave them to *Yemayá*."

"These stories are wonderful," I say.

"Yes, but they're not just stories. We believe in them. They give us hope. They keep us safe."

I touch their matching red and white bracelets. "Which one is this?" Paloma looks at Tani. She's not sure what she can say.

"Which *orisha* is this?" I ask again.

"We're daughters of *Changó*," Tani says. "God of fire and lightning. He gives protection from enemies and dangers. You know. The big stuff. All this, it's for her more than me. You know Saint Barbara in the Catholic religion? That's *Changó*. Catholicism in Cuba is really *Santería*."

Who's *Yemayá* in Catholicism?"

"Our Lady of Regla. The black Madonna."

My father's brand of religion was so plain, so austere, I had always loved the smoke and mirrors of Catholicism, the words in another language, the transformation. Bread and wine turned into flesh and blood. My mother would have liked being Catholic. All that theater. No chicken blood, though.

I hold the crystal and blue beads to the light. I see my mother's crystal wind chimes, gathering the morning sun. I put the beads around my neck. "There. Now I've done it." The necklace feels strange against my skin. I shut my eyes, then see the man in the alley. "Oh," I say. "I don't want that."

"What?" Tani says, her eyes wide.

"I saw that man."

"But he's gone. He's not here."

I let out a slow breath and look at the two of them. I touch the beads. Everything is all right now.

Tani rubs her thumb over Paloma's bracelet, walks her fingers up the inside of her arm. Paloma giggles, crosses her arms and smiles up at me. Her shyness is dissolving wonderfully.

"You were drawn to those colors because of your mother," Tani says. "Mother and daughters are often children of the same *orisha*. You said you were twelve when your mother died. It's okay not to talk about it," she says quietly. She's stroking Paloma's bracelet with her finger. "So you always feel incomplete then, like part of you is somewhere else."

"I thought I would outgrow that lost feeling."

"How could you? When you were just on the edge of everything."

I thread the beads through my fingers, then pick up my locket. My own private syncretism. Something has changed but I don't know what.

"I will always remember your Hemingway paper," Tani says.

"I couldn't have done it without you. More than the Spanish I mean."

A shadow comes over her face. "I like you very much, so I'm getting a little frightened. So much betrayal down here."

My eyes fill with tears.

Then, at last the pizza. Paloma eats slice after slice but Tani eats very little. I eat two slices but am so hungry by now I could have eaten half of it. We stack our empty plates in the center of the table. I thought maybe they'd have leftovers for home, but we've eaten it all, except for a single piece Tani wraps in a napkin and tucks in her purse. A waiter in a white apron takes the plates away and wipes the table clean. The green tile looks like satin in the light.

"Weren't you very hungry?" I ask.

"Oh, it's only the usual headache. I get them if I have to translate a lot. We have no aspirin or things so I just ignore it."

There's a bottle of Tylenol in the bottom of my bag, which I give her on the spot. She shakes out two and downs them quickly without comment. "Thank you," she says, handing the bottle back.

"No. Please. Keep it."

"Thank you very much," she says, and snugs it into her purse. "So do you want to know how to make your beads work?"

No chicken blood, she promises. Still, if you're Catholic, isn't the wine supposed to turn into blood?

"Now," she says. She spreads her hands on the table. "The first Wednesday of every month you spray a mouthful of this firewater over the beads. Then you blow cigar smoke over them. But you have to remember to do it every month. It will bring *Yemayá's* blessings to you. It will keep you safe."

"Why the smoke?"

"For cleansing. So you will be worthy of her presence." The words drift back to me from somewhere long ago.

I am not worthy that you should come under my roof.
Say but the word and my soul shall be healed.

She reaches into her purse and brings out a little pale green bottle of firewater, and unscrews the top. It smells faintly of molasses.

"Here. Try it," she says, and puts a drop into my mouth. It burns my tongue. Communion after all.

Wine into blood, bread into my body, broken for you. "Don't you say some words now?"

She laughs at me, but her face has closed up. "Now you say your secret name but only to yourself," she says almost in a whisper. "The name only you know, that you must never say out loud. The name given to you by your *orisha*."

Right then I didn't know who I was. *Laura, Annie Laurie.* I was both and neither.

Death and Resurrection
Old Havana

"Why did she give me a picture of Che?"

"Oh, well. Che is our hero, not Fidel. They found his bones in Bolivia, so now he's coming home. That's what all this television is about."

I look at the postcard of the man looking like Errol Flynn. "He was beautiful."

"He was unbelievably beautiful," she says as tears gather in her eyes.

The wound dresser, the wispy beard like Christ, the revolutionary, the idealist, the executioner. So he'd vanished out of history into myth.

"Did you know they cut off his hands? Even in death they feared him. You can't see those pictures in Cuba though. They only want to show him alive. But I think in death he is even more powerful."

I can believe it. Pop icon or not, in Cuba, Che is everywhere. It's lovely to watch the way the light comes into her eyes. Even Paloma is watching her. She knows not to tug at her mother's arm now.

"He was a man who could not live on this earth. He couldn't live with the way things were. His bones, though, I know what they mean. They mean he's really dead."

For a long time people thought he might still be alive. The nuns who washed his body took snips of his hair. They thought he looked like Christ. And people seeing him all over the countryside afterwards. In Bolivia but in Cuba also." She laughs. "You know, just like your Elvis at the mall."

Tani's watching Paloma now, but she's gone back to her portrait. She's laid it out on the table and is tracing it with her finger.

"Che is my Ernesto. Just like your Ernesto."

So Che was only his nickname. Argentinean for *Hey you*. These tiny details—that he had terrible asthma, that he was allergic to fish, that he was a terrible dancer, that he loved every woman he ever met. How he rose out of the mist of history and myth like an accusation. *J'accuse*, his eyes said from every billboard in the country.

"Where you're going on Sunday, to the *mogotes* in Viñales? He was there, in those mountains, getting ready to go to Bolivia to start a revolution."

She laughs as tears come to her eyes again. "You know what's really funny? Che's grandson is a punk rock musician."

She looks so alone, the sun to her back now, her daughter's life before her, with all the promise and sorrows of any young life urging itself forward.

"He died for us," she says softly. "For all who are *los pobres de la tierra*—the dispossessed of the earth."

She puts her arm around her child, so thin and dark, and pulls her close, and I think how fragile is her young life, and all of the incantations and charms she's gathered to keep her safe.

The sun through the palms is softening now. We grow quiet, wrapped in that light. So now Che would live forever. There was something to be said for dying young. Didn't Kennedy teach us that? Or Christ? Or my beautiful mother? There were days the light from her could fill a room, as she gathered up all the color she could.

"I forgot red," I say, unthinkingly.

"What do you mean *red?*"

"I wanted to tell you about my mother's red shoes."

"Like *The Wizard of Oz*," Tani says. "I had red shoes too."

"You saw *The Wizard of Oz* in Cuba?"

Tani laughs. "In Washington."

"Washington State?"

"When I was little I lived in Yakima, Washington."

"I know Yakima. I live in Seattle. That's in Washington too."

"I was there once."

"But how did you get to Yakima from Cuba?"

Paloma has heard it all before. She looks up from her picture and leans into her mother. You can see how much she loves this story of her mother going away and then coming home.

"Do you know *Operation Pedro Pan?* The boy who never grew up? Well that was me. I lost my childhood when I left Cuba. So it took a long time to grow up. That's why I loved that movie so much. All I wanted was to go home.

My parents thought it would only be for a little while. After Fidel, everybody thought the children would be sent to Russia to be educated. I know they did it because they loved me, but I would never do it. Not ever."

Paloma lays her head against Tani's shoulder and takes her hand.

"I was eight years old when my parents gave me to the priest. It was an arrangement with the Catholic Church that if we got out of Cuba, they would take care of us. I had this little pink suitcase and my little white stuffed dog. In Miami they tore my little dog apart to see if my parents had smuggled anything out with me."

She's stroking Paloma's hair now, a touch as necessary as breathing. I think of Pilar and Maria and wonder when this child would ease out of that touch and into harm's way.

"For ten years I was away from Cuba. Do you know how many things change in ten years? Do you remember when the world was going to blow up?"

"The Cuban Missile Crisis," I say. I remember everything about it because it was only months before my mother died. I remember school starting and how quiet my mother was. Then suddenly there were missiles. The least change could upset her, but these missiles didn't. She didn't believe in them. But my father did. He said they were "an absolute rupture of meaning."

Tani hugs her arms and closes her eyes. "It was so cold in Yakima. To live in a house where the windows were shut all the time! I couldn't breathe. It was so dry and brown and cold. But I loved the snow. Also I loved the apples and cherries in the spring. And then in the summer so hot."

It all rushes out. "I thought the Americans were going to bomb my house. We were only supposed to be away until our parents could come for us, or Castro left. But the missiles changed everything. All the Cuban flights got cancelled and nobody could get in or out. We got sent all over America. Thousands of us.

"It was the strangest time. The American papers said we were going to war against Cuba. That tornado in the movie? It picked up my house and threw it against the sky. And Rico, my real little dog? He was staring out the window of my bedroom just like in the movie. He had wet dark rings under his eyes. That movie scared me, but it saved me too, because Dorothy came home. My dog, though, she died a long time before I ever got back."

"I remember how the ships with the missiles turned back, and we weren't going to die after all." But I can conjure no faces from the news. I'm remembering a smell. It's what I was trying to remember in Cathedral Square.

"But I got my red shoes," Tani says. "Just like your mother. My new family said, 'What can we do to make you smile?' and I said, 'I would like red shoes.' They didn't know they were my secret plot to escape."

I knew all about red shoes. Dorothy's red sequined shoes clicking three times, but mostly Eugenie's red shoes, and her voice in the letter—"I was wondering if you would let me keep the red ones. You know how I am about always having those shoes." Her red high-heeled shoes crisscrossed in front of her chair, as Ella Fitzgerald spun on and on.

"It wasn't so bad," Tani is saying. "My family was nice. They gave me dancing lessons because I looked so sad all the time." She smiles at the memory. "They were saving me from Communism. So of course I secretly started to learn everything I could about it. That's when I read about Che. The Americans thought he was the devil, but I was at that age, you know, when you want everything you're not supposed to have, and he was so beautiful.

"Anyway, I was eighteen when I finally got back to Cuba. I was so mad at my parents for sending me away. Now I'm the crazy Commie in the family. Everybody either died or got out but me. I know what to do to get out of here. But Paloma's father, he would never let her leave. He would do anything to stop her. I don't want her pulled apart. So here we are."

She smooths back Paloma's hair, adjusts her hair band.

"When I was a little girl I wanted to dance with *Ballet Nacional*. But then I was sent away. We passed it on the edge of the *Prado*. That beautiful building on the corner by *Hotel Inglaterra*? The building with all the angels and turrets and the caryatids? That's *Gran Teatro*. Where the ballet is."

But I didn't remember the *Gran Teatro* or the winged angels or the caryatids. I didn't remember the *Hotel Inglaterra*. I only remembered how Paloma had not let go of my hand.

"I want her to study ballet but she doesn't like it. That's my dream though. Not hers."

"I don't think my mother ever had dreams for me." I'm remembering all the times I had tugged at her sleeve too. Here I am, Mommy, look at *me*.

"Look who's here," Tani says, pointing across the room to the boy who'd sketched our pictures in Cathedral Square. He's sitting cross-legged on the floor now, sketching a man with a Cuban girl on his lap. She must be about fifteen. She's sitting stiffly on his lap, his thick forearm around her waist, his chin burrowing into the soft place on her neck, his chunky white legs on either side of her long, long legs. She wears her beauty tentatively, despite the spandex bike shorts and the white peasant blouse slipping shyly down her shoulders, the growing sense of her own power settling with a dark radiance upon her face.

Tani's glaring at him, this man in the rumpled shorts and black socks and street shoes, his crisp new *guayabera* a size too small, a sheen of sweat gathering on his blotchy forehead.

"I know that boy is just trying to live," Tani says. "So is she." The man's gold watch flashes in the sun. "Why hate that man for it? I do, though."

The boy is working furiously now, his hand rushing across the page. He doesn't even need to look up anymore. He has everything he needs inside his head. He looks so much younger sitting on the floor, with the sun reflecting off his glasses.

The sunlight is filtering through the arcs of stained glass and over the tiles in wavering pools of colored light. I think of this boy before us, and Teresa and Antonio and Tani also—and all that might have been and was not.

Then Paloma is tugging at her mother's arm. She's pushed her chair back. It scrapes across the tiled floor. Tani rolls her eyes. "We'd better move on. How about *La Bodeguita del Medio?*"

"It sounds foreboding."

"Oh, no," Tani says. "It means 'The Little Storehouse in the Middle of the Block.' It's nothing to be afraid of."

I've come back to see it by day. I'd stood there in the dark only seconds, breathing the hot night sounds that rushed out toward the late-rising moon. What had he been doing there? *You*, he'd said, *yes, you.*

The *Bodeguita* is just opening for the day. Inside it would be cool and dark before the day heated it up. But I don't want to go in. I want to run my hand down the side of the building across the street and remember the hot, rough feel of those bricks against my back and not be afraid. I shut my eyes and breathe in. No Old Spice and cigarettes—just early cooking smells, onions, garlic, and the omnipresent smell of exhaust and insecticide. No one is calling my name. No man with the sharp, dark eyes and dark ponytail. Where is fear? In its place is a strange new expectancy somewhere between wonder and dread. But there is something else waiting in the shadows. The blue stone is smooth and cool in my hand.

We walk on and turn a corner. "Tenements," Tani says, pointing to the crumbling facades. "Thirty of your closest friends and relatives living right there with you. All the conveniences of home. No water, of course, electricity on, then off again."

A black dog pokes its head through the iron grating on one of the balconies and follows us with mournful eyes as we walk down the street, laundry hanging from nearly every balcony, beaten into submission by the relentless sun. I smile at a shirtless old man with no teeth sitting on the curb, then look away. This is the *Via Dolorosa*, the way of sorrows.

Then we turn down the last street, a dead end that leads to the bay. Long shadows from the buildings on both sides eclipse the sun to a narrow strip overhead. No clothes drying from these Old World wrought iron balconies, no people taking in this sunless air.

No music rushing out these dark windows, no people calling to each other across the street.

Then Tani stops and lets go of Paloma's hand and she skips on ahead. She's deciding whether to call her back. But Tani just stands there, watching a solitary man who has appeared at the end of the street. He's leaning against the side of the building looking out onto the shimmering harbor. A ripple of sunlight crosses our path. Tani puts her hand to her mouth and steps back into the shadows. Tears slide down her face.

"Bernardo?" I whisper. Because there he is. His flowered shirt, the shape of his head, the way he rubs the bridge of his nose. How strong and gentle his hand holding mine, how beautiful his face in the moonlight. Tani reaches for my arm. When I look down the street again, the man in the flowered shirt has disappeared into the shadows. I stand there shivering in the silent Cuban air.

"They didn't want you to know," she says. "I waited all morning to tell you. I didn't want Paloma to hear. He was hit by a car going home after the mayor's. He was thrown off his bicycle and he died." Tani looks at me from the mask that is her face, though her eyes are full of sorrow. "It was an accident," she says. Her voice has emptied of all feeling. Then she turns away and whispers, "It always is."

"Oh," I start to say but my throat closes off. I look for something to sit on but there is only the dark rough wall holding me up. "What do you mean?"

"Nothing. Things sometimes happen, don't they. He was a beautiful boy, wasn't he?" she says. "I wanted you to see the still waters before I told you." A wail rises out of the shadows and disappears into the dissolving sky.

"What does it mean that we saw him?" I ask.

"I would be glad to know the dead aren't gone."

"Me too," I say, "me, too."

Tani's watching Paloma dash out of the shadows and into the light. She's way ahead now. She's going toward the water. Tani calls out and Paloma turns around and rushes to her mother. There is something in her voice that commands her. Tani pulls her into her arms.

An old woman in a colorless dress comes out onto the balcony up ahead. She stands there for a minute looking down the street at us, or so it seems, then throws a bucket of water onto the street.

The blue stone is hot in my hand. I close my fingers around it.

We walk the length of that dark street without speaking. We have gone as far as we can go. I feel my grief and outrage settling now into a strange new calm that gathers everything up in a gentle, unguarded light.

"It didn't hurt," I say. "It was absolutely painless."

Tani looks at me and narrows her eyes. "You're different now. You see things too."

"I think so," I say, because I can see it so clearly before me. That Russian Lada rushing out of the darkness and clipping him as he rides so silently on the shoulder of the road, the flowers on his shirt blooming in the headlights fast approaching from behind, his head lowered over the bars, urging himself on into the night.

He doesn't have time to turn around. He only knows that for an instant something has lighted his way. Then a whoosh of air lifts him end over end into the night. He is higher than he has ever been. He's in a field of stars, like a field of poppies in the wind. There is nothing but this, in all the world nothing finer than this, he is thinking, and that's the last thing he knows as he slips from the tender green hold of earth entirely, and gives himself up to this holy light.

She's waiting by the side of the road for him now, her cool hands over her heart as she watches down the empty road. If something is wrong it's her fault. She shouldn't have been so careless with her speaking. She knows it. He said he had quit it all when they married. No more subterfuge, no more secrecy or intrigue. He'd leave it for others, even though she'd urged him on.

She can't just stand there waiting anymore, so she begins to run down the road, hoping this will draw him home to her. The moon is only a fingerprint of light behind the clouds as she rushes along the side of the road, making no sound at all.

The Divination
Central Havana

It's just the two of us now, making our way through the streets of Central Havana. Under this heavy, gauzy sky everything has taken on a bleached, dry feeling, with the close, musty smell of unremembered rain. Some afternoon high cloudiness has drifted in from the sea and tamped everything down into a sleepy dream. I'm glad we're going to the mountains tomorrow. I can hardly breathe.

"This is *Santería* country," Tani says. "I know what you're thinking. Where's all the color? But just wait. In *Santería* country, all the color is inside."

Here, the apartments jut edge on edge into repeated rows of narrow doorways and dark forbidding alleys. Only now and then the surprise of coming upon an old man with slow and watchful eyes sitting on a plastic chair next to a doorway, or an old woman in a faded yellow dress standing against the doorjamb, following us with her cautionary narrowing gaze, a white bell of warning—*prohibido el paso!*

"I will be translating, okay?" Tani says. "I'll hear everything you say. What the *babalawo* says also."

"Okay," I say.

"In Cuba by day everything is one thing and by night it's another. By day it's *Santa Barbara*, but at midnight, you know, it's *Changó*."

When she'd said, "Do you want to meet a *babalawo*," I said, of course, why not? I'd been edging toward it ever since the *santera* gave me my blue stone. My palm read, tea leaves or Tarot cards, just no chicken blood. Only a cleansing, a healing of wounds, as Tani had promised.

"Do you understand?" she asks again. "The minute you set foot in his house you will see the night things. But it's secret and we must be careful. I don't know if I can explain it well enough. Some *babalawos* are dangerous. Some of them are spies of the government. Who knows more secrets than they do? Some *babalawos* do terrible things. Sometimes they kill people."

She's no tour guide now and I am no tourist. My camera is buried deep inside my straw bag, and my little blue stone, and my blue and silver beads are tucked safely out of sight in the pocket of my dress.

The streets are empty of everything but the heaviness of eyes. Behind doorways and half-shuttered windows, from narrow dark alleyways, cool and wary eyes. I can feel my heartbeat in my hands, a rush of air down my throat.

Tani manages a half-smile but holds my hand as we make our way down the street.

There are people everywhere now, toward or away from the amazement of their everyday lives. The overcast is almost gone now. We stop in front of a window with a yellow curtain billowing against a wrought iron grating. Tani squeezes my hand. I can feel her breath warm on my neck. It's clear even to me that something is about to change. Tani rings the bell.

The door opens and a beautiful woman is breaking into a smile. The *babalawo's* young wife. The woman drops her smile and looks me over. Then she looks at Tani with narrowing eyes, then at both of us together, then back at me. Tani hands her the money for me.

She takes me by the hand and leads us into the house. The woman closes the door behind us and I hear the lock fall into place.

"You can go in now," the wife says. So I step through a beaded curtain into the sacred room, lit only by an open doorway that leads out into a narrow alleyway. I catch my face in the oval mirror. It startles me, and for a moment I don't know where I am. A crucifix on the opposite wall hovers in the corner of the mirror.

"Please sit down," the *babalawo's* wife says with her hands. My eyes take in the room—a couple of chairs facing a woven mat in front of the far wall, three drums wound with rope, some small ceremonial iron tools, a statue of Saint Barbara in red and gold, holding her sword, a closed, dark door.

"*Changó* by night," Tani says, nodding at Saint Barbara. Then she points to the cement statue in the corner by the door, an oval head with cowrie shell eyes, nose, and mouth. "*Elegguá.* Guardian of doorways. So no evil can enter. You know, like the St. Anthony you wear for safe passage? The same."

Then she points to the figure in blue against the wall in the corner. "*Yemayá*," she says. "I don't need to tell you who she is."

"My *orisha*. Her beads are in my pocket." My voice is shaking. "I was afraid to put them on."

"Why?"

"Because I thought it would be disrespectful not to know what I was doing."

"But you know already." Tani smiles at me strangely. "Anyway, isn't she wonderful?"

It's the most beautiful doll I've ever seen. This doll belongs in a museum or a gallery of folk art or a cathedral. The dress is unearthly, a gossamer blue, beaded in a swirling pattern of silver and blue that catches the light. A tiny iron chain circles her neck with her symbols on it—a sun, a moon, an anchor, a key. In front of her a blue and gold tureen, and inside, her sacred stones in coconut milk and seawater, and beside it, crisscrossed violet, blue and yellow flowers. *Yemayá*, goddess of the moon and sea, a silvery undulation over the waves.

Then my mother comes to me. My own Eugenie, that moon-driven girl turning round and round. And her blue castle mailbox, the silver key in the secret place, the crystal wind chimes turning in the light. My mother was a daughter of *Yemayá*. And so am I.

"Remember everything you can," Tani whispers, as the *Babalawo* enters, takes my hand, and sits cross-legged, on the mat. He shuts his eyes and places his hands on his knees. Then he looks up and smiles at me with eyes beautifully brown and full of light.

He speaks only Spanish, but what he says, he says to me. I think of my dangerous American otherness and wonder if it's all right to be here. Yet I'm not here as an anthropologist or scholar or tourist but as one of a thousand lost souls come in from the street.

He's a lovely looking sixty-five-year-old man with a carefully trimmed white beard and close-cropped white hair under a gold crown. He's wearing a Baltimore Orioles baseball jersey, tie-dyed parachute pants, and sports shoes. A hip high priest with a syncretism all his own. Around his neck is a gold cross on a chain, yellow and amber beads for *Oshún*, and a string of white beads I can't identify.

On the wall above him is the crucifix I saw in the mirror—nail holes in Christ's hands and feet, the wound in the side, the bloody knees, and a word I did not know in black letters above the cross beam. *INRI*. This is nothing like *El Cristo*, the sixty-foot white, marble statue of Christ guarding Havana Bay. This Christ is all ribs and knees and ankles, dark matted hair, eyes beyond sight.

The *babalawo* stretches out his legs, crosses his ankles and picks up his sacred book. It's full of numbers and markings and looks to be very old. He turns the pages carefully, then sets it down. "He wants to know if you are ready. He has prayed to the dead of your family and to the *orishas* for permission to conduct the divination."

"Tell him yes," I say. I unclench my hands, unfurl my heart. Now he would tell me whose child I am, and what my future holds.

"First he wants to tell you about the gods of *Santería*," Tani says. And so she translates as he points to things in the room, *do you understand?* and I shake my head yes to the rich, smooth sound of his voice, yes to the dark, luminous eyes, yes to the *orishas* and how they connect us to the things of the earth—the sun and moon and sea and rivers.

Then he touches my forehead with his *opele*, the iron chain with the eight, two-sided coconut rinds. He holds it in the middle, between his thumb and forefinger, and throws it on the mat. He studies the pattern they make, splayed over the mat—which rinds land up and which land down, like heads or tails, and in which order, and writes down the pattern in his little book. Then he throws the chain again.

I don't understand any of it. I'm watching those dark slender hands and the way the chain and medallions fly across the mat. Then his hand sweeps over the chain of coconut rinds lying in a pattern only he can read, and he looks at me and smiles. Then he says in English, "Laura. Daughter of *Oshún*."

"It's the pattern of your life. It's all written down now," Tani says.

Was I daughter of *Oshún* then? Tears come to my eyes. So I was not daughter of *Yemayá*. I was not my mother after all. I was my own self. I was daughter of *Oshún*.

"You must remember September 8," Tani explains. "It is her feast day. You must take care of her. Not just stick her in a corner in your house and forget her. You must give her things. Like pumpkin and cake. White cake. She likes coconut also. Cinnamon and honey. All sweet things. It is good to be daughter of *Oshún*. *La Caridad del Cobre*, patron saint of Cuba."

Tani sees my tears and touches my arm. "It's all right," she says. "You can belong to more than one *orisha*." She had remembered my quick fondness for *Yemayá* in Cathedral Square and my blue and crystal beads.

"No," I say. "It's not that. I'm happy to be daughter of *Oshún*."

"You must pray to her," Tani says. "Ask her for things."

I had not said any prayers since my mother died. An old verse comes to mind: "Come unto me all ye that labor and are heavy laden and I will give you rest." And my father in the doorway, a shadow in the hall light, just before he said goodnight, and left me to say my prayers. He never asked me to say them out loud. It was probably my mother's doing. She couldn't abide any violation of privacy.

"Do you have family then?" the *babalawo* asks.

"A father," I say.

"No husband or lover? No children?"

"No."

"Are you menstruating?"

I look at Tani.

"If you are menstruating," she says, "certain things have to be done differently."

"I'm not anymore," I say. How would I explain it? "I've had, you know, a hysterectomy."

Tani's eyes widen. Of course. No problem. Tani explains by cupping her hands below her waist and lifting them up.

Ah, the *babalawo* nods. So there would be no children to wish for. I wrap my arms around myself.

Then he hands me a seashell and a bone. I almost drop it when he puts it in my hand. *Bone of what?*

"It's all right," Tani says. "It's only goat vertebra." I close my hand around it and shut my eyes. It feels strange and light in my hand.

"Shake them in your hands, like dice, then hide one in each hand. He's trying to see if the pattern of your life comes with good or bad luck. If he picks the seashell hand it's *ire*, good luck. If he picks the bone, it's *osobgo*. Bad luck."

I shake them and let them divide as they will. Seashell and bone. Good and bad. Then he throws the *opele* to see which hand to choose. He points to my right hand. I turn it over and there is the bone.

Then he consults his book and writes down the *oddu*, the pattern and its legend. He throws the *opele* again, and points to my left hand. Seashell. Then bone, then seashell, then bone again and again and again. I do not take my eyes off his hands. Even from here, I can see the pattern of 1's and 0's he is making, one under the other, until they make four lines across. Upside down they are hieroglyphs—marks and zeroes which are my life.

Then I look over at Tani. Her face has clouded over. Her mouth is clamped tight.

She's holding onto the edge of her chair.

"What's happening?" I whisper.

"The bone is very bad. There is very bad luck in the bone. He's finding out how it comes to you and what can be done to remove it."

But the *babalawo's* face doesn't change. The whole time the expression of calm never leaves his face.

"Now he is asking what offerings must be made. Also what sacrifice."

I look at the crucifix that hovers above him—the head hung to one side, the bloody knees, the word INRI above the cross beam.

"Why do you come here?" the *babalawo* asks. "What is the weight to be lifted?"

A fist of panic covers my heart.

"What do you want?" he asks again.

"I want to be happy," I say. "I don't want to be sad anymore, or afraid."

The scrim of translation will shield me from nothing. I watch the *babalawo's* eyes soften at the corners, as Tani translates. I listen to my words detach themselves from meaning and shape themselves into a languid, fluid sound I do not recognize, yet understand. I don't take my eyes off his face.

"Tell me what you want again," he asks.

What do I want? I want my shattered self knit back together. I want to be whole. I don't want to be alone. Tears run down my face.

"Do you wish for love then? Do you wish for someone to love you?"

"Oh, I don't know. I don't know about that." I look at Tani.

"I know," she says. "Love is complicated."

"I'm afraid to wish for love."

"You should," she says. "You should always wish for it. However it comes."

Then I see Michael bending over Antonio, touching his face.

"All right," I say. "I can wish for it."

All these years I had tried to beat back death with such an urgent eroticism, I had come unmoored, casting filament after filament of myself into open air, then suddenly and always flung back to earth, and the loneliness after—a cold, old moon against a bleak, winter sky, a universe bereft of stars and human exhalation.

I had never been able to yield to the slow, more certain knowledge of heart touching heart, desire playing softly against my closed eyes, my mouth, the sweet plum of faith on my tongue.

I look at the statue of Christ on the wall and think of everyone I knew who had been broken on the spiny wheel of life.

What was INRI?

"You know," Tani says. "It's what Pontius Pilate said. 'Here he is. Jesus of Nazareth, King of the Jews.' I for Jesus, N for Nazareth, R for King, I for Jews. You are not Catholic, then?" she says, smiling.

"No," I say, "I'm not anything."

The *babalawo* lays down the *opele* and looks at me. "There is a river to cross," he says. "Your heart is a strange darkness. Why is joy on the other side of the river?"

"So much loss," I say. "People who have died for no reason."

"Who? Who has died?"

"My mother," I say. "And once a baby girl. There has been an accumulation of sorrows.

Also a Cuban friend who has just died. And much distance from my father."

I look at Tani. Her eyes are fierce and dark.

"Fear or joy," the *babalawo* says. "One or the other."

Then the soft, low chanting begins again, and I shut my eyes and feel that rich, dark sound ripple over my skin. Now the *babalawo* turns quiet and reaches out. And then behind my eyes I see Bernardo kneeling beside the *babalawo*, his flowered shirt catching the light spilling in from the doorway. "My son, my son," he says, and holds out his hand and blesses him.

When I open my eyes the *babalawo's* hand is raised in midair, the room shimmering with light.

Illuminata. "Now you will see things," Tani had said. The *babalawo* turns his hand over, looks at me, and nods.

"Yes," I say.

"Now you must hear a hard thing. Inside your sorrow is a great anger you have never spoken. You are angry for things that could not be helped. You have anger for your father for not safekeeping you. But anger takes up too much room. I will prepare an offering to take it away and replace it with a brand new thing. Three times a blessing will come to you. You must come back in three days."

I shut my eyes and shake my head.

"She is leaving then, for home."

"Ah! It seems you have only come here. I must do it now then. You will wait please for me to prepare. It will not be long."

He leaves the room and we sit without speaking.

Then the wife comes back and motions for us to follow her into the alley. "*Oshún* asks for a sacrifice," Tani says. "So she can help you."

"All right," I say, and step into the narrow band of light filtering down from the long thin rectangle of sky between the buildings.

Then a dark shape, just as I knew there would be, when we step into the alleyway. The dark shape tucked under the shadows—the thin black-speckled hen in the cage by the wall.

The *babalawo* does not look up as we stand beside him but continues making marks on the ground with a piece of white chalk—a smooth half-circle in front of the altar and five or six crosses through the curve. Then he stands up and says a prayer to the sky, then a prayer to the altar he has made—a tureen with dark stones, another full of a dark-green liquid that catches the light, a vase with yellow and white flowers, a single, small white lit candle.

What happened next? Who can say why some things collect in the net of memory and other things fall through?

It squawks only once, struggling a little at the beginning, when the *babalawo* first lifted it. That wild little heart against his smooth dark palms, the panicked flutter of wings. Then he strokes it into stillness. Only its eyes tell it's alive. It doesn't flap its wings or cry out. Its tiny self a willing sacrifice, its heart a slow and steady pulse.

The hen is offered to the tureen filled with that dark glistening liquid. Would I have to drink it? I'm being drawn toward things so far outside myself I'm in a country with no words I know. But I won't shut my eyes, I won't miss a thing.

Then with the hen in his hands, the *babalawo* makes the sign of the cross—high up to the sky, down to the tureen with the stones, and then crosses himself, left then right, across his chest. "It is blood that is needed," the *babalawo* says. "A sacrifice for *Oshún*. So she will help you." In that tight alleyway, the sun is edging its way down those high gray walls.

The *babalawo* bends over and picks up the knife. *Lamb of God, who takes away the sins of the world, hear our prayer.* He strokes the neck of the hen with the knife, and dark feathers drift down through the light onto the offering.

Lamb of God, who takes away the sins of the world, have mercy on us. Still, the hen lies quiet in his hands, the blinking eye the only sign of life, as the black feathers float down through the holy light.

Lamb of God, who takes away the sins of the world, grant us peace. He takes up the chant again, this time low and sweet and soft, an incantation of love and death. Then he takes the knife, and in a single, fluid gesture it is done.

I don't know what happens next. I only remember how the offering glistens with blood—how the droplets descend like little rubies in the light, over the offering for *Oshún*. Fruit and pumpkin seeds and purple flowers sprinkled with sugar and honey, and all of it carefully placed on a square of brown wrapping paper, now darkening brilliantly with blood. Then the *babalawo* lays the chicken on the pavement. I look at it lying on the dark-stained concrete before the offering, a jumble of dark, scattered feathers.

Behind me are the spade and shovel. Gardening tools, but no garden.

"Was it a worthy offering?" he asks *Oshún*. Was I a worthy daughter? He dips his hand in the dark liquid and shakes it over the offering and sprinkles it over me. Then he nods and smiles. "Yes. It is a fine offering. All that is needed."

So this is the necessary sacrifice. It seems such a slight offering. The least of these, this small, diminished life, transfigured now through the awful blood. I look at it lying there and feel the sun pouring into that narrow passageway, over my head, my shoulders, my open hands, washing me in a furious light.

And then there it is, a gift from my past, rounded and whole and undiminished by time. My first blessing. My father had brought it up from the basement that terrible Easter morning after my mother had died and laid it in my lap without speaking. A baby Easter chick. I cupped it in my hands and brought it to my face, felt its tiny beak against my lips, its warm breath on my face. I had not thought of it for so long. How did he do it? How had he managed to buy that little chick in time for Easter morning?

So there was something given back. It had not fallen through the net of memory after all. And Eugenie? What was given back of her?

I do not see him sever the head. I only see him bending over the offering, and when he stands up, I only see the eyes unblinking now, and the beak, which opens twice. Two exhalations without breath, two words without sound, the final benediction. The offering would be gathered up in the square of brown paper and cast into the sea. And my dark fearful heart brought into the light.

Tani has disappeared somewhere in the back where the *babalawo* is washing his hands. I pass the oval mirror in the holy room just before I go through the beaded curtain. For a moment I don't recognize my face—the flush on my cheeks, the strange white around my eyes, the wide dark pupils, my extravagant hair.

I wander into the living room and sit down. I can't stop the tears. Then they come back into the room, and the *babalawo* sees the tears down my face and wipes them away. "A small sacrifice for such a big thing," he says. "Your life is in *Oshún's* hands now. You must come back someday and let me know how it goes."

I have come so far. How will I ever find my way home? I know no bridge to take me there.

The Age of Knowing
St .Louis 1963

"How do you know if you're going to hell?" I had asked my father, stepping into the bar of light cast by his desk lamp onto the red Persian rug, the only extravagance in his spare, dark office. "You can go to hell for your sins when you're twelve because then you're in the age of knowing."

My mother had gone away again, and I knew there must have been something I could have done to save her. I was glad I was only ten and tucked safely outside the age of knowing.

My father's head jerked up and he turned around sharply. "Who told you that?"

It was Mrs. Blevins, my Sunday school teacher. I couldn't tell him what I feared, that my mother's fate was inextricably linked to mine, that her salvation depended upon my own.

He must have read my mind, because he pulled me close to him and took my face in his hands. He must have known even then, though we could not speak of it, of my terrors when my mother left, how I walked through my life holding my breath in my hands, hugging myself to every dark corner.

He looked at me with a strange and tender look I had seen only for Eugenie.

"You are precious to the universe, Annie Laurie. You must never forget it." I had never heard him talk like that. I was precious not just to Jesus, in that Sunday school way, but to the universe.

But then later, after my mother died and everything closed up, the old fear returned, along with the nightmares. "Daddy?" I whispered. "Can you wake up now?," I touched him on the shoulder. I had been standing there a long time. This depth of sleeping frightened me.

He sat up. "Annie Laurie, it's you. What's the matter?" It was only years later that I realized how lightly he had learned to sleep. But he had no need of sleeping like that anymore. Now he slept like the dead.

"I'm afraid of going to hell again," I said, still wrapped in the terror of the dream.

My mother had died and I could not save her. I wanted my father to wrap me in his arms, while I tucked my head under his chin. I wanted to hear how precious I was again, not just to the universe, but to him.

"Well, you go back to sleep now," he whispered, patting my arm. "You're not going to hell. I won't let you." Then he sighed a deep, involuntary sigh, and I knew he was already asleep. I sat there on the floor for a long time, my hand on his chest as lightly as I could hold it. He would not go away. He was not the one I wanted, but he would not go away.

Betrayal
El Viejo y el Mar

I wake up, thinking about ambrosia. Oranges and apples and bananas and grapes and cherries and coconut and whipping cream. "What should we serve?" the ladies at the church asked my father. "Make anything you want," he said. "But make ambrosia. Make enough to last forever." And so after the funeral service, after the gathering in the basement of the church, my father and I carried ambrosia home in yellow ceramic bowls with thick plastic shower-cap coverings. Ambrosia had been my mother's favorite.

But once we got it home, neither of us could eat it. The ambrosia sat in the refrigerator for days, until Mrs. Beswick threw it out. She didn't ask permission. That summer our brief, mutual anger at Mrs. Beswick was the only thing my father and I shared.

What about Bernardo's family? What food would they bring to comfort the heart, appease the tongue? Why does death leave us with hunger for such sweetness?

Maxine had forbidden fruit. But now it's Ernest's birthday party and I want pineapple and mangoes and papaya and limes. I want that sweet tartness, the taste that's always two things at once.

Down below a band is beginning to set up next to the seawall. More than a dozen hotel employees in their brown uniforms are moving deck chairs, setting up tables, putting up spotlights around the swimming pool. The events of the day seem a long way off. That unblinking eye, the blood, the shaft of light in the alleyway have all vanished. Maria's handwritten pages are locked away in the safe in the closet. Everything tucked neatly into place.

There is nothing on earth like this air, this light. The ocean seems as quiet and sleepy as I am. There are supposed to be steps leading down to the water somewhere along the seawall toward the Marina. But nobody's telling where. They don't want us swimming in the ocean at all. Tourists getting scraped up on the rocks or the seawall, or stung by Portuguese-man-of-war, and hardly any medical supplies. All those stories of *balseros* devoured by sharks are enough to keep most of us away. Yet there was still time, if you wanted it enough.

The late afternoon sun settles on the water in a thousand winking stars. I imagine that water washing over me. Brick comes to me suddenly, and I touch my throat and the hollow place where my locket rests, then his hand between my breasts, his tongue a brush stroke down my belly, down between my legs, light and fluttery there and there, and how I loved it.

Then how despairing and frightened he looked when he said, "You don't feel anything anymore, do you?" And I cried then because it was true. It had died with the baby. That tiny, nameless baby he had called Stella by Starlight. I didn't want to name her until I knew I would have her for good.

I take a long, cool shower, wash my hair and let it dry, while I pull myself together. My face could use some artistry. I put on pale pink lipstick, a little blush, some mascara, then I slip on a white cotton sundress, slide into my sandals, tie my hair back with a white ribbon. I dab Maria's jasmine perfume behind my ears, the inside of my wrists, in the tender place on my throat, an anointing.

I grab my purse off the bed and head out the door. I touch my locket, check my purse—room key, safe key, a lipstick—and my little blue stone. I already know the comfort of rubbing it between my fingers or holding it in my hand.

I can smell her perfume before I see her. Sweet talcum and *Jungle Gardenia*, like all the grandmothers in the world. But coming through the lobby, Maxine is no grandmother, with her glossy red lips, a rosy bloom on each cheek, her red-polished nails, her rich brown eyes rimmed with mascara. She's wearing a black dress that floats over her legs as she comes through the lobby. A black beaded purse hangs from her shoulder on a lacy, gold chain.

"You're beautiful," I say. "I love your purse. Not that I didn't like your big white one."

"I'm done with that," she says. "This is my coming-out party."

I look at her and smile. "I can see that."

Her hand reaches for mine. "What about *you*? You're glowing, my dear."

"I had a wonderful nap."

We walk through the lobby and past the bar and the dusky purple couch where Bernardo had sat with us that first morning.

"Let's sit here for a minute," she says.

I don't know if I can sit here and say nothing. There had been three of us, sitting in the shadows, looking out at that shivering light. Now one of us is gone. There had been such earnestness and worry on Bernardo's face, and such longing. I can't think how to tell her.

"Should we order drinks?" she asks. Her look has changed. The radiance is there, but also some tragic thing edging the corners of her eyes. "We need to sit here for a minute," she says. She strokes my arm and looks at me urgently. "You know about Bernardo, don't you."

I'm glad for the dusky carpet, the deepening shadows. "I was trying to find a way to tell you. And you already knew."

"They finally had to tell us *something*. Judith cried when she told us. She must have loved him."

"She frightens me," I say. "I don't know why."

Maxine takes my hand and holds it fast. "I can't believe he's gone. Of course I know he is."

"It's unbelievable, though, isn't it?"

"Completely." She strokes my arm. "You are such a dear. I have three daughters, but I love you as a daughter, too."

I lean against her softness. How I have missed those pats and caresses that say you are my deepest heart.

Now we can hear the music coming from the courtyard. The party is beginning without us.

"Such a surprise," Maxine says at last. "To find that death is an affirmation of life after all. I didn't understand it before I came to Cuba."

"I woke up from this wonderful nap hungry for everything."

"It's strange, isn't it."

"Bernardo was safe," I say. "He was safe when he died. I don't know what it means, but it's something I know."

Maxine just looks at me. "Something happened to you today, didn't it?"

I take the blue stone from my purse and hand it to her. "I'll never be able to explain this. It's a different way of knowing things. Keep it for a little while."

She turns the stone over in her hand and rubs it between her fingers.

"All right," she says. We're exchanging something outside words.

She tucks the stone in her purse and snaps it shut. "There will be an accounting. I will not let him go gently into that good night." There's a radiance to her, but it's something more—a total disconnection from fear.

We can hear the music filtering through the doorway more insistently now. Finally she says, "It's time to go to the party." She takes my arm as we walk into the courtyard washed in the setting sun. "Isn't this the most spectacular sky?"

"Look," I say. A waiter in the brown hotel uniform is holding a tray of green drinks, iridescent in the fiery light.

Maxine takes one and hands it to me, then takes one for herself. "*L'chaim,*" she says.

I swirl the drink, put it up to the light, and watch the green turn into gold. "To life."

"Oh, my," Maxine says. "Now we've done it. We should have been drinking this all week."

Sugar and lime and mint, and something else that sends a rush of warmth over my face. *Rum.* The Cuban elixir. Sugarcane, burned and cut and crystallized into sugar, and what's leftover turns to rich, dark molasses poured into oak barrels, until at last—such a surprise for the tongue, sweet mystery for the heart. The rich dark amber of *Havana Club* poured over ice, or straight in the glass, or mixed with Coke, for a *Cuba Libre*. Or the radiant green of lime juice and mint, for this *Mojito*, in my hand.

The band is playing a big-band brassy trumpet four-beat-mambo. It's Tropicana, Perez Prado, Ricky Ricardo—tourist stuff. The more exotic sounds of *claves* and güiros, and *conga* and *gourds* speaking mystery, speaking Africa, I hope will come later.

"Would you like this dance with me?" someone asks Maxine in beautiful English.

She looks startled, and turns to me, then back to this man who is so clearly offering what has been needed for so long. Anyone could see how beautiful he is, with thick white hair, a white moustache, smoothly-bronzed face. He's wearing the traditional *guayabera* and dark pants.

"Thank you," she says, and puts the long gold chain of her purse over her shoulder, and holds out her hand. Her smile says *oh yes, this was coming all along, and now I believe in it after all.* If Maxine had noticed him before, I didn't know it.

He's guiding her confidently through the crowd toward the open plaza. Then he puts his arm around her waist, takes her hand, and leads her into the dance. Together they're as smooth and elegant as dancers in the movies. The turns and dips, the syncopation, they know just what to do. My only dancing had been with Eugenie. It was forbidden in my father's church.

The music turns softer, slower now, as the sun slips toward the horizon, scattering lavender and gold into the clouds. Something draws me to the crowd on the other side of the pool. I can't stop looking for it. Then there he is, standing with a woman. Michael's hand is on her arm as she turns to look up at him. Then they turn and laugh with the two men who seem to be with them. The woman is beautiful. Then he turns back, startled to see me, before breaking into a smile I can feel all the way across the pool. Now I'm looking everywhere but at him, though I know he's moving toward me. I turn and make my way quickly into the lobby to the women's room. I lean on the counter and begin to cry. Heat rushes up my throat and over my face. I sit down on the bench and lean my head against the wall.

"Are you all right?" someone says.

There is Maxine before me.

"I saw you dash into the lobby. What's wrong?" she says, touching my face.

"Nothing," I say. "Everything. I don't know. Bernardo. My baby girl. It's her birthday party too."

Maxine sits down and puts her arms around me.

"I'm sad everything is over."

"But it's not. It's just beginning! So many things are just beginning." She hands me my little blue stone. "This. This is the beginning of something."

I rub it between my fingers. Then I tuck it safely in my purse.

"We should go to the party now," she says, then takes out her handkerchief, and blots the mascara from my cheeks, gives me a little lipstick, smooths my hair. "There. Beautiful as always."

She takes my arm and we walk out into the sky turning red.

Michael sees me and comes toward me again, then takes my hand. "Come. I want you to meet my friends. We're staying at the hotel when we're not on the boat." I look from the beautiful woman with the short, blonde hair to the two men, who must be brothers, both so tall and broad shouldered. Her diamonds flash in the sun, but the only man with a wedding ring is Michael.

"This is Juliette and Remy and Dennis," Michael says. Then he touches my arm and says, "And this is Laura. . . the professor I was telling you about."

He has forgotten my last name, but before I can say anything, I see Maria rushing toward me, a message in her tragic gray eyes. She's carrying a tray of drinks but she's not stopping to serve them. A white towel hangs over her shoulder. I smile and she opens her mouth to speak. I touch her arm and then she's face to face with Michael. "And these are Michael's friends from the boat." I have forgotten their names also.

"Are you at the Marina?" she says.

One of the men tells her, yes, all week.

"It must be a beautiful boat, then."

"We chartered her out of the Keys. She is beautiful. Just like Juliette. We're from Canada, and Michael, here, is our best friend. He's from Maine. Not so far from Quebec."

Maria is looking at them intensely. "For how long are you here?"

"We leave early Monday."

I watch Maria's eyes turn dark. Something is gathering behind them. She looks at them gravely, before she says all too brightly, "Oh then. How nice to have more time. I must be working now," she says. She turns to look back at me, and her eyes brim with tears. I rush to go after her but lose her in the crowd.

Then the music stops, and you can hear somebody clearing his throat. It's Wallace at the microphone. Nobody's listening. The music has stopped, but the dancing goes on.

"I want *everybody's* attention." He gives a short, failed laugh. "I know, I know. His birthday was on Monday, but this is his *party*." His scowl has returned and his shoulders are bunched up around his neck as always.

Then the band strikes up "Happy Birthday," and we gather to raise our glasses and toast Ernest. And if we were standing close to someone we love, we'd touch glasses and smile our secret smile and think of all the things that will happen back in the hotel room after the party's over.

I think of Michael and Juliette in their hotel room, with all their secret things, and feel unexpectedly sad. I can't see them or Remy or Dennis. Still, they must be somewhere. He can't have gone without saying goodbye.

I look over the crowd, wondering if I would see Ernest's ghost again, as I had at the *Finca*. Happy Birthday anyway, Ernest, wherever you are. And, Little Sprite, happy birthday to you, too.

Then it's over, and we begin drifting toward the pool. We've been told the mayor himself will be here. There must be more than a hundred people by now.

The sun has dropped from the sky.

Then the floodlights come on, and we're inside a blue-lit day. I edge forward, brushing the elbow of a tall man in a black linen jacket. He whirls around and makes a gesture I can't interpret. He looks me over and then he smiles and nods and turns back around. He's probably just a guest at the party, but there's something in that quick alertness when I touched his arm that tells me otherwise. In front of him sits the man with the dark lock of hair, the smile like Ricky Ricardo. The mayor of Havana.

Then the man I'd bumped steps back and puts his arm around the shoulder of the man standing next to him. His jacket falls away and there is that dark bulge under his arm.

A fanfare of music explodes through the loud speakers. An old man in a little boat slides out of the darkness at the far end of the pool, followed by iridescent mermaids, leaping high out of the water with a precision and grace I did not think possible. And before us a full water ballet reenacting, however loosely, the plot of *The Old Man and the Sea*.

It's hot and crowded around the pool, but it's as though none of us want the magic to be over, and so we stare at that water, waiting for some new miracle to rise up. But the water only shimmers under the lights. The show is over.

It's completely dark now and the torchlights have come on. The band has picked back up, but it's a different sound, a primal, unearthly sound, and you can feel a shift in the crowd, an acknowledgment of something darker and richer than Perez Prado and the cha-cha-cha. *Yi yi yi* the singer's voice cries over and over as it slips from the domination of the drums to split the air, then glides back down to merge with the guitar and the tender soft-shuffle of the maracas. Then the drums take over completely, driving an ancient song.

I feel something brush my back, hot breath on my neck. I turn around but can't see who it is. I start to back away. That smell is spreading out over the crowd now, up into the night. Old Spice, Old Spice. Smells promise terrible things. I want to run, but where is there to go? Other men must wear it. But how could he be here? There it is again—*yi yi yi* splits the air and then there is no ground or sky, only an empty falling into air.

My eyes read the crowd from right to left, left to right. The universe has upended.

He's here, all right, crossing in front of me, working the crowd. In the glare from the floodlights, I see the sharp black eyes, the ponytail, the compact, efficient body. I step back into the dark.

Now I see how other Cubans regard him—the deferential turn, the nod, the pat on the shoulder—as if he's not been expected but now here he is, importantly, and gathering such surprise and recognition, and a feigned sort of cheerfulness, or so it seems. He's making his way to the mayor, who's still sitting in a front row seat by the pool. He touches him on the shoulder and kneels down to say something in his ear. I just stand there watching him for a minute or two before I'm jostling my way out of the crowd.

Then I see Maria rushing toward me again, but this time her eyes are bright with fear. She takes my arm and whispers something desperately into my ear, but it's so quick and accented, I only know it's something to do with Pilar. Then the *Bodeguita* man's head jerks up. He's seen us together in that instant before Maria sees him too, before she spins around and dissolves into the throng.

He bends down and says something quickly to the mayor, stands up and begins searching the crowd.

I can't see Maria anywhere. Then there she is, walking across the lobby, trying not to run. Then I notice what she's wearing. No brown uniform, no brown shirt and slacks. She's in her jeans and lavender top. She's not been working the party. I think she's come to see me.

I search my purse for the blue stone. There's the room key and the safe key, and at the bottom, the little stone. Maria's manuscript is safe behind that locked door. I put my hand to my locket. The band plays on.

I slip into the scrim of dark between the torchlights and the hotel. From here the lobby is a lighted window. Now Maria is rushing across the lobby when the *Bodeguita man* grabs her arm. She whirls around. Then he's saying something furious to her, and she's nodding frantically, *yes, yes, yes* when he shakes her, and I think he's going to strike her with the palm of his hand. But she wrenches free and disappears out the lobby and back into the crowd. He stands there in the middle of the lobby, watching her go.

His fists are balled up at his sides. He needs to hit someone, he needs to hit *her*, but she's gone, and he's left standing there in all that coiled energy with nowhere to go. His eyes are slits. I remember his face close to mine, how hard, how fierce, his Old Spice, his cigarette breath hot on my neck. *Maria, Maria,* who are you that he would treat you like that?

Then I feel something running down my legs. I step back into the light. There's a spreading green stain down my dress, dripping off the hem onto my shoes. Then I notice the empty glass in my hand.

"Here," someone says, and holds out a napkin. I look up and see that brilliant hair in the trembling light, those piercing eyes that never once held a smile. "Such a shame," Judith says. "Such an ugly green stain now on your white dress." She bends over and begins harshly rubbing the front of my dress with her napkin. I can feel her breath on me. I feel a little sick.

"It's all right," I say breathlessly, but she keeps on wiping the front of my dress.

"This drink stains, you know. You will never get it out. It's ruined now." I'm trying to back away, but she won't let go of my dress. Then she hands me the napkin. It's in shreds. "Here."

I can only stand there holding the napkin in my clenched hand.

"Do you know her?" she asks. "I saw you talking like you knew her. You know she was Bernardo's dearest friend. And you. What about you?" I catch Maria, just at the edge of sight, before she vanishes for good.

"Who do you mean?"

Her face is tight and cruel. "You know, don't you."

"Oh, no," I say. "I don't know who she is." I feel my cowardice rush to my face. The *Bodeguita* man is waving his arms at someone behind the desk, but she's not watching him now. She's looking for the flash of lavender and that dark, short-cropped hair.

For a moment Judith must have forgotten I was there because the mask falls from her face, and by the flickering torchlight I see that her face has crumpled. Her eyes grow wide with rage and sorrow. It's a look so unguarded, so revelatory and absolute, I shudder for Maria and for us all.

Then she pulls me to her and kisses me hard on the cheek. "There," she says. "There. It's all finished now. The party's over."

Immersion
El Viejo y el Mar

Now we're lit only by the pool lights and the lights from the hotel. Even now there must be leftovers going home wrapped in napkins and tucked in pockets, and light for the night gathered gently in scarves or held in cool determined breath, and carried home on bicycles, through perilous, darkened streets.

The party is breaking up. We filter toward the hotel, solitary and hushed. Just the sound of a little wind in the distant palm trees. It's so late, and tomorrow we will go to the *Finca* one last time.

I feel inside my purse for the key to the safe. I'm on my way to my room to get that manuscript and fling it into the sea. It's the most outrageous thing I can think of. Those handwritten pages fanning out, the blue ink a momentary bruise on the white dissolving papers. Or I could burn them. No. After Eugenie's letters I could never burn anything. But at the elevators I make a turn and head back outside. I sit down at a table on the patio outside the restaurant. The moon is floating in and out of the clouds. I'd fling the manuscript out to sea later.

All right. Maria knows the *Bodeguita* man after all. Who was she anyway? She was working the late shift, all right, that night ages ago when she came with her daughter to break my heart. And Bernardo? Who had betrayed Bernardo? All I knew was that Maria had betrayed me. It was an old familiar feeling. My father who forgot me on the curb the day of the storm, or my mother who left me forever when she walked into the street, or Brick who could not outlast my grief.

Either the Maria in my room was a mirage—or this one was. Maybe they sent her to me that night I was sick. Maybe they sent her to befriend me, so I'd take her manuscript. Or maybe she was making things up as she went along. But what did she want from me? Everyone wanted something down here. Judith, and Tani and Paloma, playing on my American innocence and guilt. Everybody but Bernardo. In death he was safe from my shameful bitterness.

"Believe half of what you see and none of what you hear." But who could remember such a thing when you have fallen in love with the life before you? And in this air and sky that so beguiled you from the start, who could blame you for such blindness?

I look back into the lighted restaurant. Just a few couples now, finishing their coffee, hotel patrons who don't know whose birthday it is. One lone server is standing against the far wall in his wilting white shirt, black pants, a white towel over his shoulder. He looks like Maxine's waiter, Winston. He looks like he wants to go home. Now the waiter is turning off the lights, one by one. Then it's dark inside the restaurant and dark on the patio too. I'm too tired to go back up to my room, and it's so lovely here with the little breeze.

The moonlight gives more than enough light. I listen to the dark slow whisper of the waves, then get up and follow the seawall toward the Marina, looking for the steps leading to the water. They're easy to find. I walk to the edge and look down. The hem of the sea brushes the seawall and slides back into the dark. I slip off my shoes and tuck them under my purse on the ledge by the stairs and sit down. I'm thinking of all my swimming medals and how proud my father was. Of course I know what I'm doing. I'm not crazy like my mother. But a whisper of doubt says that I am, because this is exactly what she'd be doing.

The steps are rough against my feet. I don't know how deep it is or whether the bottom is rocky or stippled with coral. I take three steps down. My dress wraps itself around my knees. I take another step and it floats around my waist. I don't know how many steps there are before I'd tumble into the sea, so I kneel down and slide out into the ocean.

I turn over and my dress floats out around me. I lay my head back into a perfect stillness and turn my face to the sky. I stretch my arms out and float effortlessly. Now I'm a mermaid too. I'm a woman who went to a party in a white dress, and now I'm a sea creature rising on a moon path.

Then I think about sharks cutting through the water thirty feet out, or sting rays floating darkly over the sand, or sea snakes brushing against the seawall, and pull my head out of the water and try to touch bottom.

Mermaids
St. Louis 1961

"Lady, sometimes you just gotta throw them in," the swimming instructor had told my appalled mother. I was standing with my toes curled against the side of the pool, trying to get the courage to jump. He was treading water and shouting up at my mother, who was standing across the pool next to the bleachers, where the other mothers were sitting in a friendly clump. She stepped to the edge of the pool and shouted back. "If she doesn't want to do it you shouldn't make her! She's only *seven*."

Her high heels snapped against the tile as she rushed across the room and pulled me up to her. "That's the worst thing I have ever heard of."

"You don't want her to *drown* someday, do you?"

Then she leaned over and spoke to him in a low, dark voice I had never heard before. "Don't you ever say *drown* again." The swimming instructor stopped dog paddling and grabbed the side of the pool.

Then my mother took my hand and we fled the room, my feet slapping against the concrete next to the clickety-click of her red high heels. She would teach me to swim herself. "Just wait for summer, Annie Laurie, I'll show you how to swim. I have a secret way that nobody knows about." But she went away that summer and the next summer after that, so I spent my days in the little plastic pool my father had set up in the backyard. Why was it always summer when things fell apart? She said summers were only sun all the time.

You had to wait too long to see the moon. In winter you could see it by four o'clock.

"But you can still see it, Mommy. It's always there."

"Not really," she said. "You can't see it really."

I was ten when my mother taught me to swim. It was the best summer of my life, my mother home and everything calm and full of light. For two weeks we stayed in a big cabin close to the water, just the three of us. "Can you teach me now?" I asked every minute of the day, until one night she said, "Wake up, Sweetie," and took my hand and led me out across the grass, strange and cool and damp under my feet.

"Mommy, where's your swimsuit?" She was wearing her long silver nightgown.

"We don't need swimsuits," she said, and slipped off her nightgown and it floated into a silvery pool at her feet. "See?" she said, pointing to the sky. "It's here now. I was waiting all this time for it."

I looked up at the sky. My heart pounded.

She was waiting for the full moon, she said, for a night with no clouds, a night so warm you could walk through it with your eyes closed. But I thought she was waiting for something else too, and it was the part I didn't know that scared me.

For two summers I had watched my friends jump off the end of the dock while I floated around on my inner tube with the little church camp kids. I knew just where the water got too deep for touching bottom. Now everything would change. I would be able to jump off the dock into deep water too. But I was afraid to keep my eyes shut and hold my breath under water. It would be like falling down a well. I loved the water, but I always had to be touching bottom.

Then my mother walked out to the end of the dock, dove headfirst, and disappeared into the dark reaches of the lake. I ran onto the dock and peered over the side. It was all right. It was only my changeling mother who was here one minute and gone the next. Her timing was always exquisite. When she began to lose hold of it, she always went away until she got it back.

She knew how long she could be down there and still be safe. But I couldn't stop shivering. I kept watching the water, so smooth and still. Then there she was, the light shining on her white shoulders. She leaned back and stretched out her arms and floated on the water, her hair fanning out around her. She had forgotten I was there. "Mommy!" I called.

Then I rushed down the dock to shore. It was my turn at last. She motioned for me to take off my nightgown.

"Mommy, I can't. Somebody will see."

"Nobody can see. It's part of the secret. Anyway, it's how you have to be."

I looked behind me. The house was dark and lost in the trees. The moon had risen over the hill now and was laying a shimmering path across the water. I pulled my nightgown up over my head and tossed it to the sand. I stood there in my panties, my arms across the little buds blooming now on my ten-year-old chest.

She rose out of the water and took my hand, and we edged our way into the lake, the water inching up to my thighs, my waist, my chest. I'd never been without my clothes like this. I was holding my arms up, standing on my tiptoes. The water glistened all around me.

"Now stretch out your arms, like this," she said. And she pushed off and floated out into the lake.

"Can you touch bottom?" I called to her.

"I don't have to," she called back. She was treading water. "We can float forever if we want to. But only girls can. We're drawn by the moon. It's our wombs that make us float. Turn over and put your head back. Like this."

"I can't," I said.

So she came back to me and held out her arms as I put my head tentatively against them. "I'm holding you tight," she said.

"Can you still touch bottom?"

She gave no answer.

"Keep holding me," I said. Soon though, I lay so quiet and still, I didn't know that my mother had slipped her arms out from under me.

I was watching the clouds scudding across the sky. I didn't sink or drown or worry about what was under the surface, but floated silently, while little waves lapped against the dock, and held me in a gentle, drowsy lullaby.

"I'm floating all by myself," I called.

"Isn't it nice without clothes on?"

I had never felt anything like this cool water washing over me. I was filling up with miraculous secrets and powers. I was beautiful and strong now, too. I thought about my womb somewhere below my belly button, and how it was holding me up.

Then I lifted my head out of the water to be sure she was still there. I couldn't see her anywhere. "Mommy?" Something fluttered inside my chest.

"I'm holding you tight," she had said moments ago. "I won't let you go."

But where was she? I tucked into a frantic dog paddle and whirled around. The lake stretched out wide and dark. I knew I couldn't swim to shore. I couldn't pull myself up onto the dock.

Then she was back, cool and still.

"Where did you go?"

"Underwater," she said. "I wanted to see how far down I could go. It was too dark and too far though."

"Please don't do that again."

She didn't say anything.

"Mommy?" She didn't answer, but swam over to me and took my hand. I put my head back again and we floated together without speaking, as a thrilling hush grew between us.

We floated for a long time like this until Eugenie said, "There's a day place and a night place, and this is the night place. It's best for people like us."

I didn't know how we were people like us.

The Night Place
El Viejo y el Mar

I slip out of my dress and toss it up over the edge of the seawall, then push off through the water. I feel the water over my chest, between my legs. I roll over, turn my face to the sky, and spread my arms wide. I could float like this forever.

I'm staying parallel to the seawall, out maybe twenty feet, shifting and turning in synchrony with the waves. I don't know how long. Then the wind picks up a notch and the waves begin to rock me a little as they break against the seawall. I'm beginning to feel a little seasick. The moon has dissolved into a faint smudge.

I can't find the steps or the ledge where my things are. I try swimming back, but the current is pulling me away. Now the tide's coming in, and the waves are breaking against my back. I turn my head to keep from scraping my face against the rocks. I try to grab the ledge, but it's far above me now. There's no bottom anymore. I can see only a few lights from the hotel.

Then a wave hits me in the back of the head and I go under. I thrash my way back to the surface, gasping for air. You couldn't really drown this close to shore. Where were the goddamn stairs? But there is only the wide empty sea and this dark stony wall. Now I have to struggle just to stay near the wall because something new is happening, something more frightening than the surge of waves against the seawall. After each rush of waves, something is pulling me out toward the open sea. Then the next wave slams me back into the seawall. My shoulder scrapes hard against it as I grapple and claw but can't catch hold. The waves pull me out and down. I shut my eyes and hold my breath. When I come back up I'm farther out than ever. The waves are breaking over my head now. I try to stay parallel to the wall and catch it on the next wave.

I can't see lights anywhere. Am I dying? No answer but the slap and hiss of the sea and the vacant, starless sky. I'm breathing in time with my frantic heart.

Then I hear her say, "It's all right, see? I'll hold you up." And now my mother's hands cool and lovely, and then the smell of jasmine, and Maria's hand on my wrist, my face, as I hold onto the side of the bed. "Breathe with me," she says, "breathe with me like this." Then Maria says, "We'll breathe together, like fish in the sea. See how they turn in the current and never lose their way? Breathe as you slip away. Now hold your breath and touch the wall, this water rushing over you is nothing. Do it again and again as long as you have to." I would live inside the rhythm of the sea. I would rise and fall with that pull and tug of water to moon.

Finally my knee smacks into something. Stairs out of the sea! I grab for them, but the water pulls me out again and I hold my breath as my head goes under. But it's only seconds before the next surge of water sends me up those rocky stairs.

I crawl onto the ledge and sit with my head on my arms, while the waves climb up the wall and curl around my ankles. I try to stand up but sit back down and put my head between my knees. My palms begin to sting. I feel bruised all over. To my left the lights from the boats in the Marina, rocking in the water. I can't see *El Morro* from here. Far out the water dissolves into darkness. Maria dreamed her death in it.

But to the right, the hotel lights. Not so far. I sit for a long time The air is warm after the ocean and it's drying my skin and my hair. I'm safe now, in the dark out of sight. I'm just another swimmer by the edge of the sea. I try to stand up but fall to my knees. I wait till the dizziness passes, and then stand up slowly. I feel my knees begin to shake. I reach for something to hold to but there is nothing but the night air. The stones are still warm under my feet. I look down at the water churning against the seawall, sending spouts of sea foam up over the ledge. I'm all right now. I close my eyes and raise my arms. It's my mother's final, ambiguous nod to the universe. Under this starless sky I'm finding my way back to my life.

My dress is up ahead, wrapped around one of the flagpoles, a little white sail, flapping in the wind. And now my sandals on the stones by the same stairs I'd taken down to the water. My dress is almost dry. I shake it out and slip it on, then slip into my sandals. Even my purse is there.

The wind is blowing fiercely now, and a couple of patio chairs have blown over. I can see the silhouette of someone coming out of the hotel to move the furniture inside. The flags on top of the hotel are snapping in the wind. It's beginning to rain.

So Maria was a mermaid too. Maybe we all were. Maybe we're all one thing and another. Whatever she is doing, it's what she has to do. I would help her any way I can.

My Mother, Myself
El Viejo y el Mar

I go through the patio doors into the deserted restaurant, through the lobby, back to my room, and open the door into the dark. I smell cigarettes. The door closes behind me. My hand is on the doorknob as I try to slow my breath. I listen for the shuffle of feet, the rustle of curtains, but hear only my heartbeat thundering in my ears. The darkness hums. I flip on the lights.

No mattress upended or drawers tumbled out. My robe is on the bed, my slippers in the middle of the room, just as before. I look in the closet, behind the shower curtain, on the balcony, before I click the deadbolt. That smell is only the maid having a cigarette break. I'm just crazy from the swim.

I slip out onto the balcony and breathe in the smell of sea and rain, which is coming steadily, now. The air is still warm against my skin but I can't stop shivering. That old childhood fear, that instinct closer to the ground than sight or sound. Wasn't it always smell that announced it?

My skin is beginning to burn. I shut the drapes and go back into the bathroom and take off my dress. There are scrapes on my elbows, a big scrape across my collarbone, a little one across my cheek, on my knees and shins. I stare at my face in the mirror and put my hand in the hollow of my throat. I feel under my hair for the golden chain. Nothing but an empty place on the back of my neck. I run my hands through my hair. No locket anywhere. Of course it's lost in the sea. Still, I wrap up in a towel and go back to the bed and dump out my purse. Maybe I'd tucked the locket away at the last minute. I have the sudden urge to account for everything. A lipstick, a little mirror, my magic stone, the safe key.

I sit down on the bed and try to think. My money belt and passport and Maria's manuscript are in the safe. I go to the closet and push aside the clothes and turn the key. I hear the click, but the door won't open. I try again. Still it won't open. On the third try it opens, and then I know what the cigarette smoke means.

My fingers scramble frantically over everything—the money belt, safe, the Santería beads, safe. But no passport! And no manuscript! My heart pushes against my ribs. I lean into the clothes and hold on. My throat tightens. That sharp line of blackbirds zigzag across my eyes, then a dark shadowy narrowing at the edge of sight.

My hands start to tingle and my breath comes in shallow little pants because there's another smell—faint, but chillingly familiar. I slip down against the clothes, my back to the closet wall. Old Spice. "Maria?" I say to the air. I sit there for a long time. So this is how it is, our lives linked forever in someone's dark plan.

I go into the bathroom and run cold water over my wrists. Then I turn on the shower and stand under that gentle rush of water, which eventually quiets the stinging. I tuck my head under the shower nozzle and feel the water cool and lovely through my hair.

I didn't drown. Instead I floated on that moon-driven sea.

I turn off the shower and begin toweling off. When I try to brush my hair, something catches in my fingers—it's dark and vile, maybe oil or tar. Then that wet place against my throat comes back to me and here he is—the Bodeguita man, with his hot breath on my face, his hands between my legs, my locket in his mouth. I dig through my overnight bag for the scissors like a crazy person. Wet like that, my hair is easy to cut. It falls onto the floor like a whisper.

I remember how my mother looked that last time she came home, with her hair in ravaged tufts, as if she'd not let it go without a fight, then her final transformation at the beauty parlor. It was how she looked in the end—her blue eyes wide and dark—her face a triangle of pain and desire, more beautiful and attenuated than ever.

The scissors in my hand feel steady and sure. I take it section by section. When I'm done, I step back into the shower and wash my hair again, then towel it dry. A shorter version of Shirley Temple. I do not look ravaged. Still, I check for the glint of madness in my eyes, though I have never seen it. In my mother it was never so simple as that. I look less like her than ever.

I go back out onto the balcony. A fine rain is blowing across my face. I run my hands through my hair, across my bare neck. I can't believe how tired I am. I'm safe inside an earth-bound fatigue and the sensuous pull of gravity on my skin. The ocean air has cleared the smoke away. Maybe a smell was only a smell and no harbinger of danger after all.

The surf is crashing into the seawall. A wave of fear washes over me again, and then it's gone. The smell of Old Spice is gone too. Maybe Maria came and took the manuscript back, and smoked a cigarette while she waited for me. But my passport! Someone had to have taken it. But why? How would I ever get home? I wonder who has betrayed who. It rains steadily all night.

The Fire Next Time
St. Louis 1959

I knew it was Wednesday because I was studying for the spelling test that was always on Thursday. My father had made a fire that burned all evening. He was at his roll top desk in the corner, instead of in his study with the door closed. My mother, in her maroon velvet high back chair, was reading a book. Her red high-heeled shoes lay crisscrossed on the blue rug in front of her chair. She'd gotten up to put on "Cheek to Cheek", her favorite Ella Fitzgerald song. I loved how that voice drew you into the dance, how it slipped around the corners of the room, light and deep at the same time, an ebony sound so warm and rich it matched the radiance in my heart. Such happiness, I thought. To be this wrapped in love, our faces luminous in the firelight, where I lay stretched out on the floor checking my spelling homework.

I could hear my mother tapping the spine of her book against the arm of the chair in time to the music. Out of the corner of my eye, I could see her leg swinging to the beat. I plunged on through the fifty-word list for the unit test tomorrow. *Their, they're, there.* My father looking down at his papers, my mother looking at the fire across the room. The ruptures of our lives had smoothed themselves out and vanished into distant memory. I went back to my spelling. This room, *their* house—*their* child. *They're there!*

My mother had gotten up to stoke the fire with the long black poker, until the logs flamed up and shot a burst of sparks up the chimney, and with it a cloud of smoke. She stood there looking at it, then stoked it again. My father looked up quickly but then went back to his work. This steady, certain firelight said my father was keeping us safe, that he loved us both. This firelight would hold her to this room, to my father, and to me. But when she turned around, I could see the heat from the fire on her cheeks, like palm prints.

"Come on, Peter, dance with me." My mother was dancing in the middle of the living room now, while my father sat hunched over his papers at the roll top desk. She was singing along with Ella Fitzgerald on the record player.

She danced over to my father's desk and whisked the papers out from under his arm. I heard the sound of paper tearing. My heart tightened. I held onto my pencil and turned my face back to my tablet and those columns of words. They were all spelled wrong. But it was only the beginning of that familiar dip and rise. I shut my eyes and prayed for it to go away. Prayed her back to the maroon velvet chair, the book in her lap, the swing of her leg to that music so full of light and calm it would keep her tethered there.

"Sorry," she said and laughed, tucking the papers back under his arm. "Dance with me," she said again, tugging at his elbow. "*Please?*" She was swaying against the back of his chair, beating time on his shoulders. "Dance with me cheek to cheek or any way at all."

"Eugenie, don't."

"Peter Peter Peter. Please?"

"You need to sit down, Eugenie. You're getting all worked up."

"I can't, Peter. Can't you do *anything?*"

"Did you take your pills tonight?"

"Well somebody is an awful stick in the mud right here at this desk, who won't even dance with me."

"I'll dance with you, Mommy," I said.

"Okay, Sweetie, come here."

So I put my feet on top of hers like always, and we waltzed through the room. We were spinning, circling the couch.

She was singing faster and faster. I could feel my mother's heart beating through her sweater, pulsing wildly against my cheek as I held on tight, and we turned and turned. Then my skirt caught the corner of the fire screen and it toppled to the ground. My mother didn't seem to notice. The fire crackled and popped.

Then my father caught me under the arms as we sailed by and lifted me off my mother. She whirled around at him. I stood there between them. "You like me best on those pills, don't you?" She glared at him. "You like me good and quiet. You don't know what it's like to take those pills and have a fog in your face every minute of the day."

"I know I don't," my father said gently.

She glared at him again. She was breathing fast. Her sweater had come part way unbuttoned and her chest glistened in the overhead light. "Peter Peter Pumpkin eater, had a wife and couldn't keep her. Put her in a pumpkin shell and there he kept her very well."

"Mommy," I said, tugging her toward him. *They're, their there.* I took their hands and pulled them together. They didn't seem to be able to touch each other. They dropped their hands, but didn't stop looking at each other. Then she dropped my hand too. She shut her eyes and took a long, slow breath. She smoothed back her hair, buttoned her sweater. How desperately we want our parents to love each other, how desperately we want them to tell us who we are.

"Annie Laurie, you should get ready for bed," she said coolly, looking straight at my father. Then she turned around and walked toward the kitchen. Somehow she had caught herself just at the edge of that dark and wordless thing. I could hear the water running into the sink, into the glass, then I heard her put the empty glass on the counter. "Cheek to Cheek," she sang softly to herself as she stood by the sink looking into the pull of the night.

This was how she was, gone too long from the asylum. I knew there would be something dramatic now. It had only been a small fire and she never meant to do it.

Then after weeks so wild she couldn't sleep or rest, weeks wound up like a top careening across the floors and smashing into walls, there came a slow, sad winding down that turned her toward a place so dark she disappeared completely.

I always imagined it as some kind of elaborate rest cure, where my mother was wearing one of her white satin nightgowns, being served breakfast in bed. What was it like, back then, before the anguished miracle of lithium? My mother died too soon for that.

It wasn't until years later that I pictured the leather straps and her teeth clenched around a rubber bit. Or the Thorazine jammed into the back of her throat, or insulin shock, or the threat of an ice pick between the eyes.

Then one day I would come into the living room after school and there she was, sitting in that maroon velvet chair, half-hidden in the shadows, as if some giant had lurched out of the dark and crushed her. She was sitting there waiting for me, her cornflower blue eyes pale and flat.

"Mommy?" I said, to be sure it was really her. I had never seen her hair like that. It had been brushed sternly and pinned back with black plastic barrettes. They looked like black scars behind her ears.

"Hi, Sweetie," she said. But her voice was the wrong speed. It came out cottony and slow. "Come here. I want to hold you."

So I climbed into her lap, but her body had a frightening slackness.

"What happened where you were?" I asked cautiously.

"Oh, it was mostly boring."

"Your eyes look different." I didn't want to point out too much.

"It's just those pills. They make your eyes look funny. I had to promise to take them or I couldn't come home."

I wanted to tell her she smelled different too. She didn't smell like lavender anymore. She smelled like she had been scrubbed to death.

"Give me a hug as hard as you can," she said. "I want to feel how much you missed me."

And I hugged her hard and she hugged me back and buried her face against my neck, but her arms were loose around me.

She rubbed her chin against my head. "If I'd stayed home any longer I'd have scared you to death," she said. She touched my cheek with the back of her hand.

She was my quiet mother for a long time after she came home, before the magical mother came back. But the way she was when she first came home always frightened me far more than the way she was before she went away. We sat there watching the dark come into the room, until one of the women who always stayed when my mother went away, came in and said, "It's dark in here," and turned on every light, one by one, while my mother flinched as if she'd been slapped. Then I saw that something had worn a ruddy bracelet around her pale wrists. I traced it with my finger. "My souvenir," she said, tucking her hands into her sweater. "Make it dark again please," she said. But before I knew it, she was edging her careful way up the stairs to her room, where she stayed until Mrs. Bell called us all to dinner. It had only been a small fire.

SATURDAY, JULY 26, 1997

Red Moon Rising
Finca Vigía

The sea is flat and gray in the early morning, a mirror to the sky. The threat of bad weather seems distant now, dissolved in other threats.

I come into the room after breakfast and see the red call light flashing. I sit down on the bed, take a long, deep breath, and count to ten. It feels urgent, dangerous—to Maria and Pilar, if not to me. I shut my eyes and there we are, the three of us, gathered in hot silence, as the phone rings on, our shadows rising against the wall.

But it's nothing. It's everything. My passport was found in the dining room! But I know I didn't leave it in the dining room. It was in the room, safe under the manuscript. Why would somebody take my passport, only to give it back? How was it lost when I didn't lose it? And the manuscript? I only hoped Maria had changed her mind and taken it back. She'd said, *There are names in it. I put names in it.*

The security man at the desk hands my passport over and says sharply, "You must not lose it. You do not ever want to do that."

"Thank you," I can barely say, and take it back with a trembling hand. I rush to my room and put the passport back in the safe, hoping the manuscript had miraculously returned. The money belt and the *Santería* beads are there as before, but no manuscript. I hope it was Maria, but if she came back for the manuscript, why would she take my passport? There had been no smell of jasmine, only Old Spice and the ashy smell of cigarettes.

I slip the beads around my neck, no locket anymore, and grab my sweater.

The van is parked in the shade in front of the hotel. Six of us have signed up for an early-morning visit to the *Finca*, with special permission to go inside.

I expected great weariness but feel only a strange alertness and a sense that something has shifted in me. Something happened to me in that water that can't be taken back. So when I look up and see Judith, with her brilliant hair and that provocative chin, I'm not afraid anymore.

"I'm glad you're going on my trip," Judith says, as she sits down. When she turns to me and her shoulder touches mine, my skin doesn't prickle. Her friendliness seems genuine, even if I don't really trust it.

"You cut your hair! Why did you do that?"

"Oh," I say, as I feel the new place on the back of my neck. "Too much humidity for all that hair."

"Yes," she says, her gaze lying heavily on me.

I start to speak but she interrupts. "It will be cooler for you. Aren't you hot with your sweater?"

"Oh, I'm always cold."

She looks at me as though she's trying to remember something just beyond recall. I hope all she remembers is that I spilled something on my white dress and she tried to clean it.

The windows are open, and a little breeze drifts through the van. The sun has come out and is glinting off the water in the little pond with the sculpture of the old man battling the marlin.

"People should be on time," Judith says, turning around. "Oh yes. There they are." Two people I recognize, but do not know, take seats together across the aisle. Judith checks her list. "There are two more," she snaps. We Americans are becoming Cubans after all.

A woman wearing a wide-brimmed hat rushes across the drive and takes the stairs. "Sorry," she says, and takes the seat behind me.

Judith taps the driver on the shoulder and says, "We can't wait forever." She checks her list. Then there he is. "Oh good. Now we can go."

"Hello!" he says, smiling widely, as he comes up the stairs. "Hello."

"Michael," I say. He takes a seat next to the woman with the hat. I turn to the front and try to quiet my astonished heart.

Judith signals to the driver and we pull out onto the road. "Look at this fine day. The rain all gone now. I think it comes back tomorrow night. No matter. Are you excited about going inside the *Finca*?"

"I am," I say, touching my cheek, a developing bruise the only visible sign of my seawall encounter. The bruises on my knees, the scrape across my collarbone, my elbows, my red palms all hidden from view.

She's beaming. "I have been waiting all week for it. I am going inside the *Finca!* And now a baby granddaughter. I have a son also, did I tell you? He's becoming very high in the government. I had a daughter who died a long time ago, you know, so that's why this baby girl is so precious."

"I'm happy for you," I say, and find that I mean it. "Is it your son's child?"

"Oh yes," she says, but something quiets in her.

The sun scatters a net of light across our arms as we make our way down streets lined with palm trees.

"I liked you best, you know. I always have my favorites."

She's relaxed into whatever has settled between us. Maybe she's no longer the villain in this melodrama.

"I didn't know it would be so soft," she says, as she touches the back of my hair. But the rush of warmth down my neck becomes a shiver.

"We're the same," Eugenie said every time she brushed my hair. "Your hair is just different, and you want to be like everybody else."

"All right," Judith says. "It will grow back before you know it."

"Those shoes are very sad to me," he says softly. I'm standing in Hemingway's bedroom next to Michael, looking at the shoes lined up on the shoe rack tucked under the open window—the sandals, loafers, wingtips, white bucks.

"I thought it the first night I came here," I say quickly, before he knows I've seen him blink back tears.

"A person's shoes left behind. . . " he trails off.

I want to take his hand but do not. "I know about shoes," I say.

"I'm so glad I found out about the *Finca*. I didn't know I would find you."

"I thought I'd never see you again. You were wonderful with Antonio. I wanted to tell you."

He looks at me carefully. "I'm sorry, but I have to ask. You cut your hair. And you have a bruise on your cheek. Are you all right?"

I try to laugh but it catches in my throat. "I went swimming last night and there was an encounter with the seawall. It's a long story. But I'm okay."

Michael reaches to touch my arm but pulls back.

"I saw you with your friends. And your wife?"

He starts to speak but then looks down at his fingers which are turning his golden ring.

"I'm sorry," I say. "I didn't mean . . . . "

"I always thought it was a shame Hemingway died like he did and wondered what else could have been done to save him. In my own practice I'm always haunted by that kind of end. The possibility, I mean."

"Everybody thinks Mayo's botched it," I say, but what I really want to say is, was there anything that could have saved Eugenie? Instead I just stand there with the ache of tears behind my eyes, looking down at Hemingway's goddamned shoes.

"What was wrong with him?" I ask. "Was it manic-depression like everybody thinks?"

He nods. "It's a killer disease and one of the most inheritable. I prefer *manic depression* to *bipolar*, though. It catches the beauty and the terror." He looks down at those shoes and becomes a little stricken. "I'm talking too much, aren't I?"

"No," I say. "I'm listening to everything." I had looked in the mirror all my life and seen my mother's face looking back at me and wondered when the cracks would begin to show. The shoulders drawn tight, the unsettled hands, the eyes wide and knowing.

Neither of us say anything. The sun has risen over the corner of the house now, and the room fills with a tender light. Something passes between us, yet I can only stand there and let the tears come.

"That's one of the reasons I wanted to come here. I wanted to see if there was anything in this house to explain his death to me. It's a mystery I confront in my work way too often." He pauses and looks at me hard. "Should I stop talking like this?"

"No, please don't."

"Do you want to talk about all this in his bedroom though?"

"Yes. Especially."

He looks at me with a longing I don't understand. He clears his throat, wipes his face. "It can be a violent and despairing time," he begins, "but wildly creative too. Sometimes I wonder what's lost by treating this illness. By flattening everything out. It's a torment for the patient, but also for the physician."

My ears fill with a roaring I know too well, and I touch my beads. "My mother never had doctors who felt that way."

"I'm so sorry. I don't have to go on."

"No. Please." We're both staring at the shoes to keep from staring at each other.

"He had electro shock and certain drugs, but not 'the talking cure,' as they used to call it."

"He said the talking cure was right there," I say, pointing to the Corona ROYAL sitting on the shelf under the kudu head.

"Imagine what would have been lost on the page if he'd talked it all out and not kept it under pressure. What if all the demons had been exorcised? On the other hand, what suffering would have been avoided? I would think one writes out of joy also."

"So much of his work is filled with the wonder of just being alive and breathing in this world—but then all that despair. Why did this happen to him?"

"It could be so many things," Michael says. "The reserpine he took for high blood pressure, the effects of ECT, diabetes, all the head injuries. But my god. Look at the genetics. All the sorrows in that family."

"It's strange to be here," I say, "in his bedroom with his shoes right there."

So we walk through the house to the bathroom. On the wall next to the scales, Hemingway had penciled weights and dates of recording. A text of its own. Five years of diminishing weight. Forty pounds from 1955 to the last recording, July 24, 1960, a year before his death. In the end, maybe it was the only narrative he could write.

Kudu, gazelle, antelope, buffalo, and lion heads and animal skins, and drums and swords, the sunlight through the glass doors, the table set for six—they were one thing. This bathroom is another.

"I've read about this," Michael says. "It tells me a lot."

"What does it tell you?"

"That he wanted to live," he says.

"And terrified he wouldn't."

On the shelf above the toilet is a large jar with a lizard preserved in formaldehyde. It looks like a miniature dinosaur, turning toward the last of the sun. "It's not so strange to preserve dead things. My mother had a stuffed owl named Leon."

"I love it," Michael says, on the edge of laughter. "Why not?"

"I loved it too, but it kind of scared my father."

"I keep seeing him with a pencil in his hand, writing those numbers," Michael says.

"I know I'm being emotional, but this room feels sacred some way. I mean too private to be a museum."

"I'm glad I'm here though," Michael says.

"Me, too."

"Isn't every place sacred where there has been suffering?" he asks. "We're all crucified one way or the other. And in some way resurrected. I try to believe that, anyway." He backs away from the numbers, puts his hand against the window ledge. "I'm sorry. I didn't mean it so dramatically."

"Oh, I wish I could believe that," I say.

I look at the lizard floating in the sunlight. Suddenly this isn't a sacred place after all.

It's a horror. "Please let's go."

He touches my arm. "Why don't we walk down to the pool? And get out into this air."

So we walk down the stairs through that curtain of green. Mangoes, flamboyantes, aguacates, hibiscus, frangipani, oleander—the names dissolve on my tongue before I can say them. It's lovely here in the cool morning light. Birds quiver blue and gold in the trees, settling upon us insistent and lush.

"Is the *Finca* what you wanted?"

"More," he says. He looks out over the vacant, empty pool. "It's beautiful even without water."

"For me too." I've found my ghosts and I'm laying them to rest. The little girl in the white dress is nowhere to be seen.

"Shall we sit here for a minute?" Michael says.

So we sit down on two white wrought iron chairs under the poolside cabana. "Have you seen the *Pilar* yet?" It gleams in the shade across the way from the pool.

"It was the first thing I saw."

"You like boats, then."

"Passionately." He's staring off at that boat, all teak and brass.

I'm sitting beside this man with his elbows on his knees, his chin in his hands, the sun brushing against his arms, glinting off his watch, his ring.

"I really do think my mother had what Hemingway had."

"Manic depressive illness?"

"I know. But I hate that. She wasn't just a diagnosis."

"Of course not." He looks chastened. "But a diagnosis tells us it isn't our fault. Or her fault either."

"But I want to know what happened to my family. So it's not just some terrible thing happening for no reason." We're rushing ahead now. But we're also being careful.

"Do you want to go on?" Michael says.

I wrap my arms around my waist and lean over. "Yes," I say. "Yes."

He looks shaken, because he knows things that are going to hurt me.

The breeze washes us in an intimate, whispery sound. The jacaranda is a lavender cloud brushing the sky. "It's so beautiful."

"Maybe this isn't the place to talk about it."

"Maybe it is."

"All right." We sit there for a moment while he gathers himself. "The diagnosis often depended on where you went for it. But I don't want to talk clinically to you. I don't want to do that."

"But I have to know."

I want to take his hand, put my arm in his, my head on his shoulder.

"In New York you were often diagnosed schizophrenic, even if you weren't. And your treatment varied from place to place."

"What was the treatment for manic depression?"

He rubs the face of his watch with his thumb. "They just didn't have all the psychotropic drugs we have now. So. . . ."

"So they used savage things instead."

He pauses for a second. "Yes," he says. "They did."

"Tell me about electroshock."

"It sometimes had a calming effect. They weren't using lithium until 1970, so ECT was pretty common in the sixties."

He's found the voice that would keep us from losing our way.

"Lithium saved many lives that otherwise would have been lost to darkness."

"I have some letters," I tell him. "She wrote some letters from those places. She tried to burn them but at the last minute she tried to save them."

He takes my hand at last, and we sit there looking up through the panoply of green.

"I don't often admit it," Michael says finally, "but not everyone can be saved. Some wounds can't be healed." He looks so sad when he says it, I wonder whose life he couldn't save.

"That's so despairing."

The breeze startles the bamboo into a wild, thin creaking. The ancient bird rises up, splitting the sky with a premonitory cry.

"Do you want to go back to the house? We could sit on the verandah."

Then we make our slow, reluctant way through the lower grounds, up the narrow path edged with palms trees and ferns and philoden-drons, then up the long stairs to the verandah. The bougainvillea hang heavy and lush overhead, filtering the sun.

"Moonlight Serenade" is playing on a scratchy phonograph in the library, just as I had imagined it that first night by the pool. "That song," I say, reaching for the beads around my neck. "I thought I'd dreamed it."

We stand in the doorway but can go no farther.

Michael whispers along with the music, then slips into the song, easily, softly.

"Oh," I say, looking away. "That's your song too?"

"It used to be."

"This little band was playing and everybody had to shout over the music, so I couldn't have heard it so far away. But I did. It was my mother's song." A proctor stands like a sentry beside the record player. Animal eyes flash in the sun. "This place is full of ghosts."

"Not haunted, though," he says.

"No."

I brush back my hair, then remember I'd cut it off, and laugh shakily. "I thought this was the library. But the whole house is a library. All these books. And animals. All these eyes."

We walk back out to the verandah and sit down.

"Tell me about my mother. Tell me everything you can."

Michael clears his throat, and even then, I know it's not a customary gesture. I'm sorry I pushed him to talk when he's trying to find the shifting balance between us that would keep us steady. It's getting hot now, even in the filtered sun, but I can't seem to move.

Michael looks straight at me without blinking. "Where did you live growing up? Where might she have gone for treatment?"

"My father won't talk about it. He says it's in the past where it should stay. But we lived near St. Louis."

"She might have gone to the Missouri Institute," he says more to himself than to me.

"She went to Montreal once, to see a famous doctor, but it didn't work out. It was a kind of experimental therapy. Or something."

I can feel a darkness gathering inside my head, then something shooting up the back of my neck. "Ravenscrag," I say. I have no idea where that word came from.

"I'm sorry?" He's hoping I'll take it back, that I have tripped over my tongue. A trickle of sweat runs down his face. He brushes it off with the back of his hand. The sun is unrelenting.

"She said she went to a castle called Ravenscrag. Is that possible?"

"It was. That's what it was called."

"I thought she was making it up, like she did sometimes."

"It did look like a castle. It was one of those mansions that became a psychiatric hospital in the early forties. It was headed by a Scot named Ewen Cameron. One of my professors had seen it in the early sixties. We all learned about it later."

"I think something terrible happened there."

He doesn't say anything for a long time. Then he says, "Do you remember hearing about the Allan Institute? Do you remember her doctor's name?"

I can hardly hear him. We're rushing toward a dark thing and we both know it. "My father. . . I remember my father saying her doctor was president of some famous psychiatric organization. I think this doctor was my father's last hope."

"Laura, did your mother ever talk about her treatment?"

I'm trying to remember that awful time, the very worst, the time that had begun with such hope, in another country. And the dark weeks that had followed her return and the spring that never came.

"I remember my father bringing her home early. They didn't want her to leave, but he went to Montreal and got her anyway. She said she had seen the heart of darkness."

We sit there for a long time under that extravagant sky. "She loved Conrad. She loved the dark writers." I shut my eyes, for the sun is a red moon rising.

"What are you going to tell me?" I say. I feel my pulse in my hands.

"How much do you want to know?"

"Everything." He has the saddest eyes I've ever seen.

The Kitchen is a Sky
St. Louis 1963

The day my mother died a smell woke me up. I followed it through the early morning house down into the kitchen. Where was our yellow kitchen? It had turned into a sky! Everything was blue, with white wispy clouds scudding high across the walls, a crescent moon in the corner of the ceiling. How had she done it? The sink and the counters were a tornado of sponges and brushes and buckets of paint. But in the far wall by the back door, the old yellow paint showed through in patches. It was as if she had run out of time. Something tightened inside.

I raced up the stairs and down the hall to the guest room where my mother slept most of the time. She was asleep on top of the bedcovers in her nightgown. Some magic had finally come to us, and she would be all right and I would be all right too. Finally this long dark spring would be over. The smell of paint—like the unexpected smell of bacon and pancakes early in the morning—had conjured it.

"Mommy?" I said, touching her arm. "I have to go to school now. Are you all right? I like the kitchen."

Drowsily she pulled me to her, and I lay with my head on her pillow. She touched my face. "Thanks," she said.

Maybe we were still in the magic place. Yesterday morning she had come into my room while it was still dark and led me outside. She said it was hard to live if you were in love with the moon. It's always stronger than the sun, but it takes great faith to believe in it. On nights without a moon, she would burrow her way into the darkness like some tiny forest animal. That fragile light was my mother's life burned into the darkness.

"Look," she had said. "Look at everything." The sun was just coming up from behind the trees, turning the sky violet and gold. "This is what you miss by sleeping in. I'm going to make you a big breakfast." Then we watched the sun cross the dining room window until it caught in the crystal chimes and flashed across the room. She said the crystal was turning gold into silver, sun into moon.

I watched her sleeping there for a long time. I knew I would be late for school now. "Where's Daddy?" I finally asked.

"Oh," she said from a long way away. "He went out for something."

"Milk?"

"I think so."

"Will he be back soon?"

"Maybe it was Mrs. Beswick. Something."

I closed the door without a sound, not even the click of the lock falling into place. I gathered up my books and my sweater and my felt board for my report on caves. I hoped she would sleep all day. Then Mrs. Beswick would come and clean everything and tonight we would have dinner under the sky.

When I saw my father in the doorway of my classroom that afternoon, something turned over in me. I was standing in front of the class, beginning my report on caves. I'd fallen in love with stalagmites and stalactites, with all things underground, things secret and dark you could bring into the light if your heart was pure enough. They drew me urgently, desperately for months, and now it was spring and I would bring them to light.

If you were absent you couldn't give your report. Otherwise I'd have said I was sick and my father would have let me stay home and she wouldn't have walked into the street. She might not have stayed for my father, but she would have stayed for me. But maybe she couldn't get through another Friday with the world turning dark and breaking in two. Maybe she couldn't get through another weekend waiting for that rock to be rolled away. There was no such thing as Good Friday. Spring had unfolded in a plenitude she could not see.

I hoped she hadn't gone into the street that day in her

paint-spattered nightgown and her bare feet. I hoped the neighbors hadn't seen. I'm imagining how she said it. "I'm just going next door," she'd said to nobody in particular, and put on her Easter dress and her white straw hat with the pink ribbons, and stepped into the street. She only saw her hand against the sky, and the sun on the windshield of the car coming her way.

I stood at my locker that Monday morning after, trying the combination. My father had said it was best not to stay home, but to go to school. I couldn't even remember the first number and had to ask the janitor. He looked at me, and laughed. "Annie Laurie, it's already April and you've had that combination since September!" I walked down the hall and knew people were looking at me and saying things, but the words were just sounds that slid off my back like water off my rain slicker. I turned the corner and went out the side door into the rain because now I could hear such terrible words I could only stand by the side of the gym and bang my head against the bricks until the buzzing stopped.

Frankenstein's Bride
Finca Vigia

When it's time to say goodbye to the *Finca*, Michael comes back and touches my shoulder. I can't stop thinking about that haunted castle in Montreal, and the horrors they inflicted upon her. Tears are spilling down my face.

"Please tell me you're all right," he says, sitting down. He seems in such anguish I wish I could comfort him, but I can't stop crying.

"I'm so sorry," he says again. "I'm just so sorry I said anything." He puts his head in his hands. "The families had so much guilt. The patients had so much shame."

"My father. . . It wrenched him to pieces."

"Laura," he says, taking my hand, "your mother may not have even come close to those treatments. If she was strong he never would have chosen her. He always chose the weakest ones."

"But she was beautiful. I heard it all the time. Isn't it a shame, she's so beautiful. I knew what they meant. What a shame the inside didn't match the outside. In her own way she was strong, though. But he might not have seen it."

Then he says gently, "I think it's time to leave. People are going to the van."

But I can't let it go. "All I know is that something couldn't be fixed after that last time."

There are tears in his eyes. He blinks them away. "Sometimes I think I'm in the wrong line of work."

"Why do you say that? You're very compassionate."

"I feel my patients' sorrows more than I probably should."

"Oh, I think it would be very helpful to be understood like that."

We get up and walk down the front stairs. I look back one last time at that white house, the palm trees against that radiant sky, the tower where I had seen Hemingway's despairing face, his frightened eyes.

"She had a little burn mark on her temple. On the right side, that never went away."

The van pulls slowly out of the parking lot to the street. Michael sits beside me in the back. Judith is across from the driver, the woman in the broad rimmed hat in the seat behind her, and across the aisle, the husband and wife who look like brother and sister. That was always curious to me, how people who resemble each other fell in love. We were blonde, all of us—Brick and I, and my mother and father.

So where did she come from, that dusky little one with the dark tuft of hair, three days old forever? The dark-haired man who loved my mother?

We edge our way down that narrow little street into San Francisco de Paula. Judith leans forward and says something to the driver. She's gesturing out the window at a little wooden stand, where a shirtless old man is selling limes and stalks of sugarcane. A chalkboard is propped against it advertising tomatoes, peppers, lemons, pineapples, but I see only a few limes and three or four stalks of sugarcane.

"Would you like some sugarcane juice? It's delicious!" Judith looks at our blank faces and shakes her head. "My little chicks," she says and smiles. "It will surprise you how good it is." She shakes her head again. "You'll see!" she says, stepping out of the van.

The husband is scowling and looking exaggeratedly at his watch.

Now Judith is going through some elaborate negotiations with the man at the sugarcane stand. There is much waving of hands, then she throws her head back and laughs. She's holding up a large orange plastic cup.

"I'll bet that cup is dirty," the husband says. "There's absolutely no water out here."

"What do you think is in it?" the wife asks.

"We have no way of knowing," the husband says. "Tubercular."

"Well, we can't drink it."

Then Judith is bounding up the steps of the van. "Here it is! You must try it. *Guarapo*. Sugarcane juice." She holds up the orange cup, with two little sugarcane stalks in it. She takes a sip. "Delicious!" she says, and hands it to the woman.

"Oh, no. Thank you, no," she says and quickly passes it to her husband.

"No, thank you," the husband says. The wife knits her face into a smile, and shakes her head. "We can't," she says, looking down at her lap. The husband hands it to the woman in the hat and wipes his hand on his pants. She shakes her head and looks out the window.

A shade lowers itself over Judith's face and her eyes fill with surprise and embarrassment.

Then Michael looks at Judith and smiles. "I would like some."

"Oh!" she says. "Oh, you will!" The woman turns and hands it to Michael, who takes a long swallow.

"You're right. It's wonderful. Thank you very much."

Do I want to follow? *It's all right if you don't want to drink it,* he says with his eyes. I manage a little swallow. "It really is," I say, and hand the cup back to Judith.

Then Michael pulls a dollar out of his pocket and I do the same, and so, finally, does everyone else. Judith is blushing furiously, and waving her hand.

"Oh, no," she says. "I didn't mean for you to pay. It was my little surprise for you."

"Please take it," Michael says. "It's not for the drink. It's for everything."

Her hand goes to her throat. "Thank you," she says. "Thank you very much. It has been an honor to accompany you."

The man clears his voice. "Yes. Thank you," he says, through a pinched and fleeting smile.

Judith nods, then turns to say something to the driver. The husband whispers under his breath. "Did you see how fast she had that money in her pocket?"

Then we're turning onto the highway. We've left San Francisco de

Paula far behind. It's good to be sitting by this brave and gentle man.

"It's all right to tell me the rest of it," I say. "You were sheltering me before."

"I just don't know what good it would do to hear everything. I've known these horror stories for so long, but I've never met anyone whose loved one. . . ."

My own Eugenie was in that place. "She couldn't stand to be told what to do. Tell me again about the voices."

"It's beautiful," he says. "This place is just so beautiful. He's quiet for a long time looking out the window. "You know your mother may never have had any of that treatment."

"It's all right. You can tell me."

"This is hard for me. It's my profession that did this."

I look at him. "My father tried to bury the past. And now here it is."

"Are you sure?"

"I've come three thousand miles for it."

He's pulling a calm from somewhere deep inside as he rubs his temples, then folds his hands in his lap. "He called it *psychic driving.* He thought he could take the mind and make it a blank slate. He took a patient's anguish and deepest fears and played them back a hundred times. *A thousand times.* Sometimes in their own words, sometimes in his. They had tapes under their pillows so they would think the voices were coming from inside. In the day they wore these helmets with the tapes inside.

"He called it the *Sleep Room.* It was so dark even the nurses didn't want to go in there. He played the voices after ECT, and during sleep therapy. It was his version of brainwashing. The CIA funded it. After the Korean War when they were doing all kinds of things. They called it the search for 'The Manchurian Candidate.' They called it MK ULTRA. If you heard that name you would never forget it."

Now I start to laugh and tears run down my face. Thank God it was all made up. The mad scientist and the beautiful girl strapped to the table. Then a jolt like electricity hits my chest. Eugenie herself had called him Frankenstein. And I had seen the movie. "*The*

Manchurian Candidate," I say quietly. "In the movie Frank Sinatra's girlfriend had my mother's name." I'm almost whispering now. "'My name is Eugenie,' Janet Leigh said in the movie. 'You say the 'g' soft, you have to say it soft.'"

"Eugenie is a beautiful name," Michael says.

"She was always correcting people. But if you knew her, you'd never say it wrong."

"I know," he said softly. "I really do know."

"She had the most wonderful hair. Where did her hair go inside that football helmet?" I don't stop the tears or turn my head. "That Doctor Cameron. What did he look like?"

"Laura, he could have been anybody. He could have been a banker or an accountant."

"Did you ever see his picture?"

"I'm remembering a picture in a book and what people told me over the years. He was tall. He had an ordinary face. Thin lips, deep-set eyes, heavy, close brows."

"You haven't described a monster."

"I read somewhere that he loved Mary Shelley's *Frankenstein.* He must have known on some level that the monster he'd created was himself."

"All those doctors and nurses? How did he get them to do those unspeakable things?"

"He had so many titles and awards. He was treating what were considered hopeless cases. People called him a pioneer. My God, he was."

"My mother wasn't a hopeless *case*. She was just a person who needed things they didn't have."

"In seven or eight years . . . ." He puts his hands out as though fending off a blow. "It doesn't do any good to know this."

"Couldn't lithium have saved her?"

"It might have. Maybe Hemingway too."

I would never forget those numbers scribbled on the bathroom wall, that record of a soul trying to outlast the dark.

"Did that doctor do things to women? Did he take advantage of them?"

Michael's holding tightly onto himself. "They said he had a

deep, hypnotic voice. A Scottish brogue. They said he could be very charming." His words rush out of him unwillingly, in a soft fury. "He called the women 'Lassie.'"

"But did he?"

"People heard things. Maybe. Yes. Probably."

"Is he dead?"

"Yes. A heart attack."

"But didn't people *know* about this?"

"Eventually. But when he left the Institute, he took everything with him. Then of course he died. That's why the court cases were so important. The families wanted to bear witness. But for some, it was shame that kept them silent."

I had no idea what my father knew. He sat in his study day after day, long into the night, his eyes so sad and distant, the tender slump of his shoulders, as I watched from the doorway, his desk weighted down with books and papers, and the big black leather Bible with the gold-edged pages he kept thumbing through.

"That doctor was the one who made my mother walk into the street."

But I knew even as I said it, what my mother did was born of many things. There was no single thing that drew her toward death and away from me.

I have never seen anyone listen so hard. How it must wear him down to listen to such sorrows day after day. This unearthing of bones has exhausted us both. It can't possibly still be morning, but there is the sun, still climbing the sky.

"I like your hair," he said, "Even if I don't know the story."

"Oh," I say, feeling a rush of warmth up my face. "Now I don't look like my mother so much. Maybe just the eyes. And the shape of my face."

"You have a beautiful face."

I turn to the window and feel a little current of air across the new place on the back of my neck.

When I look back, he's staring straight ahead. He's turning the wedding band between his fingers like he'll never stop.

"My real name is Annie Laurie. That's a story too."

"Oh, that's lovely," he says. "Could I call you Annie Laurie?

"Oh," I say, because only my father calls me Annie Laurie. "I would like that."

"I'd like to see you again."

"All right."

"My friends and I. . . .We're spending the evening with some of their Cuban friends. But tomorrow?"

"Tomorrow is Pinar del Rio."

"If there's room, maybe I could come along."

"Okay," I say. I can't look at him because my heart is tumbling to him.

Then we're winding our way through the outskirts of Havana toward the Marina, as I spin my grief into a final bitter song. The owl makes a grieving sound and calls *hoo-hoo, hoo-hoo.* Tucked into its own feathery self, it turns its head fearlessly from left to right. But how strange this secret lifting, this unexpected coming into sight.

Ravenscrag
St. Louis 1963

It was the moon of a false spring, milky and cold and sending no light. Shadows filled every corner of the room as memory dissolved like a face under water. After long absence my mother has come home. Now I would dream again.

While she was gone I slept the sleep of the dead. Now I would work my way night by night through the dreams that gave shape to her absence. The first dream was always like this: My mother is walking down a dark hallway lined with stones. Her footsteps make no sound. There is no light and she holds a candle in front of her. She knows exactly where she's going. She's wearing a long, silvery nightgown that trails behind her. She's safe after all, with this candle to light her way. Her hands are cool and steady, and I know no harm will come from this flame. She has found a way to turn dark into light, and this makes her smile. Now she's climbing the stairs, but the stones are cold on her feet.

Stop! Who goes there? The voice is low and bloodless, but she isn't afraid. She slows her step, but she doesn't turn back. She's the beautiful princess bride, locked away in the castle, waiting to be rescued. When I wake up I know I have dreamed my mother into the bride of Frankenstein.

"Where is her room?" I asked my father every time she went away. "Tell me what it's like exactly. Does she have a window? Do they know she always has to be seeing out?"

My father looked stricken. He had forgotten to tell them.

"I'm sure they know this, Annie Laurie. It's their job to know how to make people better." But my father and I had never discussed in what way she needed to be better. It always slipped edgewise through language, like water through alarmed and fluttering hands.

"What was it like, the place you were?" My father looked grim, my mother dazed. He carried her little brown suitcase up the stairs. Such a tiny suitcase for all those weeks.

"Your hair," I whispered. "What happened to your hair? She stood there in that dark entryway by the coat rack, staring at her coat. I was afraid she was going to bolt for the door, so I wrapped myself around her and held on tight. "What was it like?" I asked again. But this time, she said she lived in a castle. A castle! In my dreams just the same! She said it didn't look like a hospital at all. For one brief moment, hope filled the dark place inside my head. Maybe this was a sign that she would finally be home for good.

My mother was in the kitchen, sitting at the table. She was in her bare feet and nightgown. Her hair was a pale field of wheat. I pretended I didn't notice how strange she looked without her hair and how much it scared me. "It's coming in all straight now," she said flatly. "Don't be scared, Sweetie, it's nice to touch."

She was watching the steam rise from the coffee my father had just given her. She'd been home a week. That morning she'd heroically tried to make breakfast and had burned the eggs. The blackened scrambled eggs were floating on top of the soapy water in the sink. I saw a shadow fall across her face. Then she turned her head and she was my beautiful mother again.

The burned smell and the smoke from the blackened skillet hovered in a little cloud over the stove. My father opened the window above the sink and turned off the water. Then he sat down beside her and took her hands, though she slipped them away. "It's all right, Eugenie," he said. I knew even then, that this was the portrait of a blighted marriage. It was a picture so sad I knew I would never get married.

"I wanted to make eggs," she said. "You don't know how much. At the hospital I thought about it all the time. When I was awake all night, I pretended I was home watching out the kitchen window and when the sun came out, I knew I hadn't lost track of time or anything, and if I was making eggs, I was like everybody else now.

"I kept making them in my head, so I wouldn't hear what that terrible doctor's sayings were. I tried to remember what they tasted like, but I couldn't taste anything anymore.

"I'd crack the eggs against the bowl, I used that pretty bowl I always liked, the one I broke. I listened to the sound of the whisk, *tuh tuh tuh, tuh tuh tuh,* for a long time, then I dropped the butter into the skillet and listened to the sizzle, then I poured the eggs into the skillet and it was a whispering sound you wouldn't hear unless you were really listening. Then I stirred them till they turned that pale yellow color I like, then the all-finished sound, the hardest one to hear, when I lifted them out of the skillet in the big ceramic spoon onto the plate. 'A little noiseless noise among the leaves,' that's what Keats said. It was my table spread for you all that time I was gone. I picked something hard to do, hearing something nobody ever hears. I don't see how they could have burned, Peter, I watched them the whole time."

For my mother, there was time enough for everything now. "I know this way is better," she said. "Everything went too fast before. I'm all right, though, even if I couldn't make breakfast. I'm not sad about the eggs." She smiled a secret smile I had learned not to trust. Later we learned she was stopping her pills, one by one, one day at a time.

"Where are your slippers, Eugenie?" my father asked. "It's drafty in here. Aren't your feet cold?"

She just looked at him. "Those voices he played. I never said those things." Tears were coming down her face now.

"I know," my father said gently. "I know you didn't. I know what happened to you."

"They broke me all apart and now I can't ever be fixed."

"You shouldn't say that."

She shook her head and glared at him. "Don't ever tell me what I can say or can't say."

"I didn't mean it like that. I meant that you should never give up hope."

"I know that," she said, waving him away. "Hope is a good thing if you can have it."

"Eugenie," he said tenderly, and covered her hands. Her hands lay quiet under his.

"The voices they put in my head. He put them there while I was sleeping."

"You don't ever have to talk about it."

"I know."

"Well. It would be good to talk about something else now."

She slid her hands out from under his. "He said he wanted to make me a blank page that he could write on."

My father slumped in his chair.

"I wouldn't let him though."

My father tried again to change the subject. He began to talk about me, who stood invisibly in the doorway. "She did beautifully while you were gone. You shouldn't ever worry about that. I checked on her every night before I went to bed. She must have slept twelve hours a night. I don't know why she would wake up with nightmares now."

My mother just sat there and stared at him. She wasn't really here anymore. It was weeks ago when I'd heard my father whisper on the phone. "I have hope this time. Yes. I know that. It will be a while longer. I don't know what else to do." He meant Montreal. It was French, like my mother, and whatever was in Montreal would finally make her better.

My quiet father couldn't stop talking. He was filling the silence in the room with words that spun emptily into air as my mother sat there vacantly. I was invisible to them. I had spent my whole life skulking around corners, waiting in the shadows to rescue them.

I slipped into the kitchen to make my presence known. My mother and I exchanged the secret look that always excluded my father. His white shirt was rolled up at the sleeves and the end of his tie was wet. He was wiping the steam off his glasses. He rubbed the bridge of his nose with such hopelessness I wanted to go to him and sit on his lap and put my arms around him and say, "Daddy, she'll be all right. You know she just needs time to catch up to herself."

But I was too big to sit on his lap, so I just stood there with nothing to say. I didn't want him to see that secret look again, and

I could feel my mother drawing me into it against him, so I looked down at my shoes, and blinked back the tears.

My father had always tried to make us into a little family during the calm times when she was home, but they were so short and so unremarkable I hardly remember them. When she was gone he never knew what to do with me. My mother had drawn me into her circle of light so surely, and I was so hungry for her touch, her smell, the sound of her voice, and so fearful of her absence, hers was the only face I saw.

But maybe there were no in-between times. Maybe she was always either getting ready to leave or making her anguished way home, and I was holding on for dear life either way. In the end, I don't believe she was ever truly at home anywhere.

I poured myself some cereal and sat down. My mother stroked my arm. "It's good that you're eating. I know the eggs were a disaster."

"That's okay," I said. "I didn't really want any."

Then my mother said, "You don't need to have nightmares. That place I went to. It was nice." But I could tell she'd practiced those words, because her eyes always shifted when she was lying. She looked so tiny in her nightgown, her wrists raw again, the skin stretched taut and thin across her cheeks, an indigo smudge under each eye like a bruise. It was all too familiar. Yet she was different in some profound way. Maybe it was her wheat field of hair.

She read the mistrust in my eyes. So she took my hands and told me again. "Annie Laurie, my dearest heart. That place I went to was a castle."

"Okay," was all I said.

I could see my father blinking back tears as he got up and went to the sink. I watched his back shiver under his white shirt as he stood there looking out the window. Then he began scrubbing the skillet. He jabbed and jabbed at that skillet and those burned on eggs.

"What were those voices you were talking about?" I asked. My father turned sharply toward me and opened his mouth but nothing came out.

"I just had some bad dreams," my mother said. "You know how I like to talk." I could tell they were both wondering how much I'd heard.

But I knew she had gone to some terrible place that was never a castle. When she came home, it took her a week to get out of bed. But if the castle were a lie, I would catch her in it. I would trip her up, though my life depended on believing her.

"Then what was it called?"

"Ravenscrag," she said in a voice not her own. She wrapped her arms around her waist and leaned over. When she finally looked up her eyes were dull as agates.

My throat tightened. *Ravenscrag*. What a horrid name. I knew she was weaving a fairy tale for me out of what clearly was a nightmare. Then it occurred to me that this Ravenscrag was the worst place of all, and that she wasn't making this into a fairy tale just for me, but also for herself.

She shut her eyes and when she opened them the light was back. "It really was a castle once. Or a mansion, anyway. A gray stone castle on top of a hill. You could look down and see a river sometimes and a long driveway with trees. In the fall it was covered with leaves. Somebody said they used to have wonderful parties there. But that was a long time ago, before it was a hospital. Anyway, my snowy owl came back."

It was the fifth straight night of dreams. I woke up crying again.

She came into my room and wiped my cheeks with her thumbs. "I was dreaming about when you were gone," I told her. "A terrible man wanted to hurt you. He was wearing a white coat and white gloves and when he grabbed you, you dropped your candle, and your nightgown caught on fire." She didn't ask what candle or what man but nodded like she knew exactly what I meant.

"He was chasing you and your hair was on fire and he pushed you over a railing and I tried to catch you, but I couldn't. I watched you fall through the sky. You were like a star that went out.

"I know," she said, and she lay down with me and put her face next to mine, her face wet with tears—or were they mine? It was as though she was having my dream or I was having hers. But even with her there, I was lost in a dark sorrow.

"Sweetie, it wasn't so bad; it was never so bad," she said, and she climbed under the cover. But she was cold and trembling, and

I was the one who put my arms around her and drew her close. Even then I knew this rapture could not last.

"You won't ever send me back there, will you?" she asked my father in my dream.

And my father had said, "No. Never. Never." In my dream he would be the prince who saved her at last.

SUNDAY JULY 27, 1997

Stalactites and Stalagmites
Pinar del Rio

"I'm glad you could come," I say to Michael as he sits down beside me. We have the two front seats behind the driver. There are twelve of us, and the guide, who sits down in the seat across the aisle.

"I'm glad somebody changed their mind so I could." I'm relieved when the door finally shuts and no Judith anywhere in sight.

The white skyline of Havana shimmers in the distance, as we rush on toward the clarity and cool air of the countryside.

When I turn around again, we're traveling out of the fifties back into the 19th century and eventually into primordial mists. Up ahead, a cream-colored Buick floats past a bare-backed man on horseback, a thin cloud of dust rising behind him.

We're heading west, to Pinar del Rio, to the valley of Viñales, where the mountains rise astonishingly out of the mists. We're going to the caves, and the underground river of forgetting.

"What were you going to do today?" I ask.

"Lunch with my friends at the Marina. I think I told you we're sailing back to the Keys tomorrow. Now here I am with you."

"Is it all right not to meet them?" He'd said friends. He didn't say *wife*.

"It's more than all right." He can't stop smiling.

"I thought it was difficult getting into Cuba."

"Not if you have the right nationality and enough money."

"And you have both?"

"Or neither," he laughs. "My friends are Canadian and have

lots of money. I was coming to give this paper anyway, so I met them in Miami.

"We're leaving tomorrow, too. Unless we're behind bars."

"What do you mean?"

I'm sorry I said it, because he looks genuinely alarmed. "Just hyperbole. They've taken our tickets. That's all."

"Can they do that?"

"Well they did. They're supposed to give them back at the airport. But it's very strange. Everybody's worrying about it. And there was a bit of trouble at the mayor's party."

"I don't know this. I left so soon. But are you all right?"

I begin to give him a short version, when the guide stands up and taps the microphone.

"Good afternoon. My name is Tomas. And I am your go-between from one world to another. I will be your Charon to the other side." He's a short, compact man with elegant silver hair and wire-rimmed glasses, linen *guayabera*, tasseled Italian loafers. He speaks in clear, accented English, his voice rushing up and down in curving, rolling syllables.

"We are seeing the plains now, where sugarcane and citrus fruits grow. Those are Royal Palms, the national tree of Cuba. Soon we will come into the mountains and you will see *bohios*, where the famous tobacco of Pinar del Rio is dried. And you will see the *mogotes*, the limestone mountains that rise up out of the ground into the mists. You will not believe it."

REVOLUCIÓN ES UNIDAD, ES INDEPENDENCIA proclaims itself in fading, black letters on the side of the overpass, where clumps of people are waiting in the shade.

"They are waiting for a ride to take them to Havana. Maybe an hour. Maybe never." We're passing a cart drawn by two oxen, and now a flatbed truck jammed with people.

"The highway was built in the early eighties to bring Pinar del Rio closer to Havana. Now it's all this wonderful highway but no cars and no gas."

Michael shows me his guidebook—the lush green of sugarcane fields, then rice fields and banana plantations and around some magical turn, the tobacco fields of Pinar del Rio.

"That's where we're going," Michael says. "*Cueva del Indio.* Cave of the Indian," he reads. "The Guanajatabey Indians used it for sanctuary and for burial. Also as a hiding place for runaway slaves. Che Guevara took his troops into these caves during the Cuban missile crisis."

"My father thinks Castro has weapons stockpiled in there. He warned me about the caves and the bats."

"Will you be all right doing this?"

"I need to see a dark place like that."

There is a strange, sudden quiet between us. He knows what dark place I'm thinking of. The sun ripples across the guidebook, across his hands, his arm, across his face.

"We don't always have to feel the suffering of those we love." But he says this so intensely I wonder if he's also talking about himself.

"It says the caves are not a trip for the claustrophobic. Are you claustrophobic?"

He laughs. "Yes I am. A little."

"You should be sitting in the aisle instead of me. But I'm a little claustrophobic too, so thank you."

Michael reads on. "The *mogotes* are made of limestone formed when the roof of the valley collapsed. They are riddled with underground rivers and limestone caves, dating back 160 million years ago."

"I don't know if I can do this," I say unexpectedly.

"You don't have to do anything you don't want to do."

"Do you worry about the claustrophobic part?"

"Oh, I'll be all right."

How to explain my sixth-grade fascination with caves, and the science report on stalagmites and stalactites I never gave? Where all growing up is growing down. Like two minds set into one—light speed and slow motion, manic and depressive.

"I just know I need to see them."

"Caves of the mind," he says after a moment, then shakes his head. "Oh my. Please don't think of me as a shrink."

The highway goes on and on as we sit without speaking. Then, "Would you like some water?" He hands the bottle to me and I drink and drink. I had no idea I was so thirsty.

"You remind me of someone I met yesterday who heals people too," I say.

He looks at me, then turns away. The attraction is pulling at him too. There has been too much between us too fast and neither of us has expected it. I look at his hand again and see that ring. I lean into him without thinking, my arm brushing against his arm.

Then he turns to me and says, "I really do like what's happened to your hair."

"Something did happen to my hair. That's a nice way to put it, though."

"You were going to tell me why you wanted to see the caves."

There are no breaths deep enough to steady me. But I begin anyway. I can always stop. So I describe how I had thought limestone was made out of limes and I signed up for the report on stalactites and stalagmites. How in those days I was in love with all things underground—things that needed candlelight or flashlight or torchlight. Maybe it was my mother's story of Ravenscrag, or the dream of my mother in the haunted castle.

"'Do you know the difference between a stalactite and a stalagmite?' That was my riveting introduction. 'If you lean over and put your head between your legs, down would be up and up would be down.' That explained my whole life. I was already in front of the class when I saw my father's face in the doorway. I didn't drop my report or my felt board illustrations. His eyes said, now it has finally happened."

But I didn't believe it. She would always come to me in some half-light. She would defy the sorrow of his eyes that said this is forever.

So I said, take me to the caves, Daddy. And if he had said yes, let's go find the stalactites and stalagmites, I could have said it only looks like they're frozen in place. They're changing all the time. But I wasn't growing up or growing down, I was held forever somewhere in between.

"I never saw the caves," I say at last. "And now I will."

Michael takes my hand and turns his face to my face.

Where We are Going We Already Are
Pinar del Rio

"This restroom is only for the truly desperate," Tomas, the guide, says. "No toilet paper, no soap, no water, no flushing, no light." Since I'm of the truly desperate I'm first in line.

When I come back from that dark place, I shade my eyes. Michael is standing by the little bar set up under a thatched roof, holding two drinks. He holds one up to me and smiles. I like his short clipped brown hair with a sprinkling of gray, his blue-green eyes. And his pale yellow shirt, rolled up at the sleeves.

The pasture on the other side of the road is sparse and flatly green, with a cluster of royal palms in the distance and several gaunt cows staring bleakly at the highway, their ribs sharp in the noonday sun. The little tourist shop holds the usual: Che T-shirts, a few *Santería* dolls, little bottles of pale *Havana Club*, a small collection of postcards, most of them black and white grainy reproductions of the Malecón, *Plaza de la Catedral, El Morro*, along with a few garish, colored postcards of the beaches at Varadero. None of Hemingway or the *Finca*.

"How was the bathroom?" Michael says, handing me a *mojito*.

"Very authentic."

"You look happy to be in Cuba," Tomas says. "Why not? You are wise to be choosing the mountains. You can have been going to the beach."

"Someone told me to go to the mountains to see the *mogotes*."

"Would you like another?" he says. "It is the Cuban way to find joy wherever you can."

"Oh, I already am," Michael says.

The guide's eyes flash. "Where are you two coming from?"

"Oh, we're not together," I say too quickly, and feel heat rush up my face.

"I sailed from Key West with some friends. I'm from Maine," Michael says.

"I'm from Washington. Seattle."

"Yes. The rainy place. My family is from Viñales, where we are going. It is sometimes rainy there too. My father grew tobacco in Pinar del Rio. But it was the Revolution, and everything was happening so fast. I followed Che, like everyone. I believed in reform and became a professor of economics. Also I was in love with poetry. Can you believe it? My wife died a long time ago, but my daughter lives with me now in Havana, and my granddaughter and now her little baby girl. I am sorry to be talking so much."

Then he takes my hand. His wrist is tawny, muscular, and tucked under his wide silver watchband, is a bracelet of blue and white striped beads strung together with twine.

"Oh, your bracelet! *Yemayá?*" I say, pointing to his wrist. There is such pleasure in recognition that I've forgotten Tani's cautionary tale: almost everyone in Cuba believes in *Santería*, but many must hide it.

He casually puts his arm behind his back and his eyes withdraw.

"You are very observant," he says.

I hold out my necklace.

"Yes. *Yemayá*," he says. "*Orisha* of the sea and moon. Very beautiful. That fits you."

"I'm really a daughter of *Oshún*. I fell in love with *Yemayá* before I knew it."

"You can be in love with two *orishas*. They are sisters anyway. You can't be too much in love. There are many ways to be a family, you know."

Then he raises his arms as if to embrace us. "'My glory was I had such friends.' That's Yeats. My daughter gave me Yeats."

Michael's eyes glisten with remembering:

"'I think where man's glory most begins and ends.

And say my glory was I had such friends.'

"My wife had that framed behind her desk so it would be the

first thing her clients would see. She's a social worker." He swallows hard. "She was a social worker."

"Do you know 'The Stolen Child?'" Tomas says. "It's my favorite Yeats.

'Come away, O human child!
With a faery, hand in hand,
For the world's more full of weeping than you can understand.'

"The faeries help explain our brokenness. They heal our suffering. Like *Yemaya* and *Oshun*."

Something is happening to us. Yeats in the *mogotes*. "I would have thought Lorca or Neruda," I say.

"Oh yes, of course. Yeats came as a surprise. My daughter found it for my birthday. It was left behind in a room she was housekeeping. And then of course I fell in love with it."

I point to his bracelet. "It's not *Yemayá*, is it," I say quietly.

He's studying me closely. "You know about it, then."

I want to tell him about the *babalawo* and am surprised by how much.

He nods a strange assent and holds out his arm. "It looks like *Yemayá*, doesn't it? Blue and white like her. But see the stripes? Also there are seventeen beads, not seven. It's for *Babalú-Ayé*. He's a healer too. Not so different."

"Like Ricky Ricardo," I say.

"Of course. *Babalú*," Michael says, as a smile of recognition flashes across his face. Then his eyes darken. "I didn't mean to trivialize."

"No, no, you're not. It's all right. That's exactly what he was doing. Singing to *Babalú*, only people didn't know it."

All those *I Love Lucy* re-runs with Ricky Ricardo pounding out that secret rhythm on the conga, while the musicians in ruffled shirts played big band mambo behind him. He always wound up on his knees in the end, I think now, in a gesture of supplication.

"Oh I'm a trickster, all right. *Babalú* is Saint Lazarus, you know. In Catholicism, the healer of the sick. My belief is a recent development. Economics professor, tour guide, and now mirrors and smoke."

Then just for a heartbeat, he drops the mask. "My granddaughter, she is a great believer, my guide in all things. She has finally almost half-persuaded me. Now I believe in almost half of everything."

Then his face changes again. "My syncretism is in here." He thumps his chest with his fist. "An empiricist like me believing in stones and smoke and a little poetry also. What am I coming to? I am mostly coming apart," he says, tapping his chest again.

Then he sees me looking at his elegant shoes.

"There is much going without in Cuba. But of course there is always the sky and the mountains and music, and making love. There is no need for beautiful things like these shoes. I am very vain about my perfection," he laughs. "It is an imperfect fit, so to speak. *Babalú* and this crazy tour guide."

"I think it's wonderful," Michael says. "You're a healer too then."

Tomas and I move to the bar under the shade of the thatched roof. Michael excuses himself to buy some postcards.

"*Nada*," the guide says to the bartender. "One more *mojito* and I will no longer be clear in the head. That's what *Babalú* does. He guides us to the underworld. Another?"

"Oh, no thank you," I say. "I need to be clear in the head too."

He touches the bracelet on his wrist. "You are very kind. I try too much to be funny. Sometimes, it is a great effort."

"I think you're lovely."

Then he looks at me hard. "You and Michael are not together then?"

"No," I say. "We've really just met."

"But you have family?"

"Only my father. My mother died a long time ago."

"You should see him all you can, then. Families are so easily broken."

I point to the cows in the pasture next to the rest stop. "They're so thin. I'm falling in love with Cuba and it's breaking my heart."

"It's difficult to raise cows in the summer when there is no rain and nothing to eat. They'll fatten up in the lushness to come. Everything will be all right in the mountains." He turns to walk away then looks back. "I really thought you two were together. You don't mind?"

"No," I say. "I don't mind."

"There is much restoration for the soul in the mountains," he says over his shoulder. The heat shimmers off the long empty highway and I imagine the mountains that lie beyond, cool and exotic in the mist.

Everything outside the window rushes past—a man walking toward the bridge with a string of chili peppers over his shoulder, a brilliant splash of red against the white of his shirt—an old man pulling a cart carrying a refrigerator—a cow tied to a fence post beside the highway, the owner asleep on the grass—a dusty brown horse strapped to the gas pump of a long-abandoned gas station.

Then we sail around a corner and come up fast on a woman walking along the road. Michael's hand tightens on my arm. "She's on the wrong side of the road."

Now she's walking barefoot out into the road, swinging her shoes. Her skirt flares up as we slide into a little quarter turn around her into the next lane.

I turn around and see she has stopped in the middle of the road, her hands on her waist, looking after us with angry, resolute eyes. Then she's gone, vanishing into the curve of the road.

"We almost hit her," Michael says. He's gripping the seat in front of him. The guide book has fallen to the floor.

"Cuban roads are very dangerous," Tomas says quietly. "That was very bad." He shakes his head and sits back down. "But everything will be all right in the mountains."

Michael rests his head back against the seat, closes his eyes.

"Your hands are cold," I say. He turns and looks at me with such anguish I look away.

"It was just such a surprise," he says, but can't finish. I don't know what he's talking about except that it's grave.

I brush the top of his hand, his ring.

"I don't seem to be able to take it off."

"You don't have to say anything."

He holds out his hand, spreads his fingers. "I can't imagine my hand without it." He puts his hands together, one hand holding the other. "Her name was Sophie. A car hit her."

"Oh," I say. "Oh."

You could be riding a bike, no lamplight to guide your path, no way to see your flowered shirt—or you're wandering in Havana at high noon, your white dress and beads your only help against that rushing black car—or running in the morning mist, the car behind you silent and deadly. Or walking barefoot by the road, as moonlight gathers in your hair.

We sit there for a long time, holding hands. How strange to be here with this man, memories rising up for us both.

The Girl in the Road
St. Louis 1950

My mother slept in the curve of the quartermoon. She couldn't sleep the other days of the month. Too much wildness in the full moon for that. But that curve was a quicksilver hand holding hers, or cupped against the side of her face. She was always safe tucked away in there.

How to catch that brief flicker of light that was my mother's life? When my father began to withdraw from me that summer after my mother died, it was confirmation of my worst fears. I was an orphan. I had neither mother nor father now. And if I was not my father's daughter, then who was I? And so I began to invent their lives, to prove that their love was the force that had called me into life and anchored us all to earth and to each other. Everywhere I turned I looked for stories that would let me bear my staggering loss. Who said that to live without despair we must make myths out of our lives?

But was there one secret that would explain away the darkness and bring her to light?

That terrible summer when I hated my father because he couldn't save her, it was G who loved her best. It was G who left her on Christmas, who gave her earrings instead, who was her true love. He was the man in the picture I didn't know. The serious mouth, the chin with the little cleft, the strong, square face, those dark eyes, his dark hair, when everyone else in my universe was blonde. Later, when it seemed my life depended on a different story, it was my father who had saved her that night. G had done something terrible to her.

The script of those letters darkened as my understanding of the world became more complex, but it always began with the story of what happened on a moonlit road. As she tells it, of course, she would find herself on that road.

She'd be walking barefoot, carrying her red shoes by her thumb, her white dress whispering as she walked, her blonde hair billowy and soft on her shoulders. She's walking in the gravel, but she barely knows it. Soon she steps into the road and feels the pavement smooth and warm against her feet. That's better, she thinks. The moon is a smudge of light in the corner of the sky. The heat of the day presses against her, trapped under that heavy sky. She's keeping her eye on that thumbprint of light rising now over the trees. But she's so close to the edge of the road, the headlights can't catch her in time. She's completely in the dark but for the moon, which breaks out at the last minute, and there she is, in her white dress, her shimmering hair.

Nobody knows what she's doing out there so late at night. She doesn't know she's still crying, but she feels the salty taste at the corners of her mouth. I must still be crying, she thinks. But the moon has broken free of the clouds and washes her in a pearly light.

Just then a white, luminous thing rises out of the road in front of him. Her white dress catches in the light laying itself over the road. He always wondered if he would have seen her, if the moon hadn't slipped from under the clouds just then. He shudders to think of it. It was magic, she said, the way it came out just in time, the way the headlights caught her white dress. "You might have run me over," she always said, "flat as a pancake. But you knew I was there all the time, didn't you?" And when she says this she wraps her arms around her waist and smiles a secret smile I knew even then it had nothing to do with my father or that night. It wasn't till years later that I recognized she said it partly because it terrified him. I'd watch him flinch behind his glasses, then grow quiet looking at her. My Eugenie, my own true girl, he's thinking, so many ways to keep you from harm.

When the car pulls up beside her, she knows she should be afraid, but she's not. She just thinks, oh there you are now, I'm so tired. Peter tosses the Bible he'd laid on the passenger seat into the back and his note cards spill out over the seat and fall to the floor. She picks them up and hands them over as she gets in.

"That's nice to have note cards," she says. "It's nice to have things organized so tidy and nice. All your ideas safe in those cards. I always use those yellow pads. Or sketch books. Sometimes I write in pictures instead of words. I'm going on and on, aren't I? I need to get back to school now. Can you take me?"

"Anywhere. I can take you anywhere." She just leans her head back and shuts her eyes, her red shoes with the broken heel in her lap.

"It was hard to walk after my shoe got broken," she says. "I'm glad you found me."

All Peter can think of, when her arm brushes his, is that she smells of lavender. He has never felt anything like it. He hears her breathy silence beside him, feels her cool hand on his arm when she talks. Then he realizes she's trembling.

"Oh," she says, with an intake of breath that frightens him. "I'm going to be sick please stop the car." So he pulls the car off into the gravel and she pushes the door open and runs into the grass.

"Are you all right? Can I help?" he calls into the dark. Already he wants to wrap her in his arms and say everything will be all right, but he just stands by the side of the road with his fists inside his pockets. He doesn't want to embarrass her or startle her or make her run away.

"I'm all right now," she says at last, and then she's coming across the grass toward him. Her face is damp and cool though the night is still warm. She's shivering, so when he gets her into the car, he takes his jacket from the backseat and wraps her up.

It's because of G that she's like this, why she's on this country road so late at night, why she feels sick. "Thank you, that's really nice," she says, but she can't stop shivering.

"Are you all right?" he asks again. By now he's frightened, but all he can do is drive on in the silence that has settled between them and hope his jacket will keep her warm. He wants to put his arm around her, but he's holding onto the steering wheel for dear life. Then he realizes how much he wants to kiss her.

When at last he's walked her to her dorm, she smiles up at him. He hadn't realized she was so tiny. By now it's one in the morning, and the dorm has been locked for hours. Everything is quiet and dark. "I don't know if they'll let me in," she says. "I'm so tired." So he says, "You can come home with me." He doesn't care how he would get her into his room at the seminary or who would see her. She could have his bed. He would sleep in the chair. Then the porch light comes on and a woman is standing in the doorway with pin curls in her hair, clutching her robe.

She doesn't say thank you or look back one last time. She just disappears inside. He doesn't even know her name. He just stands there staring at the closed door and the light going out. How can he lose her when he has just found her?

"Yes, I remember you," she says when he calls her a week later. It wasn't hard to figure out where to find her.

"Eugenie," she says. "It's French. You say the g soft." *Eugenie Eugenie Eugenie*, he says over and over. Such a light, strange sound that says, "Save her. Keep her safe from harm."

He is Risen
Pinar del Rio

We're climbing into the mountains now, and to the right a valley opens up, green and tropical, and dotted with palm trees and *bohios*, where the tobacco leaves lie drying under dark thatched roofs.

"Tell me how he chose them," I ask.

Michael puts down the Guide Book. "*Pinar del Rio*. What a beautiful name. Pines of the river? The River of pines? I don't know."

"I don't know either."

Then Michael looks at me without blinking. "Cameron believed every patient's illness was rooted in some dark secret. What patient wouldn't have secrets? *My God*. That's just what President Ford said when they told him about Ravenscrag."

"You know about this, don't you?"

Michael's eyes have turned dark. "I think he chose people who had some terrible secret. And then he went after it. *Relentlessly*. Such a violation, to take from a person so ill the thing they most need to guard."

"My mother had a secret," I say. "Her secret was me. I was the secret."

"What do you mean?"

"I don't know if my father knew for sure I wasn't his child, but I think he did."

Then he says, "Aren't our sexual secrets always our deepest, most precious ones? How lovely to be such a beautiful secret."

I can't stop the tears. "She wouldn't have told that terrible doctor anything."

"The metaphor of the psychiatrist digging up lost ruins is a terrible image. To get at something before a patient is ready. My God. To just sit there with your legs crossed and your notebook in your lap, reeling it in like a *prize*."

I can feel him breathing hard beside me.

"I'm sorry. That was inexcusable." Then he says, "I want you to know this. The listener must be worthy of the secret."

"No. Please. I'm grateful for your anger."

We're far into the mountains now, taking the winding road up toward Pinar del Rio. In the distance beyond this turn or the next, the *mogotes* would rise out of the valley floor, prehistoric and otherworldly. Tomas stands up in the well of the van.

"Soon we will pass the monument to Che Guevara," he says. "In 1967 he died in Bolivia of execution. Two weeks ago was the 30th anniversary, and his bones have been discovered in Vallegrande, Bolivia. It is very emotional for many Cubans, and for me also."

The remains, the bones, the ashes. "He is not there," my father had said from the church pulpit that Easter morning after my mother died. "He is risen," he said, with tears spilling down his face. But nobody had risen. Nobody had come back from the dead.

"I'm coming along, you know," Michael said.

"I thought you were claustrophobic."

"I am."

The tops of the Royal Palms shimmer in the sun as they incline toward us. "It's beautiful," Michael says. Flashes of color rush by— frangipani, oleander, hibiscus, bougainvillea. And now the flame trees—coral umbrellas of shade—the spiky tips of the dracaenas, and the patchwork fields of tobacco.

"We are going to the mountains where Che trained with his men," Tomas says. Sweat is running down the side of his face. He wipes it with a white handkerchief, then folds it up and puts it back in his pocket. "Now Che has returned, like everybody knew he would."

No more Che sightings in the countryside or in South America or Africa. In death he was so much more powerful than he ever was in his complicated, extravagant life. If you believed in his untainted passion, you could forget the executions he ordered inside *La Cabaña*. You could forget them in the shadow of the lighthouse at *El Morro*, and the sixty-six foot *El Christo* blessing the harbor and looking the other way.

Tomas sits down across the aisle. He drops the microphone on the floor and leans back. It's nothing, he's thinking, just that funny little tightness, not exactly a pain, you couldn't even call it a pain. Besides it's all too familiar. His breath is coming in little gusts, hot and close and small. There it is again.

"Is he all right" I ask.

Just then Tomas leans over, picks up the mic and turns to us. "Authentic Cuban experience. Exotic scenery, crazy tour guide. The works."

What was it, brushing against my face just then? Who was always saying *the works*?

"I am young at heart, you know. But these past weeks I have felt old with the death of Che truly now. Is it odd to be talking like this when we have just met?"

"Not at all," Michael says.

"It's like everything in Cuba," I say. "A longed for surprise."

He looks at me with dark hawk eyes, full of radiance and grief, as though some tragic resolution is just around the corner. Then he wipes his face again, stands up, and smiles. "We will be stopping soon now for the caves. If you do not wish to go down, you can wait at the little outdoor restaurant. It will be dark and very difficult walking. I myself find it formidable. But it's nice to sit in the shade of the restaurant and order *cerveza* or a *mojito*."

He puts the mic by his side and looks at the two of us. His smile is gone now. "Are you going into the caves?"

"Yes," Michael says. "We are."

"That's good. Some people get only so far, then they have to turn back. Of course soon there is no turning back. However, in their own way they are transforming."

It would have been easy to hide our holding hands in the folds of my dress. And when Tomas looks down at us, it's with a secret acknowledgment. We're deep in the mountains now. We have come to where we are going.

"Your hands are warm now," I say.

Caves of the Mind
Pinar del Rio

I feel Michael behind me as we climb down the stairs to the cave. "Are you all right?" he asks. He touches the back of my neck lightly.

"Are *you* all right?" I say over my shoulder.

"So far."

"We're not very far," I laugh. And so we leave the sky behind us and descend into the cave to make our cautious way over the stalagmites rising from the floor of the cave, ducking under the jagged, sharper stalactites above. Were they growing up or growing down? My sixth grade research had stopped short of that chicken and egg question.

The air is cool and damp and heavy to breathe. We hear the sound of water dripping and then as we come closer, the sound of water lapping against the stone steps leading down to the river.

"This gentleman is your river guide," Tomas says. "Today he is also apparently your oarsman, as he will explain."

A thin, tall man with an extravagant moustache steps out of the boat and onto the bottom step.

"Our boats have the finest of motors," he says formally. "But we have at the moment no petrol. So we have obtained a luxury row-boat for you! Did you know that Cuba has a national row boating team? I, however, am not of this team. So it will take longer today, your patience please."

"We will need to go in two trips," Tomas says. "It's not long on the river. It is well-lit and not difficult at all. You have already overcome the difficult part."

One at a time, we edge down the stone steps to the boat and the waiting river, our River Styx, rippling in the torchlight.

There are six of us—the river guide, then Michael and me, Tomas, and two others. We drift for a few moments while the guide adjusts the oars, and then pulls out onto the river.

"See there, up by the torch?" the guide says. "An Indian head. And over there. Imagine perhaps a wild boar. Also many snakes. The caves allow the greatest of imagination." But day after day, a person would grow tired of thinking of odd things to look at. Some days he'd surely want to break out. Imagine a woman's breast. A man's cock.

"The three-headed dog of Hades," he says, pointing to the stone ledge we're floating under. But it's like someone else naming the shape of a cloud.

We're floating silently down the black river, lit an eerie, greenish yellow by the torchlights, placed along the way. I want to drift down that river in silence. I want to gather some image from this place and unwrap the mystery of what had happened to my mother.

"We're inside time," Michael says.

"Or outside of it."

"It's beautiful," he says. "Caves of the mind."

But I don't see any beauty. Shapes hanging down and jutting out like tumors, like the underside of something unspeakable, or the inside of some alien creature, replicating itself in the water where the torchlight lays a trembling path of yellow-green light.

"All these twists and turns," I say. "It looks tortured to me."

"This is the underside of the *mogotes*."

"Okay, but not beautiful."

He takes my hand.

Up ahead the river forms a narrow channel where the cave walls edge up tight and hang close overhead. It feels like we should duck. I expect to see bones scattered on the outcroppings or wild, dark things with yellow eyes slithering out of sight. I feel Michael's hand tighten.

"Try to see cave paintings," he says breathlessly. "Anything beautiful."

"Are you all right? Your hand is cold."

"I'll be okay."

The torchlight throws shifting, monstrous shapes against the cave as we slide through the narrow channel and into wide, dark waters. We're deep inside my mother's castle now. We're in the Sleep Room at the end of the hall. There is no moaning and shrieking—only faint whimpering, and the eerie silence of the dead made by the living. "Take deep breaths," Michael says. "Like this."

"I am. Everything feels so tight."

Michael is squeezing my hand. I feel him take deep breaths too. He's closed his eyes.

We're far down the river now, with only the whispery sound of the oars, and dripping water. This river would have to end. Any minute now we would drift around some curve into the light and it would be over.

Then I see something flicker—not the torchlight, but a little golden winking, higher up. We drift closer and two amber eyes catch in the light. Suddenly the torchlight wavers then flares, and there it is—a dark owl perched on a ledge.

The owl makes a deep, hollow sound, and rises up—dark and wide against the torchlight. I put my hand over my face against the whirr of those enormous wings.

Michael's hand tightens again, then an intake of breath. His hand slips out of mine. A fierce, shadow rushes across the torchlight again and dissolves into the dark.

It's completely black now, just the torchlight from the boat throwing a thin, rippling path of light onto the dark water. I want to turn around to find Tomas but can't move. He has vanished into the dark. Then I feel him leaning forward and whispering in my ear, "We are in Hades, you know."

Someone cries out.

The Sleep Room
Montreal 1963

She's sitting in his office on the leather couch as far from his chair as she can get. She's wearing her street clothes and has a needle in her arm. She looks at it like she can't remember how it got there. She has refused to lie down. Peter said goodbye long ago. She watched his taxi wind its way down the long, circular drive until it disappeared. The trees are dark sculptures against the gray Montreal sky.

"I don't have any secrets," she says, now that the cycling has stopped, and she can breathe again. She has signed the consent form. The form that said yes to everything.

"Tell me your secret and I will make you well," he says again. "It's your secret that's making you sick," he says in that soft, Scottish voice who calls her Lassie like she's some kind of pet. He sits there with that grim smile on his face. His eyes are terrible.

You can't make me tell you anything, she's thinking, but she says, "How will it make me better?" His smile starts out thin and slick across his face, when she slips into a white, effortless fog that loosens her tongue. Maybe all the time it was only this. But she doesn't want to tell him anything, especially that. Still, she has come all this way and they have tried everything else. And she has never told anybody before.

"Sodium amytal is a wonderful thing. Say it. Now say it again, Lassie. Again. Say it one more time. Yes, I know it makes you cry. You want to be a good girl. It's truth serum, so you can't stop yourself. Tell me your dark secret, Lassie, then you will get well."

She is so beautiful he hates her imperfection all the more. He looks at her appraisingly. He could make her perfect. He would probably have to break her to do it. He loves this kind of work. He wants her secret. He knows it's something sexual. Most secrets are. She's crying when she finally tells him.

"I just loved him all to pieces and I couldn't help myself. His dark hair, his eyes, he was so beautiful."

He hands her the box of tissues but she won't take it. He sets it back on the coffee table and bends toward her. "You have built your life on a pack of lies."

She doesn't really hear him now. She's back inside her memory, which is her shame and her glory. "When I told him about the baby, he started to cry. He said, 'I'm so sorry, I'm so sorry.' Now I was going to have this baby that was his, but he was already married. So I never told him when she was born, this man I loved. I never told Peter either. I don't know if he knew or anything. I was sad for a long time. But then there was this beautiful, tiny baby who was blonde like Peter and me and not dark like him."

"Look at the mess you've made," he says. "You have hurt every-one around you. You are selfish. You think only of yourself. You use your beauty against men. You are a whore."

She's far from him now, still tucked safely into herself. But she doesn't know what the needle is doing to her when she goes on. "Peter had never been with anybody before and he didn't have anything with him, and he said, 'What should I do, is it all right?' and I said, 'Yes, yes yes,' and I lay there and thought of the one I loved and this baby now. Then I said *Peter*, and touched his face and I knew he was going to take care of me."

"Yes," he says, letting out a long sigh. "That's what I wanted. That's exactly what I wanted. Now you can relax, Lassie. You're nice and quiet now. You feel better, don't you? You need to cross your legs, Lassie. They're all sprawled out. It's not nice. Cross your legs. Do it." She had stopped crying long ago.

His breath is like something in the ground. He tried to kiss me in his office and I told him he smelled like death. "He gets up really close when I'm in bed, and whispers things in my ear," I told the nurse. I know because I can feel his breath on my face and that smell. I can smell him when he kisses me when I'm sleeping, too.

"Vanity, all is vanity," he's saying, stroking her face. "You know what I could do to you, don't you? I can fix it so you can never hurt yourself again. You're too beautiful for your own good. Nobody should be that beautiful with such a flaw in them. We'd have to shave your head. Not like how we cut it now. How beautiful would you be then, Lassie? And you wouldn't care if it ever grew back. We do it all the time here. For the intractable, the *incurable*. I'm not saying this in the tape, I'm whispering it in your ear. You'll remember my voice saying it forever."

"I can't move my arms and legs, or even my head," she cries.

"Why is he giving her that?" the nurse asks.

"Giving me what?" she says.

"Curare," the nurse says, and she can tell the nurse hates him too.

"I know what *curare* is. It's what paralyzes you in poison darts. So I have to hear the sayings under my pillow."

"He's crazy," the nurse whispers to her. "You should find a way to get out of here."

The white owl at the foot of her bed is silent and still. Its amber eyes are unblinking. She's Sleeping Beauty now. She's unrecognizable. Her beautiful blonde hair is gone. It lies in short, dirty tufts.

She's sleeping the sleep of the dead, even though her cheek twitches and you can see she's listening, even in her sleep, to the tapes playing under her pillow. She can't help it. This is the Sleep Room, the Zombie Room at the end of the hall, where even the nurses fear to go. There's a strange light here, everybody says so.

Nothing works. Nothing lasts but this: Her tongue swells and her throat tightens. Her hands clench, and her feet twist, then her back arches and bares her throat to the chill of dark things as lightning splits her apart.

He's stroking her arm in the dim, flickering light. She has been here so long she doesn't know anything. Her arm is outstretched for the needle that holds sweet oblivion. She's past dreaming now, and nightmares, and sayings under her pillow. The owl sits at the edge of the bed, keeping watch.

A Syncopating Heart
Pinar del Rio

"It's over," Michael says. "Look." He's pointing up ahead to a grow-ing circle of light. I won't turn around and beckon the dark thing at our backs.

Behind us the waterfall pours itself into the sun as we drift through green and dappled light. I feel the pressure of tears and wipe them away.

Tomas is the first to get onto the dock and out of the ravine. He's rushing across the footbridge, his head down, hands jammed into his pockets. Then he leans against the railing and puts his head down against his arms. The back of his shirt is soaked.

"Tomas?" Michael says, coming up now, putting his hand on his shoulder.

"Oh," he laughs, jerking his head up. "I was recovering from the caves. Souvenirs are over there. Such a nice terrace," he says breathlessly.

Sweat is pouring down his face.

"Oh my," he says and puts his head down again.

Michael touches his back and Tomas straightens up and clenches his fist over his chest. Michael's shirt is wet too. The sun is soft and green, filtering through the trees.

"It's nothing," Tomas says, and turns to cross the bridge.

"Let's stay here a minute," Michael says.

Tomas nods and shuts his eyes.

"I'm a physician." Michael takes his wrist and counts his pulse. He looks at him, then at me.

"I know," he says. "It syncopates."

"That's what it's doing."

"It will pass. It's only the caves." He tries to laugh. "All my life such claustrophobia." He shuts his eyes again.

I touch Tomas's arm. "Me, too," I say. "I didn't think I could do it."

He nods and gives me a thin smile. "It's nothing. Truly," he says between breaths.

But I can see the panic in his eyes. He keeps wincing against some kind of pain.

"Don't worry," Michael says. "I'll check it again in a minute. Try to take deep breaths. Let everything slow down. Your heart is going very fast. It just needs to calm down."

"And the syncopation to stop."

Michael nods, and touches his arm.

"And this little pain to end." He shakes his head against it. "Such an indignity. My pride is wounded," he says mockingly, as he thumps his chest.

"It's not shameful," I say. "Everybody has things that go wrong."

He looks up at the sky. "I love all this light. The caves were so dark."

"It's nice here," I say. "It's cooler under the trees."

"You are very kind," he says, then shakes his head. "This heart has a mind of its own. I have one remaining pill at home, but I must save it for when I need it absolutely."

My American guilt washes over me.

"I am trying to be philosophical," Tomas says. "But I love my life. I would hate to leave it. I have many things to do. Do you think I'm all right now?"

Michael looks at him closely, then back at me. "I think so. Sure."

"See how all right I am? A miracle of health."

Then we all walk slowly to the terrace. I take Michael's arm and whisper, "These things happen all the time to you, don't they. People in harm's way, and then there you are."

Michael just shakes his head. "Sometimes."

We sit at the far end of one of the tables and order drinks. Other tourists are in the cigar shop buying rum, or *Cohibas*, or drinking a *cerveza.* It's quiet and cool in the shade, and now a little breeze. "I will get you drinks," Tomas says, getting up.

Michael puts his hand on Tomas's arm. "It's so nice here. No need for drinks."

Tomas takes a deep breath and eases back in the chair. "Belief is a strange thing, isn't it. Did you see the owl? I tell myself it wasn't a death omen. Sometimes they go into the caves to hunt for bats. My Stygian owl. My owl of the River Styx."

And there it was—the shadow sweeping over the walls of the cave, the rush of wings, wild and premonitory.

"Once a couple of years ago, somebody asked me about the owl in the caves and I said, 'What owl?' Can you believe it? I was a realist for so long, I couldn't accept it."

"I believe it," Michael says, almost in a whisper.

"I thought I was the only one," I say.

Tomas looks at the two of us. "Of course," he says softly. He shakes his head and an odd half-smile inches across his face.

There is a green stillness in the air, and for a moment, an acknowledgment that can't be taken back. We sit there and let it settle slowly upon us.

"This owl," Tomas says at last. "It haunts me. I'm glad of your company. It has been terrible seeing it alone."

"When we came into the sun after the dark, I thought, how could there be an owl?" Michael says.

Tomas pats my hand. "Yes, I know."

"I'm glad I wasn't by myself," I say.

"But I'm becoming great friends with it now." Tomas looks away, and when he turns back to us, his official smile is in place.

We sit there without speaking, while a shadow passes over us.

"There will be rain tomorrow," he says. "For your journey home."

I don't stop to think how he could know about the journey home or where this sudden intimacy has come from. I only know that his face holds a sudden brightening. "The owl. I know what it is now," he says. "There is no translation."

"Is it life or death?" I ask shakily.

"One or the other." His voice is clipped and stern. He clenches his fist and taps his chest again. "It's happening already. I'm certain of it."

What's happening already?

Then his eyes become impenetrable behind the silver-rimmed glasses.

I want to stand under the waterfall, be washed in that innocent light, that sunstruck air. Isn't that what caves are for? All that darkness for one solitary moment coming into this fury of light?

"It couldn't have been a white owl, could it?" I ask. I had always wanted some mythology of my own.

"No white owls in Cuba. It would be beautiful, wouldn't it? To see such a thing."

"My mother saw a snowy owl in our backyard. She said it protected her. She was the only one who ever saw it though."

How many times had I seen her standing at the kitchen sink, looking out at the tree where the owl kept watch, the water from the faucet running over her raw and tender hands.

"I've seen a white owl," Michael says, blinking back tears. "Once I did."

Tomas turns sharply toward him, his eyes flashing. Something has snapped into place. Then he raises his hand in a secret benediction, or so it seems. "It's finished now," he says.

I look at Michael's hands, the glint of the ring he can't remove, and feel my startled breath gather in my throat.

"The owl doesn't only mean death. Your mother was lucky to have a white owl watching over her." He's touching his bracelet now, running his thumb over the beads. "I feel so much now the pull of earth," he says.

Then he looks at Michael. "You should love her. You should not wait to understand it."

God's Nail Clipping
Pinar del Rio

It's our last stop before Havana. Tomas is standing in the well of the van, holding onto the grab bar, as we make each turn. He looks, in some unaccountable way, restored. His voice is steady and smooth. "Soon we are going to see an artistic wonder. *El Mural de la Prehistoria*. One way or another you will not forget it. It is a painting on the side of *Dos Hermanas mogotes*. Truly, it is a sight for sore eyes. Or is it an eyesore?" He strikes his forehead with his palm. "I am confusing myself."

He goes on. "It was designed by a student of Diego Rivera. Some find it very inspiring. Some find it also very big. It is 400 feet high and 600 feet wide. You can have your picture taken in front of it."

"Go to the mountains," Maria had said. "Go to the *mogotes* in Pinar del Rio." She didn't mention *El Mural de la Prehistoria*. I thought of Mount Rushmore and our human desire to carve our faces everywhere we go.

We climb out of the van and walk across a wide field toward the mural. A giant limestone picture on the side of the *mogote* painted in swirls of color, outrageous against the lush green that frames it. Giant snails, dinosaurs, and cave men, hardly distinguishable from all the swirls of colors, shaped into a loopy nightmare. I look at the pamphlet the driver handed us as we stepped off the van:

"Mural de la Preshistoria is the creation of a group of local farmers which never before had kept in their hands a single painting brush. To do it, they hanged from parachute harnesses eight hours every day while they painted each part,

leaded by Leovigildo Gonzales, who was using a loudspeaker and binoculars. Finally it ended in 1964."

"Thank God," Michael says.

"All that color gone to waste."

"An offense to the eye."

"An offense to the heart."

"Better faded though," he says. "Imagine those colors against this landscape originally. It would have been an insult."

"We've left our cameras on the bus," I say, smiling at him. "How did we know to do that?"

He turns to me, but we stand there without touching.

I feel unexpectedly shy, caught in such a look of recognition I have to turn away.

"It's nice to feel the same thing about the mural," he says. "Do you have any idea what I'm trying to say?"

He's about to give himself over to me, but my heart is closing against him. Tomorrow all our chances will be gone.

"This mural is just crazy," I say. "I'm going back to the van."

His eyes are full of alarm. "I'll go with you." But neither of us can move. We just stand there in the middle of the field without speaking, looking at the waiting van, the mural behind us.

"Let me go with you," he says again.

I want to take his hand, kiss his face. "Okay," I say.

"Just a minute," Michael says. "I need to get something. Please don't go. I'll be right back."

"I won't go," I whisper, even as I turn from him and walk toward the van. Somewhere inside our driver is asleep behind the wheel, or finishing off a report on Tomas's deeply suspect lack of discipline.

A woman is waiting next to the door of the van, holding out a small brown plastic bowl with three shriveled mangoes. "Soap?" she says, pulling at her dress.

"*Nada,*" I say, turning over my hands. "I'm so sorry."

Then as I turn to go, she touches my arm. "*Por favor?*" she says, and carefully lifts a picture from the pocket of her dress. It's a picture of the woman herself, holding a baby girl about a year old. It's some kind of celebration, because you can see a banner in the background. The baby looks about to cry because something outside the picture has caught the mother's startled attention. It's not the kind of picture you'd carry around unless it was the only one you had.

I give her a dollar. She lowers her eyes and nods, then hands me one of the mangoes. "*Gracias*," I say, and step onto the van and take my seat. I put the mango in my purse and shut my eyes.

Nobody, it seems, has brought any soap.

A Juan Gris painting comes to mind. "Woman with a Basket." But this woman is no Juan Gris painting, with her narrow, drawn face, the dark circles under her pale brown eyes, the sharpness of her collarbone through her thin green dress. No one would ever paint her portrait or carve her features into stone. Her soft, inconsolable *por favor* is just a whisper on the wind.

Michael is coming up the steps, then slips into the seat beside me. "I wanted to get you something to redeem the mural." It's a little *Santería* doll. The blue and silver dress is unmistakable. "I know this isn't *Oshún*," he says. "They didn't have one for *Oshún*."

"How did you remember *Oshún*?" I ask. I feel the ache of tenderness in my throat.

He looks surprised. "I don't really know."

"Do you know who this is though?"

"Yes," he says. "It's the other one. The one you also loved."

"*Yemayá*." I rub the satin skirt between my fingers. Crystal and blue. Crystals in the wind, a blue mailbox, colors of the night. "Thank you," I say.

"There were some great postcards of the mural," he says.

"Better or worse than the original?"

"I could go back and get some and you could see for yourself."

"I think we're out of time," I say. "Thank goodness."

Michael looks startled. "No we aren't."

I've said it all wrong. "I only meant the postcards." But of course we are.

Then the doors of the van snap open and Tomas has conjured himself out of nowhere. He hops up the bottom step and the driver jerks around as Tomas says something low and quiet. The driver begins shouting at him and shaking his head violently. But Tomas just stands there. Then he turns around and points out the window.

"Los Jazmines!" he says sternly. Then more softly, "Los Jazmines, *por favor.*" The doors hisses shut as he takes his seat. The van pulls slowly out of the parking lot and edges toward the perilous road home.

"We are a little off schedule," he says, as he stands up. His voice is as strong and resonant as ever. "But I have persuaded our driver of the necessity for stopping at *Hotel Los Jazmines.* However, for a short time only. These roads are very dangerous at night. We must be back to the highway before dark."

Then he comes to me and leans over. "*Los Jazmines* is for you. The mural is only for tourists. You must see the *mogotes* at sunset from *Los Jazmines.* I know what it is like to see the mural when you are expecting splendor."

Hotel Los Jazmines is pink. A salmon pink three-story building with white wrought-iron balconies, overlooking the valley. We cross the empty patio to the railing and look out.

There they are, like a Japanese painting. In this light they are blue, as Maria had said, strange, greenish mounds that shimmer blue in the mists that hover in the valley in late afternoon and early morning.

"We are in time." Tomas is standing next to me on one side, Michael on the other. "This is what I wanted you to see."

The sun slips from the sky, a liquid, amber light shooting down through the mists, then the clouds just above the mountains turning gold, and then the *mogotes,* a violet darkening against that ravishing light. Tears slide down my face. In another moment it will be gone.

"It's so beautiful," I say, "to be gone so soon."

"You shouldn't be sad," Tomas says. "Now you must watch for the moon. It comes quickly here too. It will be a clear and beautiful rising before the clouds come again. You have heard it, no? The prayer of the Cuban biker? *Hope for a full moon and no rain.*"

I'd not thought of him all day, and now here he is, a grief fresh upon my heart. I wonder, was it a full moon when he was biking home to his own true love?

"Cuba is always a quartermoon," he says. "God's nail clipping. God's quarter smile. We wait for a fullness that never comes."

"My friend told me to see this. She comes from here."

"I know your friend," he says. "Your friend is Maria."

"Maria who works at the hotel?"

Tomas holds his braceletted wrist in his hand. "She is my daughter," he says softly. "*Babalu* is for Maria's child. For all children who . . . . " Tomas turns away before he can finish. "The light," he says abruptly. "It will go quickly now. We have to hurry before it does."

Is she safe? I want to ask, but he's halfway back to the van now, hurrying against something beyond the dark. I notice he's limping.

Out the window, the countryside rushes past in a flush of green, and to the left, the darkening fields below. In the soft, lavender light, the eucalyptus trees are floating in air. Soon the light drains out of the sky, and the palm trees rise darkly against the last of the sun. Then the moon rising over the tobacco fields, over the Royal Palms, over the *bohios*, shadows against the gathering dark, the thatched roofs silvery in the moonlight.

Rock of Ages
El Viejo y el Mar

I can see nothing beyond the pull of the headlights against the dark. We rock gently side to side, until the road straightens out, and I sink into a drowsy, dreamy stillness. Then it's as if we're flying down the highway, hurtling toward some appointed hour. He'd said *Maria.* He'd said, his daughter.

We tear down the road as night settles deeply upon us. Stars shower the sky. And there she is—Stella by Starlight.

"It's all going to have to come out eventually," the doctor had said. "You just can't sustain that amount of blood loss month after month." So I agreed to the surgery. And when the white fog lifted and I felt the scar like a hot wire burning across my belly and up my chest, I said *good,* and when the room tilted like a merry-go-round spun out of control, I said *good* again, and when the nausea hit and I thought the retching would split me open, I said *good good good.*

"Do you have children?" I ask Michael.

"We. . . . No. No children."

I take his hand and warm it between my palms. The dark inside that van has turned everything safe between us and so I ask, "How long ago has it been?"

Michael leans back, turns away. "I don't know," he says. "It seems like a long time. It seems like yesterday."

He's rubbing his thumb across my hand. "You can tell me if you want."

"I didn't think I would ever lose her. Then one day she was gone. Grief holds you to the one who is lost." In the dark I can feel him turning his ring. "Two years. Almost two years."

I think of the accumulation of sorrows in my life, and Michael's sorrow still so sharp and new. I want to tell him about Stella by Starlight. Someday I would, if I still knew him then. Tomorrow and all the leave-taking wash over me.

"How did you lose her?"

"Sophie. . . . " he starts to say. He leans forward, his face in his hands. "Physician, heal thyself." Even in the dark I know there are tears down his face.

"You don't have to talk about it."

But he says, "I want you to see her." Sophie with the short auburn hair that turned gold in the sun, and green eyes and lovely eyelashes and cheekbones, and pale, freckled, satiny skin. When he knew finally that she was never coming back, he rushed from the hospital, he couldn't go home, to the place where the car had clipped her as she ran along the gravel shoulder of the country road, where he stood in the bitter rain trying to call her back. "I wanted to tell her goodbye."

She had died instantly, he knew that, though he had sat in that orange plastic chair outside the ER holding her running shoe for over an hour while they did futile, merciless things to her.

They had never been religious. But then she was gone, and he knew she had to be some place, if only he could find it. He wanted to put up a cross or something, though Sophie would not have abided that. So he just stood there in the rain dripping off the pine needles of the tree, unable to move. Then he heard it, that dark, hollow sound, that deep and mournful cry, *hoo-hoo, hoo-hoo,* as an owl rose unbelievably white against the flat, gray sky. A white owl, an Arctic owl! Such an unearthly spread of wings, he had never seen such a thing. And his heart tightened, because he knew she was saying goodbye to him. He didn't believe in such things. But there it was.

When he came back to the house at last, he saw her coffee cup, the pink lipstick on the rim, a pink kiss, the coffee cold and oily and catching the light as the sun came through the kitchen window. The fog and mist and rain long gone, the rest of the day stretching out ahead, sunlit and cruel, and before him an endless number of such days.

He played that last morning in his mind like a prayer. Every detail a splinter of the cross—the hair in her brush on the counter, her slippers scattered on the floor, the juice glass half empty in the kitchen sink, her keys a jumble in the center of the table. She had wakened him in the night with her mouth slow and dreamlike, and in the morning when he was only beginning to wake, he reached for her, but she was already gone. He would have said, "Did we make love in the night or did I dream it?" And she would have smiled and said, "As if you had to ask."

Eventually, he said it was a taste in his mouth. He ran his tongue over his teeth and couldn't remember when he'd last brushed them. So he went into the bathroom but couldn't remember which toothbrush was his, and which was hers, and what was that funny taste? Which meal had he eaten or not eaten, to leave such a taste in his mouth?

He stared at the toothbrush, held it up to the light. The pale blue toothbrush Sophie had bought just last week, or the week before. He spread a fat little white strip of toothpaste over the bristles. He stared at the other toothbrush, the green one. Or was the blue one hers? He put the blue toothbrush back next to the green one in the I HEART YOU cup holder, put it in the cabinet and shut the cabinet door. He stood there for a long time looking at a face he could no longer recognize. He had come unmoored.

We can see the lights of the hotel in the distance as we near the Marina. I think of last night's sunset, the sea bronze and golden with the falling light, then night dropping like a curtain. And the crush of waves against the seawall, the stairs to safety, my life handed back.

Tomas is sitting so still I wonder if he's all right. He's just holding on, or so it seems. He'll be home soon now, can put that magic pill under his tongue, lean back into safety at last. How did he ever lead all those tours into the caves? How had he willed his acquiescence?

"He'll be all right," Michael says. "He's pretty strong. He just needs that pill."

There is a sweet, sad shyness between us now. I don't want to say goodbye. I'm holding the plum of desire under my tongue without speaking. And there it is—in the drowsy shadows of some late Cuban afternoon, the ebb and flow of light across the white sheets, the glittering earth beneath.

Michael says, "I don't want this to be over."

I turn to say *oh yes, that's it exactly*, when the van makes the turn into the compound and the lights come on like a slap across the face. Tomas gets up. His shirt clings to his back. He kneels beside me and touches my shoulder.

He leans closer and says something so softly the words vanish into air. "Maria," he says. "You should help her. Do it if you can."

His eyes are dark points.

I want to call after him, *the manuscript is gone!* But he's making his way to the back of the van, as if he's never been beside me at all. Everything is spinning and I'm inside the dark turning place. I put my hand where the locket should be and pull it away. I'd forgotten about the beads.

That terrible man had grabbed Maria so hard his hand was already a purple flowering on her arm. Such dark and ancient violence, all of it—the phone call, our shadows rising against the light, the missing manuscript, Judith's dark eyes in the torchlight, the Judas kiss.

I take Michael's hand and hold it to my face. The air shimmers over my skin.

"What did he say?"

I shake my head. "It's about Maria."

We're coming to a stop at the gate into the compound. Tomas comes quickly forward but doesn't turn around, he does not say goodbye, and when the doors open, he just hops off the van and dashes into the headlights. Then I see her by the side of the road as if she's waiting for him. Her eyes are a blood moon in the headlights. Her hair falls carelessly against her face.

The gate lifts and we pass under it. The security officer inside the booth is following him with his eyes. Tomas and Judith have vanished into the darkness.

"I wonder if he's really sick," I say. My voice is shaking.

"What do you mean?" Michael turns around to look behind.

"He isn't limping now."

"What are you thinking?"

"He said he was a trickster. St. Lazarus. *Babalú.*"

Babalú, Babalú. A hand brushes my neck. "He wants me to do something that's dangerous, I think." I take my beads off and slip them into my pocket. "Maybe he planned it all along."

Michael looks shaken. "Planned what?"

"I don't know. Everything. His intimacy. His illness. You know, 'In Cuba, believe half of what you see and none of what you hear.'"

"Or the other way around. You hear nothing but you can see half of it, anyway." He takes my hand.

"Don't let go," I say without knowing it.

I shut my eyes and see the lighthouse at *El Morro* laying an uncertain path across those dark shifting waters, the waves exploding against treacherous rocks, Maria's face, her dark hair. A woman floating on the water. "I'm probably just being melodramatic," I say. An old hymn comes to mind.

Rock of Ages, cleft for me,
Let me hide myself in thee.

Starry Night
Old Havana

I'm standing on the rooftop of *Hotel Ambos Mundos,* watching the moon rise over Havana Bay, flush and weighted with desire. The cobblestone streets glisten in the lamplight. Everything has taken on a muted, dusky glow. The air feels warm and close, a presentiment of the rains to come. Tomorrow we are going home.

There had been no sign of Judith, who has vanished as surely as Maria, into that tangled, perilous night. I think of those pages taken from my safe, and if her story would ever be told.

The music has turned plaintive and soft, as the party draws to a close. Maxine left long ago. So many Cubans still out—on go-carts, bicycles, pedicabs, or walking the Malecon, waves splashing over the seawall.

The beacon of light from the lighthouse at *El Morro* Castle is flashing across the water. *El Cristo* is blessing the harbor, lit white against the dark. I think of boat captains making their way in the storm toward the lighthouse, and seeing *El Cristo* for the first time, rising miraculously out of the fog. I have fallen in love with this place and now I must leave it.

I look out at *La Cabaña,* spread imperiously between *El Morro* and *El Cristo* and wonder what Che believed. Maybe he had only believed in himself. And revolution. Still, did he look at *El Cristo* as he ordered the executions?

On those dark October days years ago, what was it like from here, with the lighthouse dark and missiles aimed every which way?

No chain drawn across the harbor to tuck the city safely into night. No cannons at nine to announce that all is well. And *El Cristo* in the dark, blessing those unguarded waters. Missiles from America would have no trouble finding their way.

Michael is standing against the railing, talking to someone I don't know. I like looking at him from across the room, and how he's looking back.

"They're out of water," he says as he comes over. "I didn't think you wanted anything else."

"I just realized I've spent the whole day with you."

We stand there leaning against the railing.

"You're not wearing your watch." There's a thick white band around his wrist I hadn't noticed before.

"I lost it in the caves," he says, rubbing his wrist.

"How does it feel to lose time like that?" I'm being clever and stupid.

"I don't know," he says, blinking back tears. "I really don't know."

I put my hand to my throat and feel my *Santería* beads. "She gave it to you, didn't she."

"Yes," he says, and I take his hand and bring it to my face.

"Yesterday I lost my mother's locket in the ocean." I can't look at him. "I'm sorry I said that about losing time."

"She gave me other things, and I kept everything she had." He looks out. "It's all so beautiful, isn't it."

"It's over sixty feet high," I say, blundering again, as I try to find something to hold onto. *"El Cristo de Casablanca.* Sixty-six feet of Italian marble."

Behind us the music has reached the finale, as the singer holds a pure, crystalline note that goes on and on. Then he brings it to an astonishingly clear, clean stop. The applause is riotous—clapping, whistles, stamping feet.

I turn around and look out at the harbor again. "I've never heard anything like it."

"He should be famous with a voice like that," Michael says.

"Maybe he is. But then what's he doing up here?" I think of Winston, and the dancers at *Gran Teatro*, of Tani and her daughter, and Antonio and Teresa, and all unrequited dreams.

"Do you want to leave?" he says.

"Can we stay a little longer? I can't get enough of looking out. Tomorrow I'll be gone."

"I was watching you across the room. You looked so sad. Is that what you were thinking?"

"I was wondering about *El Cristo* and the lighthouse. If they went dark in the Missile Crisis." We stand there, watching the lights on the water.

"Van Gogh's *Starry Night*. Not missiles."

"Oh, that's so much better." And then a memory comes, rounded and whole and full of light. Something given back. That day in Old Havana had conjured it. Vanilla and almond and cinnamon and guava. But it was the pies I remembered. The cherry pies. Maybe it was too poignant then—or buried in the chaos that came after. Now here it was, the taste of grief unspoken. I had grieved my mother in ways so subterranean I had mirrored my father's haunted, stoic ways, silent to the end. Now here she was. My mother still.

The Last Supper
St. Louis 1962

I smelled it the minute I walked into the house. "Mommy! You're making dinner." She was boiling water for macaroni and cheese.

She was smiling at me. "Favorite dinner for favorite child."

"Only child," I always said.

"One and only," she always said.

Something was in the oven. I cracked open the door and saw two cherry pies bubbling under the oven light.

"I didn't know you could bake pies."

"Today seemed like a good day to find out. You know, with everything that's going on."

"It looks like you've been cooking all day." I smiled at her cautiously.

"I tried out some things that didn't work," she said, seeing me look over the kitchen. It looked like she had used every pot and pan in the house.

"Don't I look beautiful? she laughed. There were streaks of flour down her shirt, flour, maybe butter, on her pants, as if she'd wiped her hands on them, a puff of flour on the top of her bare foot.

"Tell me all about your day," she said. She was watching me carefully. She handed me a glass of milk and some graham crackers. She thought all children needed graham crackers dipped in milk after school, and one chocolate kiss to tide you over until dinner. Whatever else was lacking in our kitchen, at least there was this.

The milk was warm. I imagined it sat on the counter most of the day. "They probably told you at school," she said.

She wiped her hands on her shirttail and sat down across from me, resting her chin on her hands.

"They played it over the loudspeaker at lunch. Our teachers talked about it all day."

"I don't want you worrying about it, Annie Laurie. Bombs and things always sound scary, but they're not really. Lots of things are scarier than that. Anyway, it's just a stupid thing that's happened, and then we'll all get back to normal." She sighed a long, weary sigh, as if she were impatient with such posturings. "Anyway, Khrushchev looks like a pig, with those ugly little pig eyes. That's why I made macaroni and cheese. For Daddy too. You know he'll be worrying about everything. Besides, do you know how far away Cuba is? We're tucked in safe, right here in the exact middle of the country."

With my mother sitting across from me at the kitchen table, two pies in the oven, steamy smells rising off the stove, the leaves coming down in the late afternoon sun, I had never felt safer in my life.

I went into the living room to watch for my father. I breathed in the kitchen smells and laughed to myself. My mother always knew things other people didn't. I stood at the window, waiting to see my father's face, the way it would change when he saw the dining room. Then he was coming in the door, holding his coat over his arm. He turned and reached to put it on the coat rack as he always did. But tonight he missed his reach and the coat fell to the floor.

He just stood in the entryway and stared into the dining room. Candles flickered over the table, casting a watery light against the wall. Ella Fitzgerald was singing "My Funny Valentine" on the phonograph.

I always hoped that was how my father saw my mother. He'd keep his funny valentine forever.

"Hi, Daddy. Mommy made us a great dinner."

"I smelled it all the way up the walk."

"No you didn't."

"Yes I did." He was grinning at me in the way I loved, but under the hall light I could tell his eyes weren't smiling. We'd both learned, like forest animals, to be wary of anything new in the air. We raised our heads and sniffed the air for fire.

I gave him a big hug, took his coat and put it on the coat rack. He was in the kitchen now with Eugenie. He had his arms around her. She'd buried her head against his chest. He kissed the top of her head while she stood there, holding on. I could only wait in the shadow of the hallway and whisper those words along with Ella. Stay, funny Mommy, stay.

We sat in the dining room and ate by candlelight, the night coming through the uncurtained windows, the candlelight flickering across the white silky tablecloth, the good silver, the linen napkins drawn up into elegant roses on our plates.

It was the best dinner my mother ever made. She seemed to have designed the meal with color in mind. We sat and ate mounds of macaroni and cheese, and plates of green beans with bacon and pimiento, and bowls of red and green and purple vegetables I had never seen before. Our housekeepers generally stuck to peas and corn and an occasional squash.

We ate in silence, astonished at what my mother had wrought. How had she made those pies? She had never baked a pie in her life. I knew from the look of the kitchen it had taken her all day. And yet she'd made a golden lattice over the top, and little waves of golden crust lapping at the edges. And cherries in juice so hot and tart and sweet the taste kept changing inside your mouth.

"Eugenie, this is wonderful. I've never had pie like this in my life. This is a miracle."

"Thanks," my mother said, and smiled cagily at him, as if she had some secret under her tongue too delicious to swallow. "I can still surprise you, you know."

My father laughed. "You surprise me all the time." Could it be that everything really was all right? My heart rushed to believe it.

Then my mother brought out the vanilla ice cream, scooped a creamy white mound on each of our plates, and set the ice cream in the center of the table. "For eating all you want. I didn't want the ice cream to change the cherry taste."

I watched my father look at her as she worked. There was such sadness and longing and desire and hopefulness in his eyes. Even then, just on the edge of everything, I could read that look, as I tried to figure out how men and women were together, how my mother and my father were together. Achingly sweet, and then so tart it made your mouth tingle so that you knew it would never be sweet again, and then there—as sweet and lovely as before. Our lives were always changing like that, like the cherry pie in my mouth the night we waited for the missiles.

There was no radio, no television, no news bulletins that night, just the sound of our contentment and Ella Fitzgerald on the phonograph. Nobody mentioned Khrushchev or Castro or Kennedy or missile sites or the Soviet ships plowing through those waters toward Cuba, their missiles aimed at the sky. We had no way of knowing as we sat long into the evening that our lives would go on, that somebody would eventually blink, and pull us back from annihilation, that it was no Last Supper after all.

In the night I dreamed of war and air raids and missiles and bombs. I crept into my mother's room. She had taken over the guest room at the beginning of that last summer. She said that on this side of the house, the moon lay a path across her bed while she slept. I had never seen this, even the nights I crawled into bed with her, but she said it only happens when you're really sleeping.

"Mommy?" I touched her shoulder. Her face was half-buried in the pillow. "Mommy? Can you wake up? I had a bad dream."

She opened the covers for me in her sleep and I slid in beside her and we curled up like spoons. She was warm, and I lay like that for a long time, feeling her breath against my hair.

After a while she said, "Nobody should be alone when they're afraid. I'm awake now, Sweetie, you can tell me your dream."

So I told her how I'd been watching out my window for the war everybody at school said was coming. I was listening for a warning sound—a low flying bomber, the wail of a siren, a warning cry from somewhere in the dark.

Then I saw the missiles—a constellation of red and golden light streaking down out of the sky. I told her I had covered my head, because I knew for certain I would die.

"But if you'd kept your eyes open, Sweetie, you'd see what they really were. They were your gift from the universe. Your very own sign." She had wrapped us in such magic, we lay like that all night while Castro's missiles turned into falling stars. There wasn't anything in the world that could frighten me now.

That was in October. By the end of April, my mother's things had been packed into boxes and taken to the basement. By the end of May, that room where we had slept like spoons, was Mrs. Beswick's. My mother had been right. Missiles weren't anything to be afraid of.

The Shattering
El Viejo y el Mar

The three musicians and the singer are sweating hard, as they begin to pack up. Half a dozen people are finishing the last of their *mojitos*, mint leaves wilting at the bottom of the glass.

"I want to show you something," Michael says. "We can walk there, if you want."

"Okay," I say.

We take the long elevator ride from the rooftop, passing the fifth floor and Room 511 without looking back. Goodbye Ernesto, I say, as we float to the lobby.

"Where are we going?" I ask as we turn onto *Calle Obispo*. I don't want to stop holding his hand.

"You told me you'd only seen the cathedral by day. You said it frightened you."

"It was so dark inside," I say, as the moon hovers in the violet sky. *Catedral San Cristóbal de la Habana*. Water turned to stone. Those dark wooden doors heavy with time, the altar to lost children, the one-eyed woman outside the cathedral with her glass of water and Tarot cards.

"Wouldn't it be ghastly at night?" It would be Ravenscrag, I think but do not say.

"I promise you it won't be." So we walk down streets lit by lamplight, washing everything in a pink and amber glow. There is no *Bodeguita* man here.

We enter the plaza and drift toward *El Patio Restaurant* where we take a table at the edge of the square. The moon is tremulous and white against the midnight blue of the sky, the cathedral shimmery now. The lanterns in the cathedral bell towers give an ambient light, as do the lanterns strung around the square, lighting the stained glass over the humblest doorway. By day the sun filters through that arc and casts silken pools across tiled floors. By night it's a fairy lamp redolent in color.

The heavy old boughs of the world lift for a moment. The heavy dark doors have opened and now it's a castle of faith and light.

"It's not haunted anymore, is it."

Michael goes to speak then stops, because an old man with a cane and eyes as opaque as the moon, crosses in front of us, dragging a long plastic sack, his shadow floating over the cobblestones. He stops to speak.

"Oh," I say, and reach for my dollars.

Michael touches my arm. "He'll get in trouble."

The guard growls something at him and waves his stick. The old man just stands there. The guard yells at him and jabs him in the back. He loses his balance and drops to his knees.

Michael rushes to help him, then turns to say something to the guard, but he's already squared himself, his hands on his hips, his gun a dark shape in the lamplight.

"Let's get out of here," Michael says, taking my hand.

"That poor man."

"Homelessness is forbidden in Cuba," he says darkly. "So is hunger." He pulls me close as we walk down Obispo Street under a bower of lamplight.

"It feels like we've run out of time," I say, looking at the clouds rushing across the sky.

"I think we have lots of time." We cross the square and make our way into the street.

Then I stop and say what is deepest in my heart. "I'm afraid I won't ever see you again."

"Why do you say that?"

"It's so beautiful here. What would I be to you in ordinary life?"

"Oh," he says, his voice dropping almost to a whisper. "You wouldn't change." Then he says, "I haven't made love to anyone in so long."

"I haven't either," I say, and try to remember if it's true.

"I don't know what's left of me," Michael says, "but I want to love you like that."

"I know," I say, fleeing into that shyness between us, now that we have put it into words. We slow our walk and then stop altogether. I wrap my arms around my waist.

"I wanted to say it, to ask you," he says. "Not just stumble into it. Am I talking too much?"

"I don't think so. Maybe."

He's circling his ring round and round. He looks down and stops. "I'm afraid to be lost again."

"The shattering."

"Yes. The shattering."

The Third Blessing
El Viejo y el Mar

The breeze washes us over in earthly delight. We can hear the sea curl against the shore and slide away. The candle by the bed casts a soft, rippling light, the scent of jasmine in the air. We are in another country.

We are here to love each other, but we're taking our time. He doesn't know that's exactly what I need. His hands are asking permission and taking it at the same time, as though he's following a memory he has never had. He's following it over my face and down my throat, then he's kissing that hollow place where the locket was, and I know exactly where he's going, but there is no hurry, and then he slips down and down again, his mouth so soft and fine, and everything begins again only deeper now, and then I can feel where he is and where he has been, until finally he is everywhere.

I'm in a place I have never been. Oh the surprise of it! The candle pulses against the wall, then flares up, and there it is, the owl perched on the ledge of the cave against the torchlight, terrible and still. But then in a rush of breath, the owl hurtles down and out of the cave, and I gasp with the sweet ache of it, and in a flash of spreading warmth, the owl ascends into the night. It's the language of owls, the golden eye that holds everything in a dark and final knowing. Then the night settles easily over us, as we breathe it in and turn it over on the tongue, before we fall asleep.

In my dream, I'm standing on the rooftop of *Ambos Mundos* and watching *El Cristo* lighting the dark waters of Havana Bay, one hand over his heart, the other hand outstretched. I look down and there is the old lamplighter, making his way over *Calle Obispo*. He waves to me and shouts in a sonorous voice that rings out over Old Havana, "Nine o'clock and all is well!" Then in a rush, I know something terrible is about to happen, and I put my arm out to stop it. But I can't, because *El Cristo* is tilting forward off the pedestal, then a terrible falling that is the end of everything.

"Christ!" I say, bolting up.

Michael touches my face and draws me back. "What is it? What's happened?"

"The water was so dark. I'm afraid of that water, and the rocks. I see death in it." My heart begins to close up against him, and the life that had beckoned me an hour ago. Then I tell him my dream, and it's as if he had seen it too.

"That's a terrible thing to see."

I think of all those who have been broken on the craggy shores of the world. *La Cabaña, El Morro, Vallegrande, Ravenscrag.* My own Eugenie. So we are all crucified one way or the other.

Michael sits up and in the candlelight he looks like something is breaking loose in him. "You are saving me," he says softly.

I touch his back, cool now in the air off the ocean.

"I thought my heart was a cavern." He shakes his head, and turns back to me. *"La petite mort.* The little death."

I touch the hollow where my locket had been. My *Santeria* beads are lying in the bed. "Death is death," I say.

I'm shivering because now I'm breaking open too.

"This kind of death calls us to life."

"Isn't it strange to die into life like that?"

"I read once that joy is a taste before it's anything else," Michael says. "Before the heart or mind can gather it up."

I think of the soft air and violet sky, the taste of coconut ice cream, the sweet surprise of limes and plums and strawberries and cherries, tart and sweet. And all pleasures of the hand and mouth and tongue.

"The *babaláwo* said there would be three blessings." And I tell him about the Easter chick my father gave me when my mother died, and my mother's cherry pies the night of the missiles. My father and mother come back to me.

"What was the 'third blessing?'" he asks.

"You. You are the third blessing."

Then he says, "Can we make love again?"

"Now?" I say.

"Right now."

"Love me in the dream then. Make love to me in the dream where *El Cristo* is blessing the harbor."

"Like this?"

"Yes."

"And this?"

"Yes, this, and this also."

"Do you feel it? Do you feel what's happening to us?"

"I'm afraid," I say. "Could you love me? But what if you can't?"

Then he says, "But what if I can?"

We lie there for a long time, until we fall asleep again, as the breeze brushes over us, like the fingertips of someone you love touching you lightly.

Stella by Starlight
El Viejo y el Mar

A muffled knock rises from deep inside the dream. My mother's castle. And my mother herself, knocking on the heavy wooden door, her knuckles raw with knocking, the candle tilting and dripping down her wrist. *It's me! it's me! help me please!*

I touch Michael's face. "Someone's knocking," I say from inside the dream. Then I jolt awake. "Is someone knocking?"

"I think so," he says, and draws me to him. "Who'd be knocking so late?"

My stomach is a knot tucked under my heart. "CDR, or the police or, internal security?"

"Or room service."

I want to laugh.

"It's all right. Whatever it is."

"I thought I was dreaming. You almost can't hear it." But the knocking keeps on, a muffled whisper.

"It doesn't sound official, does it," he says.

"No. It's like a question."

"There it is again."

"I know who it might be," I say, shaking off the dream. "Maria." I pull on my robe and go to the door. I look through the peephole. All but one of the hall lights are out. Still, I can see someone. Her head is covered in a shawl. She moves aside and a taller figure in a hood knocks more urgently now. "Not Maria."

Michael leans over and looks for a long minute. Then he touches my hand and whispers, "*La petite mort.*"

"No," I say. "*La grand mort.*"

"That's pretty funny," he whispers, and we start to laugh.

"I wonder if we've been filmed."

I don't remember if we were quiet or loud.

Some final acknowledgment is settling upon us. The candlelight murmurs against the wall. We're safe in the shadows and this little joke between us.

"It's something terrible though, isn't it?"

"I'll get dressed," Michael says, pulling on his pants and T-shirt. Then he opens the door against the safety chain. "Yes?"

I look again. The man has pulled off his rain jacket hood, and there are the dark eyes, the ponytail. All this time and now here he is. The *Bodeguita* man.

The woman slips off her shawl. Her hair is wet. That sharp chin, the eyes, the tilt of her head. "You know who I am," Judith says. "This is my son. Let us in."

We stand there, wondering if we could manage to shut the door again.

But her son shoulders the door until the safety chain snaps and falls. And then they're standing inside the doorway, searching the room with their eyes. The cigarette smell has come in with him.

"Where is she?" His eyes are hard and unblinking.

"What do you mean?"

"You know who," Judith barks. "We saw how you were talking at the party. We know what you are doing. We have followed her here."

The *Bodeguita* man goes into the bathroom, then comes out and stands in the center of the room with his hands on his hips. I see the bulge under his jacket.

Judith is carrying a canvas bag, which she sets on the floor. She yanks open the closet doors, opens the drapes and steps onto the balcony. We can hear the rain pattering against the deck furniture.

Michael has taken a step to block him but changes his mind and stands there with his fists balled into his pockets. The *Bodeguita* man moves toward him. "Don't even try it."

Michael is trembling from the effort of control.

"You know where she is," Judith taunts.

"Who are you *talking* about?" I almost scream. I want to hit her.

Judith blinks. For a moment she can't think of anything to say. Then her head jerks.

"You really don't know, then, do you. Do you know *anything*?" Her face is twisted with fury.

"Medusa," I murmur, as a shiver cuts through me.

"What did you say?" She reaches to grab my robe.

"We're wasting our time, Ma," her son says, and takes her arm. "Come on. We'll find her."

"His name is *Raul*. He could have you *arrested*." They leave the door open, but as they go, Judith turns around and hisses, "I almost liked you." And then they're gone.

Michael closes the door, locks it, and shuts the drapes.

"Come here," he says, and pulls me into him.

I start to cry. "I want to be where we were before the knocking."

"You're still shaking." He rubs my shoulders and my arms, kisses the back of my neck. "I wish I could make us some tea. Or something. Or we could go down to the bar for a drink."

"No! I'm afraid to leave the room."

"We'll just stay here then. Whatever it was, it's over now."

"I'm afraid for Maria. She's the one they wanted." I've told Michael everything.

They've left the canvas bag behind.

"Should we look?"

"Why not?"

"I don't want it here," I say. "There could be weapons."

"It looks military, doesn't it."

"Shit. Maybe they'll come back for it."

"We'd better look," Michael says. "We can be careful. Can you get the flashlight?" He slowly unbuckles the strap and lifts the flap. Michael gently pulls the bag open while I shine the flashlight inside. Then he sits back on his heels and shakes his head. "Unbelievable."

"What is it?"

"Baby things. I don't know. Diapers, a bottle, blankets I think."

"Why don't you take everything out of the safe and give it to me."

Michael takes my money belt and my passport and tucks it under his shirt." Nobody's going to take this."

Later when the knocking returns, I tuck my head against his shoulder. He pulls me tight. "If we're quiet maybe they'll think we've gone."

But the knocking continues gently, then insistently.

A familiar voice through the door. "May we come in please?"

"Tomas?" I say, edging open the door.

He steps inside, followed by a boy in a baseball cap and poncho. He sets down the bag he's been carrying, pulls the door in after him, and turns the lock. In the rush of candlelight I see his eyes shift from me to Michael to the rumpled bed. "I am interrupting," he says without apology or surprise. The boy dissolves into the shadows.

"What are you doing here?" I ask. There is only sorrow in his eyes. My heart flutters against my chest, a rush of heat over my face.

"So much is happening now. We have been waiting in the shadows for them to leave. They have followed us here. We are in need of your help."

His face is a torment.

"Where is Maria?" A nightmare passes through me, and then as before, the waves against the rocks, the beacon from the lighthouse sweeping over a woman in the water. "She's gone, isn't she."

The boy steps out of the shadows into the flickering candlelight. He takes off his cap. There is the short-cropped hair, the silver streak, her beautiful face streaked with tears or rain, her strong, cool hands, her voice low and soft in the dark, the scent of jasmine floating through the hot, fetid air.

"Help me please," she says to Tomas, who lifts the poncho up over her shoulders, and Maria steps into the light. She shifts the baby against her chest and tucks that baby's head under her chin, her hand a little starfish against her neck.

"We are in a Cuban conundrum," Tomas says as he tries to smile wryly. But it breaks apart and he reaches for the chair. His voice is muffled with grief. "As I have said. We are in great need of you."

"Is it Pilar then?" I say, feeling the dread of the answer.

"*Mariquita*," he says softly now. "My little ladybug. That's what I used to call her. When Pilar was little, she loved that name." He stops for a minute to gather himself. "Then one day she said it wasn't dignified enough, but I could say it anyway."

My throat closes against her name, as my heart settles into a familiar lodestone of grief.

"No more pain. No more worry," Tomas says, as he takes that baby foot in his hand. "She's lost her bootie."

I see Pilar so clearly now. Her Mickey Mouse watch has told her when to cut the bonds of earth, and then her sharp and tender wings lift her into air. Her eyes, caught by moonlight, shimmer now, seeing everything.

Maria is silent as tears run down her face. She sits down on the bed and lays the sleeping baby against the pillows. She wears tiny golden hoops in her ears, her thumb in her mouth, her free hand splayed in sleep.

"This is Mia Luna. She is Pilar's child."

Tomas sits on the edge of the bed and touches her face. They are a nativity of sorrow.

"She's the one they wanted," he says bitterly.

"Why would they want a baby?"

"Only this baby. Judith wants her more than anything."

Of course. The baby granddaughter. Her son's child. For her daughter who died.

"But how can that terrible man be her father?" *I can do anything I want to you,* he'd said in a hot breath against my neck.

Tomas's face is full of grief and rage. "He violated her and then she didn't know what to do. If Maria hadn't stopped me, I would have killed him. She said we would save this child another way."

"They forgot this bag of baby things," I say, pointing to the canvas bag.

"They think they can have her for good now," Tomas says. "They think you are helping them."

"Is maybe my book still here?" Maria asks but sees my tears welling up. "They took it, didn't they."

I look over at the open closet and the empty safe. "I should have hidden it better." It's too late for everything. Everything is too late.

"And where exactly would you have hidden it better?"

"I don't know. I didn't know they could open it."

"How could you have known? I asked you to keep it here."

"Did you tell her what was in it?" Tomas says sharply, and waves his hand.

"Some of it. That my friends were in prison also and that terrible things were done to them. And some names of who did it."

A trembling runs through me, for there is Eugenie in that dark room with the owl watching over her. Her prison also.

Tomas breathes deeply. "*The disappeared.* She wrote it so they wouldn't be forgotten. Now the worst person to have it. He has stalked them. He has followed them everywhere." He looks to the closet. "Couldn't you have kept it safe?"

Maria looks at Tomas sharply, then puts the bootie back on the baby's foot. "This child is my story. The other is no matter. I know it by heart and someday I can write it again. The names will take care of themselves."

Tomas shakes his head. "I am so sorry. I didn't mean to offend. My anger has come untethered."

Michael takes my hand and pulls me toward the bed. I want to sit on the bed too, but I'm shy of it. I can only stand there, looking down.

"How old is she?" I ask, not knowing what else to say.

"Such a big girl now. Almost six months."

I lean over to touch her, then pull my hand away.

"It's all right," Maria says. "Sit down so I can give her to you."

"Oh no, I couldn't."

Michael touches her head. "You should hold her."

She's a warm weight in my arms, then no weight at all, curled against my chest. I feel the pull of tears as I breathe in her powdery baby smell.

"Mia Luna," I say. Stella by Starlight. Little Sprite.

"You should see how you look holding her," Maria says.

I kiss the top of her head. She stirs in my arms, lets out a little whimper, sighs, and goes back to her thumb.

I'm standing, now, rocking her back and forth in that way people do without being taught. Maria's face is luminous in the candlelight. The curtains pulse through a tender light.

"Pilar called you the American in love with Hemingway. Daughter of *Yemayá*." Then Maria hands me a thin bracelet of yellow and white beads. "And *Oshún* also. A present from Pilar. She has wanted you to be her godmother. A baby can't have too many mothers, can they."

I shut my eyes and gentle her head against my face.

"See how you love her?" Maria says.

I lay her back in the covers, and sit down. "She looks like Pilar already."

Tomas's eyes have turned strange and dark. "She was so sick." Then his shoulders sag, and he puts his head in his hands. His shirt looks wet. "Ay," he says, wiping his eyes. In the half-light, his face is gray.

Michael reaches for him. "It's only my syncopation. It's nothing."

Tomas closes his eyes as Michael kneels down beside him, and takes his wrist.

"Just a moment to catch up with myself. My heart is having a mind of its own again."

Michael looks to time it, surprised again that his watch is gone. "It's steady, Tomas. Just fast. No missing beats."

"Where would I go to find them anyway?" He smiles wearily. "There is no time that cannot hold a little joking."

He looks so beaten, sitting there. His beautiful Italian shoes are ruined now, the legs of his pants, wet and dark.

"Is there any tightness? Any pain?" Michael asks.

"My heart is broken," he says, completely without irony. "Why would I not have pain?" Then he looks at Maria and nods. *Go ahead. Tell them.* And then she does.

"I don't know how to ask politely," she says. "But we are desperate. I am only just barely holding myself from going into pieces." She looks at Michael. "You and your friends. They have a boat from Canada. I heard you say it at the party. Is there any way to be on it also?"

"Oh," Michael says. He just stands there looking at her. "I don't know why not. They're here. My friends are here at the hotel."

I look at Michael standing in his T-shirt and pants, his bare feet, his golden arms, the white band on his wrist where his watch had been.

The conversation is quicker than you could imagine, given all the sudden complications. "They're all right to do this," Michael says as he hangs up the phone. "We've been going back and forth from the hotel to the Marina pretty much all week, anyway."

"She sleeps wonderfully. All night," Maria says. "You couldn't wake her if you tried. Such a good baby. Such a good little girl. She loves every face she sees."

We watch her eyelids quivering in her dream. What does a baby dream? The sound of her mother's voice? The scent of her skin, the rhythm of her heartbeat, the face she seeks first and always?

I smooth my hand over her baby skin. One foot is curled under her nightgown, the other bootie lost again, her hair damp with sleep, her thumb in her mouth, her dark eyelashes brushing her cheeks. I know he wants to pick her up and disappear with Maria into the night. But then he collects himself.

"The weather is going to be nothing now. It is passing already."

"Pilar. . . ?" I try to say.

"It's good to have loved her," Maria says. "And Mia Luna? She is precious to the universe, not only to us."

Tomas looks at me closely, "*Yemayá* takes care of *Oshún's* children. So you see we all have many mothers and fathers. Yeats is our father too, you know." And he recites in a faltering voice,

> "'Come away,
> O Human child,
> To the waters and the wild
> With a faery, hand in hand,
> For the world's more full of weeping than you
> can understand.'"

We are all thinking of the waters that will carry this child to safety and for a moment, we fall silent. Then the sound of the phone, shattering the air. A lightning bolt into the heart.

Michael looks to the peephole, then turns around, shaking his head. "No one's there," he whispers, as the phone rings on. The baby doesn't stir when Maria picks her up and holds her close.

"It's midnight," I say. "Who would call at midnight?"

"Don't answer it," Michael says.

"Maybe I should," I say. "They must know we're still here."

So Michael reaches for the phone, but the line has gone dead.

"You should go. . . as soon as you can." Tomas looks to the door but can only stand there trembling. He is breaking apart. Maria goes toward him, but he puts out his hand and shakes his head. "I can't leave you, if you even look at me." She turns from him and shuts her eyes.

Then he straightens his shoulders and raises his head. He takes a breath that catches in his throat, then tries again. His voice is hushed and raw. "It will take a little longer with this weather. But you'll be in the Keys . . . . Wear the poncho, Michael, please."

Michael looks startled to still be holding the phone. And startled to be the one to carry her. "Of course. I'll tuck her under the poncho. She'll be safe and warm."

But his eyes are busy thinking. Then he says, "Juliette can have her arm around Maria, and Remy and Dennis can walk on either side. We'll just be arm and arm. No one will care, it will be so late."

"You just have your shirt," I say to Tomas.

"It's only a little rain."

"Do you have far to go?"

"Not so far."

Then Maria rushes to him and tries to hold him back, or so it seems.

He takes her face between his hands. "I'll see you soon. One way," he takes a tight, crushing breath, "or another."

Maria turns and folds into me. I hold her close.

"I won't look back. You won't even see me go. *Pffft* and I'm gone." Tomas is crying as he leaves. I look up to see him tuck his head down and plunge into the night.

It doesn't take long to pack things up. If Judith and her son are coming back, it will be soon. I'll stay behind and be honey for the hornets. It's all right. I don't know anything. And in the morning, I'll head for the airport with Maxine and Bill and Wallace and the rest of them.

"I can't say goodbye to you," Michael says as I help put the poncho over his shoulders. He's tucked the baby into his arms. She's hardly a flicker under that poncho. Maria puts on her cap and zips up her baseball jacket. All boy through and through.

He nods toward the bathroom. "I put your passport and money belt back of the toilet. Not very original. But just for the night." He's looking everywhere but at me.

"I'll see you," I say, and touch his face. I can't look in his eyes, which I know are filling with tears.

I imagine them now, as they make their way down the back stairs out into the night. Michael, with his arms full of precious cargo, Maria beside him, in her baseball cap and jacket, Remy and Dennis and Juliette, on either side. The rain blows in their faces and against their legs, as they make their way along that wild, vacant shore, toward the weaving and bobbing lights of the Marina. They're so jaunty and bold, laughing and swinging their arms, no one would dare stop them.

I sit on the bed and run my hand over the tangled sheets, put my face in the pillows and breathe him in. I go to the balcony and feel the soft rain on my face. It's cooler now. I look out toward the lights of the Marina. Now they're slipping past the guard as easy as you please. I tell myself I'm safe, but I've pulled the safety latch and the deadbolt and wedged a chair under the doorknob.

I try to lie down but can't shut my eyes. Then I do. And that's when I see him so clearly, in his guayabera and shorts, standing in the corner of the room, looking out at the ocean, his feet planted apart, his arms crossed, the beginning of a smile at the corners of his mouth. He's in his fullness now, no whispery thin hair or frightened eyes. He brought me here and now he'll take me home. Pilar believed in him and so will I.

The waves rush against the seawall, the lights from the Marina flickering in the distance. The wind quiets into a fine soft rain, as the moon, low in the sky, hides itself in the dissolving clouds. Through the gray mist, lightening with the coming dawn, the curve of the island in the far distance declares itself in winking lights across the wide expanse they float upon, the gray despair behind them, a sheet of Cuban tears.

Precious Cargo
Havana, Cuba

The next morning, Tomas will wake to the drowsy sweep of the island curled against the sea and think of all the children forsaken under this heavy sky. *Loss*, he'll think, *Is there no end to it?* He'll finish the preparations as Pilar had wished, and then take her with him back to Pinar del Rio, where he will scatter her ashes.

He'll call the hotel and say Maria is sick. When Judith and Raul come back looking for them, they'll be over the waves and waters and on their way to the Keys. Already he can feel Pilar with him. She has never left him. He'll go to Pinar del Rio and wait for the owl to call his name. He's heard it twice already. The third time he'll let it lead him away. All he has to do is shut his eyes and take her hand.

And me? I'm only a go-between. Even so, now and forever after, this child will be a starburst of grace in my arms. What are parents anyway but the bearers of precious cargo from one place to the next, to be left to life as each child finds it? I think of Tani and the cold, harsh winters of Yakima, the sky drained of light. But this child will be no Peter Pan. One day Maria will come back and show her the sapphire sea against the curve of Havana, that arc of color and light, an invitation to the eye and restoration of the soul. She'll be no quartermoon, lonely in the sky, waiting on the edge of night. One day, however that may come, she'll rise to complete herself, and hasten the stars.

ACKNOWLEDGEMENTS

I came to Cuba as part of the first Ernest Hemingway International Colloquium, sponsored by the Cuban Ministry of Culture. I fell in love with Cuba and then it broke my heart. What else could I do but return again and again, adding to the story that was taking shape in my mind and heart? Many guided my way: Gladys Rodriguez Ferraro, curator of the *Museo de Ernest Hemingway;* Dr. Maria Valdez Fernandez, researcher and resident expert on *Santeria;* Frank Fernandez, researcher and maker of Cuba's best black bean soup; Professor Carmen Cusa, Hemingway and feminist scholar; Nicola Shangrow Reilly, my exemplary research assistant, who found answers to questions I didn't even know I had; Dr. Marisela Fleites-Lear, many thanks for help with factual accuracy; to the late Dr. Gordon Biele—for information on how ECT was used in the 1960's, and for directing my attention to the Allan Institute in Montreal, formerly named *Ravenscrag,* and to the appalling work of Dr. Ewen Cameron, its director. Thanks to the beautiful, sixty-four-year-old *babalawo,* who blessed me with my first *Santeria* cleansing ritual. And to Dr. Luis Vasquez, philosopher, physician, and tour guide, who gave me my book's title, when he said, "Cuba is like the quarter moon, always waiting to complete itself." Then he asked: "What happens when you fall in love with a country that is not yours?" Now I know. And so many along the way whose names have slipped through the net of time but who live on in these pages, and others whose names I hold close but fear to say, because even with its all its beauty and splendor, there is fear in Cuba also.

More thanks than I can say to Dr. Linda Patterson Miller, who gave this book its finest editing, and for her life-long friendship and love; to Dr. Sandra Spanier, friend of my heart through Cuban dramas big and small; to Dr. Loly Alcaide Ramirez for the generosity of her time and care in reading this manuscript; and to the late

Professor Bickford Sylvester, who kept dreaming of a Hemingway Cuban conference until it became a reality.

I read many books during the research phase of writing *Cuban Quartermoon*, but most helpful were: Gordon Thomas' *Journey Into Madness: The True Story of Secret CIA Mind Control and Medical Abuse;* John Mark's *The Search for the Manchurian Candidate: The CIA and Mind Control;* Dr. Harvey M. Weinstein's *Psychiatry and the CIA: Victims of Mind Control;* Yvonne M. Conde's *Operation Pedro Pan*; Migene Gonzalez-Wippler's *Santeria: the Religion*; Hope Edelman's *Motherless Daughters*; and Dr. Kay Redfield Jamison's *An Unquiet Mind: A Memoir of Moods and Madness.* Anyone looking for more information on such topics would find these works a fine place to start. I will always be grateful for my writing residency at *Hedgebrook Writers Colony*, where I wrote a share of this book; and to the University of Puget Sound for numerous research and travel grants, helping make my field research possible. Thanks to all—both inside and outside the pages.

And infinite gratitude to Beverly Conner, writing soulmate and reader of this manuscript way too many times; to Beth Kalikoff, who saw the manuscript in early forms and later ones, and never faltered, many thanks and much love. And to my family, Robb, Courtney, Walter, Chris, Maureen, Nicholas, and to David—editor extraordinaire, a wordsmith himself, and caretaker of my heart. All love, all love. Nothing without you.

ANN PUTNAM is an internationally-known Hemingway scholar, who has made more than six trips to Cuba as part of the Ernest Hemingway International Colloquium, sponsored by the Cuban Ministry of Culture. Her novel, *Cuban Quartermoon*, came, in part, from those trips, as well as a residency at *Hedgebrook Writer's Colony*. She has published the memoir, *Full Moon at Noontide: A Daughter's Last Goodbye* (University of Iowa Press), and short stories in *Nine by Three: Stories* (Collins Press), among others. Her literary criticism appears in many collections and periodicals. She holds a PhD from the University of Washington and has taught creative writing, gender studies and American Literature for many years. She has two forthcoming novels, and lives in Gig Harbor, Washington.

www.annputnamwriter.com

Made in the USA
Las Vegas, NV
16 December 2022

62946768R00204